The Swan-Daughter

The Swan-Daughter

Carol McGrath

Published by Accent Press Ltd – 2014

ISBN 9781783753376

Copyright © Carol McGrath 2014

Printed and bound in the UK

For Tara and Tim

Acknowledgements

My sincere thanks to Stephanie, Alison, Bob and Hazel at Accent Press for bringing this novel to the reader.

My thanks to Jay Dixon, my indispensable editor who has been superb with this novel and to Nikki Fine who was my only beta reader and pre-editing stage copy editor. Nikki you were a canny reader!

The Benedictine Hours
Les Heures Bénédictines

Matins	Between 2.30 and 3.00 in the morning
Lauds	Between 5.00 and 6.00 in the morning
Prime	Around 7.30 or shortly before daybreak
Terce	9.00 in the morning
Sext	Noon
Nones	Between 2.00 and 3.00 in the afternoon
Vespers	Late afternoon
Compline	Before 7.00 as soon after that the monks retire

Glossary

Hippocras – a sweet honey wine
Thegne – an Anglo-Saxon nobleman of middling rank
Villein – peasant
House coerl – the elite corps attached to an earl's household
Palisade – the protective fence that circles the estate buildings
Seax – a short Anglo-Saxon knife sometimes double sharpened
Skald – a poet but one of Viking origin
Relics – saints' relics were an important part of Christianity from the seventh century onwards
Old English riddles – short poems
Burgh – town
Handfasting – a secular and legal form of marriage universally used before the advent of church reform during the 11th Century

Alan of Richmond's Family Tree

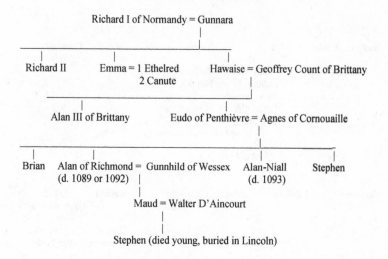

Richard I of Normandy = Gunnara

Richard II   Emma = 1 Ethelred   Hawaise = Geoffrey Count of Brittany
                      2 Canute

Alan III of Brittany   Eudo of Penthièvre = Agnes of Cornouaille

Brian   Alan of Richmond = Gunnhild of Wessex   Alan-Niall   Stephen
         (d. 1089 or 1092)   (d. 1093)

Maud = Walter D'Aincourt

Stephen (died young, buried in Lincoln)

Gunnhild Godwinsdatter's Family Tree

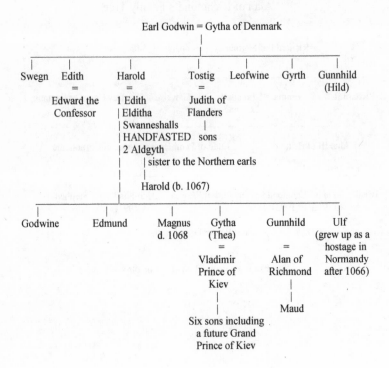

Earl Godwin = Gytha of Denmark

Swegn	Edith	Harold	Tostig	Leofwine	Gyrth	Gunnhild

Edith = Edward the Confessor

Harold =
1 Edith
| Elditha
| Swanneshalls
| HANDFASTED
2 Aldgyth
| sister to the Northern earls
|
Harold (b. 1067)

Tostig =
Judith of Flanders
|
sons

Gunnhild (Hild)

Godwine	Edmund	Magnus d. 1068	Gytha (Thea)	Gunnhild	Ulf

Gytha (Thea) =
Vladimir
Prince of
Kiev
|
Six sons including
a future Grand
Prince of Kiev

Gunnhild =
Alan of
Richmond
|
Maud

Ulf
(grew up as a
hostage in
Normandy
after 1066)

Epitaph for Count Alan

A star nods approval at the kingdom; Count Alan our
companion is dying
And England is saddened as its first leaders are now
turning to ash
Count Alan was the flower of the kings of Brittany,
And that he, too, is dead, allows decay to threaten the
order of nature
With unsettled law.
In the beginning the Conquest shone with the blood of
noblemen.
But this great lord grew strong as he followed our king
So, listen to us, as we say, 'May he have rest',
A great noble who has fought so bravely in Britain.

Ascribed to a 12th-century monk who wrote it in his copy
of work by the Irish monk Marianus Scotus (1028-1083)
and translated from the Latin by Dr Mat Harris of Malvern
College and loosely rendered more poetic by myself,
while hopefully preserving the original meaning.

Tristram and Isolde

They both laughed and drank to each other; they had never tasted sweeter liquor in all their lives. And in that moment they fell so deeply in love that their hearts would never be divided. So the destiny of Tristram and Isolde was ordained.

Tristram and Isolde, excerpt from *The Death of King Arthur* by Peter Ackroyd, 2011.

Prologue

Christmastide 1101 AD

As the musicians' music dies away I step up from my place below the salt. Sweeping back my cloak, I draw out my flute and play a few notes. I stop, and bending forwards say, 'Listen.' For a moment everyone shuffles on their haunches. The hall falls silent. They all love a story.

'Listen well,' I say, 'for this is a true tale of elopement and a princess's romance.' The men and women seated behind the white cloth raise eyebrows. I now have their complete attention. 'My lords and ladies, this story is about a great scandal, one that happened to Gunnhild, the youngest daughter of King Harold of England and his hand-fasted wife, Edith the fair, she of a swan's neck white as the feathers on an angel's wing. Ah, so you have heard of her beauty I see. Then fill your drinking horns, my friends. I shall be some time. For this tale we cast back to the year ten hundred and seventy-five when Gunnhild, a maid of eighteen, lived in Wilton Abbey, her hair hidden under a postulant's cap – though she had no desire to take the veil, nor did she wish to live out her life amongst those who had fled into abbeys for care of their hymens after the great battle. No, once her aunt, the Dowager Queen Edith had died, this young lady wanted her freedom and she was determined to have it.' I pause. The Yule log crackles and sparks in the hearth. 'Perhaps this was a mistake, perhaps not. You can decide for yourselves.'

Candles splutter and flicker in the recesses along the wall as I begin to recount my tale in a voice as clear as reliquary crystal.

Part One

St Margaret, the Virgin of Antioch

(Picture from Wikipedia)

1

Wilton Abbey, December 1075

It had been so easy to take it.

As Wilton Abbey's bell tolled for her dead aunt's midnight vigil, everyone – priests, nuns, novices, postulants and girls – passed through the archway into the chill of St Edith's chapel. Gunnhild hovered near the back of the gathering. When the nuns' choir began to sing the first plainsong, she lifted a candle from a niche close to the doorway, cupped her free hand around it and slipped out into the cloisters. She hurried along a pathway through overhanging shadows until she reached her aunt's apartment, rooms that were set away from the main abbey buildings, elegant as befitted a queen, albeit a dowager queen. Pushing open the doors, she crept into the reception hall, crossed the dead queen's antechamber, the great bed-chamber and finally into Aunt Edith's vast wardrobe. *I must find it because when I do I shall have a suitable garment to wear when I leave this place. I must take it before it is given to that dwarf, Queen Matilda.*

Gunnhild set her candle in an empty holder on a side table a little distance from the hanging fabrics and stepped into the space between wooden clothing poles. Frantically her fingers began fumbling amongst Aunt Edith's garments. *Which one was it? No, not those woollen gowns, nor the old linen ones either. No, look again.* She moved along a rail by the wall fingering linens and silks until finally she found what she sought at the very end. Reaching out with both hands she touched the overgown, pulled it down and took it out into the candlelight. Its hem was embellished with embroidered flowers – heartsease or pansies – in shades of purples and blues with centres of glistening pearls. Her aunt had worn it when Gunnhild had first travelled to be with her in Winchester for the Pentecost feast of 1066, just after Aunt Edith's husband, King Edward, had died and Gunnhild's father was crowned king.

Their family had risen and he had wanted his nine-year-old daughter to be prepared by her aunt for an education fit for a princess, to learn foreign languages, play instruments and embroider. She had remarked then to Aunt Edith that heartsease was her favourite flower and Aunt Edith had lifted her hand, smoothed it along the silk and said, 'One day, this dress will belong to you.'

Gunnhild peered closer, examining the clusters of tiny flowers, noticing how perfectly they were edged with gold and silver thread. Her eyes darted about the fabric. There were no moth holes. The green silk dress was as fresh as it had been ten years before. She laid the overdress on a stool, returned into the depths of the wardrobe and with both hands shaking lifted down its paler linen undergown. With a cursory glance she saw that it, too, remained in perfect condition. *Make haste and hurry away*. She folded the overgown into the linen shift and pulled her mantle over them both. Carefully closing the wardrobe's leather curtains she blew out the candle and sped from the apartment, fleeing back through empty cloisters to the postulants' building.

Pausing to catch her breath, Gunnhild pushed open her cell door with her back, slipped inside and spun around. Her every muscle tensed with fear. Eleanor was standing in the middle of the room.

'Christina sent me to find you ...' Eleanor, who had been her friend since she had entered Wilton Abbey, broke off. 'What, by the Virgin's halo, are you hiding under your cloak?'

Gunnhild pulled out her bundle and dropped the garments onto her cot. Eleanor held up the silk overgown and then dropped it onto the tiles as if it were poisoned, her face pale with shock. 'This,' she gasped. 'Where did you get it?'

'I took what is mine by right,' Gunnhild said in a quiet voice.

'You stole it.'

'No I did not. My aunt promised that one day this gown would belong to me. All her clothes will be shortened to fit the dwarf queen. And anyway ...' Gunnhild glanced down at her grey postulant's robe and her hand flew to the hideous black cap that Christina, the assistant prioress, forced her to wear, 'I need something better than these.'

'Whatever for?'

'You will know soon enough, Eleanor, I promise.' Gunnhild scooped the gown into her arms, folded it and placed it back on her coverlet beside its linen undergown. Her mind working quickly, she searched around her chamber for a suitable hiding place. The garment chest had a strong barrel lock and a key, though she rarely secured it, but now ... She crossed the room, flung open the coffer's lid and bent down. For a moment she inhaled the pleasant scent of cedarwood chips and felt around with both hands, rooting amongst her plain linen until she plucked out a green fillet embroidered with a golden pattern and a pair of red deerskin slippers decorated with twisting, fire-spitting, Godwin dragons. Both had been gifts from Aunt Edith for her sixteenth birthday. She lifted the head band, turned it around and around in her hands and faced Eleanor again. 'These belong to the daughters of my family; my aunt gave them to *me* to keep, not to my mother who is in a convent, nor to my sister, Thea, who is far away in the lands of the Rus, but to me,' she said, clutching her hands together so tightly her finger bones felt as if they would crack. 'No, Eleanor, the real sin is to imprison one of us in this abbey, to expect her to wear dull gowns day upon day, and order her to wed with God.'

Eleanor leapt up from the bed and pointed at the headband. 'Where in heaven's name would you wear that? Christina will find you out. No one is forcing you to take vows. You chose your own path. You have broken two vows already, obedience and poverty. If the abbess finds out ...' She caught her breath and rasped, 'Oh, for heaven's sake, Gunnhild, take them back to your dead aunt's rooms and leave them there for Queen Matilda before you break the third.'

'And that is unlikely here,' Gunnhild complained and tucked the fillet and slippers back in the coffer. 'No, I shall risk Christina's fury.' She plucked the gowns from the cot, laid them neatly on top of the fillet and slippers and covered the lot with two everyday shifts. Turning back to Eleanor she said,

'Christina must not find out. Please say you will not tell her. Besides, I have not yet taken any vows, nor shall I take them … I have changed my mind … My father, King Harold, remember, how he was once king of the English? Well, I shall never forget it, nor that the dwarf queen's husband, that bastard, William, killed him on the field at Senlac. I shall never forget that *King* William stole our kingdom.' She gasped for breath, almost choking with fury. 'My father never intended me for the church. He sent me to serve my aunt, to learn to read, write and embroider. Now Aunt Edith is gone to God's angels there is nothing left for me here. I intend to be free.'

'Gunnhild, how will that happen?'

Eleanor's voice was very, very quiet. Gunnhild breathed deeply and said, 'Eleanor, I am a princess. When my knight comes to claim me I shall be waiting for him in that dress.' She climbed up on to the chest and slipped her hand behind the statue that sat in the wall niche above it. She felt around for a small key and grasped it. Carefully, so as not to knock over her plaster St Edith, she climbed off the clothing chest. Kneeling on the cold tiles she secured the barrel lock with a loud clink, stood on the chest again, replaced the key and set the statue back into its original position. Looking over her shoulder she called down, 'Now it is hidden and only you and I know where. Promise me you will not tell.'

'I will not. Gunnhild, your secret is safe, at least on earth if not in Heaven.' As Gunnhild jumped from the chest Eleanor reached over and caught her hand. 'Hurry or you really will be discovered and I hope God forgives you because if Christina finds out she will not.'

'Bah, I am not afraid of Christina.' Gunnhild hesitated momentarily, and added, 'No, not a bit, even though I know she will beat me with her rod through the cloisters and lock me in the ossuary if she ever discovers my intention to escape.' She reached out for Eleanor's hand. 'Thank you. You are a true friend.'

Eleanor drew her close and whispered. 'Be careful what you wish for, Gunnhild. Now let us slip back into the chapel before

8

the dragon comes looking herself.'

Hand in hand they sped back to the novice stalls in the chapel where they took their places amongst the other postulants and novices and bowed their heads in prayer. The vigil was drawing to its end. The bell in the abbey church was already tolling. It would only be a few hours until Prime. After morning prayers Gunnhild was to travel to the funeral in Westminster Abbey because she was the only surviving Godwin heiress dwelling in England, but once Aunt Edith's royal funeral was over she would return to Wilton to be buried alive as deeply as the winter that was gathering about the cloisters.

Touching the course hemp of her plain gown she sighed. No knight would ever look at her dressed in raiment as pale as the shroud that covered her aunt's once lovely form. As Gunnhild's eyes swam with tears, she wiped them away from her cheeks using a corner of her cloak. She whispered into the candle smoke, 'Aunt Edith forgive me; I want to be of the world, not apart from it.'

2

Westminster, December 1075

'And the Lady Edith passed away in Winchester 7 days before Christmas and the king had her brought to Westminster with great honour, and laid her with King Edward, her lord.'
The Anglo-Saxon Chronicles, translated and edited by Michael Swanton, 2000

Their long wagon clattered into the palace courtyard, almost too late for Aunt Edith's funeral. The palace of Westminster was smaller than Gunnhild remembered. Even so, the new church still drew her awed gasp as she peered out at it from the nuns' litter. She recollected how Aunt Edith's smooth face had become riveted with anxious gullies on the night that the King, Gunnhild's uncle, collapsed at the Christmas feast of 1065. He had lingered in a shadowy place between worlds for days, rambling terrible prophecies, foretelling, to those gathered at his bedside, of fire, sword and destruction.

It was this fear that drove Uncle Edward to give care of his kingdom to Harold of Wessex, her father, who was the strongest of all the earls. After all, the other earls had elected her own father to be king because the obvious choice, young Prince Edgar, who had been born in exile, was foreign to their people and was inexperienced.

During that long-ago Christmastide the freezing palace had seemed to creak and groan with the weight of her aunt's sorrow. She remembered Uncle Edward's funeral on the Epiphany and how, on the same day that he was interred, her father had been crowned King Harold II. On that day she had become an eight-year-old princess.

Now, ten years on, she climbed from the wagon into the icy courtyard to stand in her thin woollen mantle amongst the nuns from Wilton waiting to join her aunt's funeral procession. It

11

would move in a stately manner out of the palace, across the snowy courtyard and into the long pillared aisle through the Minster's west door. She was not a princess today, of course. As she surveyed the noble Norman ladies, clad in rich furs and gathering around the palace yard in elegant groups, she could not help but long for someone to love her, someone to free her from Wilton and sweep her into her own elegant existence in the world beyond abbey walls.

She shivered and watched, her face as unsmiling as those all around her. King William, who led the procession, looked ahead sternly. The tiny queen who stepped neatly beside him owned an alabaster complexion as white as polished ivory. Gunnhild knew that she was, of course, far beneath the dwarf queen's notice.

At last the Wilton nuns slipped into place to join the walk to the cathedral and Gunnhild took up her position alongside Christina, behind the knights and nobles, bishops and monks. As they moved forward over the palace's icy yard towards the church, the monks' censors swung back and forwards through sharp winter air in a slow, methodical rhythm. After what seemed an endless time, they were at last crowding into the nave of the great Minster. Others pressed in behind them and Gunnhild found herself moving forward with a crowd of mourners all about her. They thronged every space from the altar to the West Door. She could smell the musty damp rising off their furs, hardly masked by the heavy oily perfumes that they wore to conceal the stink of their sweat. Her throat was irritated by the pungent smoke from the golden swaying censors and she began to cough. Christina glared at her through bead-like jackdaw eyes that missed little. Gunnhild clamped her hand to her mouth.

Turning away from the censor-swinging monks, she tried to breathe slowly. *In, out, in, out. Try not to inhale the sickly perfume, worse inside than out, just breathe.* As she recovered, a deep sadness overcame her and her mind wandered. Aunt Edith was telling her to sit by her charcoal fire on a stool, teaching her to read from an illustrated book with tales of animals – stags with thorny crowns, red foxes and long-eared hares. Shaking herself from such memories, she focused hard on where she was now. Looking about the nave, she began to scan the sombre faces of others. So many people had gathered at Westminster. *Did they really care about the dead old queen who had straddled two worlds, the beautiful world she had known before the great battle and that of the Norman conqueror. How could these strangers possibly care about her clever aunt?* She closed her eyes, and by squeezing them tightly shut, she captured an older recollection. This time she saw her mother embroidering a fine tunic with golden thread. It was for her handsome warrior father, Earl Harold, in their happy time before he was king. Perhaps her mother, the once lovely Edith Swanneck, was here too. She opened her eyes and glanced around again, peering hard through gaps in the groups that crowded the nave. Her mother was not there. *So they never invited my mother. I am still not permitted to speak with my mother in case we plan together to bring my brother Godwin back from Denmark and help him to kingship. Aunt Edith never allowed me to write to her. 'For your own sake, Gunnhild,' Aunt Edith had once said when she had begged to write to her mother. 'Forget you ever had a mother. I am your mother now.' Gunnhild knew the true reason. Simple. The bastard king is afraid of my mother, ever since her part in the rebellion at Exeter. She is like the rest of the mothers of Hastings, shadows in the corners. This is what becomes of passing your days on your knees in prayer.*

Gunnhild chased another memory. Ulf, her little brother, was still a hostage at King William's other court in Normandy. He had been fleet of foot and so filled with mischief. They had glided together over frozen ponds on bone skates and climbed tall spiky trees on the estate of Reredfelle that winter before her father had sent her to Wilton for her education. She felt herself smiling through damp eyes until a moment later a finger was prodding her, pushing her forward. Christina was hissing in her ear. 'Wake up, look down. This is a funeral, not a wedding.'

Four nuns stood in a tight group around Christina, their

sweat as stale as rotting fish, their breath foul. Gunnhild looked away from them and swallowed. She glanced across at the other side of the nave. A knight who stood by a statue of St Mark's lion was looking straight at her, watching her. As she caught his eye he turned to the canons who were gathered about the coffin chanting prayers, helping Aunt Edith to Heaven. Had he really looked her way, or was her imagination tricking her?

'Gunnhild, what are you doing now?' Christina pinched her arm. Gunnhild bit her lip to stop a retort. 'Look down, girl. This behaviour does not become the daughter of a man who was once a king of the English.'

'I am just trying to find my mother, Lady Christina.'

Christina hissed. 'She would not be invited.'

Sweat trickled down Gunnhild's back and soaked into the coarse linen she wore under her gown. She must find fresh air before she vomited in front of them all. 'Excuse me a moment. I ...' Gunnhild clapped her hand to her mouth and turned around, almost knocking the nun behind her over in her haste to escape. She pushed back through the great gathering of nobles, weaving a way around groups of strangers until she sensed clearer air from an opened side door. She ran out into a small courtyard and retched. She used her sleeve to wipe the spittle from her mouth and leaned against the stone wall, gulping cold air. Once she felt a little better, she edged her way back along the wall. The same knight stood there with his back to her, hovering just inside the doorway, blocking her return. He shifted his stance and glanced out. From her place of safety she observed him through the slits in the stone tracery of the portico. She realised that she had seen him before. His red hair was less bright than when she had last observed him during the nightmare year when other women of her family fled England. She had only been ten years old and had chosen to stay at Wilton with Aunt Edith.

Many foreign ambassadors and great knights had visited Aunt Edith. This red-headed knight, known to them then as Count Alain of Brittany, had lingered deep inside her memory. Her mother had behaved in a scandalous manner, agreeing to

14

wed the knight then breaking her promise. Aunt Edith had been angry and had never mentioned her mother's name again. Momentarily the knight stood still as the effigies that graced the side chapels inside the minster and, watching him slowly scan the courtyard, she felt a delicious stirring of something she longed for – his world.

He moved out of the doorway, strode around the portico and looked straight down at her. Trying to reclaim her dignity, she stood up, swept her hand down her gown and pulled her rough mantle closer.

'Are you unwell, my lady? Can I fetch someone, one of your order, perhaps?'

She did not reply. He spoke again. 'Who cares for you? Can I find that person for you? Ma petite, you are a novice, yes?'

Stretching up to her full height she found her tongue. She fixed him with as stern a look as she could manage. 'No, my lord, I am not yet a novice nor do I ever intend to be one. I am Gunnhild, a daughter of King Harold of the English.'

'I thought as much. Lady Gunnhild, you are grown since I last saw you in Wilton. You must be … what age?'

'I am eighteen years, and I am quite recovered, thank you. Please allow me to pass.'

The knight scrutinised her face. *Is he looking for my mother in my countenance? My mother was right to deny him, of course. This man could never replace my father.*

He said, his voice so low she hardly heard, 'And at eighteen you should be wed.' He bowed, inclined his head and moved aside to allow her passage.

'You are bold, knight.' She looked up at him, refusing to let his remark pass unnoticed, even though she agreed. She should indeed have a husband.

'And you are fair, my lady. I mean it as a compliment.' At that, Gunnhild pushed past him into the church and hurried back through the crowd.

She turned at a pillar and glanced back, her eyes searching hard for him but others had closed him in and he was gone.

When she returned to her place, Christina tugged her mantle

and she fell to her knees. They rose again as everyone was beginning to leave, drifting towards the great door, following after the king and queen and Lanfranc, the Archbishop of Canterbury, the Bishop of London, monks, nuns and nobles. No matter how hard she peered through gaps in the great gathering she could not see the red-headed knight and, by the Virgin, she could not remember his name.

'Where were you, Gunnhild?' Christina said.

Gunnhild pointed to an alcove close to the narrow doorway. 'Praying to Our Lady for my aunt's soul.' The lie slipped from her tongue as easily as the liturgy she knew by rote.

'Sooner you are shriven the better, my girl.' Christina took Gunnhild's arm and hurried her back out into the brightness of day. Turning to her group of nuns she dropped Gunnhild's elbow and said, 'There are too many temptations at a funeral feast. Prioress Winifred will see to our needs in the women's hall and there we shall rest.' With that she turned on her heel. Dutifully the four nuns of Wilton followed as Gunnhild trailed behind them. Glancing backwards, Gunnhild now saw that the knight was leaning on his sword by the choir stalls, once again observing her. Feeling a flush of colour creep up her neck she drew her mantle hood close and hurried after the others.

3

Wilton Abbey, Winter 1076

While snow and hail and frost all fall together
The heart's wounds seem by that yet heavier ...
The Wanderer – A Choice of Anglo-Saxon Verse edited by
Richard Hamer, 2006

'Gunnhild, I must speak with you and with Eleanor,' Christina
announced after Nonce on a snowing day in January. The year's
first snowfall always reminded Gunnhild of how her
grandmother, Gytha, had told them of how a white raven who
had belonged to the Norse god Odin scattered feathers in the
cold of winter, feathers that fell to earth as snow.

Obediently bowing their heads, they trailed behind Christina
through the icy cloisters, exchanging anxious glances. Gunnhild
wondered what was waiting for them. Had they not been
diligent enough? Would Christina punish them for some silly
misdemeanour with more time on their knees in the chill chapel
in prayer, finger-pricking embroidery, or, perhaps, the worst of
all punishments, fumigating blankets for the abbey's guest
house? She shuddered. The extra blankets were stored in fusty
chests where fleas mysteriously multiplied in their woollen
seams.

She huddled into her mantle and longed to climb the twisting
stairs behind the cloisters to the scriptorium where a basket of
coals glowed in a charcoal brazier. There, she could lose herself
in drawing tiny acanthus leaves which she loved to touch with
gold. Tucked away in an alcove set aside for her use she drew
and coloured little figures with such talent that visiting monks
remarked that they could never better her work. She trampled
snow as she plodded behind Eleanor and Christina, escaping in
her mind into her miniature depiction of the Wedding at Canna
with its small roses that crawled up a pillar beside the kind

Jesus who reached out his hand in blessing.

They had arrived at Christina's door. She ushered them inside, pointed to a bench and ordered the girls to be seated whilst she placed herself behind a table and arranged her gown. Once she was comfortably seated she looked at them both across the top of a prominently positioned box and a book.

Gunnhild did not recognise the largish box but she knew that the book beside it contained the names of postulants and their possessions, those belonging to girls with great fortunes and some without. Eleanor was without, but then she was an accomplished embroideress and embroidery was of great value. Christina leaned forward and opened the codex, spoiling the perfect arrangement of box and book. Ignoring Gunnhild she glanced up at her friend. Eleanor was a novice. 'Yes, I am correct, Eleanor, my dear,' she said with a thin smile, 'the book indicates that you will take vows next year.' *Christina looks like a hawk today.* Christina screwed up her eyes and sat back in her chair. 'I consider you in need of no further instruction, Eleanor. You may take your vows this Easter.' Her thin lips broke into a smile. 'Until then you will work on our tapestry panel for Bayeux. Bishop Odo is anxious this is completed before Pentecost. Canterbury is ahead of us with their panels and this we cannot allow.'

Eleanor's shoulders visibly relaxed. Christina turned to Gunnhild. Her thin smile became a frown. 'Gunnhild, we are not considering you as a novice, not just yet – though I expect you to be ready by summer.' Christina sat up straight and drew herself taller. 'In preparation you shall attend four services daily.' Gunnhild let a sigh escape her lips. 'Not so fast my girl,' Christina continued. She tapped the mysterious box. 'You will remove yourself from the scriptorium since you, too, must work on our tapestry panels. The Bishop is sending one of his designers to check our work. It has to be perfect. You will be stitching the vow that King Harold took in Bayeux when he acknowledged Duke William as the rightful future king of England.'

She heard Christina's pronouncement as if it came from a

distant world. These were hard words. Her aunt often said that Harold had ignored a promise made on holy relics to be Duke William's man and that when King Edward had died her father had by-passed Christina's brother, the Atheling Edgar, and had accepted the English throne. Gunnhild wanted to cry out, 'This is all past, long, long ago. It is nothing to do with me.' But she swallowed and bit her bottom lip, the physical pain helping to ease her anger. Christina continued, 'As you well know, Gunnhild, a vow on holy relics is sacrosanct. Your father's broken promise brought us to war, caused his own death and has brought God's wrath on us.' She lifted her hand and again tapped the box by her elbow. 'In this chest are your inks and brushes. They will remain in my possession since there is no need for you to revisit the scriptorium.'

Gunnhild inhaled and silently exhaled. She could feel her heart beating like that of a wounded sparrow she had once held in her hands, trapped within the cage of her fingers. For a moment she could not breathe. She watched horrified as Christina moved the box to one side, leaned forward and remarked, 'By the way, Gunnhild, there is a visitor here today, one who wishes to speak with you. I cannot refuse this interview since he is a cousin to King William. So ...' she leaned back in her chair and sighed, 'You may see him in the abbess's antechamber after Vespers. Since our beloved abbess is unwell and I am working on the tapestry today, Sister Marte will chaperone you.' She waved her hand in a dismissive manner. 'Now, both of you go about your day.'

Eleanor bowed her head. 'Thank you, Lady Christina,' she murmured. Gunnhild rose to follow Eleanor but stopped and turned at the door. 'My visitor's name?'

'Count Alan of Richmond. He knew your aunt and says that he has a gift for you, something that belonged to your grandmother, Countess Gytha. Now go.'

'I see, Lady Christina. Thank you.'

'Go. I am busy.'

Gunnhild drew another long intake of breath and did not exhale until she was back in the snowy cloister.

*   *   *

Marte led Gunnhild to the abbess's receiving chamber and placed her in a chair behind a wooden lattice screen that had been especially imported for the meeting. Marte and Beatrice, both of them lowly nuns, sat behind her with embroidery in their laps. Soon after, Count Alan was ushered in by a servant and shown to a winged chair close to the screen. Since she had seen him last he had sprouted hair on his chin. His brush of a red beard was nodding this way and that. If she put a finger through the screen's lattice work she could touch that beard. She peeped up and saw too how his close-cropped hair gleamed in the candle-glow and how his long face was criss-crossed with a light and dark latticed pattern.

He leaned in. From behind her chair, Marte clucked her disapproval. Gunnhild ignored Marte and she, too, leaned in towards the screen. His eyes were intense, the colour of amber, fox eyes, but it was difficult to tell in sconce light. Perhaps they were just brown or even tawny.

'Gunnhild,' he said in a quiet voice. This time she noticed his pronounced foreign accent. 'I have come to ask forgiveness for what my people have done to your family. I was responsible for the destruction of Reredfelle. I did wrong by your mother. This sin has lain on my conscience for many years. Since the destruction of that estate, we have burned and taken lands from hundreds of those who once farmed them. If the people rebel they lose everything. These have been cruel years. Take the north for instance. There was a great rebellion there four years past and the lands of Lords Edwin and Morcar – do you remember them?– have been laid waste.' She nodded. He went on, now sounding impassioned, his voice hoarse with irritation. 'The punishment was harsh. Laying waste the north is not the way to win the tenants' loyalty.' He breathed hard and said, 'I live in the north and by Christ one day I shall bring peace to that land. People cannot work the land if they are not at peace, Gunnhild.' He lowered his voice. 'And, I am Alan now, not Alain. I think it may help me win my tenants loyalty. I try to be fair but if they cross me ...'

'I see,' she interrupted. She had listened to enough of this. Gunnhild had not seen the destruction of the north with her own eyes but she had heard of the rebellion and about King William's revenge. If Count Alan intended to help its recovery then perhaps not all foreigners were bad, that was if he meant what he said. 'I hope you will act as you say,' she said aloud. Thinking for a moment, she added, 'You wanted to marry my mother.'

He steepled his hands. 'A great wrong was done to her. But no one can turn this tide back from time's shore line, nor should they. Together, my people and yours will make this land strong again. We will build great abbeys and bring it peace and God's forgiving grace.' He opened his hands, palms up. He smiled at her. 'Gunnhild, I have no wife. I am a soldier and one day I shall need children to inherit my castles. I ...' He stopped and looked down at his hands.

She waited for him to continue, wondering if he was about to ask for her? He was much older than her. He must be around five and thirty. She felt her eyes widen as a whisper of hope flitted past her. He was, after all, a king's cousin.

He was studying her face, a ghost of a smile playing at the corners of his month. 'There is no point in asking for you, my lady, because the abbey here does not intend to allow you to leave. Lady Christina says you are about to become a novice, but I believe they have their own motives for holding on to you.'

'Which is?' She heard her own voice creak.

He lowered his so that the nun seated behind could not hear. 'Through you they can hope for the prosperity that once belonged to your mother. Her estates are legally her lands.'

'Surely the abbey at Canterbury will claim them, I mean, well, since she has become a Bride of Christ, surely they must claim what was once her property?' she said in an equally low tone.

'The King, my cousin, will decide their future. Odo of Bayeux and Kent and the Archbishop of Canterbury, Lanfranc, already have a great fortune. He will not allow more to fall that way. So … well … enough …' He shrugged his broad soldier's shoulders. 'What must be must be, Gunnhild.' He lifted a purse from his belt, drew open its silk cord and removed a small object. 'I hope you accept my concern for your welfare.' Confused, she lowered her eyes again. He went on, 'I came to see you today because I am on my way south to the coast and I want to give you this.' He pushed a golden chain with a jewelled cross attached to it through the latticed grill. As she took the fine chain their fingers touched, the glittering cross dangling between them. He allowed his fingers to linger. Although only a finger touch, there was strength in it. Behind her she heard the intake of breath and the clink of a dropped spindle. He withdrew his fingers and said, 'It belonged to your grandmother. I discovered it when they departed the palace at Exeter.' Gunnhild started.

After the great battle, her grandmother Countess Gytha had withdrawn to Exeter with Thea, Gunnhild's older sister. Months later, when Grandmother had refused to pay King William's tax, the King had marched on Exeter and besieged it in the middle of winter. Countess Gytha had closed the gates on the King and his army, hoping that they could hold out until Gunnhild's brothers came from Ireland with an army. After three weeks of siege the burghers of Exeter and their bishop saw the way their future lay and made peace with King William. Aunt Edith had said at the time, 'Sometimes, my dear Gunnhild, it is best to be pragmatic. My mother can be very stubborn.' The noblewomen of Exeter had been allowed to go into exile in Flanders and Denmark. That was when her mother, Elditha, had refused to leave England and instead retired to Canterbury.

Suddenly Gunnhild realised that Count Alan had stopped speaking and was looking at her curiously. She smiled and he went on, 'I kept it safe thinking one day I might return it.' He paused. 'One day, if you do not take vows,' he added quietly, 'you will be able to wear it outside the cloister.'

She searched for hopeful meaning in his countenance but sadly found none. His beard was concealing; his face was neutral. She whispered, 'I forgive you for Reredfelle's destruction, Count Alan.'

'Thank you. It means everything to me. Goodbye, Gunnhild. May the Lady Mary protect you.'

He rose from his chair. There was something she must ask, and she might never have such an opportunity again. She clutched the screen. 'Wait, Count Alan.'

'Yes, Lady Gunnhild?' He sat down again.

'I had a brother called Ulf. He was taken to Normandy. He would be fourteen years or so now. Does he live?'

She felt a moment of hesitation before he said, 'The youth is well. He dwells in the Norman court with the King's son Robert. That is all I know of Ulf Godwinson.' He rose and bowed to her. 'I hope we have occasion to speak again, my lady.'

'I hope so too,' she said quietly as a sister appeared from the shadows. He turned away and the nun ushered him out of the chamber.

Marte reached for the gift. Gunnhild held the cross tightly. 'No, Sister Marte, this was my late grandmother's crucifix. It is a gift. It belongs to me, not the Church.'

'Then it is kind of the knight to return it.' Marte snatched it from Gunnhild's fingers and stroked it, saying, 'Fine gold and little sapphires: much too valuable for a novice. Sister Christina must place it in the treasury.'

Gunnhild had no choice but to hand over the crucifix that linked her to her grandmother, who had lived out her life far away in Denmark and who had died just a year before Aunt Edith.

Later, Christina called Gunnhild to her chamber and said that when Gunnhild had taken her vows, then and only then would her grandmother's crucifix be returned. For days Gunnhild mourned the loss and wept in the solitude of her chamber. She hated Christina more than ever.

Every day following a painful period on her knees at Sext, Nones, Vespers and Matins, her anger threatened to rise to the surface. As Gunnhild's frustration grew, Eleanor patiently bent a dark head over painstaking embroidery. When Gunnhild was in difficulty and about to descend into a tantrum, Eleanor gently reached across to correct her stitches or to guide her hand into the correct position.

At the end of a particularly difficult day Gunnhild closed the door to her chamber, edged her key from its hidden place, opened her coffer and pulled out the green silk overgown. The knowledge that Christina was eating honey cakes in the same private garden where *she* had once spent treasured hours with Aunt Edith drove her into a fury. As she stood in her chamber with the embroidered silk dress skimming over the paler undergown, soft shoes on her feet and her hair loosened, a momentary wildness possessed her. The dress swirled about her ankles and as she spun around and around in the Godwin slippers she felt beautiful. She would have her freedom for one day her knight must come for her.

Throughout the hungry Lenten season Gunnhild watched the road from her opened shutters hoping that the knight would pass this way again and seek her out but he never came. The only visitor was the tapestry designer from Canterbury who rode into Wilton on a mule during the third week of February.

The designer, a small man with scarred fingers, whose breath stank of garlic and who spoke in a high voice like a boy singing plainsong, stood behind her from Terce until Sext on the second morning of his visit, watching over her shoulder as her needle ploughed slowly back and forwards embroidering the caskets that allegedly had contained holy relics. He leaned over, touched the fabric and told her to make sure that Earl Harold's fingers touched both caskets.

She looked up with fury in her eyes. 'Earl Harold was my father. The promise was a lie,' she said quietly. 'His fingers never touched those caskets. He never promised to recognise Duke William as King of England after my uncle, King Edward, died.'

'Insolent girl,' the master designer said. 'How dare you question?'

He called Christina over, and, whispering in her ear, drew her away to the far side of one of the charcoal braziers that heated the barn-like room.

Christina crossed the flagged floor and yanked Gunnhild from her stool. 'How dare you say such an untruth?' she hissed through her yellowing teeth. 'Those words are treason words. Come with me, my girl.'

Gunnhild spent the rest of that day in her shift on her knees in St Edith's chapel shivering, teeth chattering, pretending to pray for forgiveness for her rudeness. That evening she received a beating from Christina herself, six strokes of a willow rod across her bare shoulders. She wore stinging red stripes for days, long after the master designer had departed. It took a whole week for the soothing balm the abbey's herbalist rubbed into her shoulders each evening and morning to ease the vicious streaks on her white skin. The salve of cowslip and goat's grease could not heal her pride.

As the weeks slipped by, her hopes of rescue slowly faded. Eleanor would enter the Benedictine order and then she would be utterly alone. She thought about escape when she was in the chapel, when mending hose, another task she disliked, and during the tedious silent meals. For a time she squirrelled away bread and cheese thinking that she could walk out into the chill of winter and just leave, but snow lay deep about the abbey and the bread went stale. She had to feed it to the birds. If she had taken Aunt Edith's jewels rather than the pearl-trimmed overgown she could have sold them to a jeweller for silver coin and used that for a passage to Flanders and freedom, but she had not. Now it was too late. Queen Edith's jewels were locked away in the royal treasury.

By March the weather turned gentler. Postulants were sent into the gardens to plant onions and carrots and to gather herbs to flavour pies and soups. Christina supervised her charges with diligence. 'Hurry,' she chided. 'The abbess says we are to have more visitors. They will expect to see our gardens neat and our workshops as productive as their own. Here, Gunnhild, take this basket of greens to the kitchen and you, Beatrice, take the others to the lane by the weaving shed. There is a great crop of nettles there.' Gunnhild glowered but held her tongue.

Christina wiped soil from her hands and said, 'Girls, be in the abbey church in time for Vespers, clean and neat. No mud on your shoes.' Christina shoved the basket into Gunnhild's hands and marched off in the direction of the abbess's apartment.

On her way to her chamber to change her work overgown, Gunnhild caught sight of one of these visitors, a man who looked more like a messenger than a monk. He was of middling stature and dressed in a long, dark blue tunic that was belted at the waist. His hair was cropped short and was greying. He smiled as she passed. She did not hesitate to return the smile but afterwards she cast her eyes downwards and scuttled off to the novice quarters wondering who he was.

He was in the church at Vespers with Christina but he never looked her way. She was just another girl in a brown linen mantle and pale coarse habit. Closing her eyes she dreamed of wearing the green gown and of showing the world how she could speak in foreign tongues and not just write letters but also cover them with drawings of delicate flowers and tiny animals touched with magical brightness.

After Vespers she sat in the silent refectory playing with her spoon. Challenging the Rule's imposed silence the girls had worked out a code of hand signals. When they saw that the nuns were not watching they moved their hands, gracefully sending messages between each other in a language all of their own. That afternoon Emma received a message from Greta and passed it on to Beatrice who passed it to Gytha who finally nudged Gunnhild. Gunnhild gasped when she caught its meaning. Greta had traced an M for Marte, two circles for her eyes and a rectangle for their building and sent her fingers walking into every corner of her palm. Marte was searching their chambers.

Gunnhild dropped her spoon. It clattered on the stone floor and she dived under the table. The nun seated at the lectern glared around the refectory seeking the source of the disturbance. As Gunnhild retrieved the spoon she felt herself flush as scarlet as the blood painted onto the crucified Christ figure that hung from the wall behind the lectern. She scrambled back on to the bench and bowed her head. The nun glared at her and resumed her reading. Eleanor was sitting with the other novices. She glanced over and placed a finger on her lips.

The meal stretched out in one long agony. What if Marte demanded the key to her coffer; what if she had actually discovered the key's hiding place? As soon as she could, Gunnhild rushed from the refectory to the postulants' building, her heart hammering hard against her ribs. The moment she placed her hand on her own cell door she sensed that Christina was waiting behind it. She hesitated before pushing the door open. If Christina had discovered the dress she must confront her and refuse to take novice vows.

She opened her door wide. Christina stood in the middle of the chamber but from a cursory glance Gunnhild could see that nothing had been disturbed, nothing.

'Ah, here you are. Come with me,' Christina said, clearly not aware of Gunnhild's discomfort. 'You have a visitor.'

Gunnhild let out a long relieved breath. 'Count Alan?'

'Certainly not. Compose yourself.' Christina snapped and turned about, not even looking anywhere near the locked coffer. 'The abbess has news for you.' She scowled at Gunnhild. 'I am not to tell you it. Our lady abbess wishes to tell you herself.'

The nun hurried along through the cloisters like a busy spider, scuttling so quickly that Gunnhild could hardly keep pace with her. They passed into the small courtyard and through an archway that led to her aunt's once lovely rooms. She had not entered them since the night she had taken the dress. Now she felt nervous.

'Wait here.'

She stood outside the door, her hands clammy with sweat as Christina knocked on an inner door. A servant opened it and stood aside as they entered. Gunnhild modestly glanced down. When no one spoke she lifted her eyes. The abbess sat very straight in Aunt Edith's chair, smothered in a cumbersome wimple with a heavy shawl-like veil. Even though the evening was warm, she wore a thick mantle, her bony mottled fingers stretching out from her cloak like little shrubby branches. The stranger whom Gunnhild had met earlier was seated on a cushioned bench by her side. She felt his eyes scrutinise her and dropped her head again. Though she had washed her hands before supper, scrub as she had tried, she simply could not get the garden's green marks off them. She clasped them under the folds of her cloak.

'Christina, thank you. You may leave.' The abbess dismissed Christina with a little pennant-like wave of her hand. Gunnhild watched with surprise as Christina exited the door, her lips pursed because she was not asked to stay. The abbess turned to the man seated on the bench. 'This is Gunnhild whom your mistress, Matilda of Mortain, sends for, daughter of Harold of Wessex. She is her mother's heiress so, in time, understand that her lands must come to the Abbey at Wilton.' Her stare at Gunnhild was steely, clearly never kindly when property was a topic of conversation.

Gunnhild tried to still her twitching hands.

The abbess went on, 'We have educated her in languages, in the art of writing and reading and in English embroidery. Indeed, I must remind you that the child was educated by Queen Edith herself.'

Gunnhild remained very still. The old abbess's clear voice was still strong enough to slice through the soft twilight.

'Will she do?'

Gunnhild started. *Do for what?*

The visitor scrutinised her and at last said, 'Gunnhild, I am Sir Edward of Winchester, steward to Robert of Mortain's wife Lady Matilda. My Lady of Mortain desires you as a companion for her daughters until they return to Normandy next year.' His voice was almost, though not totally, pompous. 'Lady Matilda is of English descent and sister to the Earl of Shrewsbury. But as wife to the king's brother, her household is from Normandy and she wants a native noblewoman to teach her daughters

28

English as they will spend more time here in England than in Normandy. In a year's space she will deliver you back to Wilton. I understand that you are to take novice vows.'

Gunnhild opened her mouth to reply but the abbess was already speaking for her. 'It is an honour for us.' She shifted her weight in her chair and addressed Gunnhild.

'You depart for Winchester in the morning. Christina will travel with you as far as Romsey Abbey. We have St Helena's relic to deliver to the abbey church there before Easter.' She lowered her voice into a tone of deep reverence. 'The relic belonged to your aunt, Dowager Queen Edith, as you know.' She looked at the steward, Edward, as if he did not know. 'It is a small fragment of the holy cross carried to England centuries past by none other than St Helena herself. There is no one more suited to carry it there for us than Lady Christina who is much loved at Romsey.'

'I see,' the steward, said. 'We can accommodate the relic and Lady Christina under my protection. No doubt there will be a nun from the great Romsey Abbey who can chaperone Gunnhild on to Winchester and watch over her until she is settled in Lady Matilda's household.'

The abbess glanced back at Gunnhild. 'Yes, a Romsey nun can be trusted to watch over her. She is a sensible girl.' She pointed her stubby finger at Gunnhild. 'You will be ready to make the journey tomorrow, Gunnhild. Yes, you should learn much in the household of such as Matilda of Mortain, but do not neglect everything we have taught you here. May St Edith protect and guide you, my daughter.' She raised her hand and made the sign of the cross.

Gunnhild fell to her knees. 'I shall do my best, Lady Abbess.'

The abbess pulled something from her voluminous mantle and proffered it to Gunnhild. 'You may wear this as a token of our trust and your status.'

Gunnhild reached for the fine gold chain with the sapphire-studded cross, its small stones glowing in a thin ray of afternoon light that slanted into the chamber. 'It is fitting that you wear your grandmother's cross but do not lose it. Keep it on you always.'

Without a word Gunnhild slipped the delicate gold chain over her head, allowing it to fall below the neck of her dress where no one could see it. *They have decided for me but I would never have objected anyway.*

'Good,' the abbess said. 'Now go and pack your bag.' She called for a waiting nun who ushered Gunnhild out of the chamber.

Moments later Gunnhild was back in the cloisters where Christina was waiting with a thunderous look on her face. Gunnhild knew better than to show her delight to Christina. She wore a serious look to conceal her delight. No one would ever return her to Wilton. This would be her goodbye at last.

'You will be glad to return here, Gunnhild.' Christina loomed over her. 'Matilda of Mortain may be English but I have heard she is a demanding mistress.' She prodded Gunnhild along the cloisters. 'Hurry, we leave at dawn. Bag packed and into the wagon. Father Antony will drive us. Mortain's man will ride ahead of us.' When they reached Gunnhild's cell in the white building, Christina gave her a push through the open doorway. 'No shilly-shallying and no need for goodbyes. You will soon be back here.' She took the thin wool of Gunnhild's old mantle between her finger and her thumb and pulled her hand back, clearly disgusted. 'I shall send you a new one with a fur-trimmed hood, one of my own, and two clean gowns, two undergowns and fresh linen from the store chest and a cloth bag to hold them. Leave the old ones here. Be ready to depart after Lauds.'

Gunnhild ran through the abbey corridors to the chapel where the nuns were at prayer. In the courtyard a servant was sweeping the pathways. She could hear sounds from the refectory building, the thumping of platters, tables being laid for supper. From the church plainsong floated into the twilight. This was her chance to say goodbye to Eleanor. In a week her dearest friend would take her vows and then she would be gone from Gunnhild's life for ever. Gunnhild blended into the shadows of a side chapel. First the nuns filed out, behind them the novices, the postulants and finally girls from the school at Wilton. Eleanor walked alone. Gunnhild waited until she came close, stepped out and touched her arm.

'Did they find anything?' Eleanor spoke, her head bowed as if in prayer. They had practised the technique for years.

Gunnhild stepped into place beside her companion and said through lips that were almost closed. 'No, but ... oh Eleanor, something good has happened.'

'What, do tell,' Eleanor's eye brows arched up into a perfect high curve. 'And hurry, I have to attend Christina.'

As they walked through the fading daylight Gunnhild whispered her fate.

Eleanor stopped walking. 'And those things! What will you do with them now?'

She could almost feel Eleanor's shudder. 'If you mean my aunt's dress, it will travel with me. I do not intend to return. I shall discover my new life now.'

Eleanor looked straight at Gunnhild. 'What foolishness!' Then she reached out and clasped her hand. 'But may the Queen of Heaven protect you.'

'I shall never forget you, my Eleanor.' She squeezed Eleanor's hand. 'The abbess has returned my gold chain,' she added.

Eleanor squeezed her hand back. 'Good.' Gunnhild saw sorrow in her grey eyes. 'If you do not come back to us then I shall pray for you every day of my life,' Eleanor said.

'And I for you, Eleanor. Though, perhaps, we are not entirely lost to each other.' She lifted the cross from her neck, placed it to her lips and kissed it. 'My grandmother was patron of St Oswyth's Priory near Exeter. My mother was patron of St Benets in Suffolk. I shall be patron of an abbey one day also.' She tucked her cross safely back into her gown. They had reached the fork in the trackway.

Eleanor gestured towards the nuns' hall. 'If God wills it, it will be so.' She lifted Gunnhild's hand to her lips. 'I have to go now. Christina will be waiting for me. Remember, I shall have you in my prayers, always.'

Her joy saddened by loss, Gunnhild watched for a moment as Eleanor's thin grey-cloaked figure followed the pathway to Christina's chamber. How could she bear this loss? Yet she must think of the future and pray that one day they would meet again. Choking back tears, she hurried in the opposite direction back to her cell to throw her scant belongings into the linen sack.

As she lifted the silk dress from her coffer she felt a tear escape and trickle down her cheek. She wiped it away and tried instead to be practical. How could she bring Aunt Edith's dress? There was only one possible way – she must wear it.

4

March 1076

'You loved Count Alan Rufus and he loved you.'
Archbishop Anselm, 1093, to Gunnhild, quoted from 'King
Harold's Daughter' by Richard Sharpe in
Haskins Journal Vol. 19

Father Antony, one of Wilton's five priests, lifted the
carthorse's reins into his aged hands while Edward of
Winchester climbed on to a brown gelding. This was no tall and
powerful knight encased in armour like Alan of Richmond,
Gunnhild noted, as he took up his position to ride in front of the
wagon. The aging steward wore a simple brown tunic and a fine
woollen mantle with a hood that lay across his shoulders. For
protection, a dagger was tucked into his belt and a valuable
jewel-encrusted scabbard that contained a knight's sword hung
from it. Did he not worry that it might be stolen from him? She
felt for the seax Christina had given her, saying as she handed it
over to Gunnhild, 'The woods are full of dangers. Use the knife
if your maidenhead is under threat. Remember, it belongs to
God alone.'

Gunnhild took up her place on the faded cushioned seat
opposite Christina. As she eased on to the stained side-bench
she spread her clothing with care, making sure that her mantle
covered her new grey overgown and the silk dress that she wore
beneath it. She had concealed the Godwin shoes and the gold-
embroidered fillet amongst undergarments in the linen sack that
lay by her feet.

Followed by her servant who carried her sheepskin
travelling bag, Christina climbed in and sat on the bench
opposite. She wedged a box between her and the elderly
servant. With a flick of Brother Antony's whip, the wagon
rolled forward and they were off. As they exited the abbey gate

and rattled along the track towards the woods that took them in the direction of Romsey, Christina kept a bony hand on the reliquary as if it were likely to fly off at every jolt that rocked their litter. They travelled for miles in this way, without conversing, and with Christina's hand hovering over a fragment of the true cross, her lips moving in silent prayer.

Gunnhild tried to peep out of the covers to see what lay in the world beyond the abbey. Labourers had not yet come out into the fields and the land was still. Mist hung in the air, shrouding the country-side and hushing everything except the sighs of their breathing, the clippity-clop of the horse and the rolling of wagon wheels. It was so eerie that Gunnhild wondered whether ghosts would slip out of the hedgerows. But nothing sinister crossed their pathway and the wagon rattled on and on along lanes overhung with hedges of white hawthorn until, at length, they dropped down into deep woods from where they would take the old route-way towards Romsey Abbey.

Christina's hand fell away from the relic as the wagon's steady rhythm lulled her into a doze. When they trundled into sunken lanes filled with new growth, Gunnhild listened to the sound of cuckoos, blackbirds and the woodland scuffles of small creatures in the verges. Eventually the servant's eyes also closed.

Gunnhild sat up, alert, excited and silent, imagining what new experiences she might discover in Winchester. Would Matilda of Mortain take her to court in London? Could she ask for new brushes and inks or would she be forced to embroider day after day in the bower hall just as she had had to lately at Wilton? Was she to be ordered about as she had been at Wilton or would those who had care of her in Winchester treat her as the princess she truly was? She tilted her head up; she would behave as a princess. No one would treat her otherwise now that she had escaped the confines of the abbey. She reached up and touched her grandmother's cross where it lay about her neck for comfort. Yes, Grandmother, you had pride and it was no sin, she whispered to herself. Trees rustled in the light spring breeze and birds sang amongst branches that stretched tall in a woven canopy above the wagon. She watched the sun glinting through beech trees that opened in endless long marches before them.

For a time they met no other travellers until around midday when the sun rode high above the trees, she heard voices edging closer towards their wagon. Wood pigeons rose up high into the trees rattling branches and squawking down. A pheasant screeched. There came a great swishing of foliage close by, followed by human shouts, horse neighs and clanking armour. She lifted the wagon's curtain to peer out. As she did, horses clattered past them, shaking the litter's frame. She felt a great shuddering sensation and reached out for the side of the litter, clutching at the curtain, nearly pulling it down. Christina's eyes snapped opened. The hitherto silent servant shrieked, 'St Edith, save us.' Father Antony yelled, 'Christ's sainted bones!' The precious relic box dropped onto the wagon's floor with a great thump. Gunnhild's linen bundle tumbled forward as the wagon dropped down on its side with a jolt.

'Out,' Father Antony's voice reached through the curtains of the litter. 'There is a Devil's curse on this useless wagon! We need to fix a wheel and it can't be done with your weight inside.'

By now, men were shouting and horses were stamping around them. Gunnhild leaned forward and grabbed the opposite wall of the unbalanced wagon with both her hands. She peered out. The beech trees had slid to a tilt. They were collapsed against a bank of nettles. Christina roughly pushed her aside. 'You stupid girl, get out. We have lost a wheel.'

Christina and her servant were too distracted by the stinging nettles to notice the drop of silk as Gunnhild lifted her skirts to climb out. With the forest floor safely beneath her stout shoes, Gunnhild tugged at her dress trying to pull it over her silken gown. Freed from the wagon and the bank, she followed Christina around the litter to the back.

Behind the tumbled litter, a band of soldiers wearing glittering mail were climbing off their horses. Father Antony was kneeling by a dislodged wheel. Edward the Steward was down from his mount and was ruminating with a tall knight. As Christina advanced, the priest's head jerked up from behind the wheel like a puppet's at a fair. 'I was only trying to allow the soldiers passage.' He struggled to his feet clearly meaning to face up to Christina's wrath.

Turning from the steward, the knight spoke calmly to Christina. 'The priest steered your wagon's horse too far into the deep bank of the track. He was allowing us passage but the outer back wheel came away from the bed of the wagon.'

'You should have given way to us, or come past us one by one, not in a crashing huddle,' she snapped, glaring at the knight, her eyes widening with recognition. Gunnhild, too, at that moment saw who he was and found herself smiling at him.

Edward of Winchester lifted his hands and said, 'Lady Christina, peace, peace, please, please, kind lady.' His voice rising each time he spoke the word. 'No harm done. This is the king's cousin, Count Alan of Richmond. He offers to help get us back on the road.'

'I know very well who he is. No introduction is necessary.'

'Ah, Christina of Wilton, greetings.' Count Alan bowed low and smiled beguilingly at Christina. Gunnhild was sure Christina's frost must melt and glanced happily at him. She could not believe her good fortune as Count Alan turned to her. In that moment all she could see was his even features and his eyes that had been amber in candlelight, glowing as brown as treacle, and his red beard glinting like a woodland fox's bristly tail in the sunlight that fell through gaps in the canopy. This meeting surely promised her a future. She sent a silent prayer to her name-day saint, St Brigit. *Let him ask at Winchester for me.* Count Alan bowed to her. 'And so, we meet again, My Lady Gunnhild, daughter of Harold. Edward tells me you are travelling to Romsey Abbey.'

Christina spoke before Gunnhild could reply. 'She is to join the household of Robert of Mortain. We are delivering a gift for the Abbey at Romsey. After that, Gunnhild must continue to Winchester, so if you can help us get this wagon back on the road, we can be on our way.' She shook her cloak impatiently and looked about her with a sharp shudder. 'By evening there will be wolves in these woods and heaven only knows what other dangers.'

'Is that so, my lady? Then we must give you our protection. Nightfall in the king's forest can indeed catch travellers unawares.' Steadying his prancing stallion, Count Alan called over to two of his soldiers and spoke with the men. They immediately tethered the horses to a tree and began to work on the wagon's wheel. Father Antony grunted his thanks, wiped his hands on his robe and sank down on to the verge to watch. When the wheel was securely in place Count Alan said to Christina, 'Now, Lady Christina, accept us as an escort. We, too, are set for Romsey tonight.'

The nun drew herself up in an imposing manner. Gunnhild could not help but admire Christina's sense of dignity as she said, 'Well, Count Alan, I shall accept, but I insist that you ride two wagon lengths behind us and Sir Edward must ride before us. Remember, I am a Bride of Christ, and she is ...' Christina paused and waved her hand towards Gunnhild, 'make no mistake about it, destined to become Christ's bride.'

Count Alan inclined his head, 'As you wish, but should we not ride before you, to proclaim your arrival, My Lady Christina?'

Christina snorted. She surveyed the wagon which was now upright and with all its wheels firmly on the road again. 'I would prefer you kept your distance, my lord. Behind is best.' She gathered up her cloak and, straight-backed, helped by her silent servant, she clambered back into the litter.

Gunnhild started. Count Alan was staring at her, well not exactly at her, but down at her feet. She followed his gaze. An inch of green silk hemmed with flowers and pearls had dropped below her mantle. She tugged her plain dress over it and gathering her cloak close, looked boldly at him. There was a little smile about his mouth. His beard twitched. He said in a whisper so quiet that only she caught his words. 'Pearls for a virgin.' With a flurry of her mantle, she turned and climbed back into the wagon after Christina's servant.

Christina arranged herself on her cushioned seat once again. She rescued the reliquary from the floor and placed it with care between her and her maid-servant. She said, 'We shall reach Romsey in time for Vespers. Only after we see this,' she pointed to the relic, 'safe in the abbey church do we eat.'

Gunnhild nodded obediently, though her stomach grumbled. She had eaten nothing since they had left Wilton hours before. As Christina and her servant once again dozed, Gunnhild peeped out through the curtain at the back of the wagon, watching Count Alan ride on his stallion, his large troop behind him and his elegant pennant, chequered gold and azure, carried by his squire before him, fluttering whenever a breeze snatched at it.

As Christina had predicted they rattled into the abbey yard shortly before Vespers. The distance between Count Alan and his troop and their litter had gradually narrowed on the approach so that both parties arrived at Romsey simultaneously. Priests and nuns poured out from the main building to greet them. The abbess, a portly woman, stepped from the crowd of sisters and stood in the yard waiting for them to descend from their litter.

One by one, they climbed out. Abbess Hilda at once clasped Christina's hands in delight and fussed around like a clucking pigeon, as if Christina was not a drab princess from an old forgotten royal family but a queen. Christina could claim descent from King Alfred himself, and naturally the English clergy would bow and scrape to her. She was old royalty and even now she was connected to the Scottish royal family through her sister's marriage to King Malcolm. Her brother, Edgar, the Atheling, was currently at peace with King William and often at court, a fact that Christina had liked to crow about when they had been stitching that dreadful tapestry for Bayeux.

Christina wasted no time in proffering her gift and as they walked towards the abbey's hall, she explained the purpose of her visit. Abbess Hilda took charge of the precious relic as soon as they were inside. Her white tapered fingers held the crystal reliquary with great care and reverence. She turned it round and round examining and exclaiming at the beautiful jewelled reliquary, inside which the fragment of the cross was enfolded in purple velvet cloth. *How many such fragments were there in abbeys, minsters and shrines all over Europe? That reliquary must have cost my Aunt Edith a great fortune.* Gunnhild, bored with the fuss over the crystal-encased gift, turned her attention from Christina to Count Alan who had followed them inside. His expressionless face gave nothing away. He watched, unsmiling and not speaking. Gunnhild realised with a jolt that he was not really looking at the reliquary at all but beyond it, surreptitiously watching *her,* glancing away when she noticed.

The abbess handed the relic to her priest, turned to Count Alan and said, 'We are busy here and have little enough room for guests. Pilgrims are arriving for our Easter feast, but Sir Edward and the priest can have space in our priest's house and we can provide you and your men with shelter in our guest hall.'

He thanked her and smiled at Gunnhild as, looking with humility at Christina, the abbess purred, 'And you must, of course, have the only available chamber inside my own dwelling. There will be a pallet for your servant.' For a moment a smile played on her mouth. 'I can give Gunnhild a cot in the infirmary. The chamber is private with a view over our herb gardens and since there are nuns' cells all around her she will feel safe. It belongs to our infirmary sister who is visiting the sick of Michelmersh and won't return before tomorrow.'

'I am sure the girl is grateful,' Christina said.

Gunnhild cast her eyes downwards. 'I am grateful, Lady Abbess,' she said humbly. She would not have to share a narrow bed with Christina. She raised her eyes again. The Count was stretching his hands towards the blaze in the central hearth and was watching her again with bemusement in his eyes. She glanced down again but from the edges of her sight noticed how easily he shifted his attention, thanked the Abbess and with a sweep of his mantle, bowed and departed.

The abbey servants carried Gunnhild's linen bag into the

infirmary. She followed them and sank exhausted onto the cot. Minutes later, she heard the bells ringing for Vespers. Shaking off her aching tiredness, she hurried back into the yard. When she arrived in the abbey church, Christina was already kneeling beside Abbess Hilda near the altar.

A choir stood as if to attention in the choir stalls and the abbey's priest began intoning prayers over the crystal reliquary. The abbey church was packed with monastery guests, a collection of merchants, pilgrims most likely on their way to Southampton to set sail for Compostella and, finally, Gunnhild observed ahead of her, half way to the altar, Count Alan kneeling beside six of his companions, with bared heads bowed and their armour gleaming in the candlelight. Gunnhild moved up the nave past them, but could not resist glancing at his shining head as she passed. He looked up and pointed down. Her embroidered hem had once again crept below her plain overgown. She adjusted her mantle and boldly looked back. He ignored this and brought his hands together in prayer.

After the Mass, as she followed Christina out of the nave, Count Alan reached out as she passed, touching her arm. 'Wait,' he said so low she could hardly hear his words. She paused and bent down to adjust her mantle. 'Can you slip away from her?' he said. 'I wish to speak with you.'

'After supper. I can excuse myself, maybe.'

'Yes, do that. Go to the privies during the meal. They lie behind the hall.'

It was a momentary exchange but Gunnhild's heart lifted with excitement. They filed from the church into the refectory and all the time she looked ahead as if nothing had happened. Christina was talking to Abbess Hilda, and her servant was absent, probably preparing Christina's chamber for the night. Gunnhild hurried forward past Christina, losing herself amongst the other nuns.

Inside the long refectory hall, tables were laid with white napery and wooden platters, cups and spoons. All was hushed except for the rattle as servants set jugs of water and panniers of bread on the snowy cloth. Talk was forbidden here, as at

Wilton, so she silently slipped into a position of her own choosing before Christina caught her up and bade her sit beside her and the abbess. She found she had seated herself amongst a group of nuns directly across from Count Alan, his six knights and the pilgrims. She was thankful when Christina sat by the abbess, flanked on both sides by dark-gowned priests. There was no room there for Gunnhild.

After a long grace was intoned from the corner lectern, Gunnhild broke her hunk of bread and ate ravenously, mopping the juices from her bowl of pottage as if she had not seen food for a week. It still being Lent, dishes of baked eggs, custards and plates of cheese arrived in succession on to the table. She thankfully ate all placed before her.

Gunnhild's sense of anticipation mounted as the meal progressed. What had he to say to her that was so urgent and secret? From time to time her hand flew to the golden chain and the jewelled cross that Count Alan had brought to her months earlier. Her hands twitched nervously and her spoon seemed to make an exaggerated scrape. The suspense was excruciating and the wait terrible, especially as he never looked her way but ate in the required silence slowly and deliberately, not dropping a crumb on the cloth. Glancing towards Christina, she saw the nun's head was bowed as if in prayer. Gunnhild turned to the nun by her side and whispered her need to go to the privy. The nun never spoke but pointed to a side door halfway along the refectory wall.

Gunnhild climbed over the bench, slipped out of the door and without once looking back passed safely through the refectory's back porch into a muddy yard behind. She hurried towards a row of wattle and daub huts that had been erected over a running stream. There was usually a stink about such places but these were obviously kept clean since the usual evil smell was absent. She hovered amongst a clump of withies by the stream hoping he would come soon and find her. Christina might note her absence and send someone to look for her. Moments later she heard strong footsteps tramping over the cobbles by the refectory wall. Holding her breath she retreated into the shelter of an elm tree. She recognised his russet mantle as he made his approach. She breathed freely again and stepped out onto the path. Moments later he was by her side.

He lifted her hand to his lips and she felt a new sensation shiver through her as his touch lingered on her hand. He spoke softly. 'My lady, there is little time so I must be brief.' Her eyes widened as he said, 'It is clear to me that your vocation is not strong.' He paused. She suddenly felt overcome with modesty. He continued, 'But I can save you from the cloister.'

'My lord count, I am to be taken into the household of Matilda of Mortain. Though, perhaps she will be kind and help me. What do you think, my lord?'

'It is all a plot. I think that Robert of Mortain will have plans for a Godwin heiress and if you do not agree to his schemes you will be swiftly returned to the abbey cloister.'

'What might be Lord Robert's plans for my future?'

'He will give you to one of his sons as a husband. And if you refuse you will indeed find yourself returned to Wilton where you will take vows and live your life out behind convent walls. Clearly that fate is not one you desire?'

'Perhaps I might agree. Perhaps, my lord, I would welcome marriage with a great-nephew of King William.'

He took her hand, bent down and kissed it. 'Would you? He has a mean reputation.'

He held her hands, enclosing them with his, a strange sensation, indeed, but, though she felt she ought, she could not pull away. She caught her breath and swallowed. She breathed again, slowly. He continued, 'Would you find me acceptable, my lady, because I can save you from either fate? There are many who will take what they can always, but a good man would marry you for love.' His words sounded truthful. Momentarily her mother's image flitted past her eyes. He would have married *her* and *not* for love. She glanced up into his eyes. They contained an aloof look, not reflecting the love of which he spoke. They lacked passion. Yet love her he must. He had to if he said a good man would marry her for love, and she was longing for love, so in that moment she decided that he did and sealed her fate. She gathered her courage and matched his cool look with a bold one of her own. 'What are you suggesting, Count Alan? Is it that I marry you?'

'Yes, my dear lady, and I would willingly come to Wilton Abbey seeking your hand but you know that the nuns will not agree. None the less, our marriage can be arranged.' He let go of her hands. 'Before morning we can be on board my vessel at Southampton and by mid-morning we can be far away from here, sailing across the Narrow Sea. I am set for Brittany on the king's business. If we are married by a priest in God's House it does not matter if Christina objects. She cannot undo it.' He reached down and plucked up the hem of her dowdy gown. Below it a hem of gold embroidery and seed pearls glowed in the moonlight. He pulled her plain gown over the hem of her silk dress and let her mantle fall back over it. His face lines creased with laughter. 'This tells me much about you, though I am puzzled by its provenance.'

'It belonged to my aunt. Now it belongs to me.' He moved so close to her again that she could feel his breath on her cheek and his touch on her arm. He was the answer to her prayers. She would disappoint so many. And could she trust the man who had only eight years ago pursued her mother? Still, it only took her a heartbeat to whisper, 'How can we marry, my lord?'

'You agree.'

She nodded. 'I do.'

'Come to the Abbey's chapel. I know Romsey Abbey well. There is a latch gate in the garden wall behind the infirmary. Follow the pathway through the pear trees behind the abbey buildings until you are by the chapel. Another gate will lead you to a side porch. The door will be ajar. After the midnight bell rings I shall be there, waiting for you inside.' There was a rattle close by. Breaking off, he glanced about. She followed his eyes. It was only a blackbird rustling through a clump of withies. He turned back to her. 'There is a priest here who is from Brittany. He will do as I tell him. I shall bring witnesses. Do you pledge me your troth, Gunnhild?'

He lifted her fingers and kissed them one by one and as he

did she whispered, 'I do, my lord, it is what I want.'

He clasped her hands and said, 'I, too. I pledge my troth to you.' He took her face in his hands and kissed her lightly on her lips. 'Return to the table and act as if nothing is amiss. I must see to my horses.' He stroked his beard thoughtfully. 'Gunnhild, you will not regret this.'

As if an invisible thread had broken leaving no trace, Count Alan had gone. It was as if he had never been with her, except that he had left on her lips the imprint of a kiss and in her heart hope for a new life. For a candle flame's flicker she felt the enormity of what she was about to do. She could still go to Christina and confess her sin, but as she slid back on to the bench to sit beside the dark brooding nuns of Romsey she dismissed any sense of regret.

Gunnhild lay wakeful under a coarse blanket on her lumpy cot. She had put aside her plain gown and unbound her hair. When the bell rang she found herself moving and dressing as if walking through sleep. She wore her aunt's undergown and rich overgown. With haste, she stuffed her ordinary garb into her sack. Pulling on her cloak, and clutching her linen bag she slipped out of the infirmary into the herb garden. She picked her way through pear trees that lined the garden wall until she discovered the latch gate which led to a path behind the abbey buildings. Moments later she was passing the guest house where Count Alan's soldiers slept. She paused, glanced up at the curved sliver of a moon and stopped, starting at an unexpected sound and nearly dropping her bundle. It was only an owl's hoot. She caught a breath of chill night air and steeled herself. Hurrying on, thankfully she reached the church without meeting anyone. When she pushed the side door open she found herself again in the narrow nave. Count Alan was kneeling by the altar where earlier the relic had sat, now gone. The priest must have locked it away. She tiptoed to the rail and knelt down beside him. His armour glinted below his russet cloak. Bareheaded in the candle-light he looked noble and honourable.

He reached out for her hand. 'My lady, I thought you might not come.'

'I am ready,' she whispered.

'There is little time. We must go into the porch.' She turned her head towards him. He was smiling at her. He had called her '*my lady*' again. No one ever called her 'my lady' except Count Alan. It had always been simple Gunnhild or the girl or Swan-Neck's daughter. This man, who had once wanted to wed with her mother, and who was fifteen years her senior, surely had gentleness in his heart.

Count Alan took a deep breath and looked down at Gunnhild. He stared at the gap caused by the falling back of her mantle and smiled. 'Christ's holy bones, that dress is indeed suitable for a princess to wed in.'

Gunnhild stood, letting her mantle hood fall back. Her hair was loose and it cascaded around her shoulders, rippling into a golden fall of waves. 'I am ready, my lord.'

He called out, 'Father Adolphus, we are waiting.'

An aged priest appeared from a curtained enclosure beyond the altar and was followed by a small woman in a dark cloak and a man clad in armour. The priest led them into the alcove by the porch. It opened into a small side-chapel to Our Lady.

Alan made the introductions in a low voice, 'Gunnhild, Father Adolphus and Hubert of Ridgley. Hubert is the commander of my troop. The lady is Hubert's woman, Ann.' He nodded at the priest and said in a firm tone, 'Father, there is no time to spare.'

The ceremony was brief. They plighted their troth and Alan placed a narrow silver ring from his smallest finger onto the third finger of her right hand. To Gunnhild it was exquisite. As she looked closely she saw that it was engraved with tiny curling flowers. Ann produced pale linen ribbons and tied her hands to Alan's. The priest gave them his blessing and it was done. Alan of Richmond was her husband, handfasted to her as her mother had once been handfasted to her father. However, it was different because she was also wed in a church porch by a priest of the Church and no one could change what had passed.

Count Alan towered over her. 'Draw up your hood. Your hair and gown would attract a praying monk. Keep your mantle close,' he warned. 'Listen carefully to what I say to you.'

As the priest merged into the church's shadows, Alan took her arm and walked with her back through the nave to a side door. 'Wait with Ann and Hubert for me behind the church. My men must get out of the guest house and into the stable before that fool Edward of Winchester wakes up, comes prowling and puts two and three together. With luck and stealth we can be on the road south well before Matins. With fortune on our side we can be on my ship before anyone misses you.' He kissed her on both cheeks. 'God forgive me for this.' He traced his finger along her face. 'You are a beauty and a trusting beauty. When we are in Brittany I shall write to the King. He owes me much, including peace in his northern kingdom. But let us pray that his half-brother does not object and attacks my castles, not forgetting that the Lady Christina wants your inheritance for Wilton.' Lowering his voice further he said, 'You are wise to trust in my protection, Gunnhild.' He removed the linen bands from her hands where they still dangled loosely and handed them back to Ann. 'Now wait.'

With a sweep of his mantle he hurried back around the church towards the guest house, leaving Hubert to watch at the gable corner. Ann watched from the further end of the church. Gunnhild was alone again. Folding her cloak about her she leaned into the wall, glad the moon was not bright. If she kept very still, nothing could find her. She remembered that when she was a little girl her father had told her about Brittany's castles, about marshlands and a great abbey on a rock dedicated to St Michael. He had recounted tales about dragons and magical creatures that lived by the shore and sirens that lured sailors. She prayed silently to St Brigit that she would soon see those shores. Footsteps approached, a cloud crossed the moon and Hubert disappeared.

The cloud passed, the sliver of moon glowed again, the stars shed light over the brooding trees beyond her stony refuge and he returned. 'My lady Gunnhild, come. Our horses are in the lane.'

Ann hurried from her post by the bell tower, took

Gunnhild's arm and guided her behind the building. Once they were amongst trees, someone reached out for her. Alan had come to meet them. She allowed him to hold her close and lead her past a stand of dark elms, along a track and through a large gap in the hedgerow into a meadow where a score of shadowy men and horses waited. Alan took his horse from a soldier and gently pulled the stallion forward by its reins. 'Can you ride pillion behind me?'

'Yes, though I have not ridden in years.'

'Hubert, lift her up into the saddle.'

Moments later she was clinging to Count Alan's sides, her gown bunched up about her thighs, heels close in to the stallion's withers, and they were cantering along trackways southwards over the Downs. Gunnhild experienced sublime exhilaration as they flew south, as if ancient dragons had awakened and were in pursuit. She was not a postulant now, not even a companion to Matilda of Mortain's daughters. She was the wife of Count Alan of Richmond and Penthiévre.

5

'Then a sail, a great sea-garment was fastened with guys to the mast ...'

Beowulf, a verse translation by Kevin
Crossley-Holland, 1968

Shortly before dawn they rode off the hills to the shores of the River Itchen where an assortment of small craft was waiting for them by a jetty. Hubert helped Gunnhild to drop from the stallion. She struggled to her feet, stiff and exhausted. Count Alan threw his leg over and slid down with ease. He lifted her into his arms and carried her on to a waiting skiff where he sat her down beside Ann, Hubert's woman. The small boats would take them out into the deeper water of the sound where Alan said his ship was anchored.

'We'll have a north-westerly, so we are fortunate,' she overheard Count Alan say to Hubert when he climbed back on to the landing stage and called for two of his men to come and row them out to his ship. He leaned down from the jetty to Gunnhild and touched her shoulder. 'My love, may I call you that?' He paused as she nodded. There was merriment in his countenance as, rocking the craft, he clambered back in and on to the side bench, abruptly gesturing to Hubert to sit opposite him. 'Well, my love, you will soon see the ship.' His voice sounded animated. To match his enthusiasm, her feeling of excitement increased. When he added, 'And when we reach my homeland you will have your own castle,' she thought she would swoon with delight. He was her prince.

It was a fairy-tale coming true. Their two soldiers rowed them along the River Itchen and into Southampton's sound. The others followed in a small fleet of rowing vessels. Alan pointed out his ship to Gunnhild, saying his was called the *Mermaid*. It was taller and bigger than the others that seemed to crowd about it like miniature painted beasts. As dawn broke over the sound, Gunnhild saw that the ships rocking on the sea all possessed brightly decorated sails and carved animal heads at their prows. So many vessels were gathered there that it was difficult to know how they could possibly navigate their skiffs through them. Yet she watched thrilled as Count Alan's men wove their tiny rowing boats effortlessly around lesser ships, all smaller and squatter than the *Mermaid* until, at last, they reached it.

'Can you climb, or shall I hoist you up in a net as we would a sea creature?' Count Alan said to her. In front of them all he chucked her under her chin as a parent would a child. She was embarrassed by this overly familiar gesture in front of his men. They had known each other for less time than it takes for an hour candle to burn from top to stump.

'I am perfectly able to climb,' she responded and considered the knotted rope ladder.

'Then up you go.' There was a twinkle in his eyes as he added, 'If Christina and her pack of hounds including that low creature Edward of Winchester are not to catch us you had best make it quick.'

She looked up again at the dangling rope and remembered how she and Ulf had climbed trees years before at her father's estate of Nazing. As she stood up in the rocking skiff to seize the rope she felt Alan's hands on her waist. Before she could protest he had lifted her up and she did what came naturally to her. She grasped the rope ladder tight with both hands.

'Climb carefully, my lady, I am behind to catch you.'

He reached up and pushed her gently from behind and she began to move. Though this ascent was undignified she could not complain of his hand on her backside or the way he guided her legs. It felt firm and secure. A shiver ran through her as his hand momentarily crumpled up her gown and creeping up touched the naked part of her above the ties that held her leggings closed. If she had not been so terrified of falling or others noticing, though he was so close behind her he was completely shielding her back, she would have quite enjoyed the physicality of his hands on her thighs. She must hold on and move her hands upwards one after the other. *Remember the tree climbing. No hesitation. She must not look down. She could not look up.* Her dress fell back again. He allowed her to climb on ahead. She concentrated on her arms, moving her hands up the knots one after another, catching the shaky rope cradles with her feet until a sailor leaned over the side of the vessel, grasped her wrists and hauled her on board.

Moments later Alan was up behind her. He placed an arm about her shoulder to steady her on the rocking deck, held her close and turned her around to look back to shore. 'Look how small the land seems now. Once we are all of us on board we can catch the wind.' He touched her face. 'Don't look so scared. I thought you wanted this.'

She nodded and said earnestly, 'Oh, yes, I do.' She did want this. She had won her knight and nothing could change it. She felt his strength as he squeezed her arm and was pleased when he said, 'Then, no return, my love. Let us get you comfortable.' Before she could reply he turned her round again and pointed to a wooden shelter in the poop end of the ship. 'That will be your bower. Later Ann will serve you, but for now you should try to sleep whilst the water is calm.'

'In a while,' she said her voice high with the thrill of being on such a magnificent vessel. 'I want to wait until everyone else is on board. I want to see everything. I was a child the last time I was on a ship, you know, and that was only my father's dragon-ship that sailed on the River Thames when my Uncle Edward was king.'

He looked down at her, his mouth curving into a smile. For a moment he hesitated, then said, 'As you wish, Gunnhild, but once everyone is on board I must make sure the men are ready to hoist the sails. This is a cargo vessel, a sailing ship. We only use oars in narrow channels, sometimes in manoeuvres such we must now make to get us out into the Narrow Sea. Look at the oar-holes.' He pointed to either side, to the fore and aft, where there were oar-ports and benches. He then waved to the mid-deck area where there was a gaping hole. 'And below us, there is a great hold for cargo.'

Gunnhild looked to where Alan had indicated the oar-ports, situated to either side of where they were standing and then to where a ladder went down through the great hole into the heart of the vessel. While they were talking, his men were boarding, clambering up the rope and over the side in the same way as she had. The cacophony of sound would have terrified her had she not been so thrilled by all the movement around her and the knowledge that at last she was free of Christina and Wilton.

There was shouting, clamouring, clanking, a screeching of seagulls, creaking of ropes, unfamiliar accents, noise, so much of it. By now, many of Alan's men were stowing their gear and bundles in the hold amid-ship behind them. He put a hand on her arm and called over to the last of his soldiers as they climbed over the ship's high walls. He picked out two of them to take up spare places on the oar benches to the fore and aft. He tested the ropes that secured the great sail.

When the men were all on board he left her. Calling for Hubert to accompany him he made his way to the ship's prow to speak to his sea captain. She wondered where Ann was. Looking around she saw the woman lift up the leather curtain that protected the poop-end wooden shelter and come on to the deck. Mantle flapping, Ann crossed to a great sea chest. She opened it with the help of a seaman and seemed to be inspecting its collection of cooking gear, lifting up a skillet and a few bowls. Replacing these, she took out two wooden cups, nodded to the seaman and vanished back through the curtain again.

Gunnhild turned her attention to Alan who, along with Hubert and the captain, was watching the fleet of empty boats being rowed back to land by men who were not to accompany them. Her excitement was mounting again because now she knew they were about to sail. At last he returned to his place beside her. The sea captain called, '*En avant, allez maintenant.*' As the oarsmen began rowing in a rhythm, the ship slowly moved forward. She stumbled and he caught her. 'The shelter,' he said. 'Hold on to me. If it stays calm you can come out later and see for yourself how wonderful it is to be on the sea. The stars at night are magical to behold. Can you swim?'

She felt an invisible chill wrap her round. She could swim if only she could remember how. She had learned to swim as a child. From the depths of her memory she pulled out a picture of her older brothers, her sister, Thea, and her tiny brother Ulf. Her mother was laughing as she and her maids helped them into the river and taught them to kick and move their arms. She had taught them to stay afloat and swim like a row of moor hens ploughing the stream. 'I can swim perfectly well, but surely it will not be necessary?' She felt a frown crease her forehead.

'No indeed.' He held open the leather curtain to reveal that the shelter was in fact a room with a sleeping couch that was piled high with sheepskins and cushions. There was a table fastened to iron deck rings by leather straps and three folding stools secured to the floor planks, as if they grew out of them. A hook on the wall held a heavy, hooded cape of hard material. She reached out to touch it.

'It is oiled linen, hardened to withstand the worst of the weather. Use it if it gets stormy. It will take us a day to reach the ports on the Cotentin. After that we ride south to Brittany. Rest and sleep. There has been none of that these last twelve hours.' The boat lurched and she fell against him. She trembled at the contact. He held her close to him. 'You are so lovely.' Drawing her even closer, so close she felt crushed by him, the sensation delicious, he said into her hair, 'Gunnhild, we can make this real now. My men do not need me. No one will disturb us.'

He let the leather curtain fall behind them and took her in his arms. As she flowed into his embrace, her hair fell around her face and tumbled about her mantle. When he said, 'How beautiful,' she felt that she was wanted. When he placed a finger under her chin, the gesture felt intimate and she lifted her face towards his. She was tall, almost as tall as him, so when his mouth claimed hers it was as equals, his face against hers, his lashes flickering close to hers and his body folding around hers. Moments later her cloak slid to the planks by her feet and he was expertly unlacing her gown. It shivered from her into a soft silken pile on the floor. 'Mermaid,' he whispered.

She whispered back, 'What if anyone hears? I cannot bear for anyone to know ...'

'Hush. No one will dare come near us. Do not fear. We are wedded and this is what married people do. They are all busy about their own tasks. My men will stay away. Ann is out on the deck helping the cook. If we had a wedding feast afterwards everyone would crowd into our chamber to see us bedded.'

'Yes, that is true.' She opened her eyes wide and glanced down, almost surprised that she was standing in her linen undergown. No man had ever seen her so disrobed and few women. He lifted her on to the couch. He knelt by her feet and removed her boots, her leg bindings, then his own boots and leggings. 'Help me from my tunic,' he said as he unpinned his cloak and allowed it to drop from his shoulders.

Timidly she unlaced his tunic and helped him to pull it off. He kissed her fear away, her face and her lips as he laid her out on the bed. She had never seen a naked man before, not in real life. There were tapestry pictures and religious paintings in books depicting a nearly naked Christ on the Cross, Jonah in a whale, St Sebastian's martyrdom, but she had never seen a real naked man. She opened her eyes wide, tossed her heavy hair away and boldly stared at his risen manhood. What was this? Was this how men penetrated women? Was it the evil some nuns spoke of in hushed tones saying, 'It is a married woman's duty to make children.' They had shaken their heads, not thinking she was listening from her place weeding the marigold beds in the garden. 'What a shame that Queen Edith failed in her duty. If she had not, the Normans would still be in their own country.'

She reached out and touched his risen penis. This was probably forbidden by the Church, not part of her married duty, but she did not care. She was curious. She had seen dogs do it but never humans, though she had heard them, and in that moment she remembered her mother's shooing her off before she saw too much. He responded by moving her hand onto it and then by wrapping his arms around her. The boat rolled and rocked as she became liquid beneath his caresses: his soft kisses on her breasts, his stroking, sucking and touching. In the distance she could hear the sailors' voices, the plashing of their

54

oars on the water, their shouts and the clanking of a cooking pot. Then he was gently removing her shift and she was as naked as him. 'Now we are equal,' he said. 'Believe me when I say that you are lovely, Gunnhild. I promise I shall try not to hurt you.' He lifted her hips and gently entered her, not from behind as the hounds in the hall yard did, but facing her and right into that place her monthly courses flowed from. She felt her body rip apart. 'Hush,' he said as she cried out. Then she was moving and sliding in rhythm with him. Somewhere distant, out on the water, seagulls were screaming and she felt her own call rise from the depths of her throat. 'Hush, my love.' His voice melted into her. She managed to control her cry. He reassured her. 'No one will listen, nor would they care. You are my wife, Gunnhild.'

'But I care. It is not seemly,' she whispered tearfully.

'You are my wife. I say it is seemly.'

Afterwards he pulled the sheepskin rug over them both. 'Next time, it will be in a proper bed with fine linen and I shall give you a morning gift.'

'What would that be, my lord?'

He caressed her naked breast. 'Umm, a castle or a manor.'

She removed his hand and turned to look straight into his eyes. 'I would prefer new gowns and shoes and mantles, clothing I have never owned. Things I have longed for. I need inks and paper and books, too …'

He silenced her. 'All these will be yours as soon as it can be arranged. Now sleep.'

She dozed in his arms, too tired to pay attention to the aching in her groin, the moisture on her thighs and the hymen blood that streaked them. As she fell towards dreaming she heard him say to her, 'You are my mermaid of the seas, a sea creature to grace my ship.' She tried to speak but words seemed trapped in her throat. She could not reply. Somewhere beyond the rocking boat a sea bird screeched, as if to warn her that all would not be as it seemed.

When she awoke, a thin light penetrated the gap in the curtain.

It must be afternoon. She pushed herself up. Alan was not by her side but Ann was sitting on one of the stools with a piece of mending in her lap.

The woman stood up, leaning against the wall of the vessel to steady herself. 'My lady, you should eat. I can bring you something.'

Gunnhild nodded, though she felt queasy. It was possible that the cause of the nausea she felt was hunger. After all she had not eaten anything for hours. Her clothes had been neatly placed on the small table, not the silk overdress but a plain gown from her linen bag. Embarrassed, she clutched the cover about her to protect her modesty and looked with a question at Ann. 'My gown?'

Ann said, 'You will ruin that silk you were wearing on this ship. I put it away.'

Gunnhild nodded and pulled on everything Ann gave her, the plain hempen gown she had worn leaving Wilton and the serviceable linen cap under which she tucked all her hair, tying it tightly under her chin. Ann ducked out of the opening. Gunnhild was lacing her boots when she returned with a bowl of soup and a hunk of rough bread. 'It is not much but it will stave off hunger.' Ann began to fidget. She was frowning. Her eyes darkened. Gunnhild wondered what she had done to cause such anxiety.

'What is it?' she asked as she reached for the bowl and began to drink the thin gruel.

Ann's face paled as she whispered, 'My lady, the water is very still. The light is strange too. Everyone is gazing into the horizon as if the Beast himself is set to emerge from it. There is fear in their eyes.'

Gunnhild thrust the bowl back into the woman's hand and pulled the sea cape from its hook. Dragging it about her shoulders she pushed past Ann and out through the heavy curtain. Out on the deck, Alan was watching the sky and talking anxiously to the captain. His soldiers were gloomily staring out to sea. The oarsmen were resting their heads on their forearms. Their faces reflected the same dark anxiety she had seen on the soldiers' faces, the same as was on Ann's. She reached out and touched Alan's arm.

He turned round. 'Gunnhild, go into the shelter, there will be a storm. We cannot outrun it and we must not row closer to the coast lest we are dashed against the rocks before we reach Honfleur. This is the way of it, calm first but the devil comes with his winds. Get back under the shelter and pray; pray we are kept safe.' His eyes were fearful. 'Pray for deliverance.'

'How can you tell? The sea is so still.'

'Look into the horizon.'

Gunnhild followed his eyes. The sea was flat, so flat that it looked like the watery lowlands around Glastonbury Abbey, a place remembered from when as a child they had visited the west, and the ship, like the abbey itself, was becalmed in a silty pool.

'Look again,' he said.

Clouds seemed to push the vessel deeper into the sea. It was too still. She glanced up at the sky. The seagulls of earlier had vanished. They were the only living creatures above water, on an exposed ship on a huge sea. 'St Brigit protect us,' she said.

Count Alan grasped her hand. 'Do not fear.'

She heard the captain's roar of 'Drop the sails.' The sky blackened and the sea began to stir. The sailors rushed to the mast and struggled desperately with the sail, managing to drag it down just in time, stumbling and falling over each other as they tried to fold it and finally tie it to the ship's floor. The wind began to push through the sky, causing the boat to shake from side to side, tossing it upwards. *Was God punishing her for her sin?*

Alan dropped her hands. A sailor close to her looked up from the great sail and called out, 'Mermaid's curse.' And a streak of yellow lightning crossed the sky.

'Get into the shelter now,' Count Alan thundered. 'Do as I say, Gunnhild.'

She struggled backwards as the prow of the ship rose up again and again. It was as if it were being pushed from beneath by a conspiracy of sea creatures determined to toss them into the turbulent depths below. Suddenly she thought, I can't swim if we go down. I won't have time to swim. The sea will snatch us like a giant long-necked goose reaching for its dinner. And we are all going to drown. A feeling of panic gripped her. She clutched the curtain that protected the shelter. As water swilled about her ankles, she looked back towards the sea. It was coming over the boat's walls. It was coming for them. There was another lurch as the boat rose and fell and she was thrown inside the cabin. Ann grabbed her arm and stopped her crashing into the ash planks of the wall. 'Hold onto those iron rings,' she yelled above the storm's banging. 'And pray.'

Tossed onto the soaking plank floor they both clung to the iron rings that lined the wall of the shelter. The ship reeled and reeled over and over, again and again. Water poured from the deck around their knees. She could hear Alan calling to the sailors to scoop it up and bail it out. But still the sea swirled around them, catching at their gowns, drenching them through.

Gunnhild clung on to the iron ring for her life, fearing all the time that it would rip away from the side. The water kept gushing in. No amount of swimming would save her now. If the ship capsized she would not survive. None of them would. They would be dashed on to the rocks, lost for ever, dropped into the Devil's cauldron from the middle of the sea. The ship would break up and they would all die.

'Lady Mary, save us,' she prayed over and over. 'St Brigit, hear my prayers. Save us.'

Every time the ship leapt up Ann called out, 'God spare us.' Her voice was lost because of the thundering noise outside the cabin.

The ship continued to heave and rock. Alan yelled above the storm at his men to lash themselves to their posts. There was nothing more after that but the heaving, creaking and shouting and Ann's mumbling of pater-nosters. Gunnhild clung to the iron ring, trying to think herself somewhere else, in the garden at Wilton, safe in her own chamber in the postulants' building, in the scriptorium, talking about her dreams to Eleanor, and as a child at Reredfelle before the great battle that had destroyed her father.

Night began to fall, and as suddenly as the storm had begun the waves started to become quieter, the sea more of a roll. The vessel was still tossing about but the wind was gradually dying down. Eventually the vessel stilled and she felt the sailors begin to row. Ann stood up and told Gunnhild to stay in the shelter. She reached for the hanging and flung herself through it.

'Find my lord,' Gunnhild cried out after her.

After a while, when Count Alan came to the cabin, Gunnhild was wringing out her dress. She tried to stand up but he told her to sit. He lifted her damp mantle, placed it around her, and handed her a cup of heated wine. 'Drink this. It will steady your nerves. We shall be in Honfleur by daybreak. We have the fire up again. When you are ready, come out and get dry. We have a ship to get into port. I want to make sure there is no further danger to us. Such a storm can blow enemies up into our waters.' His voice was soldierly. He was concise, determined and lacking emotion, a warrior steering them all to safety.

With that he was gone. She gulped down the spiced wine feeling it warm her stomach. As she leaned back against the planks too tired to care about anything, a wave of nausea overpowered her. She pulled herself to her feet and stumbled through the curtain into the air away from the fetid shelter. Once outside she leaned over one of the leather buckets used to bail out sea water and retched and retched until she thought there was nothing left to lose from her stomach except her insides. Too ill to warm herself by the charcoal fire, she crawled back into the shelter, collapsed onto the couch and pulled a damp sheepskin over her, thinking that she had survived the storm only to appear cowardly, weak and useless in front of the soldiers. Ann returned with a cup of water and wiped her mouth. There was a dry blanket in a chest. She warmed it by the brazier and wrapped it around Gunnhild.

'You are as white as a shroud, my lady. I hope he is not planning to make you ride when we reach shore.'

Gunnhild clutched her stomach again and squeezed the words out between her teeth. 'If my lord insists, then I must.'

Ann made a clicking sound of disapproval but otherwise kept silent. Gunnhild tried to think of a warm room, a fire and the company of women. She thought of the colourful letters she had illustrated and imagined her unfinished miniature of the Wedding at Canna with its pretty acanthus leaves climbing around a pillar and the handsome Jesus who turned water to wine. The picture distracted her until at last they heard shouts of port and land, the sound of the sail lowering again, sea gulls cawing, the thumping of feet around her and calls of 'Pull into the jetty'. There was a great rattling and after it a jolt.

Alan pushed his head into the shelter. 'We must disembark first, Gunnhild. Since we are now lord and lady you will smile for them all, no matter how you feel. We shall lead a procession of sailors to the Church of St Matthew and give thanks for our deliverance. Afterwards we ride to Bayeux. I have business there.' He saw her look of dismay and frowned. 'It is a two and a half day's ride into Brittany.' His tone was brusque. As Ann adjusted Gunnhild's mantle on her shoulders, she said, 'Poor lady, he is a soldier and unaccustomed to a woman's needs.'

Gunnhild ignored Ann's words and instead turned away from her, throwing a frown in the woman's direction first. She was a princess after all, her great father's daughter, so she raised her head, gritted her teeth and followed Alan on to the deck.

6

Bayeux, April 1076

But he [King Edward] also at a later date, sent to him Harold, the greatest of all earls in his realm in wealth, honour and power that he should swear fealty to the Duke concerning his crown and, according to the Christian custom pledge it with oaths.

The Gesta Normannorum Ducum of William of Jumieges, ed. and trans. by Elizabeth M. C. Van Houts, 1997

Gunnhild awakened out of a deep sleep and leaned against her feather pillows. She stretched her arms above her head, remembering where she was but still not quite believing it. Their bed was soft and comfortable with its own curtains and a luxurious coverlet embroidered with vivid green tendrils, yellow flowers and brown birds.

Gently drawing aside the bed curtains, Ann peered in and whispered that she had brought soft rolls and fresh milk so that Gunnhild could break her fast. Gunnhild glanced around. Their chamber was spacious. Braziers glowed in each of its four corners, the windows were closely shuttered and candles glowed in tall holders.

Ann set the wooden tray on a side table. 'You must rise, my lady, and make haste. Count Alan's soldiers are gathering in the courtyard.' Hearing the note of insistence in Ann's voice, she hurriedly swung her legs over the edge of the high bed and slid onto the tiled floor.

'Here is your clean linen. You have a quarter hour to ready yourself.' Ann laid out her shift and gown, pointed emphatically to the marked time candle that flickered on the corner chest and proceeded to busy herself brushing down Gunnhild's mantle.

Only when she had eaten every crumb did Gunnhild pull on her shift and undergown and reach for her green overdress. When she had tied her belt over the silk folds, Ann made her sit still as she combed out her hair and plaited it into two long thick braids. 'You had best wear this too,' she said and lifted the Godwin headband from a stool and handed Gunnhild a fresh veil from her bundle. 'Count Alan sent into the town for a horse for you to ride today. It is a long way to Mont St Michel.' She clicked her tongue against her teeth in her usual disapproving habit. 'He expects you to ride all the way south after only a day's rest.'

'I wonder what nature of animal he has found for me.'

Ann softened. 'I am sure the beast will be gentle-natured. My lord Alan knows horses.'

Gunnhild thought of her aching thighs after their previous night's coupling. Alan was a considerate lover but after they had made love he left her alone and went down into the hall to sleep amongst his men. She would have liked him to stay but he had shaken his head and said, 'My men need me. They expect my company. After all I must keep them from losing all they earn through dice games and drinking competitions, unless, of course, I join them and take all. Gunnhild, I am a soldier first, a merchant second, and now that I am a husband I must divide myself three ways. You must learn to share me.'

She sighed, lifted her bag and stuffed her used linen inside and handed it over to Ann. By the time the cathedral bells had rung for Sext, Ann had thrown her freshly brushed cloak about her shoulders and, now ready, she climbed down the stairs into the hall and hurried out into the courtyard. Alan was mustering his men by the stable block near the gate house. Gunnhild crossed the swathe to the mounting block and waited patiently for him, determined not to show fear of a horse to any man, even though she had not ridden her own mount in a dozen years.

As she waited she contemplated the great motte that loomed up above her, the tall stone tower on the top and the flying bridge that led up to it, sloped at a gentle angle to make it easy for horsemen to ride up from the bailey and enter the keep's courtyard. Alan had held a conference up there in the tower with Bishop Odo and other Norman lords. He told her on his return to the bailey hall where they lodged that he had asked

Bishop Odo, the King's half-brother, to write to the King on his behalf concerning their marriage. Odo, he said, would hope to achieve something for himself out of it. He was always happy to upstage his brother, Robert of Mortain, if he could add to his own considerable wealth.

Alan had informed her the night before that the keep up on the motte hill contained stores and sleeping chambers and a great hall, saying, 'When you live in my castle of Richmond, you will find it has a great keep, fortified and strongly built of stone and for good reason. In the north we need to be protected. It will withstand sieges, so if the rebellions start up again the rebels will not even try to attack me. You and our sons will be safe when I am away fighting or on business with my wool and salt merchants.'

Our sons, she thought to herself. What about our daughter? Aloud she had said, 'And so the old timber palaces of great lime-washed walls painted with birds and beasts will fall into disrepair and vanish as the seasons pass.'

'That is change for the better.'

She shrugged and frowned. 'Maybe, but they were beautiful.' She recollected the smell of pine and the warmth of their hall at Reredfelle and had distracted herself by looking out of the window at a small robin pecking about the soil in the bailey hall's garden.

Now she waited patiently for Alan by the mounting block thinking that the bailey was in fact a village with filled stables and workshops, cobbled yards and houses with tiled roofs. Yesterday they had ridden out of it and through streets which surrounded the new cathedral, radiating out from the castle walls down towards the river. They had attended Vespers in the church and as they entered she had asked, 'My lord, have you heard of Bishop Odo's tapestry?'

'I have heard talk of it. What do you know of it, Gunnhild?'

'We embroidered panels for it at Wilton.'

He stopped short, almost causing her to trip as she walked beside him, her hand on his sleeve. He narrowed his eyes and snapped at her, 'I have heard stories about that tapestry from a visitor to Canterbury. So tell me please, what precisely does that embroidery show?' There was suspicion in his voice, as if she was plotting subversion by even knowing about its existence.

She removed her hand and replied in a tone as cutting as sharpened quills, 'My lord, the tapestry tells the story of my father's defeat and the theft of his throne.' Determined not to betray any weakness she took a breath, met his concerned gaze and continued even-voiced, 'The embroidery tells that my father promised away my Uncle Edward's throne to King William in that castle up there, over holy relics gathered from all over Normandy. Was it true, my lord?'

Alan drew her into a side chapel. His tone was gentler than before as he said, 'I saw your father take an oath to the King in the church here. He made it over two caskets that I do not believe held such a great number of relics, if any at all. He made an oath to be Duke William's man, to owe him fealty. Earl Harold was England's greatest earl and as such your father controlled King Edward's policy. It was not an oath that spoke of kingship. Yet, we followed the Duke to England because many years before your Uncle Edward promised that my cousin would inherit the throne of England. That promise was the talk of King William's court for years.'

Gunnhild felt tears sting the back of her eyes. He took her hand, raised it to his lips and kissed it. 'This all happened a long time ago, more than ten years past, before the battle at Senlac. Do not allow these things to come between us now, Gunnhild. It is the past. What is done is done. We are the future. As for Bishop Odo's embroidery, they say he intends it for this cathedral so that people can see how his brother came to be king of England but I have heard a rumour that it is no ordinary tapestry.' He paused and lowered his voice further. 'I hear that your English have embroidered it with wiles. Earl Waltheof of Northumbria was in Canterbury once and saw them working on it. He claimed that if you look closely you will see hidden stories.'

Two grey-cloaked monks passed close to where they were

standing in the shelter of the Madonna's chapel. She shuddered as if air that was already chill had become bitter. If the cathedral's ghosts or its monks heard her speak of the embroidery's true messages it might bring about the tapestry's destruction, so she waited until the monks moved out through the great door and then she confessed to him, 'Yes, there are secrets concealed in its panels, in the borders, but I cannot explain them as I did not work on them. I know of one and there are others. There is the image of a fox and crow repeated three times when my father and Duke William appear. The fox steals the cheese so, my lord, who stole the kingdom, my father or the duke?'

'So Waltheof spoke truth.'

'I think Aunt Edith knew more and I know she had helped decide the tapestry's design but she never discussed any of the secrets, except it was she who told me about the fox and the crow.'

'Then it is best they remain secret,' he said and led her from the church.

For a moment she pondered those secrets. What she knew was that the tapestry borders contained sympathy for her people and for her father. She heard that when her father, King Harold, was setting off for Normandy from their hall at Bosham, on the tapestry he wore a moustache as he always had in life and he held his hunting hawk, Elidor, on his wrist. This hawk travelled everywhere with her father. Aunt Edith said he told everyone he was going over to Normandy on a mission, a secret mission to bring his nephew, Hakon, home. Also he hoped to get his brother, Uncle Wulnolf, freed. He had no quarrel with Duke William, but, many years earlier, Hakon and Uncle Wulnolf had been taken hostage by Duke William to ensure that their family did not get above themselves and that the Godwins did not stand between him and King Edward.

Aunt Edith had suppressed a laugh. She had pointed to the border below the scene and had said in a whisper, 'Look at the wolf and the crow, Gunnhild. Now who do you think is which?' Gunnhild remembered how her own eyes had widened as she realised that Aunt Edith had cared deeply for her brother, King Harold, and that, in truth, she had perhaps been suspicious of Duke William rather than unquestioningly sympathetic. Aunt Edith had smiled at Gunnhild's moment of realisation and put her finger to her lips as Gunnhild had opened her mouth to speak, then snapped it closed. But Gunnhild knew that Aunt Edith meant that King William was the wolf, even though cleverly it depended on who was looking.

She was startled from her reverie by a shout. 'Gunnhild, Gunnhild.' Alan came striding towards her from the direction of the stables leading a grey mare by its reins. Bells jingled as he walked the horse forward. Dazzled by the beautiful creature approaching her, she forgot her puzzling thoughts.

'Here he is,' Ann complained from behind her. 'And with that beast.'

'Be quiet, Ann. It is a horse, not a monster, and a beautiful one by the looks of it.'

Alan led the animal up to her. It pawed the ground as if in a greeting. Alan said, 'You are ready, Gunnhild. We have a long day's ride ahead.' He turned to Ann. 'Hubert is waiting for you over there.' He waved in the direction of the stables and took the linen sack with its scant possessions off her. He secured the bundle behind the mare's saddle. Ann took heed of him and obediently hurried off to find Hubert, weaving her way through barking dogs, stamping horses, grooms and soldiers. Alan said to Gunnhild. 'Can you ride this horse?'

'I can try.'

'Don't hesitate, never show fear and always let the mare know who is in charge. Take these. I think they will fit you well.' He slipped his hand into his mantle and withdrew a pair of soft leather gloves. She was delighted and pulled them on, holding her gloved hands forward for him to admire.

He ignored her proffered hands. 'Climb on to the mare's back.'

'Does she have a name?' she said quickly pulling back her hands.

Alan turned to the groom who said without hesitation,

'Ombre, Shadow in the English tongue.'

She crooned into Shadow's ears and stroked the mare's nose. Shadow bent her head to nuzzle her. 'You know you are mine, Shadow,' she said and turned back to Alan. 'She is mine to keep, isn't she?'

'I have paid good gold for her. Up into the saddle now, Gunnhild, there is no time to waste. Show us you are a lord's wife and not a nun who is transported everywhere in a wagon.'

The words rankled. Gunnhild immediately placed her foot in a waiting groom's open hands and hoisted herself into the saddle. She took her time arranging her skirts so that they spread out to fall to the top of her boots. Fortunate, she thought, that Aunt Edith's dress has so much material that it billows about my legs. The undergown beneath was comfortably loose. Their groom helped Alan to set Gunnhild's mantle over the back of the mare so that it fell around her. She took hold of her reins and deftly turned Shadow around.

The memory of riding as a child returned effortlessly. Her mother had taught her to ride. As the groom led her into the yard she felt a lump lodge in her throat for the loss of Elditha. She recollected how her mother had promised that she would not always be at Wilton, that Gunnhild would come home often to Reredfelle. But it was not to be. War was cruel. They had all suffered. Her mother was forbidden to see her and she was forbidden to write to Elditha. Was it the same for her sister Thea who was now in Kiev? She had hardly known her elder sister who had been so much in their grandmother's household. She bowed her head to hide the tears of sorrow that escaped and slid down her cheeks. Wiping her face with her mantle, pushing back the past, she forced herself to focus on now.

With the groom walking by her side, Gunnhild easily gained confidence. A flick of the groom's switch and Shadow began to trot. She found her rhythm as the groom watched her circle the bailey and return to Count Alan's side. This is freedom, she thought, as she mastered Shadow. For such a future, she had escaped Wilton, had married without any permission and crossed a stormy sea to Normandy with nothing but trust in a stranger's love and the clothes she stood up in. If Christina could see her now trotting forward to the head of a column with her husband by her side and only days passed since she had run away, what would she say?

It occurred to her that she should write to Wilton as Alan had written to the King. She must explain why her calling was not the cloister. She would write to the abbess of Wilton once they reached the abbey at Mont St Michel because there should be monks there who sent messages throughout Christendom; she must send hers before she was considered an ingrate to the abbey and, hopefully, they would grant her grace and forgiveness.

Frowning, she trotted out of the castle gate by Alan's side, under the archway with carved dragon heads just like the one that hung over the doorway into the bailey hall and which Alan said also adorned the great doorway into the keep. They stopped at the cathedral and dismounted.

'Only a quarter hour, Gunnhild,' her husband said as he ordered all of his men into the nave. 'We must pray for God's guidance and for a safe journey.'

She heard a lark singing in the beech trees by the cathedral wall. No, it was a cuckoo mimicking a lark. I swear to the Virgin, she thought to herself as they entered the cathedral, my husband is even more devout than Aunt Edith ever was.

She sank on to her knees before the altar. As the priests blessed their journey she found she was dreaming of its end in a tall castle by the sea, one with pinnacles, a bed chamber that she would make fit for a Godwin princess, an ante-chamber where she would use inks and vellum to make her own books, and a great hall where they would celebrate feast days. She would have a herb garden as beautiful as the one her mother had loved on her estate at Reredfelle.

They stopped overnight at Coutances and then at two other manors belonging to Count Alan on the route south and west. It gave him the opportunity to introduce Gunnhild to his stewards, enquire about the manors' safety in case of attacks from the border with Maine to the south-west, and to check on the yearly planting.

On the final part of the journey, marshes loomed ahead, mist-shrouded and ominous. Slowly they moved in twos along the narrow pathways that threaded through the swampland. Gradually the mist burned away. In the distance Mont St Michel rose up high above the tidal flats, soaring into the heavens. She drew breath as she saw it. It was a magical place set upon what appeared to be a craggy rock lost in water that looked smooth as silk. The tide would soon retreat from the island allowing access to it. Alan had said that they would pass a few nights at the monastery and would continue to Dol after he had sent out messengers to announce their arrival. It would not do to ride into that fortress with armed men. He did not want a fight with Ralph de Gael.

'Why are we riding to Dol rather than to your father's castle at Dinan?' she asked.

He thrust his red beard down towards her. 'Gunnhild, you are innocent of what has happened out in the world.' He hesitated before continuing, 'Last year there was a rebellion. It was led by two of our Breton earls, Earl Roger of Hereford and Ralph de Gael and by the English Earl, Waltheof. They wanted to seize the kingdom and place Earl Waltheof on the throne. The other two would rule with him as his dukes.'

'But Earl Waltheof is married to Judith, King William's niece. Would he be so disloyal?' she said.

'So you know that at least,' Alan said. 'But he lost favour with the King because he attended Ralph de Gael's bride ale at Exning. When he was in his cups he agreed to their rebellion, then regretted it later and confessed all to Archbishop Lanfranc.'

'And it was over?'

'The Earl came over here to see the King and throw himself on his mercy. The King took him back to England and instead of forgiving and setting him free he threw him into the gaol at Winchester. There he remains until his trial.'

'And the others?'

'Last year Earl Roger armed and set off from the west to join together with de Gael in the Midlands and cut the country in two. They thought other English lords would come to their support but no one did. Earl Roger was captured and Earl Ralph fled back to his castle of Dol leaving his bride, Roger's sister, Emma, to defend Norwich castle. She is a brave lady and Ralph does not deserve her.'

They were now riding along the causeway some way in front of the rest of the column. Alan reined up and she slowed Shadow down, being careful to keep him on the firm track though the tide was retreating and a causeway to the monastery was opening. 'So the rebellion was quashed in the end?' she said.

'Yes. Emma was allowed to go into exile. She is at Dol with her husband.'

'What does this have to do with you?'

'I need to know what is being planned at Dol. Earl Ralph's lands border those ruled by my father. His wife owns a swathe of land in Brittany. The King hopes that I can bring him intelligence of Ralph de Gael's movements. This was why we stopped at the castle of Bayeux. I had conversation with two of my Norman allies there who have lands here in the south and are concerned about Earl Ralph's presence at Dol.'

'If he hates the King he will not trust you,' she pointed out.

'Bretons suffered much after the rebellion. Earl Ralph brought most of the discontented Breton lords of Eastern England into the plot. They fought hard at Hastings for little reward, the poorest lands and no political power. Archbishop Lanfranc has a deep contempt for my people. He called the Bretons who joined Earl Ralph "dung". After the rebellion was brought down and Earl Roger caught and imprisoned and Earl Ralph fled, the Bretons who had joined them were allowed safe conduct into exile if they left within thirty days. Many did and there is a nest of them in Dol with Earl Ralph plotting revenge. Those who stayed, mostly the rank and file, the mercenaries, those amongst them whom had shown great courage ten years before at Hastings, faced dreadful punishments.'

'What punishments?' she whispered hoarsely.

He studied Gunnhild's shocked countenance before continuing, 'Many were blinded or had limbs cut off. And, before you ask, the English stayed out of the rebellion, apart from that foolish young Earl, the great Gospatrick's son, Waltheof. And why was I not with the Bretons, Gunnhild? Because I am loyal to my cousin, King William. I was raised in Normandy and I know rebellions are useless against William. They will not succeed and will only bring more destruction to a land already suffering.'

'Where were you?' she asked, thinking of how he had been in England at the time of Aunt Edith's funeral.

He seemed to pull up his horse with a jolt. She deftly moved Shadow away, though not too close to the marshy land to the side of the trackway. She reined her horse in. Out in the marshes a heron took flight. For a moment they stopped, both watching its trajectory through the pale sky. It came down onto a raised tuft of grass amongst quicksands further on and bent its long beak into the mud. Alan glanced from the creature back to her, narrowed his eyes as if he was deciding how much he should tell her.

'You are fishing like that bird,' he said.

'You can trust me.'

'Can I? I see I must since I have a task for you. Listen carefully. I was with the King fighting in Maine at the time. When you saw me at your Aunt Edith's funeral, we had just returned to England. Earl Ralph will view me as non-partisan.' He flicked his whip lightly against his horse forcing him to step away from the dangerous side of the track where the tide seeped about the quicksand. 'When he sees that my wife is King Harold's daughter he might even be welcoming. After all, we shall visit Dol in peace. My men will hand over their weapons at his gate. He will try to seek information from me, though, indeed, I shall have none to give him.' He took her reins in his hands and drew Shadow closer to his horse. He leaned over and said, 'Gunnhild, you can help me.'

'How?'

'Befriend Emma.'

She could not refuse though she disliked his subterfuge. She nodded her head. A moment later a great neighing further back along the column was followed by shouts of 'Halt.'

Gunnhild twisted her head around to see what caused the commotion. A baggage horse carrying bows and quivers had strayed off the pathway into the quicksand that straddled them on either side. Two men were trying to throw a rope out and over the animal's neck but kept missing.

'Don't go in,' she heard Hubert yell out. 'Don't step off the path.' Everyone had halted. Horrified they watched the horse as slowly it was eaten by the mud, its weight weighing it down so heavily that it was sinking fast. The other animals, mares, stallions and a couple of hounds that ran along beside them had begun neighing and barking in collective dismay, their bridle bells and collars ringing. Ann was standing on the edge of the quicksand beside Hubert. Count Alan told Gunnhild not to move Shadow until he returned. Keeping his own horse, Thunder, well away from the quicksand he rode back through his men to where the dying horse was submerged almost to its neck. He took a bow from Hubert, set an arrow into it and fired it. With a howling shriek the horse reared its neck as if to receive the arrow. As it did its head dropped. It fell back into the watery sands.

'Move on,' Count Alan ordered. 'And you, woman, get back up behind Hubert,' he yelled at Ann. 'Do not dismount again until we are safely over that drawbridge and behind those walls.' He pointed in the direction of the monastery citadel. He handed the bow and quiver back to Hubert and without another word turned Thunder's head round towards the front of the column. When he reached Gunnhild he said, 'There was nothing else I could do. The dolts were about to step into the sands to pull him back. Weapons and horses can be replaced. Good soldiers cannot.' His face was stony. He waved them forward and they moved on slowly, their column growing quiet now that the cacophony of barking and neighing had died down.

'Even the hounds have more sense than to go into that sand,' he remarked as the monastery walls grew larger.

She shuddered and they rode the rest of the way up to the monastery in silence.

7

'The archangel loved heights. Standing on the summit of the tower that crowned his church, wings upspread, sword uplifted, the devil crawling beneath, and the cock, symbol of eternal vigilance, perched on his mailed foot, Saint Michael held a place of his own in heaven and on earth ...'

Henry Adams, *Mont Saint-Michel and Chartres,* 2004

Gunnhild and Ann shared a tiny chamber in the monastery. Alan slept in a guest dormitory with his men. Two days passed and there was no messenger from Dol. Awaking after Ann each morning, she would hear a howling wind rattling the shutters. The wind's whistling was frightening at night but when she opened the shutters to behold the view beyond she felt elated. The sea stretched out for miles, but suddenly it would come racing in, swallowing up the sands around the monastery and cutting off the causeway. As it went out again it left behind menacing patches of devouring sands, those that dragged a man down through them before he could finish saying his paternoster.

On the third day, she lifted a little book of poems the abbot had sent for her consideration. He had explained in the refectory on the previous afternoon that the work undertaken in his scriptorium was of a nature both secular and religious. He said that he understood that she was a skilled artist herself. She had looked down at her bowl, too modest to reply. Then, after she had broken her fast that morning a messenger from the abbot had arrived at her chamber door with this beautifully illustrated book for her perusal. He told the monk to tell her that this would entertain her during their delay. So, since the day was calm, Gunnhild decided that she would examine the small volume in the monastery herb garden.

She prowled around the pathways with the little book secured in a linen sack, searching for a bench. At last she found one and, sinking on to a stone seat close to a stumpy oak where she could hear seagulls calling, could smell herbs growing around her and feel the sun's warmth on her face, she slipped the treasure from the linen bag, opened it randomly and began to examine the illustrations. In the picture she paused over, a tiny cloaked man with curling locks stood by a tower that seemed oddly smaller than him, his arm raised as he looked out to sea. A miniature boat bobbed on white wavy lines that represented the waves.

She scrutinised the writing on the opposite page. This was the story of a knight, Tristan, who brought a great gift to Cornwall, a beautiful lady from the kingdom of Ireland whom his king would marry. The poem was scribed in French and not Church Latin. Even so, she had to work to decipher the French. She read the words 'But the knight and the princess fell in love.'

She stopped reading it. Jackdaws rustled about the branches of the tree above her bench and began chattering loudly. The sun was in her eyes but she saw that a cloaked man had pushed in through the shadowed arched door. As he came from shadow out into the sunlight she saw that it was Alan himself and felt her face broaden into a smile.

She had last seen him at dinner time on the previous day. Since they had arrived he had attended every service in the monastery church and had insisted that his men do likewise. She and Ann attended also, but the church was large and they chose to remain at the back, slipping back to their cell before the services ended. At other times Alan was in conference with the monastery's abbot.

He approached her slowly carrying a long box in his big hands as carefully as if it were a present for Our Lord in the stable at Bethlehem. 'I have something for you,' he said as he sat down beside her. 'It is a gift from the monastery to King Harold's daughter.'

'The abbot has already been too kind.' She closed the book and Alan placed the long box between them and told her to open it. Laying her book aside, she carefully lifted the box on to her knee. She bent down and smelled it. 'Sycamore wood.'

He nodded. 'Open it.'

She lifted the lid to peer inside, gasped and raised her hands, allowing the box to slip forward from her lap. He quickly reached out, caught it and placed it securely back on to her knees. She wrapped both of her hands around it. 'I never thought to possess such things again,' she said, her eyes flickering along a row of small glass pots. She balanced the box carefully on her knees, lifted up a tiny vessel, pulled out the stopper that sealed it, sniffed it and held the ink pot up to the light. It was filled with a shadowy dark green ink the colour of yew. She examined the other five containers. They held blue ink as deep as the sky on a perfect day, a red ink, the shade of a dense, blazing sunset, ochre, the colour of earth, then a black paint as dark as a crow's coat and, best of all, precious gold with which to delicately touch capital letters and allow their decoration to reflect beauty.

She replaced these pots with great care and lifted brushes one by one from a gully that was carved into the seat of the box to hold them. Each was headed with a fine feather. She looked into the hollow again. There was a pen sharpened to a point which she could use for plain letters. She looked up and gasped, 'My lord, this gift is a fabulous thing. It is really for me to keep?'

'Yes, the abbot was astounded when I told him that you could write, draw and decorate letters. You must wrap it in leather cloths and carry it to my lands with great care. It will not be easily replaced. I have bought you sheets of vellum, not many as there is little to spare here, but maybe there is enough for you to make a small book of your own, perhaps one like this.' He lifted the small book from the bench and opened it carefully. He glanced up at her, his forehead creasing into a frown. 'What is this book, Gunnhild?'

'The abbot gave it to me to read.'

'These poems are certainly not suitable.'

'Why not?'

Alan turned the little book over and said, 'They are ballads. Some call them lays. I had heard that there is a monk here who

77

has taken commissions from as far south as Spain. They are writing poems in the south, love poems. The monk says that one day the idea will wend its way throughout all the courts of Europe and such verse will civilise us all. I see he writes in French not Latin.' Alan snorted and set the small book down again. 'It is against Church teaching. The abbot here is a good man but he is lax. You will not write such poems. I prefer you, Gunnhild, to write of Genesis and of Adam and Eve and original sin. It will be a suitable project to occupy you in my absence … until you have children to occupy your days … I shall be away often.'

She considered for a moment. This was exactly how she wanted to pass her days, though not writing the biblical story of a woman's sin. That she would not do. Aloud she said, 'In that case, I shall make stories of the saints, Alan.'

'And so you must, Gunnhild.' He smiled his approval. He rubbed his hands together. 'Now, my dear, I have other news. We are to proceed to Dol tomorrow. We set out early when the tide is safely out beyond the sands and the route clear. I want no more accidents. If we ride around the coast we should arrive before Vespers.' He stood up, stretched and rubbed his neck. 'We shall celebrate Easter with the people at Dol. My men hope for a good table there. Beans, lentils and fish at Lent weaken a soldier. They complain even though I tell them that the Lenten diet clears the mind and purifies the soul.'

'If we are to set out tomorrow I must send a letter to Wilton. Would there be anyone to take it?'

'Yes, use one of the vellum sheets and I shall seal it for you and give it to the abbot. If no one from here sails to England this side of Easter, I have no doubt that your letter can be delivered later.'

A bell was ringing from the church with echoes that reverberated around the Mont. 'The Annunciation Masses,' she remarked and returned the book to the linen sack. 'My lord, there are services here all the time.'

He looked at her sternly. 'Yes, and the Annunciation Mass is one we must attend together, kneeling side by side.'

Gunnhild scooped up her box of pens and inks, and scrambled to her feet. 'Ann will attend me. Do you realise that she is angry with you for shouting at her on the path the other day?'

Alan folded his arms. His eyes darkened and she imagined too that his beard stiffened. 'Maybe so. I have no room for women on campaign. She is Hubert's woman. He has rescued her from what he says was a miserable situation. Ann is widowed and a burden on her family, Hubert tells me. ' She felt him studying her and then to her relief saw a semblance of a smile follow. 'But if you will have her as your house-keeper, then I can allow Hubert to marry her when we are safely in Brittany.' She nodded her agreement, but before she could speak he went on, 'I shall send you the vellum. Write your letter but do not take too long over it.' He lifted the linen sack from the bench. 'I shall restore this to the monk who wrote it. It is not suitable for my wife.'

She felt disappointed at the loss of the little book, and, for the first time since her marriage, she felt a hint of despair. 'I shall be brief in my letter and to the point.'

They separated at the garden gate. He leaned down and lightly placed a kiss on her cheek. 'Pity it's a saint's day,' he remarked with meaning. 'Now take the box back to your chamber, fetch Ann and meet me outside the chapel. Be quick about it.' The bells began to ring again as they came to the low door leading into the guest house where she was lodged.

She made no reply and turning her back hurried through the doorway, clutching the precious box of inks to her chest.

The following day was bright and clear. As they rode out, a gentle breeze brushed Gunnhild's face and she determined to enjoy the day's ride since now her conscience was clear. She had delivered her letter into the abbot's keeping. They rode past the quicksand and retraced the route they had followed to Mont St Michel. As Gunnhild twisted round in her saddle and stared back, she thought the monastery a place of extraordinary beauty, a serene group of tiled roofs and pinnacles where the roosting jackdaws now looked like specks of black against the grey stone, and white gulls careered about pinnacles like a tiny angelic host.

The greater group of Alan's men separated from them and rode off towards Dinan. With Hubert, Ann and six of the best soldiers with them for protection, Alan and Gunnhild followed the twisting coastal trackways into Brittany. They paused at noon to eat bread and cheese and drink cider from the leather flasks which the monks of St Michael had provided on their departure. The abbot had promised Gunnhild that when two of his monks journeyed to Winchester for Whitsun they would carry the letter for the abbess of Wilton with them. Count Alan had sealed it with his personal seal, one that declared his family motto, 'Live in Harmony,' and placed it into the abbot's hands with a letter of his own. 'Of course, I have written to King William declaring that I have wed Gunnhild Godwinsdatter who, by her own free will, has united with me,' he told the abbot, before turning to Gunnhild. 'I reminded the King that since he had previously sought my union with your family and that this was in fact a pleasing and suitable union, we both beg forgiveness for our haste and we humbly desire his blessing.'

The kindly abbot raised his brush-like eyebrows and blessed them both, but added before they left, 'Guard your back at Dol, my friends. You are entering a viper's nest.'

Gunnhild prayed to her name-day saint that they would not remain for more than a few nights in Ralph de Gael's fortress.

Late in the afternoon, they clattered over Dol's drawbridge and into a bailey which was filled with restless activity and strident noise. The whole yard echoed with soldiers' yells and servants' shouts. They wove through people hurrying about tasks: unloading carts, carrying pails, and groups of watchful men who lounged by the bailey walls polishing weapons. As sharpened swords gleamed in the afternoon sunlight, Gunnhild felt their owners' eyes follow them as they rode past to cross a second drawbridge that led them up the slope of the castle mound. There they met bands of fierce-looking soldiers making their way back down the hill. They dismounted in the courtyard outside Dol's great battlemented keep where eager stable boys ran forward to take charge of Thunder and Shadow. Count Alan ordered them to rub down the animals and care for them as well they would their own lord's beasts. Shadow was filthy with sweating flanks and her white left forefoot needed a new shoe.

'See to it,' Count Alan barked at a groom. 'There must be a blacksmith here.'

The groom nodded, 'More than one, my lord Alan.' The wiry man took Shadow's reins and led the mare towards the upper stables.

Alan grunted to Gunnhild and pointed to the watching guards. 'I see we are expected. No secret arrival here.'

Count Alan's soldiers dismounted and with their helmets dangling from gloved hands gave their horses to the care of a band of eager stable boys who raced forwards to receive the reins. The soldiers followed Alan and Gunnhild through an arched doorway to an inner courtyard where they handed over their studded scabbards and sharpened swords to two waiting guards. The great keep door loomed up before them. Of a sudden it swung opened and Gunnhild saw Ralph de Gael looming out of the half-light, standing just beyond the shadowed threshold; beside him, Lady Emma. She was visibly with child.

Ralph de Gael stepped forward. He was a bearded young man built like a bull, his dark hair shaggy like that of hounds employed to guard sheep pens from wolves. Gunnhild could not take her eyes off his mantle brooch-pin that was intricately cut with swirling patterns of Celtic design. Nor could she take her eyes from the man who wore it and who spoke to her in a mix of English and French.

'La belle Gunnhild, fille du roi Harold, my lady Emma will see to your needs while you rest here ...' He turned to Alan. 'Et avec Alain Rouge, mon cher ami, soyez bienvenus à mon château, bien, bien.' He threw his arm about Alan's shoulder. 'Come, come, Emma and I have prepared a great welcome for you both.'

Lady Emma stepped forward and offered them a silver bowl filled with water. Maids rushed to stand by their mistress and proffer linen cloths so that Gunnhild and Alan could bathe their hands and faces before entering the hall. Gunnhild glanced up and held out her hand for a towel. As she did, she saw how Earl Ralph stood back while all this was going on, but also how he watched Count Alan closely through narrowing eyes as Alan rinsed the dust of the road from his face and carefully dabbed the cloth about his beard. *He does not trust my husband.* Gunnhild dried her hands and thanked Lady Emma. *But I have no doubt that my lord recognises this, too.*

He sent Alan's men off to the kitchens except for Hubert whom Alan insisted stayed with them. The Earl led them through the hall towards the raised dais platform where a brazier glowed and a table was covered with fine linen napery. Gunnhild looked hungrily at the plates of food – cheeses, pies, breads and tarts. Then Earl Ralph ordered a servant to draw a heavy leather curtain across to separate this part of the hall from the greater hall. He dismissed his servants saying that he would see to his guests' needs himself. When Earl Ralph placed them about the table Gunnhild found that she was sitting opposite him, beside Lady Emma whom she liked immediately. A comfortable sense of homeliness and intimacy pervaded the board and she began to relax. At first the conversation was neutral as they spoke of their journey from England, the storm and their visit to the Monastery of St Michel. Count Alan told them how Gunnhild had left the Abbey of Wilton to marry him and had refused to take vows or go into the household of Matilda of Mortain. He said that he was travelling into Brittany to introduce Gunnhild to his father at Dinan and to visit his own estates at Penthiévre.

'So the King accepts your marriage?' the Earl remarked with surprise, looking hard at Alan to his side. 'You had permission to marry a princess of the Saxons? It is more than he gave me for Emma. It was my bride-ale feast at Exning in Cambridgeshire that started my troubles.'

'He does not know yet, Ralph. He will, but he does not know yet,' Alan said in an even tone as he took a slice of fish pie onto his dish and stabbed at it with his eating knife. 'But this was no bride theft either. The lady consented.' He smiled at Gunnhild. She lowered her eyes and said nothing.

The Earl let out a guffaw. 'Then you should join me.' He choked on a piece of bread which gave him a coughing and sneezing fit, recovered, wiped his nose with the napkin Emma passed over the table and declared, 'Merde; that Norman Bastard is distributing the land we fought so hard for in such a manner that only he controls all.' He cleared his throat again and wiped his mouth again. 'Why, he is even giving a number of sheriffs from Harold's brief year more power than his own Breton earls who offered him their fealty and who fought so hard for him at Hastings. All the English sheriffs have to do is prove their loyalty to him, that they did not take up arms on the field at Hastings and that they are efficient. William is wily as a fox. He wants to keep English laws, and have the English abbeys running well. That way he can have control. Then there are all these castles he has been building with huge barracks of soldiers occupying them at his own earls' expense. You know what, he fears us Bretons, Alan.' He suddenly stopped and looked at Gunnhild, clearly remembering that she was, in fact, King Harold's daughter. 'King Harold,' he added, clearing his throat again and emphasising the kingly title with clarity. 'King Harold was a great king and a noble leader of men.'

She looked back at him firm and square and raised an eyebrow deliberately for effect. He ignored her and went on with his rant about King William's injustice towards those who had fought for him in the great battle. 'Your Honour of Richmond is not the best land in Yorkshire is it, Alan? Faugh! We, his earls and barons, are supposed to be in charge of our lands but our own lands are simply his leftovers, veru gallice, goose spit! I may have been created Earl of Norfolk but, with what I have, in truth I cannot afford my own knights; the same for Earl Roger. We are young men in our prime, good leaders, tough fighters and we are deprived of any real power.' He thumped a fist on the table shaking wine from their cups. '*C'est un abus du confiance*! We Bretons were better off under King Edward than we are under this king. *This* king is power-obsessed and church-hungry.'

'And was not King Edward distributing power to favourites?' Alan said.

'He had the church appetite.' Earl Ralph let out another guffaw. 'But it was others who were power-hungry for him.' He stopped, took up his eating knife and chopped at a piece of cheese. He glanced at Gunnhild.

She looked down at her heaped plate. Her family naturally had been very powerful and rightly so as they had held the kingdom together. Her father took the crown of England after King Edward died with the approval of England's earls and bishops. Earl Ralph's father had been a staller, an administrator and he had been valued and rewarded by her father when he was Uncle Edward's advisor. But he saw the way things lay and threw his lot in with the Conqueror once her father was crowned king. It was the same with Earl Roger, the other great Breton earl who had already placed a boot in England during Uncle Edward's day. Gunnhild looked up at Ralph and studied him. She could not feel sympathy for him. He had betrayed her family. Earl Roger had betrayed them, too. As for young Earl Waltheof, the third noble in the plot, she could not really understand why he had become involved with the rebel earls. He had been well rewarded by the Conqueror for his loyalty.

Ignoring Earl Ralph, she ate silently, pretending lack of interest. She was hungry and, after all, the fish pie was delicious.

Earl Ralph, after his momentary pause, ran on, 'I cannot accept that Mortain dared to besiege my wife in our castle at Norwich. Look at her. She is fragile, a flower, a beautiful woman and she stood up to him.' He banged down his cup spilling his red wine again. It ran in a great puddle across the table. Gunnhild slapped down her napery on the rivulet of crimson that threatened to reach her side, before it dribbled onto her precious green silk gown. He raised his voice so he was almost shouting. 'If a woman can hold her castle for three months until there is barely a thing left to eat and disease claims lives, why then I owe it to her to fight the Bastard in any way I can!' He thumped the table again. 'And you, Alan, you should be a true Breton, like your older brother Brian, and have nothing to do with him.'

'Dangerous talk, Ralph. Brian does not care for the English or the Normans but remember he inherits the greatest part of our lands. I only have a small castle in Brittany, a manor farm or two as well and no more.' Ralph raised his brows at this lie. Alan noticed. 'Yes, also a few other estates in Normandy, a house in Rouen, not great. There is, of course, the Honour of Richmond and some lands in East Anglia, Lincolnshire and Cambridgeshire. My half-brother Alain-Niall has nothing. He serves me, loyal to the King, and he is loyal to me.'

'Blah, you two Alans, kings' men, both, and my heart saddens to know it, and both named so in case one of you died.' He looked even more darkly across the board at Alan. 'Listen, Alan Rouge, if my own wife can stand up to the Bastard so can you.' He paused and then spat out his next words. 'Are you prepared to fight for what your wife has lost?'

Alan remained quiet for a moment. The candle flames flickered. Earl Ralph refilled Alan's cup and then his own. Alan finally said, his tone measured, 'I shall regain her lands, but there are no ambitions on my part to wear a crown. She will be as a peace-weaver uniting mine and hers. She, too, will be a loyal wife to me and honourable and I hope she will give me a son for Richmond.'

Gunnhild swallowed. She quickly sent a prayer to St Brigit that she could rise to these expectations.

Ralph narrowed his eyes. 'And do not think to take Dol, Alan. I have allies in many places. You will see. Take that information back to your king.' Alan glared and began to rise from the table. 'Sit down, man, you are in my castle. No harm will come to you here.' Alan sat down again, though he looked uneasy as Earl Ralph refilled his cup.

Emma folded her napkin and placed it on the table.

'Gunnhild, come with me up to the solar.' Seeing a question on Gunnhild's face, she explained, 'My bower is above the hall. We call it the solar because it catches the sunlight. Come and see it for yourself. We can send for a dish of stewed pears with cream and I have a jug of honeyed wine to accompany it.' She rose decorously gathering her wide skirts about her with the confidence of a mother cat and pointed to a doorway behind the dais. Gunnhild stood, relieved to get away from the table where she could see there would be a tense discussion before Alan sought his rest. She nodded. Emma placed a slim hand on her arm. 'There is a chamber there where you and your maid can sleep tonight and beside it another for Count Alan.' She smiled at Ann who had risen to follow Gunnhild. 'Perhaps she can make it comfortable whilst we get to know each other.'

Ann hurried behind the hall to prepare their sleeping places as Gunnhild gathered her cloak about her ready to follow Emma. As she slipped away from the table, Alan was saying, 'It was not a forgivable rebellion, Ralph, not when you invited the Danes to sail to our coasts to invade us. You must try to make peace as best you can. Even with help from Anjou or Flanders you will not ever be safe, not here in Dol or anywhere else.' Gunnhild did not stop to hear more but hurried after Emma up a narrow, very rickety wooden stairway positioned conveniently to the side of the dais.

As she came off the stairway on to a short platform and entered the brightly decorated solar, she gasped at how beautiful this room was, with its fall of tapestries and carpets on the floor. The uncomfortable tension apparent in the hall fell away from her as she looked around the chamber. Embroideries covered the planked walls with hawking scenes and flowers. Emma's bed was curtained with embroidered linen hangings. For a moment Gunnhild thought sadly of Reredfelle. Although she had lived there only a few months, her mother had made it beautiful and now it was gone. What a brief moment we have in time, she thought to herself. A hall of great beauty may be here today but if there is an attack or a siege it can become ashes on the morrow.

'Look about you, Gunnhild,' Emma broke into her thoughts. 'Look at everything here. Do not hesitate to touch whatever you wish to see closer.'

Gunnhild crossed the rush-matted floor to a table of light wood. A looking-mirror of polished silver, several combs and dainty little painted pots with cosmetics and salves covered its surface. She lifted a bone comb to examine the tendrils of leaves and gilly-flowers carved into its surface. She replaced it and when she glanced up, Emma was smiling at her. Gunnhild's wide eyes scanned the room once more. Bolts of dyed linen casually lay on chairs. Floor baskets spilled braiding in colours of yellow, red and varying hues of green. For a moment she yearned for beautiful things of her own. She shrugged the longing away. Alan had promised that they would come to her, and she would insist that he kept his word. She must be patient.

Emma said quietly, 'I am with child and we are cutting and stitching two new gowns for my pregnancy. They must have laces at the side that I can let out as I grow even bigger.' She paused, took a breath and added, 'I hope my first is a girl so that she can remain untouched by war and grow into a companion for me.' Then she swept the cloth from two of the chairs and told Gunnhild to sit by the window where she could watch the sun set.

Gunnhild was glad to be close to the opened shutters, away from the stuffy dais where conversation had grown uncomfortably intense. They sat companionably for a while, watching the sun tumble towards the sea in a great orange disk until it set far beyond the castle palisade. Leaning over the sill to watch the land below the castle, she exclaimed with delight on seeing tiny figures seated on a wagon driven by an ox slowly cross the landscape. She watched them move towards the miniature village that grew like a long piece of rope from the bailey gates.

As the sun dropped into the sea beyond the land, Emma called for candles and for a maid to stow her bolts of cloth away into a coffer. At her command her ladies seemed to appear from the room's farthest shadows as if their only purpose was to dance attendance on their mistress, and as candle tapers lit up the room, Gunnhild realised that there was another chamber beyond the solar. This was where the women had been seated busy with their needlework and spinning.

'I like being so high above the ground,' Gunnhild said.

'Castle keeps like these have three, even four floors. My lord sleeps in the chamber above mine close to the roof so if there is danger he can get quickly above and see all around us. We are on the second floor here. I chose it because of the view. Above my lord's sleeping chamber the roof is guarded with thick battlements and a guard remains on duty all around, all the time. These are dangerous days.' She studied Gunnhild meaningfully. Gunnhild met her look steadily.

'I understand now why the soldiers in the bailey looked menacingly at us,' Gunnhild confided.

'They are prepared for attack and any stranger entering the bailey with an armed guard makes them wonder if there is an army outside waiting to destroy us.'

'I understand,' Gunnhild replied, though she did not like the thought that they were constantly surrounded by a military cohort that presumably resented their presence in Earl Ralph's castle.

Emma chattered on describing the castle. 'Below my hall there are stores and a great kitchen. And you came over the bridge from the bailey. It is another place where we have placed a guard. Gunnhild, this place is a fortress, a much stronger castle than Norwich ever will be.'

At the word fortress, Gunnhild shuddered. Now she felt as cold as the sea that lashed the coast beyond the castle. She was supposed to discover Earl Ralph's intentions through conversation with his wife but it seemed to her that Emma had already had sensed her mission. It clearly was why she was saying so pointedly that Dol could not be penetrated. Gunnhild concentrated hard on not feeling fearful.

She said, 'Do you ever wish to return to Norwich, Lady Emma?'

Emma looked at her curiously and shook her head. No,

never.'

She called for hippocras, a sweet honey wine which Gunnhild loved, for sweet pastries and the dish of stewed pears. Removing her head covering, Emma remarked that there was no need to wear a wimple in the company of women and Gunnhild saw that she wore her chestnut hair in a coil at the nape of her neck. It was held in place with a pin that was identical to the one that her husband wore on his mantle. They were clearly in love with each other.

Relieved to be on such companionable terms, Gunnhild removed her fillet and veil. Emma smiled a very warm and genuine smile. 'Why, Gunnhild, you are your mother's daughter, though I think I remember Elditha was a little taller than you.'

'You remember my mother?'

'Yes, and I remember you at King Edward's Christmas feast ten years ago. I was sixteen and my father was seeking a husband for me. The King died and then that year became all about war. My father sent me into safety to our estates in Brittany. Betrothal was discussed but it came to nothing. The nobleman he chose was ...' she paused. 'Well, never mind, it came to nothing.' She laughed. 'Yes, well, I must tell you since my father's choice was, in fact, Godwine, your own brother. I stayed here until my father died. Then *my* brother called me back to England and decided to wed me to his friend. It was at my wedding feast that they planned their rebellion.'

Emma touched Gunnhild's arm. 'I have no taste for war, Gunnhild, but I am loyal to my lord. He is a good and loving husband.' As she said this Gunnhild wondered how the hardened, dark, and angry Ralph de Gael could ever be a gentle husband.

Emma clasped Gunnhild's hands and held them tightly. 'This is my home. I shall be very happy to stay in Brittany if Alan can make peace between King William and my husband. If only he can get my brother released from his dungeon and seek forgiveness for that foolish young earl who lingers in a prison cell in Winchester. If he cannot, then I fear for our future. Ralph will seek help from the King's enemies, from either the French court or from the House of Anjou or both.' She loosened her grip on Gunnhild's hands and placed her hands protectively over her stomach, as if in doing so she was hiding her unborn child from their enemies. 'If that happens there will be war.'

'When is your baby due?' Gunnhild asked, noting mentally that war was what Ralph meant when he said he had allies.

'By June, two more months.' Emma was saying as she lifted the bowl of pears on to her lap and offered Gunnhild a silver spoon. 'Let us enjoy this moment together, you and I, for too soon it will have gone.'

As dawn began creeping through the shutters, Alan came to her and shook her awake. 'Gunnhild, rise, dress, get ready to ride. It is not safe for us here.'

'I know,' she said sitting up in the bed wide awake. Though sleep had eluded her, Ann was snoring quietly in the cot beside her bed. 'I shall waken her.' She looked over at her companion.

'Hubert is gathering the men. Earl Ralph's visitors are arriving today and they are no friends of mine. He revealed as much when he was in his cups.' She saw dark circles under his eyes and concern in them. 'I do not trust him. He may not stop us leaving tomorrow but we must not give him the opportunity.'

Gunnhild scrambled out of the bed, shivering in the early morning chill.

Alan said in a low voice, 'If we linger, we could find ourselves hostages, no matter what promises he gives regarding our safe passage. He will not expect us to depart so soon and if we go now we can get on the road before the morning light is full. Get dressed and wait here until I return. My men are retrieving our horses.' He slid stealthily back through the doorway. Shaking Ann into wakefulness Gunnhild explained that they were riding to Dinan.

'He will miss the Good Friday masses,' she snorted. 'Well, I, for one, have no desire to spend the morning prostrate in prayer.' Ann clambered from her bed and eagerly began to ready their clothing.

'He is just concerned for our safety. Hurry,' Gunnhild insisted.

As the bells in the chapel began to ring for Prime, Alan ushered the women through the guarded gate house. He called out that they were in a hurry to attend Mass in the bailey chapel and to let them pass. Moments later their own guard had retrieved all their horses and they were mounted again, riding down towards the bailey followed by their small escort. With their weapons recovered they were fully armed again. No one prevented their departure. Nor, thankfully, thought Gunnhild, did anyone rise to delay them.

On the route to Dinan, Alan said, 'There is the likelihood that he knows we have gone and intends to ambush us. He let us go too easily. Gunnhild, we are not riding to my father's castle after all. We shall take the trackway south past St Malo to my own estates and get well away from here into Penthiévre. He does not expect that I would ride away from Dinan, not on Easter Friday.'

'And will that be safe?' Gunnhild asked, thinking sadly that she was sorry to leave Emma whose company she had enjoyed and with whom she had hoped to pass more time over Easter, though certainly not as a hostage. She looked down at Shadow's hoofs. 'He is shoed now but he is a tired horse.'

'We are all of us tired, never mind our mounts. It is longer but safer than travelling the road to Dinan. When we arrive I shall send word to my father and he will send my troops south to us. I am afraid, my dear, you will find my castle is not as comfortable as Dol. I have not lived there for a few years.'

'As long as it has food and a warm hearth.'

'I am sure you will soon set about that,' he replied. 'It is for you to put it to rights. It needs a woman's command and at last it will have it.'

Gunnhild glowed with pleasure. Like Lady Emma, she was to be the mistress of a castle. She determined that she would make sure her keep was even more beautiful than that at Dol. It would be a place filled with romance and beautiful tapestries. Her solar, too, would be filled with sunlight and have a view of the sea. As they rode along the coastal route, bells for Easter Masses rang solemnly from distant churches and Gunnhild dreamed of a perfect future. Eventually, Alan slowed from a canter to a trot. He was certain that they had evaded pursuit. By midday a plump spring sun had broken through white puffed-up clouds and the day grew warmer. As they moved further along the coast, Gunnhild felt increasingly excited. Before night fell, her dream castle would materialise for her.

From St Malo they struck out onto a promontory. Their trackway narrowed and they were riding by cliffs that dipped steeply down to the sea. A wind had risen and it was no longer a warm afternoon. A squall of rain snatched at them and soon Gunnhild was chilled and wet. As she stared out of her hood to the sea lashing wildly against the cliffs she felt its desolation and wondered if this wild landscape could ever be kindly. The cliff road wound endlessly round inlet after inlet until at last she saw Alan's tall grey stone castle rising out of the wooded landscape. The wooden stockade rose into pointed spikes interrupted by spaces from which archers could shoot down at any stranger who rode too close. Count Alan's colours of azure and gold flew from the tower. He ordered his outrider to unfurl his matching standard so that anyone guarding the bailey would know that he was approaching.

When they reached the lower palisade surrounding the bailey, she observed guards shrugged into their hempen cloaks against the biting wind. Closer to, she saw that they were desperate-faced men, who stood in an uneven row around the wall like penitents waiting to be permitted entrance to a shrine. They looked every bit as fierce as the soldiers who guarded Dol. At least they would have protection should Earl Ralph ride south to Penthiévre to harass them. Moments later, after they had passed through the gate, she realised that their castle was a place for soldiers. It was not a home.

They avoided a pack of prowling miserable dogs that sloped around the yard looking for scraps by weaving to the left of them. Their train followed behind as they rode past soldiers' barracks, a cooking house and a miserable-looking hall where ivy crawled up the lime-flaked exterior. It was an old feasting hall that lacked windows and it was clearly unloved since no smoke curled from the slatted roof above. They rode by a small chapel but there was no sign of a priest. Nor were people attending an Easter Mass. Surely it was already time for Vespers? Why did the church bell not sound? Alan was a deeply religious lord, yet this place felt terrifyingly heathen. In the corner of the bailey she noticed a stunted beech tree leaning against the palisade fence struggling to survive. As they passed a solitary tree on the path up through the motte she saw that clouts of white cloth were hanging from the tree's branches, blowing wildly in tatty streamers.

Alan said coldly, 'Look away, Gunnhild. There will be changes here. These are tokens, scraps of garments worn by men and women tied onto that old beech tree intended to invoke the help of the old Celtic gods, maybe for the care of a sick child, or to announce a death. That pagan nonsense will be the first to go.'

Repressing a shudder, Gunnhild rode Shadow behind Alan's stallion as he followed a narrow lane that wound its way up the hill and entered the gateway into the upper courtyard that fronted the keep. Their soldiers filed after Hubert and Ann, cursing the dogs that seemed to constantly snap about their horse's forelegs. Sadness clutched at Gunnhild's chest bringing with it a deep sinking feeling that her new home was not to be the romantic castle she had imagined.

8

Castle Fréhel, Easter 1076

Gunnhild took one look at the castle's one serviceable bed chamber and choked at the smell of damp and dirt. 'Do we have to sleep there?'

'Yes, but not on that linen,' he said. 'There must be better somewhere.' He opened a chest and allowed the lid to crash shut. The stench of decay clearly sickened him. 'It has been years since I stayed at Penthiévre instead of Dinan. Had we journeyed to Dinan first I would have sent Hubert and Ann ahead with some of my troops to see how things were, that there was fresh linen for the beds, food for my table and the castle swept. This is worse than I could have expected. The steward here will have to go.'

She surveyed the chamber. It was a mean room with bare plastered walls and little furniture, a cupboard of woven sallies, a dusty space with a clothing pole behind a dirty curtain, a chair, a long bench, a roughly hewn table and, in a corner, a makeshift altar holding a crude wooden cross and the stinking linen chest.

Leaving her alone, Alan thumped back down the stairs. She opened her bag and hung her few gowns on the clothing pole. A scruffy maid came up with a bundle of linen, stripped the bed and remade it.

Alan returned and they went down into the hall together to a mean supper of salted fish and a thin, unpalatable gruel. Ann frowned throughout the meal. She was to sleep in a curtained alcove in the hall. *Her* bed was even worse, a straw pallet crawling with vermin.

'There will be changes here,' Gunnhild said to Ann. 'The journey down here was better than such a filthy castle. Even a ship's shelter is sweeter than this place.'

'An animal's byre is better than this castle,' Ann agreed. 'You will have your work cut out bringing changes here, my lady,'

Gunnhild repressed a sigh as she undressed by the light of a wax taper. Though Alan had demanded a brazier be set in their chamber, its glow was small and dull. They retired for the night with only the one thin candle, all that could be found spare. Alan fell to his knees before the small corner altar and bowed his head, rattling off prayers at speed before the candle burned down and they were cast into darkness. She wondered if he expected her to join him but he never spoke and she knew that he would resent her speaking to him as he prayed. It was Good Friday and she realised that, to his chagrin, the dangers presented to them at Dol meant that he had missed the services for that deeply holy day.

She was so cold that as she lay down in her shift she thought that she would never get warm again. When Alan had finished his pater-nosters and Hail Marys he crawled in beside her but pushed her gently away when she tried to snuggle close to him. 'Not now, my love, it would not be right, not on the night of our Lord's agony.' With those words, on that night in his chill castle, he began to shut her out.

She lay back against her dirty pillow. The new linen was no better than what had covered the bed before since the sheets smelled of stale human sweat; as if they had not been laundered since last used. Alan turned over and began to snore. She lay on her back under moth-eaten covers and tried to sleep. She was tired but sleep eluded her. Fréhel was a sorry place, a disappointment. There had only been a few miserable servants to light the fire below and cook them a lukewarm meal of salted mackerel and the lumpy gritty pottage of peas and onion which she had picked through. Food was prepared here at Fréhel in the old style; everything was cooked over the long central hearth and as a consequence the hall below them reeked of fish. She was hungry, very hungry.

As she could not sleep she lay still as a coffin under the musty coverlet and made a number of decisions. They must install a separate kitchen and a bread oven cut off from the hall.

Their servants must be trained to dress neatly and they would care for the castle properly by washing linen and cleansing the living spaces thoroughly. No one should have to tolerate slovenly maids and such appalling cooks. Wilton was a paradise in comparison, even if after Aunt Edith's death she had spent much of her time in the Abbey church in prayer.

Alan had promised that in the morning he would send out to the nearby village for a priest. He had already ordered the clouts removed from the tree in the bailey. Before supper he had called their new household together, told them Lady Gunnhild was their mistress now; they must obey her. Then he said that after their priest arrived he would open the chapel. Everyone at Fréhel would attend at least one mass daily. Three masses would be conducted in the chapel – morning, noon and evening, and the serfs would have a rota. Hubert was to organise them.

She lay awake for hours mulling it all over, stroking her grandmother's small chain which she had securely kept about her neck since the Abbess of Wilton had returned it to her. Her grandmother had been formidable. She, Gunnhild, must be equally determined to rule. The sullen Bretons *would* do her bidding and she would only show them kindness once they improved their manners. On the positive side, she had Ann to help her. She was young. Counting her blessings, Gunnhild thought that, at least, she was not tossing in a ship at sea, though on the *Mermaid* her bed had at least been clean. Towards morning, as rain lashed the rattling, shuttered window she finally drifted into an uneasy doze.

She dreamed of Reredfelle. Her father had granted them the old Godwin hunting hall after he had set Elditha aside for a new marriage and her mother had built up the estate in months. She had cleaned every building and won over the peasants who served it. They had been willing to obey the woman they saw as the king's lady and within weeks of her changes they had admired her. She dreamed of her mother sitting in the upper chamber reading to her and her brother Ulf from a book of riddles that had belonged to her father. In her mother's household everything owned its place, neat and cared for, as a hall should be. When Gunnhild awoke, her face damp with tears, she was not at Reredfelle. Her husband had already risen and Ann had not yet come to her. She examined her skin. Red welts were rising where she had been bitten. She scratched and then remembered why – the mattress had fleas. She leapt out of bed. There was a bowl of cold water waiting on a small bench and a cloth. Anxious that she did not scratch the bites into oozing blood, she dashed the water about her face and arms, glad that it was freezing since it eased the itchy bites. She examined the drying cloth for ticks, decided it was clean enough and dried herself off. Dressing hurriedly, she quickly knotted her hair under a veil and climbed down the narrow stairway into the castle hall.

Alan was seated at the bare board munching a hunk of bread with one hand and drinking a cup of small beer from the other. The Hall looked neater than it had on the previous night – there was no evidence of the sleepers; mattresses had been put into chests. She looked towards her feet. Dirty rushes had been swept away. The floor planks were bare and a team of four young girls had begun scrubbing them. Back and forwards they moved, their backs bent, their hair neatly tucked below tight linen bonnets, their hempen-clad skirts rising and falling in rhythm as they worked. She looked around her hall, pleasantly surprised. The central hearth had a fire glowing in it and an old woman was stirring something that smelled like a vegetable stew with herbs in the pot that hung from brackets above the blaze. Another was bent over what looked like griddle cakes. As Gunnhild smelled them, hunger rose in her belly.

Alan stopped eating. 'I have been up for hours but did not wish to disturb you. As you see I am beating changes into them already.' He waved his hand towards the hearth. 'However, even though they will do my bidding without question and I can order a clean-up of Castle Fréhel, it will be for you, Gunnhild, to manage the servants and see that they do not slide back into slovenliness.'

'What tongue do they speak here, my lord? Will they understand me?'

'They speak their own tongue amongst each other, just as they seem to want their old religion, but believe me, Gunnhild, they have French enough to understand you. Don't take any of their dumb nonsense from them.' He lifted an ash switch that lay on the bench. 'Walk around with this and use it if necessary. Do you understand? Show them no weakness. They are horses to be commanded.' His tone was sharp.

She had never seen her mother carry a switch to beat disobedient servants. Elditha had won servants' loyalty with firmness and patience. However, she remembered that Elditha had travelled to Reredfelle with a great household of her own and there was devotion in her peoples' hearts. She must be a chatelaine as efficient as her mother and organise these sullen servants.

Alan reached for her and seated her beside him. He placed a cushion at her back. 'Now, tell me, what would my lady like today? How about griddle cakes with butter and a cup of warm frothing ale?' Not giving her time to reply, he clicked his fingers at the women below and immediately they brought the cakes, butter and ale that he demanded. He smeared butter over a griddle cake and held it up to her. She took it and began to eat ravenously.

'Better than last night, and I ordered this too,' he said, lifting up the flagon of ale and pouring her a cup. 'We have a brewery where they make apple cider and beer. There is a buttery and a dairy. It is, without doubt, neglected but you will soon set it all to rights. '

'But there is no separate kitchen or bake house?'

'There are both kitchen and bake house down in the bailey, but up here, well, no need. We have a hearth.'

'No, we must build them. I will not have cooking done over the hearth here.'

He considered and said firmly, 'That depends on the cost. It was good enough for our fathers and good enough for us if they cook over it with care.'

'It is not good enough for me, Alan. There must be new furniture and a fresh coat of lime on all the walls.' She pulled back her sleeve and showed him the bites. 'I cannot sleep in those filthy sheets again.'

'Then they must be boiled and dried today.'

'They are past boiling. Burning would serve them better. And the mattress is full of vermin.'

'I shall see it beaten and aired.' He sighed. 'Gunnhild, it is a woman's work. After today I shall not organise any of the domestic arrangements in this castle.'

'*I* shall,' she said quickly. 'Where is Ann?'

'Ah, now there is a woman who can organise. I sent her down to the dairy and already she has sent these up.' He pointed to the cheese and butter. 'They are scrubbing the dairy clean.'

'Good,' Gunnhild said with a twinge of irritation that Ann was cleaning the dairy already at *his* behest rather than at her own. She drank a long draught of her ale. She might prove herself to be efficient, but he must pay for new things such as linens and furniture. The changes she planned would cost him and he had already indicated that he was tight-pursed. She surveyed the hall, recognising that once it was whitewashed it could be attractive. They could have scenes painted on the walls: ships at sea with borders of mythical creatures; mermaids and mermen frolicking in waves. Perhaps, too, they could commission a set of tapestries to hang in the hall and in the new solar that she intended to have as her bower. She made the suggestion.

'Such scenes cost the earth and, in any case, are fanciful. They may belong to a bed chamber but they are an inappropriate waste of money here in the hall where the business of governing is done. I grant you permission to have it lime-washed. That should suffice, my dear.'

'And the bed chamber too?'

His tone grew terse, almost resentful at the thought of any improvement, as if he considered her a scold. 'That will be done in time.' He laid down his cup and called for a woman to clear all away. He stepped off the dais, moved through the hall and spoke with the women who had just finished scrubbing the floorboards. When he returned he said, 'Now, if you are finished eating, let me show you my falconry. Perhaps you would like to choose a bird for yourself.'

Momentarily she forgot the dingy castle, the miserable yard and the sorry church that should have been opened for Easter and every other day, too. The prospect of a falcon was the best thing that had happened for her since they had arrived at Castle Fréhel. If only Harold, her father, was alive and could see her with her own hunting bird. He had loved these birds and often moved between his manors with falcons and hounds that wore decorated collars and musical bells; but then, she reflected as she walked with Alan along the muddy, winding pathway down into the bailey, what would her father think of her marriage to his enemy? Oh my father, she thought sadly, times are much changed.

First, Alan gave her a tour of the bailey. As they entered the church, she saw how lovely it was, even if cobwebs clung everywhere and it was dusty. Her eye was drawn to a high, small oriole window of painted glass depicting the Virgin and her child. Above the figure of the Virgin were two angels, one blowing a trumpet, another holding scales. She took an inward breath. These angels heralded the coming of the great judgement. She had seen such images on manuscripts in the scriptorium at Wilton. The coloured glass threw painted shadows on the tiled floor by their feet. A sweeper bowed deference to them both and Alan signalled to him to continue his work. 'He is making the chapel ready for Easter Day masses,' he said to Gunnhild.

'What happened to the priest who served here?' she asked.

'Father Alfonse was very old. He died a year past. They buried him in the cemetery. The seneschal that I put in charge a year ago never sent for another. Most people here have, of late, neglected the Christian way. That will change. There are many saints in Brittany and these people will remember to observe their special days with prayer and reverence. Believe me, I intend to root out sinful ways and destroy the perpetrators.'

'And the castle's seneschal?'

'He has been the first to go. I sent him away this morning. I have no need of such a neglectful man. Hubert will be in charge of the soldiers. Hubert and Ann will have the use of the hall down here and the bedchambers behind it. Since they are betrothed in the eyes of God, they may co-habit. When the new priest arrives from St Malo he will marry them.'

'You have made so many changes quickly,' she remarked, amazed at how much order he had instilled at Castle Fréhel within the space of a morning.

They crossed themselves before the altar and he said, 'I expect the priest to arrive tonight or at least in time for Nones tomorrow. This afternoon the church must be cleansed of dust and vermin.' He traced a finger along a wall ledge and held up a filmy cobweb. He grimaced and wiped it on his cloak, indicating that his sharp eyes would miss little. 'I have ordered the cooks to prepare an Easter feast though heaven only knows what they can provide. There will be fish and more fish, simple but suiting, though I hear there may be a lamb slaughtered for us, too.'

Gunnhild longed for meat. 'I am hungry at the thought of it,' she said as she followed him from the chapel.

They passed the hall which was to be Hubert and Ann's dwelling place. Hubert was there, leaning on a broom. 'I have ordered new grasses to be spread in here, my lord.'

'Hubert, keep the key to this hall whilst we remain at Fréhel. My wife will have charge of all the other keys to stores and domestic buildings. And send the sweepers into the church. There was only one evident.'

When Hubert hurried off to do his bidding, Alan turned to her and said, 'When I return to Normandy to meet with the King, Hubert will remain to protect you. You will be in no danger. Now, follow me. We shall look at my birds and I shall show you yet another place, one I think you will like.'

Gunnhild hoped she would find something to like in this desolate place. She glanced up at the four square watchtowers that rose at each corner of the palisade. Already the soldiers above appeared more alert than they had on the previous night. Aloud she said, 'My lord, when will you leave?'

He shrugged his shoulders. 'One reason we departed Dol so quickly is because Earl Ralph is planning to harry Normandy's borders. He let slip, albeit when he was in his cups, that he had support from the Angevin court and from the King of France himself. He has been part of a wider conspiracy to destroy our King, so I have sent a messenger to my father in Dinan and another to the King's council in Rouen.' He cupped her chin in his hands and looked into her face. 'I will have to go to the King when he returns to Normandy but it may not be for another few months.'

'Let me travel with you, Alan. I am your wife.'

'Until King William extends his blessing to us, you cannot travel with me to Rouen, but we shall weather the storm.' He threw opened a barn door. 'Now let us see these birds.'

Birds roosted on perches inside wooden cages, a half dozen of them, all looking healthy and well cared for.

'Better than the humans here,' she said to Alan, as he allowed her to choose one for herself.

They carefully pulled on leather gloves, Alan taking her small hands in his and then encasing her left hand into the hard protective glove. The boy, Enmon, who cared for the birds withdrew the creatures one by one from their cages and set them, hooded and chained, onto perches. 'How do I choose?' she asked, looking up at Alan.

'A goshawk would serve you well. Choose one of those two goshawks.' Alan pointed at the creatures, one by one, as the boy showed them off to Gunnhild.

She chose one with small sharp eyes that met her own as if the creature understood her new mistress, and then she asked the bird's name. Enmon released the goshawk and took her on to his wrist. He said in Norman French 'You have chosen Nighthawk, my favourite of them all. It is a fine choice, my lady.'

She took Nighthawk onto her own wrist then, keeping the goshawk on its attached chain.

Alan was looking over his favourite sacret with great care. 'I swear she remembers me,' he said to Enmon as he took the bird on to his wrist. The bird puffed up and seemed proud to be on his master's arm once more. 'You have taken good care of them.' Alan showed the sacret off to Gunnhild, 'I called her Lady Matilda after the queen. I shall teach you how to hawk. Do you think you would like that?'

'I would like it very much.' Gunnhild said, enjoying the feel of Nighthawk on her leather-gloved hand. She thrust up her chin. 'With Nighthawk on my wrist I may better you in the woods, my lord. Hawking is in my blood.'

'Ah, Gunnhild, I like your competitive spirit but don't count your geese yet. And now, let me show you somewhere else.'

He led her through a gateway set into the palisade, not the main gates into Fréhel but one on the seaward side of the small fortress. It had two watchtowers. Once they passed through these they were on a pathway edged with gorses and sea grasses. Alan led her to a set of stone steps carved into the cliff beyond. 'Take my hand. I do not want to lose you so soon.' He offered her help to descend into a sandy cove that lay at the base of the cliff fall. The steps were steep but Gunnhild had no trouble gathering her skirts into a bunch and clambering down without his help.

'You are as agile as a Breton pony,' he said as she jumped deftly onto the sand.

She breathed in the air. It tasted of salt and smelled of gorse and wild flowers. 'It is heaven itself,' she breathed. 'I shall come here when you are gone and I need to find solitude.'

They walked along the beach. When they reached the cliff at the other end, he drew her behind a group of small rocks. She hesitated. There were rocks and little pools that she wished to explore.

'Explore them another time,' he said, pulling her down onto a patch of soft sand. He kissed her hard. 'I have a better idea for today,' he said. 'Though it is Easter Saturday, I think the Lord will forgive us.'

She found herself melting into his embrace, her eyes slowly closing as his mouth possessed hers in a possessive kiss. Feeling an urgency that matched his own, she sank down with him onto a patch of silvery sand. Out of sight of the watchtowers he made her his own again and afterwards when they rose and swept the sand from each other he said, 'Gunnhild, I never gave you a morning gift but, today, I want you to consider Castle Fréhel as my gift to you. After all, you may already be carrying my heir. We must return to Castle Richmond, but if anything happens to me, come back here. Fréhel is your dower. It will be a place of safety.'

A shadow crossed the sun and she shivered, momentarily chilled. She was not sure that this was a gift she wanted, nor was she sure that if anything happened to her husband that she wished to raise children here. The castle felt less threatening by morning light but she wondered if she could ever subdue the Breton servants who dwelled here. None the less, she managed to smile and say, 'My lord, you are too generous.' After all, he had just made love to her as if he was in love with her. Although he never said the words: 'I love you,' she met his amber eyes thinking how fortunate she was.

9

Beltane May 1076

By the time they climbed back up the castle hill and entered the keep, the chambers had been swept and the mattress on their bed aired and beaten with switches, filled with foul-smelling flea-bane.

She begged him to purchase a new mattress. Eventually he said, 'Maybe, Gunnhild, we do need a new one to make my heirs.' He was frowning at her as he said it, as if he really considered a new mattress to be an extravagance.

Brother Geoffrey arrived that very evening to serve at Fréhel until another priest could be found. He was slim and of middling height, had kindly blue eyes, a ring of sandy-coloured hair around his tonsure, a pleasant smile and a soft way of speaking. He conversed in English as well as Breton and Norman French. When he told her he had met her mother in Canterbury and that she was in good health, Gunnhild felt happy and relieved. She decided that she and the priest would get along well. In Wilton no one, not even Aunt Edith, had ever spoken of Elditha.

On Easter Sunday, Alan and Gunnhild observed all three masses, Prime in the morning, Sext at noon and Vespers in the late afternoon. Father Geoffrey sent the falconer's boy to ring the chapel bell. He sent out a warning that all castle servants who could be spared must attend Nones at midday and the others must attend Vespers. Alan insisted that his soldiers attend at least one.

As she entered the chapel for the noon service, Gunnhild noticed several sullen faces amongst her servants. She sighed. It would be a challenging task to turn them away from their heathenish practices. At Vespers, as the sun came into the west behind the oriole window, Gunnhild found herself day-dreaming. She smiled up at the Lady Mary and wondered if soon she would ripen with Count Alan's child. Her eyes wandered about the congregation. There were children present. Not far away from where she stood, she noticed a boy with bright red hair. Beside him a small girl with fat yellow plaits was clinging to her mother's hands. Gunnhild stared at their parents. The father was burly and bearded, possibly a field labourer, though his mantle was of green wool, like a huntsman would wear. He stood patiently as the priest intoned endless pater-nosters, as if absorbed by the ceremony.

The children's mother must have sensed that she was observed because she turned sideways and held Gunnhild's stare with one of her own, boldly countering look for look, locking Gunnhild's eyes with her own. Gunnhild saw they were a hard, ice-blue but still refused to look away. Who was this woman who regarded her with such insolence? She will blame me, Gunnhild thought, for the changes Alan is placing around the castle. The little boy, who must had been about five years old, twisted his neck around and smiled at her. He had soft brown eyes, red hair, fine features and a knowing wise look on his countenance. *How did that peasant woman give birth to such a lovely child?*

Later, as they were feasting, Count Alan remarked to the priest, 'Thank the lord they did not neglect the fields last September. The grain stores are full.' He lifted a wheaten cake and grunted at the mutton that lay on his bread trencher swimming in a sauce of cinnamon and berries. 'They can bake a decent cake here.' He turned from the priest to Gunnhild. 'But they need to know who is in charge, Gunnhild.'

'So you tell me often enough, Alan,' Gunnhild retorted, her voice anxious. Gone was his gentleness of the day before. *He is all efficiency now, even with me his wife.*

Brother Geoffrey smiled sympathetically. He further endeared himself to her when he offered to help her tame them. 'They will respond to Christian ways and firmness and I can help with one, you with the other, my child.'

Gunnhild wanted to ask Alan about the family she had seen in the church, but just as she opened her mouth to speak, one of Alan's men took up a harp and began to sing an old Breton song. She glanced about the benches. The family was not in the hall for the Easter feast and by the time she had returned to their chamber to undress for bed she had forgotten about them.

Gunnhild felt her new life had truly begun when she became the keeper of keys to all of their private chambers: the stillroom, the strong room within the keep and the room above her own that was to be transformed into her solar. She was in charge of the kitchen, the kiln-house for drying grain, the cow byre and a private privy, a room set into the keep's walls beyond their chamber and which protruded out over a midden.

In the weeks that followed Easter, carts came to Fréhel with provisions, a great new feather mattress which Alan had grudgingly ordered; stools and benches for her chamber and solar; in addition to these comforts he had sent for two embroidery frames, bales of material and two seamstresses from Rouen to make her new clothing. He complained all the time that the cost was too much and she was not to expect anything else. 'They are from a merchant who owes me money. I said I would take part of his debt in kind and he should throw in his seamstresses. Gunnhild, you must be clothed as the Lady of Penthiévre ought to be. Just do not expect more.' With those words he departed for the hall, leaving her to examine the bales of cloth.

Ann and Hubert were to marry on the Feast of Beltane on the fifth day of May. Count Alan said grudgingly that it would be a gesture to this ancient celebration that was so loved in Brittany. The day would include Christian practices since they could unite a Christian wedding supper with the Beltane feast.

A few days after the seamstresses arrived, Gunnhild stood by the solar window. She held up a swathe of pale blue linen so that sunbeams slanted on to it and said, 'Ann, this is for your wedding gown.' She reached for silver braid. 'And this can edge a pair of flowing sleeves. The rest can be worked into a girdle.'

'My lady, I cannot, it is too fine.'

'Nonsense.' Gunnhild lowered her voice. 'You have helped

me with the servants, with the dairy, with the still room. I would never have known how to run this household without your help. And, yes, I know, I still have much to learn.' She laughed. 'At least I have no need of an ash switch. They obey me now, thanks to your guidance.'

'My lady, that is all due to your firm way, though perhaps the fact that you are taller than most of them and can look down on them helps, too.' Ann smiled, her dark eyes twinkling with happiness at Gunnhild's praise.

'No, I think you know that without your help I would have failed here and disappointed my husband. He does not tolerate waste. He is unwilling to allow improvements such as a kitchen,' Gunnhild pointed to the bolt of pale blue linen, 'yet he permits us fine cloth.'

Ann laughed. 'Your lord, my lady, is a wealthy man. He has trading interests that surpasses those of the kings in the east or the merchants of the silk roads. These fabrics –' she fingered the blue linen, '– he has kept stored away in warehouses in Rouen to resell. Your husband organises trade.'

Gunnhild had not known that. There were things that Ann revealed in their conversations within the territory of the solar that she must have gleaned from Hubert, though it would not become her status as Alan's wife to discuss him with her servant. 'Well then,' she said aloud, loath to allow Ann to see just how little she really knew about her husband, 'since he does not begrudge me cloth, you shall have this linen for a new gown.' Gunnhild called the seamstress over to them. 'You will measure Mistress Ann for a dress fit for a marriage. Bring me over the crimson silk.'

Gunnhild had been pleased when Count Alan had come into the solar a few days before with the bolt of silk, insisting that she had it made into an overgown and cloak. He was specific in his instructions. It should be decorated with gold embroidery. She would wear the new gown for the wedding feast.

The little seamstress lifted the bolt of crimson silk and bustled back over the rushes to Gunnhild. Gunnhild told her to leave it on the table beside them and return to her work.

'So you see, Ann,' she said, pointing at the crimson silk, 'I have already chosen my dress.' She lifted the fine blue linen. 'This blue will illuminate the dark gleam in your eyes.' She went over to a box on a small table by the window. Unlocking it, she said, 'My lord gave me three necklaces when that merchant from Friesland rode into our courtyard last week. I want you to have this one as a wedding gift.' She pulled out a string of pearls. 'I do not need it.'

When Ann's face filled with joy she knew that she had done the right thing, though she had been loath to part with the pearls. Such precious possessions were a pleasure after years of desiring such things that belonged to the world beyond the cloister.

The festival of Beltane was observed throughout the countryside. The servants discarded their sullenness and, for days leading up to the first day of May, passed their precious free hours plaiting gentians, bluebells, cornflowers and early hedgerow roses into garlands in preparation. The bailey hall smelled pleasantly of flowers and grasses. Every chamber and object was cleaned, scoured to within an inch of survival.

Gunnhild marched around the castle, up and down the wooden stairway, looking furious, holding her switch. She never actually hurt anyone with it but she used it to point at corners that were dusty or at cobwebs that hung from door lintels. Her servants were so good-humoured about the celebrations that they were cooperative without her having to raise her voice to them once. None the less, she wore a stern look. When they did a job well such as mixing the floor grasses with dried fennel at her request, she thanked them. That way she and the castle servants rubbed along together without friction.

The day of the wedding arrived. After Hubert and Ann had exchanged their vows, and were exiting the church after the mass that followed their ring giving, Gunnhild noticed the little boy with red hair standing amongst the small crowd outside. The child's mother, sister and father stood behind him. She

glanced sideways and saw that Alan was watching them, too.
This time she noticed Alan's brown eyes softening as he looked
from child to mother. The woman looked away. She was not
boldly meeting his stare as she had done Gunnhild's during the
Easter service. With startling revelation Gunnhild realised
whom the boy resembled. She glanced uncomfortably about the
gathering of soldiers, servants and villagers, wondering if others
saw it, too.

Once the feasting was over, Gunnhild watched the elfin
woman as she tripped lightly about the Beltane fire, never once
glancing Gunnhild's way. Though she wore a plain kirtle of
russet linen and an over tunic of similar material, she held
herself like a small queen, her flaxen plaits swinging as she
circled the flames, her two laughing children dancing at her
side. Unlike many of the other countrywomen she was not
barefooted. Her dainty feet were shod with leather shoes.

Cries were directed towards them. An agile, pigtailed little
musician began frantically beating his drum and was sidling
over to where she sat with Alan, whilst another, a plump man,
followed him playing a large recorder, bending forwards and
backwards sucking, blowing and puffing. A goblin-like man
completed the trio. He danced about them as he played his
bagpipes, his short green cape flying behind him until he
stopped close to Gunnhild, tugged at her hand and tried to pull
her into the circling dancers.

'They want us to dance, too,' Alan said, and took her other
hand.

'I can't,' she replied looking down at her slippers, the leather
dyed to match her scarlet dress. 'These are silk slippers.'

'Come on, Gunnhild.' Alan's tone was impatient. 'They are
waiting.' The crowd had fallen back and Alan pulled her
forward, away from the bearded goblin man.

'Who is that woman who so insolently stares my way?' she
asked furiously, on seeing the elf woman stop to watch them.
'The one wearing red leather shoes.'

'She is no one,' Alan said sharply, as he pulled her into the
circling dancers. 'Her husband is my game-keeper. They care

112

for the hunting hall. You will see it on Saturday when we take the falcons out.'

Others joined them but not the woman from the hall in the woods. As they melted into the great dancing circle, Gunnhild looked out to see where she had gone. The family were hurrying towards a cart that was waiting by the stables. The man threw a sack over a horse and climbed on to it. The woman lifted the little boy up and sat him in front of her husband, then helped her daughter into the cart. As Gunnhild wove through the dance exchanging one partner for yet another, passing a word to Ann as she swirled by her, she lost sight of the woodland family. They were gone by the time she glanced towards the barn again. Though she could not think why, she felt glad of it.

Gunnhild now threw herself into the dancing forgetting her shoes, forgetting everything except the pipes playing faster and faster as she whirled around and around. 'You are a true chatelaine tonight, beautiful in your scarlet gown,' Alan called to her as they swung by each other. He caught her and kissed her in front of everyone. She felt their approving glances whilst they clapped in time to the music.

Later, as they walked up the hill to the castle, leaving Ann and Hubert to their bedding ceremony, they could see flickering fires glowing beyond the palisade. Alan pointed and said that there was an ancient stone circle out in the woods. The country people would drift to it after they left the bailey. She had overheard the servants talk and knew that they would celebrate Beltane far into the night. Women and men would couple. Promises would be made and trysts kept and broken. She wondered how many bastards would grow in peasant girls' wombs before dawn.

They drank a cup of warmed buttermilk and sat companionably in the antechamber where a fire glowed in a hearth set into the wall. As she sipped the soft milk that was pleasantly laced with honey, they discussed how successful the wedding had been and how proud Hubert was of Ann. It was long after midnight when she and Alan climbed the stairway to their bed chamber. By then she was too tired to ask him more about the huntsman's family, especially the boy.

Later, she lay comfortably in Alan's arms, sated by their passion. They sank back into the new feather mattress resting until Alan raised his head and looked thoughtfully down at her. He whispered into the golden sweep of hair that covered his chest, 'Gunnhild, I must tell you something.'

'You have already told me that today I looked beautiful.'

'No, something else, Gunnhild.'

'Well?'

'That little boy you saw at the wedding – well he is mine. I am telling you because I see that he worries you.'

She pushed him away and sat up, wide awake. 'What are you saying, Alan?'

'It was five years ago and I have seen that they are well cared for. Agenhart is a merchant's daughter from Dinan. She is now married to my woodsman, Brieuc.' He paused, waiting for her to say something. When she remained silently tense beside him, he added, 'You must accept this. Soon we shall have sons of our own. Agenhart is a mistress; she is not my wife.' He sat up beside her, put his arms about her stiff, angry body and kissed her gently. 'Promise me that a mistress and an innocent child will not destroy your happiness. Rise above it as other women do.'

She grasped the hand that reached out for her own but she could not speak. He entwined his fingers with hers and stroked her hair. He soothed her, but though she knew he spoke the truth and was honest when many a man was not, she felt uneasy. *Agenhart is a mistress not was a mistress*. She choked back tears that threatened to flow. What was she to say to this? Everyone must know of it. The boy's parentage was obvious, so much so that even she had wondered.

'It must never ever happen again.' She turned to him.

'I do not make promises I cannot keep. You will ignore this,' he said hardening. 'Agenhart is a beautiful woman but she is not my wife and you are. As such you will behave as behoves a noblewoman.'

She choked, swallowed and looked angrily at him. *And the boy is your son.* She was royal, a princess. The boy's mother was a mere merchant's daughter.

'I shall try to understand,' she said aloud though in her heart she felt jealous that any woman had lain with him before her. She suspected that many others had lain with her husband before Agenhart and that he was telling her that Agenhart remained his mistress.

'And the boy is named?' she asked at last, hoping that this was not Alan.

'Dorgen. She called him Dorgen.'

Fréhel was her dower gift. Never would Agenhart or the child, Dorgen, enter her keep. Furious, she eventually turned away from Alan and fell asleep.

10

And the king was at Westminster that midwinter; there all the Bretons who were at the bride-feast at Norwich were condemned ... Thus were traitors to the king laid low.

The Anglo-Saxon Chronicles, 1076, translated and edited by Michael Swanton, 2000.

The day of the hunt dawned bright and clear. Gunnhild felt sad at Alan's revelation but, though it had disturbed her deeply, she held her own counsel, determined to survive the day ahead and maybe, just possibly, enjoy the hunt. She rode into the woods clad in a simple linen gown that was fuller than usual, one she had the seamstress make for this purpose so that she could ride astride Shadow. A little way into the beech trees, Alan allowed his sacret to fly free. She watched its progress as it soared high above the canopy into the blue sky.

'Let your goshawk go,' he shouted over and she released it as he had taught her over the previous weeks.

His sacret was moving in on a wood pigeon. She gasped, thrilled, as both birds swooped and chased.

'So which will bring it down, yours or mine?' Gunnhild shouted gleefully.

'The answer is there,' Alan pointed and pulled on his reins so that Thunder pranced around to face her, adding, 'The goshawk has it off her.' He whistled a long high sound that was eerily similar to a bird's cry and his sacret seemed to float towards them through the canopy. 'Now you,' he added. 'Let us see if you can call your goshawk home.'

She tried to imitate his sound but her efforts were lost amongst the rustling branches. She could not reach the note needed to call Nighthawk in. Then, as if it had simply sensed her calling, it appeared from the sky and dropped its prey close to Shadow's forelegs. Shadow shied backwards, almost throwing her, the movement was so sudden, but she spoke to him gently and held fast. A beater with a basket rushed forward past her to scoop up the kill.

Alan came close. 'Well held, and who would have guessed that your goshawk would better my sacret. She knows who her mistress is, though you must practise that whistle.'

The beater stared up at her as he moved forward out of their way. She looked down at him. He glanced at Alan with what she saw was a sour look on his face.

'Who is that man?' she said.

'He is Brieuc, master of the hunt, Agenhart's husband.'

Of course he was, she thought bitterly, but he looked so different today, confident in his brown hunting cloak, not green this time, looking quite unlike the diffident man she had seen at the wedding feast. 'He seems to resent us even though he clearly has the privileged position in charge of all the beaters,' she remarked with acidity edging her tone.

'Not so.' Alan said and nudged Thunder's flanks with his heels, moving him forward. 'He is always that way,' he threw back at her. 'Brieuc is a good man and loyal.'

'Then it is me he resents,' she said just loud enough for him to hear.

'Your imagination runs away with you, Gunnhild. You do not know him.' Stiff-backed Alan gathered his reins and cantered ahead.

There is much I do not know. She remained silent as they rode along a woodland track through the trees until they approached a clearing, and she saw the standing stones leaning into a circle, some larger than others. Although the Beltane festival had been two days before, the fire in the centre of the stone circle was still smouldering. She shuddered, sensing an atmosphere here that chilled her to the bone.

'My lord, why are the stones here in this place?'

'Ah, I wondered if you would ask. No one knows but a legend attached to them is often told by Breton jongleurs. Those stones were here before the saints came in stone boats, fought dragons and evil leaders and Christianised the land. It is said that they once enclosed a place of sacrifice. Some call them the Devil's stones and swear that if a man angers the old gods in this place he will be cast into stone and never move again. It is old magic but it pleases the woodland people to bring offerings to the stones here on Beltane and appease them. I think there is a more rational explanation. They are ancient tombs and that is all, nothing to frighten your dreams or enter your pretty head day or night.'

Pretty head indeed. As they rode past she stared back, unable to avert her eyes, fascinated by what she thought were faces carved into them. She felt them watching her, but after they passed into the woodland beyond the clearing and on to a sunlit path, the fearful feeling she had possessed in the glade gradually dissipated. She shook her reins and Shadow's bells jangled reassuringly.

The goshawk sat calmly and obediently on her gloved wrist and for the remainder of the morning Alan rode close to her, keeping Thunder's head neck and neck with Shadow's. *There was really nothing to frighten her.* She would avoid the woods when Alan was away from the castle. Sensing her disapproval, Alan called to the others who followed that he was taking a new route and to keep sight of him so they did not lose the path.

He tactfully skirted the hunting lodge where Agenhart dwelled, bringing them on further to a picnic place where the woodland thinned out and they could rest amongst the bracken and heathers to eat as they watched the sea swirl around the cliffs far below their perch. Their guards joined them and the servants who followed them in a rattling cart unloaded picnic baskets filled with pasties and meats, a fermented apple drink and stone flasks filled with clean, clear well water. Gunnhild realised how hungry she felt and fell on the food, praising everything the cooks had prepared. For the rest of the hunting expedition she tried not to think of Agenhart and Dorgen.

Later in the afternoon they were back in the chamber behind the hall. The day had turned cooler. A small fire was burning in the hearth, a long trail of wood smoke twisting up through a smoke tunnel that was set deep into the castle's thick wall. Aching, thankful that she could rest, Gunnhild relaxed. The picnic had been enjoyable, Alan attentive, and they had hunted again on the way back through the woods. Their kill was now hanging in the bailey and the birds were back on their perches in the barn. Alan sat in a winged chair by the window where he had begun to unlace his boots. Gunnhild lifted his cloak. She was looking forward to sinking into cushions by the hearth and to a simple private meal with no distractions and noise. She would not speak of Agenhart and she would win his heart. He was her husband now. Nothing could change that. The woman must be outlawed from her castle and from her presence.

Her comfort was to be short-lived. Commotion, the neighing of horses, shields clashing and dogs barking seemed to drift up towards them from the bailey. Alan leapt to his feet, threw the shutters wide opened and thrust his head out.

He turned back, exclaiming, 'By St Gildas's holy bones, I swear that is my father, Count Eudo, riding over the ditch. The red serpent flies before him.' He looked down again and called back. 'He has a train of people with him, two of my brothers, too.' Alan left the window embrasure, swept a hand up to thump his head. 'By Christus, how are we to feed them?' He returned to the window. 'He has all of Dinan with him.'

Gunnhild threw the cloak over a chair. She hurried to the window and stood beside him looking down towards the bailey. Alan's father, mounted on a black stallion, was now riding up to the castle. Beside him two other men trotted on fine mounts with sturdy saddles and gleaming ornaments studding their horses' harnesses. One held the reins of a pure white gelding. He was tall and slender, a green cloak hanging in folds from his shoulders pinned with something large that glinted in the light. She noticed how he sat erect and proud and that his hair was black as a raven's coat. The other, a stockier man like the father, was seated on a piebald mount. They disappeared as they took the path round to the castle entrance, followed by a train of horses and carts and what she was sure was a great bedstead and mattress tied to one of the wagons. She pointed it out to Alan. He moaned. 'They are planning a long stay here, but I wonder why?' He gripped her shoulder. 'He should have sent an outrider to warn us.'

'There is no time to prepare. Sainted Brigit, just look at his baggage train!' she cried.

'Gunnhild, though we are tired, we shall greet them with the customary welcome. Order food and drink to be prepared. He will just have to have this chamber.' Alan looked around. 'There is nowhere else. Tell the maids to boil up cauldrons of water. He will want a bath.' Alan sank down onto his chair again and pulled on his boots. 'Jesu, I hope there is no trouble at Dinan.'

Gunnhild hurried off into the hall to instruct the maids to build up the fire and boil up great pots of water. The guests would be stabling their horses now. Glancing down at her gown, she realised that it was still very dusty from the ride that afternoon, but there was simply no time to change. She mounted the stairway and found Ann up in the solar where she was helping the seamstress hem another new gown. Gunnhild looked at it longingly. It was to be her best summer gown of pale linen. The dun-coloured lining for the trailing sleeves lay beside it. In a state of panic she ordered Ann down to the bailey kitchens. 'We have company. Tell the cooks to put up a side of beef, a half-dozen chickens and whatever they can in the way of pasties and griddle cakes. It will have to suffice. The birds we caught today need to hang. And we shall just have to eat later than usual tonight.' She groaned. 'Brother Gregory must hold Compline this evening.'

'Who is all this for, my lady, surely not the King of England?' Ann said calmly, handing over her long sharp needle to the seamstress who stuck it into a small sewing cushion.

'Worse. It is for Alan's father, Count Eudo and his train.'

Ann pushed her sewing chair back with a scrape. 'In that case I had better get myself down into the bailey and set up the trestles in the feasting hall.'

'And I shall send maids for water and cloths.' Gunnhild turned on her slippered heel and ran ahead back down the stairway.

She reached the hall just in time and, giving sharp orders to

121

her maids, waited for them to return. Alan grumbled, 'Hurry, hurry. They are dismounting.'

She walked with him through the hall still wearing her red squirrel furred slippers. Two maids followed her carrying the swiftly purveyed washing bowls with a servant boy, who was carefully holding two cups of wine, trailing behind. Gunnhild was exhausted, her happy mood soured. As Alan led her through the hall she whispered a prayer, 'St Brigit please may we not dine past the midnight hour.'

The hall's great carved door was flung opened and the dark-headed man was standing before her in dusk-light, staring down at her feet. When he smiled up, his eyes crinkled at the sides and his wide smile was mischievous. 'My lady, I am Alan called Niall. I thank you for welcoming us to your castle. Since we have descended on you without warning, it is generous of you to greet us.'

Awkwardly clutching the washing bowl, she started at Niall's greeting. She had a strange sense of recognition, an absurd, almost incomprehensible feeling that this brother was going to become a friend. He had spoken to her first before even acknowledging her husband. Count Eudo grunted something incomprehensible in her direction but immediately turned to speak to Alan. When the older brother, Brian, limped forward she felt nothing but antipathy for his rudeness since he nodded briefly, glared at her and looked away. He was fish-cold. She called the maids forward and instead of offering the washing water herself to Count Eudo she told the maid to offer him the second basin. She held out her basin and cloth to Niall.

She wore her green silk gown, the Godwin fillet and an embroidered veil. After Compline the hall was ready to receive its visitors to board. Gunnhild sat demurely at Alan's side and Count Eudo now politely thanked her for thinking of his bath and for giving him and his company hall space. Alan Niall sat on Alan's other side, studying her, smiling through dark eyes that danced with fun. They had brought a marzipan bear with them and after they had dined on beef, pasties and broiled hens,

122

Niall had passed the great bear to her on a platter covered with strawberries so that she could break off the first piece. He said solemnly, as if this was a feat of great courage, 'We rescued the beast from the kitchens before we left Dinan and now we can use it to celebrate your marriage to my brother.' He laughed and she warmed immediately to his bantering manner. 'What a lovely lady my brother has chosen to wife,' he added. 'That gown is very fetching, my lady. Green suits you.' He looked down at the hem. 'Those pearls must be worth a fortune. My brother is generous.'

'It belonged to my Aunt Edith, who, as you must know, was once queen of England.'

Count Eudo turned to Alan and said in a cutting tone, 'Do you have King William's blessing on your marriage? I pray you have not brought down a coffer of trouble on our house.'

'I hope for the King's approval,' Alan said.

'What are you thinking of, Alan? Is a Breton wife too low for you?'

Gunnhild felt diminished. How dare he?

Alan Niall interrupted, 'No, Father, leave off. Can't you see how fortunate he is, married to a princess of the English?'

Count Eudo's shoulders relaxed. 'You are right, Niall. No merchant's daughter for our Alan.' He lifted his cup and called for a toast. 'To Lady Gunnhild of the Saxons. May she bear many sons, fine boys with Godwin's warrior blood coursing through them.'

Gunnhild winced at the reference to the merchant's daughter. *They knew.* She bowed her head, sipped the bitter wine in her cup and recovered her wits sufficiently to look up and give Count Eudo a measured look. 'Thank you, Count Eudo. I shall do my best by my duty.'

'That's the spirit,' said Count Eudo. 'My wife, Agatha, bless her sainted soul, bore me three boys before she died birthing young Stephen.'

I hope I have daughters just to spite them all. Gunnhild was even angrier at this oaf of a father-in-law.

Her husband laid a hand on her arm and, turning the subject

of conversation, said, 'So, Father, and my brothers, what occasions your visit? Was it only to meet my wife?'

Brian, the taciturn eldest son, spoke for the first time. She remembered now that she had heard that he had done battle with her elder brothers in Cornwall. He had sustained an injury to his sword arm. Maybe it also explained his limp.

He turned to Alan, 'Earl Ralph is harassing King William's borders between Normandy and Maine. He sees us as William's main support south of Dol. If we don't support him against the King our lands here in Brittany will be in danger from his attacks.'

Alan drew a breath and put his cup on the table.

Brian went on, 'They used English law on Waltheof because he is English. Last month they executed him at Winchester. And he was the least guilty. When I saw the way it was, I sailed away from Cornwall. I have had enough of England. I shall never return.'

Alan exhaled a breath in a low whistling of air, lengthy and measured. 'I never knew they had executed Waltheof.' He turned to his father. 'So, Father, you are here because of Earl Ralph?'

'If Earl Ralph attacks us we have not enough men to repel him without help. I have brought my treasury to Fréhel for safe keeping, and a part of my household. I want you to send what troops you can spare to Dinan. We can break a siege from their rear.'

'Is he about to attack Dinan?'

'He has been harassing the borders of my lands for weeks.' Count Eudo looked at Alan with a decided glint in his grey eyes. 'Can you help?'

Alan did not hesitate. 'I shall lead my men out against Ralph. If Earl Ralph harasses Normandy, the King will be here on the quickest tide down the channel. And King William needs our help.' He turned to Brian. 'Will you ride against Earl Ralph, brother?'

'No, I must ride east to guard my estates. '

'And you, Alan Niall?'

'I am with you, brother.'

'Father, where is young Stephen?'

'Learning Latin and Greek and how to be a knight at Conron's court in the south. He is safe there,' Count Eudo said. He scratched his bearded chin pensively. 'When will you ride out, Alan?'

'Tomorrow,' Alan replied and turned to his older brother. 'And you, Brian, we understand that you will protect Penthiévre to the south and east?'

'With my life,' Brian grunted. 'If Earl Ralph gets help from France our estates on the borders with French vassal territories could be endangered. I have salt pans to see to and the vineyards near the Loire. And I shall send for our little brother, Stephen, just in case Conron sides with the Earl. It is as well one of us stays here in Amorica and watches our back.' He pointed accusingly at Gunnhild. 'And as for the Danes and your brothers, Madam, they are no match for us. They may have caused my injuries but they are useless rebels. We drove those brothers of yours out of the west.' He growled and turned away from her. 'As for that Norman toad, Bishop Odo, he is a wolf. He plans to place mercenaries in every castle and estate in England – bleed us all dry. I want none of what he gave me in Cornwall. Too expensive for too little return. I am done with William of Normandy and his English subjects.'

Alan said. 'Make sure your mercenary fighters are kept on the alert in case of attack from Picardy.' He turned to his father. 'Gunnhild will see to your every comfort, Father. You only have to ask. My wife is my representative on my estate here. If I die, she is to be in complete control of Fréhel. It is her dower.' Brian muttered something under his breath that sounded like 'English bitch'. He pushed away his plate and without excusing himself shoved his bench back, rose and limped out of the hall.

Gunnhild sighed. Brian was insufferable and, clearly, she was to be left alone with Alan's father at the castle until it was safe for him to return to Dinan. She glanced at the glistening white subtlety that they had hardly nibbled. *At least the servants can eat the precious sugar when we send the remains of this feast back to the kitchens.*

The news flew swiftly to Fréhel. Earl Ralph's army was already moving south into Brittany. Two days followed with Gunnhild experiencing the same sinking feeling and panic she had felt when she first saw Count Eudo and his train approaching her castle. Alan and his brother Niall made frantic yet thorough preparations. Assembling troops into a cohesive mobile fighting force was a task that both amazed and baffled her because of the speed with which Alan executed it. He amassed weapons, equipped horses, loaded wagons with tents, sent out to his outlying estates for food, armourers, fletchers, bakers, a bevy of washerwomen and a blacksmith. Finally he ordered carpenters to prepare siege weapons and to follow with them in his army's wake. Alan and Niall had in the space of two busy days gathered together enough troops from Alan's own garrison and from neighbouring estates to incite terror in their enemy.

On the third morning Gunnhild felt helpless and not a little frightened when she watched Alan and Niall pull on their hauberks and armour. Father Gregory was called up to the Hall to bless their swords and lances. Arriving in his flowing dark robes and holding forth a wooden cross that he usually kept dangling from his belt, he alternately prayed and placed it to his lips. Gunnhild could not repress a shiver. She feared that within a summer she was to be made both bride and widow.

They assembled in the upper bailey with all the castle servants gathered to wish them Godspeed. With a cursory goodbye to Gunnhild, his brother Brian and his father, Alan turned in his saddle and, followed by Niall, he twisted Thunder's head round towards the lower bailey where his army and wagons had gathered. With his pennant, chequered gold and azure fluttering before them, Alan led them north.

To Gunnhild's relief the visitors had arrived with provisions as well as the bed for Count Eudo. Since Alan had taken both cook and baker with him on campaign, she sent Ann and Hubert to find her replacements and extra help from nearby villages.

There would be more laundry, more to cook for. Count Eudo remarked grumpily that the floor rushes needed replacing and complained that her servants were lax. Brian, as was his form, scowled. Her relationship with this older brother had not improved and she was relieved to see the back of him when he departed for his own properties, and, hopefully, to set guards on their ports and salt pans.

Thankfully, the new servants arrived shortly after Brian left with a number of Count Eudo's own servants and guards. Gunnhild desperately needed this assistance since those remaining with the Count ate much and contributed nothing to the running of her castle. Within a few days the floor grasses were changed again, the cooking in the keep hall improved and the copper cooking pots were scrubbed with sand until they were spotless. Great candles scented with spice were placed on iron spikes in Count Eudo's chamber and the wall-fire burned with well-seasoned logs. At last he seemed comfortable and his mood improved.

Even so, Gunnhild was overjoyed when he said that he preferred to take his meals with his steward in the antechamber. This was his territory and she kept her distance. Her territory was her solar and bedchamber, the small cove below the castle where she walked in the hot afternoons and the garden which she was planning below her solar window.

Gunnhild entered the keep one dinner time soon after Alan's departure and sent her servants to lay the table in her solar so that she and her maids could take the midday meal above where the breeze cooled the higher chamber. Since meals had improved on those that the departed cook had provided it occurred to her that she must acknowledge his replacement.

This cook had made new arrangements for cooking and was busy supervising their dinner over a fire in an alcove curtained off from the hall. When Ann had asked her to sanction this, Gunnhild had agreed but never thought to inspect the make-shift kitchen, thinking that Ann would supervise and instruct the cook. Now, five days after the cook had arrived, Gunnhild slipped through the leather curtain to see what these new arrangements were.

Smoke coiled up to escape through an opened window aperture. The cook was a woman who appeared to be neat, with a clean linen apron wrapped about her small frame and her hair concealed under a tidy white wimple like those worn by nuns. When Gunnhild entered she was bending over a bench chopping vegetables but, sensing Gunnhild's presence, she spun round on her heel. Seeing her rival, the faery-woman, again and in her own hall, Gunnhild gasped. Agenhart lowered her eyes and gave Gunnhild a shallow curtsey. 'My lady, I hope you will be pleased with today's dinner. I am roasting the fowl you caught a week ago during the hunt.'

Gunnhild cast a glance over at the row of pigeons and sundry catch that two boys were methodically basting over a spit. She lifted a spoon from a copper cauldron that was balanced on a chain on a trivet and attempted to control her anger by giving it a stir. A pleasant smell of herbs drifted from it. 'The stew is seasoned with herbs from my own garden, my lady,' Agenhart remarked gently, as she watched Gunnhild.

Gunnhild gave her a curt nod, pulled back the heavy curtain and moved away from the makeshift cooking area, letting the curtain drop again behind her. She found Ann sweeping the stairs that descended from the solar. 'Ann, can we have a word, now.'

'My lady,' she said and followed Gunnhild up the staircase.

'Ann,' Gunnhild began, 'how are the new servants, do you think?'

'My lady, they are obedient and efficient.'

Gunnhild paused before speaking again. This would be difficult. She had determined never to confide to anyone her knowledge of Agenhart but now the story came pouring out.

'My lady, it is only while Count Eudo is here. She is from Dinan and he speaks well of her.'

'So he asked for her?' Gunnhild felt her face redden in fury. She could not speak further for anger at the conniving spider, Eudo. No doubt his eldest son had conspired with him to install Agenhart in the kitchen to spite her.

Ann confirmed it. 'Lord Brian told me to find the woman from Dinan called Agenhart because she can cook, and she has organised a kitchen efficiently since I fetched her here yesterday. Had I known ... if you want me to send her home ...'

'Count Eudo should have spoken to me first,' Gunnhild interjected.

'Perhaps he does not have the knowledge you have of her.'

'Maybe not, but I wonder if his son had.' Gunnhild pondered her dilemma. She did not want to offend Count Eudo, who seemed content to wander about the bailey and play chess in the evenings with his scrap of a steward, Torkill. She must rise above his mischief-making. She paced up and down the chamber. It would only be for a week or two. The woman clearly could cook and sensibly she had organised this new separate preparation kitchen in one of the hall's alcoves, carefully curtained off from the hall. Finally, Gunnhild said with firmness. 'Ann, she may remain temporarily but her children are not to enter my castle, nor is she to be here when my lord returns. Then, no matter the need of a good cook, I want that woman gone.'

Ann nodded her head in agreement. 'There is no one can hold a candle to you, my lady, and I doubt he would look her way in your presence.'

'We shall see if you speak true on my lord's return,' Gunnhild said, with bitterness creeping into her voice.

Time passed quickly. Agenhart returned to the hunting lodge at night protected by the falconer's boy who had become her shadow. She returned early each morning with fresh herbs and new spices. Life continued evenly in the castle keep without further disturbance. It was nearly a month since Alan had left. One beautiful July morning when Gunnhild entered the temporary kitchen, she found Agenhart busy pounding a nutmeg with pestle and mortar. No one had yet begun to prepare the game she had ordered for dinner that day.

'My lord Eudo has requested a posset,' Agenhart said.

'I see,' Gunnhild said. 'I hope this posset will not delay our dinner. The Count is clearly as fit as I am. He has no need of cosseting. See to our dinner now, Agenhart. Brother Gregory will dine with us today.'

Agenhart said in a low tone. 'I think, my lady, it is in your interests that we keep the Count happy whilst he is here. I knew him in Dinan.'

'This may be so, Agenhart.' Gunnhild clicked her tongue with impatience. 'But, let us be clear on who decides on meal times here. I want dinner on the table when we return from noon prayers. I see nothing ready but vegetables.'

She swept through the curtain and climbed the stairway. When she reached the solar she opened the coffer that contained her inks, a wax tablet and a stylus. There was an hour left until Sext. She needed something to occupy her mind apart from Count Eudo's visit, the maids and Agenhart. When she entered the chamber she found her servants had been busy in the solar. The seamstresses had finished making gowns and were stitching a new altar cloth for the chapel. The air was close, the day stifling and she had no inclination to embroider nor was she ready to write anything, though she felt she must. Since Alan had given her inks and parchment she had only looked at them, occasionally caressing the parchment, not knowing what to compose or draw. Alan disapproved of the new verse spoken by the poets of Brittany which called out to her heart – stories of King Arthur, Tristan and Iseult. She slammed the coffer shut, making the seamstresses jump and drop their needles.

'My lady,' the pair chorused in unison. 'Do you wish us to leave?'

'No, carry on. Do not mind me,' she said and went to the window and threw open the shutters. Sunshine streamed in. For a few moments she stared out over the bailey towards the sea. The morning was filled with sunshine, the sea was beckoning her and there was just enough time before mass to climb down to the little cove. 'Let the air in. Keep the shutters open and douse those sconces,' she threw back at the women as she left the chamber.

She hurried down into the hall and outside, down through the gatehouse to the bailey. Everything was as it should be there. Maids were still busy milking cows as she passed the byre, stable boys were exercising Shadow, leading her around the yard. Father Gregory was entering the chapel, and further on, close to the barracks, a group of soldiers left to protect the castle were polishing their armour. Hubert's long sword flashed in the sunlight as he practised slashing at a straw dummy. Quivers were neatly stacked by the barrack entrance. The hall door to the bailey hall was opened and Ann was in there today, sweeping out old rushes. Gunnhild paused to ask her to send small beer up to the keep later.

Gunnhild slipped out through the door in the palisade and followed the steps down into the sheltered cove. As she sat on a rock staring at waves lapping the stones below, listening to gulls cawing, watching distant fishermen cast out their nets from small coracles she remembered the figurines of female saints she had once possessed at Wilton. They had been her tenth name day gift from her mother. What had become of them? They were most likely placed in Wilton's chapel now that she was gone. An idea came to her, one that was pleasing. That was it, their replacement, a connection between her and the mother she hardly knew now that she was far away in Canterbury, hidden in a cloister, safe from the world. She would make a book inspired by female martyrs, their name day saints. She felt bile rise. Surely it could not be the thought of martyred women, horrific as it was?

Her hand hovered over her stomach. It lurched and bubbled again. For several days she had been queasy in the mornings and she had ignored it as resulting from her nervousness over Agenhart's presence in the castle. Now she recognised what explained both her sickness and her restlessness. With joy and relief she ignored her queasiness, leapt to her feet and cried out, 'Thank God, I am with child!' She called out to the sea that swirled with a rhythmic gushing sound, sending fans of spay up around her. She held out her arms and shook her head defiantly. 'I want a girl child. Heaven, grant me this wish.'

Ann, usually so observant, clearly had not noticed that rags for her courses had lain untouched in the basket sent up by the laundresses over a month before, and Gunnhild had lost track of time passing. So much had been happening that she had not realised she was with child. Now that she knew that she was, she could settle down, lift her pen and create a book. Her book would be a gift that she could pass on to her daughters.

Wandering aimlessly about the shore, she scooped up her skirts and collected periwinkles and butterfly-shaped shells into its folds. She would draw them into her work. She gathered her mantle up in her hands, anxious to protect her treasures and climbed the steps up from the shore and hastened into the bailey hall to tell Ann her news. As she climbed the steps she made another decision. There would be improvements made to Castle Fréhel whether Alan agreed or not.

11

Lammas 1076

On Lammas day, the first day of August, Gunnhild was engaged in conversation with her new stone mason and a carpenter about a proper new kitchen area to replace the makeshift one, when, through the open shutters of her solar she noticed an outrider clattering over the bridge. She left the pair by her table looking at a drawing and leaned over the thick sill to peer down into the courtyard and get a better view. The rider leapt off his steaming horse and tossed his reins to a stable boy. Gunnhild turned to the mason. 'Go down to the kitchen and see if your plans will work.' She gave the mason his plan. 'It seems a good drawing to me.'

All summer messengers had ridden into Fréhel with regularity seeking news from Dol. They came from the women who dwelled in outlying castles hoping for news of husbands who had rallied to Count Alan's call to arms. Hubert could deal with this one. Her new kitchen was much more important.

The mason suggested building it in stone so they could have a bread oven and a fireplace built into the outside wall over which her cooks could more successfully use their spits and hang pots. He said that he had seen fireplaces set into the walls in Norman castles and he pointed out that there was already a wall-fire in the antechamber beyond the hall. A vent took smoke out through the walls, but if she had the kitchen alcove roof tiled the masons could create a chimney.

Gunnhild now followed the mason and carpenter down to look but on seeing the rider enter the hall she stopped at the bottom of the staircase. Her heart thumped and her hand went protectively to her belly even though the rider who approached with Hubert was smiling at her. Hubert called out, 'Never fear, my lady, he brings good news.'

'In that case, Count Eudo can hear it, too.' She climbed onto the dais, pushed the antechamber curtain aside, and when Count

Eudo called out, 'Who is outside,' she opened the door and brought Hubert and the outrider into the chamber.

Turning to Count Eudo, who was half rising from his armed chair, she said, 'A messenger from Dol has ridden in, from your sons.' The Count sank into his chair again.

'My lady, you should sit, too,' Hubert said.

Count Eudo rose again and offered her his chair. She sank into the cushions on the comfortable winged chair that was drawn up close to the fire even though the day was already warm. Count Eudo took the bench by the window. His forehead was creased with concern. 'Well?' he said gruffly.

'Please tell us the news,' she said more politely to the outrider.

The young messenger shook his long locks. 'My lady, Count Alan is safe and he sends you his greetings. The danger to Dinan has been averted. King William landed in Normandy a week ago and he is besieging Dol. Your husband is planning strategy with the King and the Duke of Mortain.' He turned to Count Eudo. 'They will continue to fight until they break the Earl's hold on Castle Dol.'

Gunnhild stood up shakily. 'Thank you,' she said. 'I will send a letter back with you for my husband.' Count Eudo heaved a sigh of relief. She was happy for the old man but even happier now that she knew the count would return home. He should have gone weeks ago. There was no need for him to be at Fréhel, none at all after Brian had left to protect their estates and towns. Count Eudo rose to his feet, knocking over a half-played out chess game that lay on the bench, scattering bishops and pawns over the tiles. Ignoring the fallen pieces he declared, 'Then we must pack at once. We are returning to Dinan.' His joy was almost childlike. 'I have overstayed my welcome, my dear. The King of England will destroy the bastard Earl. I wish I was fit enough to fight, too, but I am past fighting now. My sword arm is useless. I never crossed the Narrow Sea ... but then you should be glad that I didn't. In my day, two decades ago, when I could ride like a winter gale into battle, I slew enemies in scores.' He smiled jovially at Gunnhild and then thoughtfully tugged at his beard. 'And your husband will no doubt be back in time to see his son born. We must thank our good Lord in heaven. Get Agenhart to order us up a feast to celebrate.'

Gunnhild said with authority seeping into her voice, 'It is Lammas. There will be a feast this evening. Agenhart is already busy with preparations.' She said to the messenger. 'Did my lord send me anything?'

The messenger pulled a folded sealed letter from his gambeson. 'My lady, forgive me. Here it is.'

She took it from him and held it tightly, gazing down at the seal. Looking up she said to the messenger, who was diffidently waiting for her instruction, 'You must stay for our Lammas feast. Hubert will show you a chamber where you can refresh yourself and rest.' She turned to Hubert, 'There is an empty store room with a pallet upstairs. Tell Agenhart to give him fresh linen, drink and food and water to wash off the dust of the road.'

'But I need her to help us pack,' Count Eudo insisted.

'She will come after she has finished cooking,' Gunnhild replied firmly.

When the messenger had disappeared into the hall with Hubert, Count Eudo said, 'Now, read me my son's letter.'

'My lord, please excuse me. I must read this in private. If anything concerns you I shall come back down to report it.' She turned on her heel, leaving the Count with his mouth open like a frog's about to catch a fly. Setting her back, she raised her head and, holding her letter tightly concealed below the drop of her wide, flowing sleeve, she marched out of the antechamber. He would be a good riddance and after he was gone they could get back to normal at Fréhel. Agenhart could go, too. Clutching her letter she ran up the stairway into the privacy of her own chamber.

She sat in the cushioned seat by the window and broke the seal. Unfolding the parchment she ran her hand over it and smoothed it out. He wrote in English. Reading quickly she saw that he was well and that for the last two months his troops had stalked the borders of Brittany and Normandy. Finally, they had pursued Ralph back to Dol where he was holding the castle. She raised her face and sent a prayer to St Brigit. Penthiévre was safe. The King had come to their aid and was laying siege to Dol. Alan wrote, *'It will be a lengthy siege. Earl Ralph has looked for support from the Angevins. The French might become embroiled in the struggle.'*

As she read further she learned that her husband and Niall, his brother, were both safe. Reading the next bit brought her joy. The King recognised Count Alan's help against the enemy Earl Ralph, the traitors from Maine and Anjou and his loyalty to the crown. *'He gives us his blessing. He must give us your lands.'*

Alan added that he had to do penance for his violation of a postulant of Wilton and it would cost him much. *'Archbishop Lanfranc demands that we donate a coffer of silver to Wilton Abbey. Now that I have heard that you are with child, Gunnhild, take good care of my unborn son ...'*

How did he know? She had not written because she had not known where to write to. Who had known how to find him. Agenhart? Surely not. Then she remembered how three merchants had stopped at Fréhel on their way to Alan's cloth warehouses in Rouen. Perhaps Alan had departed Dol and had been in Rouen, too. But a son, he could not possibly know that. Sweeping her hand over her belly, she felt in her heart that she was carrying his daughter. Perhaps though, she considered wickedly, the wish for a daughter lay in the hands of the sea gods.

On a hot, dry day in the middle of August, followed by his baggage train, Count Eudo of Penthiévre rode away from her castle. Before he climbed on to his stallion, he gave Gunnhild a gift from his coffer, a golden oval-shaped brooch with a great ruby in its centre. 'For your mantle, my dear,' he said gruffly, 'And with my gratitude for your hospitality.'

'This is too valuable, my lord Count, are you sure?'

He had a tear in his rheumy eye. 'It will remind you of me

after I am gone,' he said as he pressed it into her hands. Then with great grunts and puffs he was hoisted by a groom on to his waiting horse.

As she stood clutching his gift, watching him trot from her bailey, she felt guilty for resenting him. She turned back to the pathway up to the keep. Now he was gone she would reduce her household servants. There was no need of extra servants and their place was with their families making ready for winter, slaughtering animals, salting pigs and preserving fruit. And though she had grown used to Agenhart she would always find her presence in the castle a threat. Agenhart must return to her own hall that very week. The assistant she had trained would take over.

Gunnhild climbed back up to the keep feeling light-hearted for the first time in weeks. Now he was gone the castle was quiet. At Wilton she had enjoyed much peace, though never did she regret her choice to leave the abbey, not even with Agenhart in the shadows of her new life. In her bed-chamber she would stumble upon maids busily folding linen, cleaning the privy set into the wall beyond her door, beating her feather mattress, changing her linen sheets or freshening up the garments that hung on her clothing pole. It was her castle, though here she was rarely alone. She sank into a chair by the window and sighed contentedly. Her seamstresses had returned to Rouen promising to come back nearer her time, to loosen her gowns and make swaddling for the child. If I am still here, she thought. Now the King has forgiven us perhaps we shall return to England for Christmastide.

She contemplated Eudo's gift. Was it a precious heirloom or should she sell it to a jeweller for silver to contribute to that coffer for Wilton Abbey? It might bring her enough to pay for her building work. She turned it over and over, examining it closely. It was finely crafted but she preferred her own simple cloak pins fashioned like animal heads with their jewelled eyes and garnet-studded enamel work.

She glanced about the solar. Soon she must bring a painter from Rouen to paint scenes on the walls, and painters cost money. Tapping her fingers decisively on the table, she realised that the ruby itself could buy her a great deal of needed work in the castle. Fréhel was her castle, her dower castle, and it should be beautiful.

'My lady.' Ann hovered in the doorway. 'Do you wish me to sweep out the antechamber behind the hall now that the Count is gone? Shall I put things as they were?'

Gunnhild stood up. 'Yes do, and Ann, I shall eat dinner there.' She took a few steps towards Ann. 'Can you tell the village servants that we have no more need of them now Count Eudo is gone. It is harvest. They can go home and I expect they will be glad to.'

'Agenhart? What about a cook?'

'Especially Agenhart. She has trained up our own kitchen servants to cook for us. She is free to return to her family.'

'As you wish. I shall tell her.' Ann thought for a moment and added, 'My lady, do you intend to pass the afternoon here or in the still room?'

'Neither. I intend to ride out on Shadow this afternoon. A stable boy can use the roan and accompany me.'

Ann's face contorted into a frown. 'Is it wise in your condition that you ride over the countryside?'

'Do not fear for me. I need the exercise.'

After Count Eudo departed, life at Fréhel fell into a gentler rhythm. Gunnhild took regular exercise on Shadow and as her body thickened she wore wider skirts so that she could comfortably ride astride. There would be no hunger this winter. The harvest was already being stored away in great barns about the estate. This efficiency was all due to Hubert. Hubert not only kept an eye on the castle guard, regularly supervising their training, keeping them primed for attacks, but he also acted as a reeve, ensuring that the castle's crops were brought in, the mills operated efficiently and the fisheries close to their part of the coast paid Count Alan's dues. He operated a successful system by which he delegated responsibility to experienced loyal men. Yet he kept close watch over them, and over the castle's own store houses and barns. He put Ann in charge of the fish salters and the drying of cod. For days that autumn the bailey smelled of fish. Gunnhild found herself repelled by the stench. On those days she took herself down to the small bay beyond the palisade where she collected shells to decorate pathways about her herb garden. As September moved into October she felt her baby grow in her womb and soon the emerging bump necessitated the loosening of the laces on her dresses.

One evening in October she asked Hubert if he could send for a jeweller from Rouen.

'My lady, do you want a jeweller to make you a jewelled cup for your baby?' Hubert asked, politely laying down a scroll concerning the religious properties on Count Alan's lands.

'No, I want to raise money to fund the decoration of the solar. Then there are kitchen improvements. I owe the mason and the carpenter coin. The new kitchen is almost complete so I thought to sell one of my jewels.'

'I see. We can send for such a person. But, Count Alan might not be happy if you sold one of his gifts.'

'Not one of his gifts, Hubert, I promise. It is something else.' She considered. Should she tell him she might sell a Penthiévre ruby? No, it might be best to speak with the jeweller first since all might come to nothing. She fingered her best brooch, a sapphire pin she was wearing on her short mantle. This had been the only valuable jewel she had herself owned before her marriage to Count Alan, a gift from her aunt. It might be better to sell that.

12

Christmas 1076

The jeweller arrived from Rouen on a blustering day in October. He was a wizened elf-like man who reached to Gunnhild's shoulder. His face was puckered like the skin of a dried apple and his eyes were as sharp as needles. Gunnhild opened her exquisitely carved, bone-plated jewel casket and laid her two treasures on a trestle. He asked that a cushion was placed in the chair to raise him up. For a moment his eyes moved over the casket and his long fingers traced the leaf tendrils and the flower carvings along the sides of the small chest. 'Lovely craftsmanship,' he sighed with longing in his voice. He wriggled about in his seat and flipped his mantle under his tunic. He became still as the statues in a cloister as he examined first her sapphire pin, then the ruby brooch. Laying the silver stick fastener aside he turned the elaborate ruby brooch over and over, holding it up to the table sconce. He jumped down from his cushioned seat with the agility of a man of younger years, rushed to the window with it and held it up, exposing it to the rays of sunlight that poured into the chamber. Nimbly, like a dancer at a feast, he spun around and studied her. She remained by the hearth and raised a quizzical eyebrow, waiting for him to speak.

At last he said with a gleam in his astute little eyes, 'It is an exceptional jewel. I can offer for the ruby brooch, that is, if you are selling. I know of an abbot who might like to purchase it as a gift for his German bishop. He has been seeking such a thing for a finely engraved silver crozier.' She leaned forward to hear him. 'Blood of Christ,' he lowered his voice. 'The ruby will remind him of Christ's passion.'

Gunnhild crossed to the trestle and put her sapphire pin back into the casket. It would have to be the ruby. Then the haggling began. After the first offer she deliberately lifted up the glinting jewel from where he had laid it on the table between them and

141

returned it to her casket. After this form of negotiation occurred twice the jeweller offered more and she raised her eyebrow again. 'Not enough,' she repeated. He lifted a second bag of silver from his leather satchel and added it to the first. She lifted the jewel, considering putting it away, but thought of her debt to the stone mason, replaced it and said that she was satisfied. She did not think he would offer a fourth time as his eyes had narrowed and his mouth was set into a determined purse. Looking at her thoughtfully he said, 'You strike a hard bargain, my lady. I hope whatever you need this silver for it is worth the loss of that ruby.'

She opened her hands, palms up, allowing her trailing sleeves to fall back. 'Master jeweller, look about you. I need much work done here. It is certainly more important than a ruby for a German bishop's crozier,' she said.

He grunted something about hoping her lord knew what she was doing selling off her treasures, but none the less, his greed for an abbot's approval won. He gave her his bags of silver in payment and she accepted them, wondering as she did so whether Count Alan would agree that the sale of a jewel was worth it.

In November, a messenger rode in again with news from Dol. The fight was not going well for the Normans. The French king had ridden out to break their siege, and with the help he gave to the rebels it was unlikely King William would destroy the castle. He would never humble Earl Ralph. The messenger looked deflated as he told her that the King might withdraw his trebuchets and his siege towers before Christmas.

'The fighting has been fierce. Count Alan is safe though he has lost some of our men to French arrows.' This time there was no letter from Alan.

Gunnhild thought of Emma. 'And what of Earl Ralph and Lady Emma?'

'The lady left Dol before the siege. She is with her own people in Burgundy now.'

'And her child?'

'That I do not know, my lady.' He shrugged his shoulders. 'Count Alan says that he hopes to return for the Christmas feast.'

Gunnhild felt joy at this news. Her heart lifted as she surveyed her Hall, which smelled pleasantly of wood smoke and of fresh camomile and sage leaf which had been scattered amongst the floor grasses that same morning. The new kitchen meant that there was no need to cook over the central hearth. Surely Alan would approve her changes? It was her castle and she had financed everything herself though she wondered about the wisdom of selling the Penthiévre ruby. Uncomfortably, her hasty action had begun to prick her conscience. She glanced from the messenger to the doors at the side of the hall, closed as the cooks were roasting November geese for dinner. The Hall's kitchen possessed bread ovens, a cooking hearth, great smoke vents and its own large door that led out to the well in the castle yard, to the vegetable and herb gardens. She thought of the other work that was in progress that autumn. The painters had finished decorating the walls of her solar with woodland scenes, nymphs and satyrs, trees with broad oak leaves, blue sky glimpsed between the foliage and steep life-like banks of spring flowers. They would now paint a religious scene in their bedchamber. She favoured the Golden Mass, the Virgin and the angel Gabriel for one wall and for another she decided on the Fall of Adam and Eve. That should please her husband. When they started painting it the following week she must have her bed carried up into the solar whilst the work was underway. If the painters from Rouen worked quickly all should be completed in time for the Christmas feast.

Calling for food and drink for Count Alan's man, she hurried into the antechamber to write to Alan without delay. Selecting a fresh piece of parchment from the coffer by the window, she first smoothed it out on the table and ruled faint lines with a rule and her sharpened pen. She dipped her goose-quill pen into a pot of black ink and began to write. Her words took shape on the page as she wrote of her forthcoming child and of her work on St Margaret of Antioch, Aunt Edith's name-day saint. She had begun to scribe it and she would decorate the capital letters with pictures. She finished her letter by saying that she prayed for his safe return. She hoped that they would soon be reunited. *Keep safe and come home to us soon, my husband. I miss you more with every day that passes.*

On a grey cold day with snow fall threatening but not yet come, Hubert sent out into the woods for the yule log. With great cheer a group of villagers wrapped in heavy woollen cloaks dragged the thick tree trunk from the forest into the bailey. When they processed with it up the castle hill Gunnhild was waiting in her hall amongst servants who carried, from cords hung about their neck, large wooden trays laden with refreshments. She offered everyone cups of warm cider and freshly baked honey cakes. Most of the villagers stood quietly sipping the drink as they looked towards the doors into the kitchen in awed admiration. Servants kept entering holding fresh trays of pastries. Gunnhild circulated amongst the villagers, stopping to pass words with each of them as she refilled their cups from a jug. She knew that she was admired by them now as she was large with child and she smiled her benevolence at them all.

Agenhart had come with them. The woman hung back from the hearth with her two children and her mother-in-law by her side. When Gunnhild approached she said quietly, 'My lady, the fighting at Dol. Have you heard any news?' The question was direct and Gunnhild answered just as directly, 'No bad news, Agenhart, nothing yet about your children's father. But I think he may be home soon, maybe for the Christmas Feast.' She moved on. The little boy ran after her.

'Madam, may I play with the kitten?' he asked. A little black cat was scurrying after a miniscule bundle of wool that had fallen from a bench. She nodded. The lad raised his bright eyes to her, smiled his thanks and then raced off to scoop the small ball of fur into his arms. He looked back at her, cuddling the wriggling kitten, still smiling and in that smile she saw Alan and her heart felt pained. Automatically her hand found its way to her great belly. She was nearly seven months carrying their child.

On Christmas Eve the snow storms began. Gunnhild attended both morning Prime and noonday Sext. The feast was to be held this year in the keep hall rather than in the bailey feasting hall. It brimmed with activity. The aromas of spices for sauces and cakes and the deep, rich oily smells of roasting fowl seeped into the air, filling the castle hall with warmth, passing through cracks in the doorway to the antechamber behind and drifting up the keep's staircases to her bedchamber and into the solar. She indulged herself in a sense of anticipation, both for the feasting that would follow and for Alan's return. Her castle was welcoming, so filled with her own particular sense of beauty that surely he must be embraced by it and welcome her changes. She held that comforting thought close to her heart.

It was heavily snowing by evening and as she looked out through the drifting white screen she wondered if Alan would battle through the gales to reach them or would he have to retire to Dinan, which was an easier journey. Climbing slowly up the stairway, clutching onto the rope rail and half pulling herself up to her chamber, she knew there was nothing she could do to bring him home that night. The villagers, too, were facing similar disappointment since those who had joined Count Alan's troops would not be returning either.

Not really interested, she pulled underskirts and over dresses from her clothing pole. Nothing fitted her now. They could not be let out any more. There was just not enough material in them. The seamstresses of Rouen had never returned but perhaps Ann could help her create a wider dress. She looked longingly at the green silk dress she had brought from Wilton and taking it from the pole, held it up to the candle light to enjoy once again the lustre from the tiny pearls at its hem. Ah, she thought wistfully, maybe one day I can wear this once more.

'My lady, tut.' Ann had slipped into the chamber and was staring at the pile of clothing she had pulled down. She began gathering them up into her arms.

Gunnhild lamented. 'I am grown too big for this.' She threw the green gown onto the bed.

'I have not let out the scarlet wool yet. It has more material in it than the others. I can do it now in time for the feast.'

'Well then, it will have to be that. It is a good colour, reflecting courage.'

Ann unpicked the seams. She had just begun to re-pin them together when they heard shouting on the stairs. Gunnhild dragged herself to the doorway and, paying no attention to the fact that her head was unveiled and her hair falling loose, overjoyed, she pulled it open.

Alan was at the bottom of the stairway shouting at the servants. 'My men must eat now. They have had nothing in their bellies for two days, nothing do you understand, nothing since we left Dol.' Then he bellowed, 'Where is Lady Gunnhild?'

Ann grabbed a mantle and threw it over Gunnhild, who had begun struggling down the stairway crying out, 'I am here, my lord. If only you had sent word.'

He swept Gunnhild into his arms as she came off the bottom step but immediately drew back. 'What, by the rood, are you wearing, woman? You will stab yourself and my child if not me.' He drew out a fine bone pin from the loosened side seam and handed to her.

'Oh, Alan, please give me a moment. We are letting my overdress out.' With that she hurried back up the narrow stair-case, hoisting herself clumsily up by the rope rail. She flew into the chamber where Ann was frantically clearing away underdresses, gowns, slippers and hose.

'Let me help you get that gown off before you injure yourself.'

Gunnhild opened her hand and presented Ann with the pin she was still clutching. 'I nearly stabbed my lord.'

Moments later Gunnhild was back in the hall and Ann had retired to the solar above the bedchamber to finish pinning and stitching. The yule log was blazing and the hall was busy with

146

Alan's soldiers seeking bench space. Servants busily put large platters of pies, bread and butter on roughly set trestles. They all seemed entangled with each other but then through the mêlée she spotted Alan standing by the hearth, holding a pasty in one hand and a cup of wine in his other. She hurried to him.

'Let us go into the antechamber. I have much to tell you, Gunnhild.' He gave his cup to the pageboy who hovered close by them, sent him away, took her hands, leaned back and stared at her. 'Pregnancy suits you well. You are carrying my son!' He dropped her hands and strode towards the door to their private chamber.

'How did you know, my lord? The letter ...'

'Ah yes, I had to go to Rouen to organise more weapons ...'

'The merchants?'

'Yes, the merchants. You look well,' he repeated.

Gunnhild asked a servant to bring fresh food and wine into the antechamber before following Alan through the doorway. Behind her she could hear his men talking and the clatter of eating knives. She closed the door on the noise and with joy in her heart she knelt by the hearth and began to unlace his boots.

'No, Gunnhild, you are in no state to do this now.' With a tug he had the boots off. He sat back into his great winged chair and held his feet out to the blaze. 'Gunnhild, it is a fine thing to be toasting my toes at my own hearth.'

'Tell me all, my lord,' she said, sinking onto a stool.

The servant brought them a platter of pasties and a fresh jug of wine. Alan pulled himself to his feet, padded over to the table and filled two cups. He handed a cup to Gunnhild, retreated to his winged chair, and with a fire poker stirred up the logs into a greater blaze, leaning forward to gaze into the flames.

He turned to look at her through sorrowful eyes. 'We took many losses. Some of our men have not returned.'

'Who?'

'Brieuc for one. He lies in the churchyard in a village near Dol. We gave him a Christian burial. And we lost our smith, too. They both died in a storm of arrows from the castle

147

battlements as my men tried to launch a counter attack … hopelessly because the French were attacking us from the rear. We had to pull back. When night fell we retrieved their bodies. Brieuc was killed by an arrow fired straight into his belly.' He covered his face with his hands. 'It was terrible,' he said at last. 'To lose Brieuc. He was a good man.'

'Does Agenhart know?'

He nodded, lifted his cup and drank the wine in one draught. 'Yes, I have sent word to her. Hers will be a sad Christmas, I fear. She must come into our Hall. They were happy together. The forest hall will go to a new tenant, a new woodsman, but I cannot turn her out with nowhere to go.'

Gunnhild said quickly, 'Her father lives in Dinan and I know that Count Eudo would like to have her there. She cooked for us here and I think he would welcome her and …' she paused and her voice became a whisper, 'the children, too.'

'Perhaps, but the boy …'

Gunnhild waited. There was an edge to that moment of silence that she would not slice.

Alan could not meet her glare. 'I would have the boy here, Gunnhild. He will be trained as a page and then he can squire for me and perhaps he will make a good knight.' Alan's voice sounded distant. This was the realisation of a terrible fear. Though why she should fear a small boy who was cast in Alan's image, a child who was polite and kind, she did not understand. To have Alan's son by Agenhart raised alongside her own children, to have Dorgen so close to her family was not something she could have ever imagined.

He reached out and touched her arm. 'Please accept this for my sake.'

His decision, she knew, would not be gainsaid. There was no point in making a protest. She replied carefully, 'Alan, I cannot refuse you this. If Agenhart is happy for him to live here with us, then I must accept her child into our care. But, what will happen when we return to England?'

'He will be part of our household and I promise you, Gunnhild, that I shall not favour him above our own children.

Our sons inherit.'

'And if we have daughters?'

'If so, they will marry well and bring more wealth to us, but if we have girls, then it is written that my properties will revert to my brothers. When I return to Rouen, I shall ask King William for your mother's lands to be added to my own.'

'I see.' As Gunnhild sat silently, Alan poured them another cup of wine. She sipped it but now it tasted sour. 'So be it, Alan, but in no way is Dorgen to be favoured above our own children.' She rose from the hearth. 'Come, my lord, come up to the solar and see what has changed there and in our bedchamber. I had a painter brighten the walls.'

'Who gave you permission? I have just spent a deal of silver on Castle Richmond.'

She swallowed. 'Then you must hear my plans for this chamber, too. That is, unless we are returning to England before we can paint it,' she added defiantly. 'And there is a kitchen.'

There was a hint of anger again in his eyes. 'Have you drained my coffers, Gunnhild? When I gave you the keys to the treasury here I did not intend that you were profligate with my silver.'

'No, I did not touch the silver. I used my own resources.'

'What resources?'

'I shall explain later,' she said hoping if he saw the work, understanding would follow and with that forgiveness. 'First, come and see for yourself.'

He rose, and she led him, awkwardly moving before him, feeling a sinking dread as she slowly climbed the stairway to the solar. Ann came rushing down the narrow steps. She bowed her head and waited flattened against the wall as Alan pushed past her.

Gunnhild slowly edged the heavy oak door into the solar open. Alan stepped inside and stood rooted to the rushes gasping his shock at the woodland scenes painted on two of the walls. 'Flowers and trees, more decorum would be correct, the Virgin and Child, perhaps, or one of the miracles!' he said. He waved his soldierly hand at the painting. 'How did you pay?'

'I shall explain later,' she said again, worried now. *He will approve my labour on a saintly manuscript.* 'Come, my lord, come and see my new work.' She took his hardened hand and led him to her work bench. On it she had laid out her inks and her pens. Alan prowled around the piece of parchment that lay weighted with stones on each corner.

'So you have begun God's work at last. What is it?'

'It will be the story of St Margaret, a lady who suffered much when she refused to wed with a Roman noble and wished to remain a Christian and a virgin. She was my aunt's name-day saint.'

Alan stared down at the tendrils of flowers that twisted about some of the letters. Celandines, tiny purple daisies and wild rosebuds peeped out from miniscule leaves. His eye moved to the standing stones which she had painted along the page margins, the sea that caught at rocks and the angels she had drawn behind St Margaret's name. 'When she died and ascended into heaven, God made her one of his angels.'

'It will be a treasure.' He gathered her into his arms and held her close. 'Can you order me a tub filled with hot water? I leak vermin and reek to high heavens.'

Alan bathed in the great wooden barrel by the charcoal brazier and admired the Golden Mass with Mary wearing her traditional blue robe, the angel that rose above her and on the other wall, the Adam and Eve fresco above their bed. 'Much better,' he said approvingly, 'but the cost. Still it is well-executed and a gentle frieze.' He reached out for the soap and began to scrub away the dirt of the journey home and then reached for the towels she held out. He ran his great hands over her belly and then pointed to the Virgin. 'And soon you, too, will give birth, my dear, and to the Richmond heir. May the Holy Virgin bless him.'

Harmonious, they descended into the hall for the feast. It was a joyful meal and after it was over, they trudged down the hill to the bailey chapel wearing fur-lined mantles, shivering despite them, to give thanks for his safe return.

Later he cradled her head in his arm and said, 'Gunnhild, before I fall into sleep, tell me please, what monies paid for the wall paintings and the kitchen end to the hall? We owe the Church money for our penance. That should be a priority.'

She moved his hand over her belly so he could feel the child's movement. 'I am going to give birth sooner than I thought. It will be February.'

'This baby feels like he is a swordfighter already. He is so anxious to meet the world. Gunnhild, please answer my question.'

She swallowed. He would be disappointed with her. She said, 'I paid for the work with a gift your father gave to me. I thought you would not object as it was my property, because you have granted me this castle which was inhospitable until I made changes. Our child must have a comfortable castle from which to greet God's world.' She twisted to face him. 'My lord, changes cost silver.'

'What gift?' He removed his hand from her belly, raised himself on an elbow and gave her a penetrating look.

She shuddered. God help her if Alan became her enemy. She whispered, 'Your father gave it to me – a ruby made into a pin. The jeweller told me it would be set into a German bishop's crozier. It will go to the Church.' She hoped that this at least would soften the loss of the jewel.

He heaved himself up, his face thunderous. 'That ruby is priceless. I cannot believe you would sell off such a gift. Worse, I should think that you have been cheated.' He clenched his fists above the covers, and she saw no sympathy in his face. She could not bring the ruby back. What was done was done. 'My father must not find out.' He sank back into the pillows, clasping his hands behind his head and looking up towards Adam and Eve. 'How could you? Who knows of it?'

'No one, none except Ann and Hubert know what I sold. I offered the jeweller my sapphire cloak pin but he wanted the ruby. I should have given him my grandmother's cross, too, and maybe he would not have chosen the ruby.' She felt tears well up at the back of her eyes. She would not cry. She said quietly,

151

her voice still hardly more than a whisper, 'There is enough silver left to pay most of our penance.'

'Gunnhild, no penance should cost a Penthiévre ruby. That ruby belonged to my mother's house. My father must think highly of you if he gave you it, and you, Gunnhild, disrespected that gift. Go to sleep for I am too exhausted for this tonight. I wish to hear none of it again, nor must you ever speak of it to anyone.' He turned on his side away from her. 'Do you understand, Gunnhild, you have disappointed me.'

'It was mine, my lord, since he gave it to me,' she said to his stiffening back.

'Let us not argue that point now. I shall have much to say about possessions and who owns them another time.'

Gunnhild bit her lip until the acrid taste of blood hit her tongue. She had been foolish thinking she could do as she had wished.

'I am sorry,' she said quietly. 'I am truly sorry.' He never answered her.

13

'Coral suspended from the neck is good.'
'On the Regime for a Woman giving Birth', from *The Trotula*,
ed. and trans. by Monica H. Green, 2002 (dates from the 12th
century)

Alan never spoke of the ruby again that Christmastide. The preparations for the festivities between Christ's Day and Twelfth Night passed without further argument and although Gunnhild seethed inwardly, with supreme self-discipline she managed to remain smiling and pleasant, even when on the day following his return Alan summoned Agenhart up to the castle hall.

He greeted her in the antechamber where logs blazed in the wall hearth. He seated her on a low stool and offered her a cup of hippocras and little cakes. Gunnhild bent over a piece of sewing, struggling because her belly was constantly in the way. At least she was seated in the cushioned armed chair closer to the hearth than Agenhart on her stool. After she gave Agenhart her condolences she sipped her warmed wine in silence, allowing her needle to slip through a long piece of linen, pretending great concentration.

Alan spoke of ordinary things, Agenhart's comforts, both of her children, not singling out Dorgen as an object of particular interest. Then he said, 'Agenhart, you must stay with us for the feasting week, though I know you feel much sorrow. It will help to lighten your heart. I would not think of you alone in the hunting manor at this sorrowful time.' He stood, reached for her, drew her up to him and kissed her on both cheeks. Gunnhild stiffened and looked closer at the linen in her lap, but her hands shook with annoyance. He went on, 'I shall send a sleigh for your mother and the children and whatever clothing you will need. My knight will bring them safely into the castle. I shall not hear any argument.' To Gunnhild's chagrin he hugged Agenhart closer to his breast, saying, 'Welcome,

welcome, my lady, you will be amongst friends.' The woman was no lady, thought Gunnhild uncharitably. She was a servant.

To Gunnhild's relief, when they were all seated together at the high table that evening, the subject of Agenhart's future was raised. She knew what Alan would say but would Agenhart agree? She must because there would be no future for her here, not once Alan returned to the war. When Alan made his suggestion, Agenhart sat looking into the middle distance seemingly with no interest in his generous plan. Gunnhild held her breath until she was near to choking on the bread she could not swallow. Finally Agenhart turned her huge eyes on Alan, smiled her usual doleful smile and agreed to set off for his father's house at Dinan after Epiphany.

'Count Eudo will provide you with your own house at my expense, of course. I shall send a letter to him as soon as the roads are passable. Cook for him on feast days. That is all he will desire.'

'Thank you, my lord,' Agenhart replied. 'You are generous. I would like to return to Dinan and if Bruiec's mother can accompany me she will care for my household.' She turned to Gunnhild. 'My lady, I thank you also. You are kind.' She looked at Gunnhild's enormous stomach. 'I am skilled with medicine. When you are near your time, send for me.'

Gunnhild bit back her retort. Agenhart was glowing, slim, fair and beautiful, whereas she had grown large and weary. She was tired of this pregnancy and longed for her child to be born. And when her time came she needed midwives, not the hocus pocus of a wise woman of the woods, and certainly not Agenhart. She replied evenly, 'Thank you, Agenhart. I hope there will be no such need to bring you back here all the way from Dinan.'

Throughout the remainder of the twelve days of Christmas, Agenhart's little family were long-faced, visibly saddened by their great loss, spending endless hours in the chapel in prayer for Brieuc's soul's safe passage to heaven. Alan granted the family a chamber in the bailey hall and Agenhart busied herself, when she was not in church, in the kitchen overseeing the cooks whom she had trained during Alan's absence. Gunnhild admitted that her rival was helpful during the feasting time, and observed how she was greatly admired by the cook who had returned with Alan from the wars. Had he not a young wife already he surely would have offered for the beautiful Agenhart.

The season passed peacefully. Much time was spent in the chapel with sombre candlelit prayer for those who had not returned from Dol. Alan did not communicate more than was necessary with Gunnhild, nor did he show Agenhart particular favour. Gunnhild felt his displeasure. He was often terse and long-faced and so, thinking of her own family and her own losses of years before, she was reticent to ask him the one question that played on her mind as they prayed for the souls of those soldiers lost to Alan. What about those souls lost to her – her father, her brother Magnus, the other two brothers she hardly knew, her mother, her sister and Ulf, her childhood playmate. Christmas always brought back memories of the year her uncle had died and her father was crowned king. Where was Ulf now? Surely Alan could discover her brother's whereabouts? But the opportunity to ask this favour never presented itself. She remained in disgrace because of the sale of a jewel, and she knew that it must wait until his mood improved.

On the morning she was due to depart, Alan summoned Agenhart to the antechamber for a talk about Dorgen's future. 'Agenhart,' Alan began. 'I would like Dorgen to remain at Penthiévre and travel with us to England when we return to my lands there.'

Agenhart's face revealed her hurt at this suggestion. Her eyes swam with tears. 'No, I would keep him with me. *She* will not give him a mother's love,' she said softly. Glancing sideways, she looked up at Gunnhild, stood on her toes and whispered into her ear so low that Dorgen and his sister did not hear, 'You do know who his father is?' Her almond-shaped eyes slid towards Dorgen, who was playing with his sister and a puppy by the hearth. Soft though it was, it was a brutal remark.

Gunnhild replied just as quietly and with a sense of loyalty to Alan that she did not really feel, 'Yes, Agenhart. I do know it and I still wish to raise Dorgen with our own children. He will become a page when he is old enough. One day he will be a knight. Do you not want what is good for his future? I promise you that I shall care for Dorgen as if he were my own son.' She stretched out and tentatively took Agenhart's hand. 'It would make us both content and we shall make Dorgen happy.'

For the first time in days, Alan smiled at her but Agenhart pulled her hand from Gunnhild's. At this Alan's brow darkened towards Agenhart. Gunnhild quickly withdrew her offer of friendship concealing her hands under draping sleeves that tailed down each side of her great belly hanging as if they were tired, wilting vines. Agenhart turned to the hearth and called her small son over. Reluctantly he left the puppy with his sister and came to his mother's side.

In a hesitant manner, Agenhart said, 'Dorgen, this is your choice.' She blinked away her tears, stopped speaking as she swallowed. In a calmer voice she continued, 'Would you like to stay here with Count Alan and the Lady Gunnhild and have the opportunity to visit new lands?'

The child looked from Count Alan to his mother. 'I would stay in the castle, Mother,' he said solemnly. 'I want to learn to be a knight like Count Alan.'

Alan laughed. 'There is your answer, Agenhart.' He knelt down to his son. 'Little Dorgen, now that you have no father, you must see me as your father.'

Gunnhild swallowed a monstrous breath and thought her heart would stop beating but Dorgen was still a child and Alan had promised that he would be no threat to their own children. Gunnhild studied Agenhart closely. A curl of chestnut hair had escaped from behind her wimple and lay provocatively on her cheek. Agenhart smiled with a generous mouth, though her almond-shaped eyes remained cold. She would remarry, for she was actually very beautiful when she bothered to smile. Gunnhild leaned down to the child and said, 'Dorgen, give your bundle to Mistress Ann and she will take you to the chamber where you will sleep.'

Ann had hovered close to Gunnhild throughout the interview and now the child took a step towards her. She embraced the boy and took his bundle. Alan said to Dorgen, 'It is near our own bedchamber and there will be someone to sleep with you until you are older. Ann will take you to this lady and if you are not happy with your nurse we shall find you another.'

'And Madam?' the boy said looking at Gunnhild. 'Will she care for me, too?'

'Yes,' Gunnhild said softly. 'Of course, Dorgen, I shall care for you and,' she looked over at Agenhart, 'your mother will have news of you. I can write to her. And you must learn to write also.'

'And read,' Dorgen said.

'I shall teach you.'

Later that morning, Agenhart departed on a covered cart. Her mother-in-law and her small daughter sat tucked under thick white furs beside her. The wagon was driven by a loyal servant who had secreted about his person a letter to Count Eudo and a purse of silver, Alan's parting gift to Agenhart. If Agenhart was heartbroken at losing her husband and son, she never betrayed her feelings. She sat proudly, like a princess of legend, wrapped in a new felt-lined mantle of warm red wool. Gunnhild observed that Alan's mistress never looked back at the small group that stood by the bailey gate waving her goodbye.

As January passed Dorgen rarely spoke of his mother. The little boy held wool for Gunnhild as she spun. He asked her to show him how to make letters. She promised him that after her baby was born she would teach him to read and write. She liked to see him laugh when he played. The kitten grew fat with the treats he slipped to the creature which he affectionately christened Smoke. He liked his nurse, a Norman widow named Amelia, who spoke Breton and who immediately proceeded to improve the boy's poor French. Alan took him to Hubert down in the bailey and Hubert began to teach him to ride a small Breton pony. He made him a wooden sword and shield and taught him fighting moves with them. Occasionally Alan took him out riding beyond the castle palisade but never into the forest which had once been his home and where another family had quickly replaced Brieuc and Agenhart.

During January, Alan rode to Rouen. He found the dwarf-like merchant and returned with the ruby. 'Rubies are rare. He was still negotiating a price for it. His bishop story was a lie. This, Gunnhild, has cost me a fortune. If I had not threatened him with the King's displeasure and prosecution for cheating my wife of that which she had no right to sell, I would have lost it. You will never sell anything without my permission again. Do you hear?' His face grew florid with anger and his eyes burned deep into her own with a fury she had not countenanced in him before, even in his most enraged moments. 'Do you hear me?' he repeated when she did not reply. 'All your jewels will be put in my strongbox for safe keeping.'

She said, 'Yes, I do hear, and I do not like what I am hearing. The Penthiévre jewels you may have, but my cloak pin from my aunt, my gold chain and sapphire cross you will not take from me, nor the trinkets I have purchased from the merchants who pass our way.' Her hand instinctively went to the cross that lay under the neck of her gown.

'I hope my father never hears of this,' he said and with those words he turned his back on her. She heard his armour, which he had not removed on entering her bower, clank down the staircase. As she listened to his retreat she could not help but feel mutinous.

Ann muttered something under her breath at the departing noise. 'I always took him for a heated man, my pet, too much heat, too dry,' she said comfortingly. 'Still waters flow silently until they are ruffled; then men like him are not so still. They are used to having their way and they know how to rub salt into others' wounds. He ought to have more sense than to upset a wife gone almost to her term. Come now, sweet lady, put your feet up on this stool and I shall make you a honey posset.'

Gunnhild felt better as Ann fussed about her. She was simply too tired to protest, too exhausted to feel more than

158

passing resentment towards Alan.

In the last week of January a messenger rode in from King William. Peace had been drawn up between him and Earl Ralph. The King was retiring to Rouen to make ready for a new campaign against Philip of France. He ordered Count Alan to return to England to secure his castle at Richmond and report on Lanfranc's and Bishop Odo's care for his kingdom.

'So we are returning to England at last.' Gunnhild laid her pen down on her table and glanced up from her work on St Margaret's white mantle.

'You will give birth soon. You must remain in your chambers. I forbid you to leave this keep before you are churched,' he said grimly.

'How long will I wait here?'

'That depends. I shall send for you, and for my son. *My sons*, both of them.'

She replied in a gentle voice, 'You will miss our daughter's birth?'

'You are so sure we are to have a daughter?' He laughed. 'Well if it is a girl I want you to call her Matilda after the queen and for my sister, Matilda, who married a Norman with English lands.'

'I had thought of Edith for my aunt.'

'It would be diplomatic to name our first daughter Matilda. We can call her Maud if you like.'

'Then Maud she must be. When will you depart, my lord?'

'In a few days. There are things I must do first.'

'I shall ask Ann to pack your travelling coffer,' she said thinking of the well-worn leather chest that was tucked into a recess near the door to their chamber. She had been storing baby swaddling there. It would have to be emptied. She smiled now, bemused. Alan might not like the scent of rose petals she had scattered amongst them.

'And Gunnhild, whilst I am away, you are not to sell anything else, not without my permission. I have taken the most valuable of your jewels and locked them in my strong-box and I

159

shall keep the key with me.'

She looked down at her enormous belly and said, 'I cannot not sell any more of the family jewels since there are none here to sell, but I do have a request.'

His mouth pursed and his rufus beard seemed to twitch. 'Not more expense?'

'No, what I ask will not cost. I want news of Ulf, my lord, my brother who was taken into Normandy eleven years since.'

'I know nothing of Ulf except that he is being raised at court where he will learn to become a good Norman. Do not ask me again. He has a new family now, the King's family in Falaise.'

He was harsh. She turned away from him and lifted her finest miniver-tipped brush. Alan had trampled like a war horse all over her feelings, first her jewels and then her love for a lost brother, her concerns dismissed as if they were of no consequence. She added a touch of scarlet ink to the blood stains on St Margaret's shift.

He said, 'Before I set off to Rouen, the other task I must do is to send for Niall.' He rapped his fingers on her table. 'He has been spending enough time touring my estates in Normandy. He will come to England. I shall need him to help me with Richmond. If we do not have a son, Gunnhild, Niall is my heir should I die first, which is likely since he is a decade younger than I; nearer your age as a matter of fact. He had a wife who died in childbirth, her first pregnancy.' Gunnhild shuddered. He ignored her visible anxiety and went on, 'And they lived in England on one of my estates but after she died he had no heart for England and returned to Dinan. On campaign at Dol he expressed a wish to return to Yorkshire. He is a sound leader of men. I can trust him to manage the garrison at Castle Richmond since I shall often be with the King.'

'Is he coming here?' Gunnhild looked up at him. 'And remember that you are fortunate, Alan, to know your brother.'

Alan glared. *He refuses to understand*. He just said, 'No, but Niall will accompany me over the Narrow Sea.' He pulled on his boots and disappeared out into the hall. From a distance she heard him calling for Brother Gregory to pen a message for

160

Niall. She could have done this for him had he asked but he had not. As she put away her own work she felt a twinge grip her belly. She stood clutching the winged chair by the hearth and breathed deeply.

Leaving the air of bitter disappointment behind, she slowly went into the hall to look for Ann. The servants must make ready her chamber for her lying in.

Their quarrel passed and with its passing her anger towards Alan faded. She could not easily change a man such as he, one she was discovering was determined to dominate her. Such are men, she thought, such is a wife's lot. She was about to give birth. She must not allow bitterness to taint it or worry to make it difficult. On St Brigit's Day they celebrated Gunnhild's birthday. She was nineteen years old. Alan gave her a coral necklace saying it would protect her during her lying in. She held up the string. It had a silver clasp and little shells fashioned from silver amongst the pieces of coral. 'Thank you. I shall treasure it, Alan.'

'I expect to see it on my return,' he said.

Thankfully this birthday gift was not to be kept hidden in a treasure casket. Gunnhild wore it around her neck where it nestled beside her grandmother's sapphire cross. She glanced in the polished brass mirror that lay on the ash wood table. The coral glowed against the soft sage of her woollen overgown, a garment so voluminous that she felt it flow and swish against her ankles as she walked to the table. Although this necklace was a small compensation for the jewels he had locked away it was by far preferable to the Penthiévre ruby. That had been tainted by his displeasure.

On the day following her saint's feast, Alan was packed and his coffer was strapped to a second horse on which his young squire had perched. 'When I am in Rouen, I shall see that the seamstresses return by spring to make you garments for your churching. Hopefully I shall be able to return then also.' He leaned down and kissed her hand.

They had reached a place of calm and she did not want ill-will to linger between them. 'Godspeed, my lord,' she said warmly. 'Return soon.'

Dorgen ran around Alan's stallion, keeping well away from the horse's back legs as he had been firmly warned to do. 'Can I be your squire soon?' he asked, looking up at Alan with great pleading eyes.

He is an endearing boy, Gunnhild thought to herself, but how are we going to cope with his persistence when he is older? 'I am sure you may,' she said aloud. 'But first you must learn to handle a horse as well as Count Alan. I think a groom is coming now to take you riding so say goodbye at once, and then off you go, Dorgen.'

Dorgen waved wildly at Alan who was turning his horse and beginning to ride towards the gatehouse. He glanced back at the child with a look of pure adoration. *I hope he loves our daughter as much as he loves Dorgen.* She bit her lip. *Soon, Dorgen will have to know that Alan is his father.* She shrugged. *It is for the father to tell his son who he is, not me.* Pushing that thought away she watched Alan and his squire canter out of the bailey gate to clatter over the ditch bridge. She waved and hurried from the yard back up to the keep and, though she had difficulty catching her breath, she rushed to the antechamber behind the hall to watch him ride down the trackway towards the road to Rouen. Standing by opened shutters she followed his progress until he became no more than a distant speck on the landscape, until he had disappeared completely.

A week later, Gunnhild was clenching her teeth. She gathered together all her willpower and bore down. In constant pain, she had been labouring since Vespers of the previous day and now from the distance she could hear the chapel bell ring out the midday angelus. Her contractions were painful and she was exhausted. When she opened her eyes, through the fug of the chamber she could perceive concern on her midwives' faces. She closed her eyes again to sense Ann leaning down over her. She felt cool water as Ann bathed her brow. As if from a great distance she heard her voice. 'It will be well, my lady. We sent to Dinan yesterday for Agenhart. She is more skilled than all of us here.' Gunnhild was too tired to complain. Another contraction swallowed her and she cried out again.

Agenhart arrived early in the afternoon. Gunnhild groaned, imagining she was lost in a night so dark and long that surely God Himself had forbidden day to ever return. She had sinned; she had turned her back on God and the abbey that had nurtured her. This was her punishment and her unborn child's misfortune to have such a mother. She was doomed. Sensing Agenhart by her pillow, she could hear her voice from far away. The sweet oil of lilac, a perfume that Agenhart had worn at the Christmastide feasting, floated in the air. She felt Agenhart touch her. The woman never spoke a word. Gunnhild saw from the edge of her vision that Agenhart had crossed to the window and was clattering opened the shutters. 'If only for an hour, my lady needs air, fresh air.'

Gunnhild could feel the mild March afternoon air caress her face. She breathed in the aroma of rosewater as Agenhart bathed her. It soothed her until a midwife gently put a long, thin hand up inside her private, secret place towards the neck of her womb. All was agony there. 'The child wants to be born. He is coming,' the midwife whispered. 'My lady must push him to life.' Agenhart raised her, placed a cup with a sweet liquid to her lips. 'Drink,' she said, and, praying for relief, Gunnhild sipped the sweet honey drink. 'You need your strength. Soon you must push.' Gunnhild felt as if she had no energy left to push.

Agenhart was insistent. 'My lady, when I say so you must push.' Another contraction came and she felt racked with a pain so profound she was sure she must die.

'Push now.' The order came to her as if from a great distance. Supported by Agenhart and the other women she heaved and pushed. It was hard. This great effort devoured the last remnants of her strength. Yet as she pushed she felt calmer.

'You will be delivered soon, I promise, my lady,' she heard Agenhart's distant voice say. She clutched the woman's hand and gasped, 'I know I must. If I do not then I shall die.'

'Strive again, my lady, I can feel the baby's head,' a midwife said. 'He has crowned at the end of the passage.' Gunnhild felt as if everything inside her was compulsively moving. She could not stop the sense that waves were swelling and crashing onto the rocks below the castle, except that she was part of the swell. Then she felt pain and enormous relief as the baby was eased from her passage.

'You have a girl, my lady,' Ann was saying. The sound of her voice was far away. 'She is a great strong baby. What will be her name?'

'Matilda,' Gunnhild managed to whisper hoarsely. 'Maud.'

It had all been so awful that she knew that she never wanted to have another child. The last twenty-four hours had been the worst she had ever known. A bundle was placed into her arms and she looked down on her daughter. 'Maud,' she whispered despite her exhaustion, 'I shall love you with my last breath.' She kissed the baby's forehead, and after that she could feel nothing, see nothing. Agenhart had given her something to drink, honey and wine maybe, she thought sleepily. She faintly heard the words, afterbirth, bleeding, and wet nurse. Someone put the baby to her breast. She had felt the washed and swaddled bundle root and then felt her suck. After that she was sure that Maud had been given the second breast. There were whispers around her, something about too much bleeding, a rip, strain, small passage.

She heard Agenhart say, 'Hush. Ann, send into the village for the wet nurse. Lady Gunnhild cannot continue to feed the child. She is too weak. Drink, my lady, again, just a little. It will expel the afterbirth.' This new concoction tasted bitter; it smelled of parsley, of leeks and she could smell vinegar. It woke her up. They were holding her legs, though she could not see why. She tried to resist but soon realised that her limbs could not move of their own accord. Now they were dripping vinegar into her secret place. She could smell it and it stung.

After that, she knew no more for several days.

* * *

When she awakened her feet were supported on cushions so

they were higher than her body. Ann told her that they had had to heal a rupture in her vagina with powder made of comfrey and daisy and cumin which Agenhart had carried with her from Rouen. They had packed her passage with a suppository of musk oil, camphor and rue. Every time the midwife changed it she was aware of warmth. The rupture was healing and she had passed through a terrible danger, Ann insisted, as she spooned mouthfuls of milk and softened bread to Gunnhild.

'Where is Maud?' Gunnhild tried to ask.

'We had to put her with a wet nurse. I shall send for her. She is a beauty. She will make a grand marriage one day.'

'I shall nurse her; none other must. Return her to me,' Gunnhild muttered and fell back against her pillows. 'My lord?' she said. 'Has anyone sent him word?'

'Yes, my lady. But as yet we have not heard back. It is too soon.'

'How long have I been …'

'A few days, you have been near death but Agenhart has nursed you to health again. I knew we were right to send for her.'

'Where is she?'

'She returned to Dinan today.'

'And Dorgen?'

'He has asked for you every day. He looks at the crib, as if Maud was the Queen of the Silkies, her tail shed and she has come amongst human kind to steal his heart. He is besotted with her.'

'Good, but he must continue with his lessons and ride every day.'

'He will.' Ann patted her arm and removed the spoon and bowl. 'Tomorrow we can allow your feet to lie on the sheets and dispense with the cushions. Your passage is healing well. There is no more bleeding and no need now to pack it with the poultice.'

'Thank St Margaret for that.'

'St Margaret?'

'Ann, don't you remember? She is a helper to women in

165

labour, just as St Cecilia represents refined womanhood and St Brigit protects our castle.'

'Ah, of course, and all three helped you survive?'

'I believe Agenhart saved my life because they willed it so.' Gunnhild felt for her coral necklace. It still hung around her neck. It must have helped, too. The door rattled and she started as she heard a mewing like a kitten's sound. When the wet nurse put the baby into her arms, Gunnhild started. Her child was tightly wrapped in swaddling and tied to a board. This seemed such a cruelty, even if the nurse intended to straighten Maud's limbs. 'Remove that. I do not want her strung to a board. I want to see her as she was born,' she said. The nurse hesitated but when Ann said, 'Do it,' the woman obeyed and reluctantly removed the straightening board. She placed the baby into Gunnhild's waiting arms.

'Now, Maud,' Gunnhild summoned all her slight strength, 'I want you by my side, your cradle by my bed, and more than anything, I want you to give suck.'

A disapproving expression settled on the nurse's countenance. She glanced at Ann with frog-like eyes that begged for support. Ann shrugged. Gunnhild repeated, 'Do as I say, both of you. Either I can or I can't, and unless I try I will not know. Unbind me, Ann.'

She sat up, despite her weakness, and kicked away the cushion that supported her feet. 'I shall try,' she said, summoning her most commanding tone. 'She will take suck from me. *I* am her mother.' She kissed Maud's fair-coloured down and smelled her comforting smell. *She is beautiful and she is my child, more precious than any jewels.* To her delight after a short time, though she felt it painful at first, Maud began to give suck. The bond she felt with her baby was worth any amount of initial discomfort.

From then on Gunnhild kept Maud and Dorgen close, watching over both children like a tigress would her cubs. She was churched in Alan's absence and for a time was saddened by the fact that he never sent her word from England. She did not even know if their messengers had reached the wilds that lay beyond York in her native country where Castle Richmond stood guarding the troubled North. Almost four months passed. The Beltane festival came and went, a quieter occasion than that of the previous spring and still nothing. She told herself daily that she had healthy children and the company of women and that her garden overflowed with flowers, herbs and salad. Her cup was half-full. She must be patient.

There should be different kinds of pictures, cloths of diverse colours, and pearls placed in front of the child, and one should use nursery songs and simple words; neither rough nor harsh words should be used in singing in front of the child.

'On the Regimen for the Infant', *The Trotula*, ed. and trans. by
Monica H. Green, 2002 (dates from the 12th century)

Alan returned on a June morning filled with the scent of wild rose and celandine. Not thinking about him, Gunnhild pottered through her herb beds filling a reed basket with fat, newly ripened strawberries. She glanced up at the cerulean sky and gasped with pleasure. It had not a single cloud to mar its perfection. Maud was alternately squawking and batting at a row of dangling shells with her fists. Her mewing grew into an insistent howl in the moments it took her mother to reach her. Cradling Maud in one arm, Gunnhild eased herself onto the bench and with her free hand unlaced the ties on her gown. Maud attached herself to her mother like one of the limpets that clung to the rocks below the castle.

Gunnhild had come to enjoy her houseful of women. Her home hummed with contentment. Now that summer had come to Fréhel the seamstresses had returned. They mended her gowns and filled linen bags with shapeless baby shifts of so many sizes that Maud had enough to last her for several years. The wet nurse remained at the castle with her own child until Gunnhild sent her away, paying her off with a purse of small coins, glad to see the back of her dour face. Throughout the spring months, as Gunnhild grew stronger, the bower was filled with the noise of singing, sewing, scissor clinking, maids chattering, and the small thudding sounds of spindles dropping as her women exchanged stories of babies.

Gradually Maud's hunger was sated and she let loose the nipple and began to doze. Gunnhild gently lifted her back into her crib. Rising slowly she saw with amazement that Alan was standing by the gate. She blinked, thinking that the sunlight was deceiving her, but he was no imaginary being. He was fully human and moving along the garden trackway towards her.

She sank back onto the bench. Tears of frustration threatened to flow as the happy moment she had just felt vanished and, instead, she remembered how she had nearly died bearing his child. He had not sent word to her since his departure months before. Wiping her tears away with her sleeve, she watched him cross the path but did not move to greet him. Her anger at him prevented her. Her disappointment was deep-seated. He was wearing a light blue wool mantle, hose that was clean and his overshirt looked new, a rich garment woven of natural linen decorated with gold embroidery. She suspected that he had not come to her straight from a ship.

He spoke first, 'I heard it did not go easily.'

Looking up she widened her eyes and said with all her pent-up fury, 'It has been four months, Alan.'

'Gunnhild, it took a month for the message to reach me. I was on the borders up in Northumbria saving our lands from the Scot rebels,' Alan replied quietly.

'No message from you and yet we sent you many.'

'Yes, I knew that you had survived as did our daughter.' He looked puzzled. 'I sent you word that I would return as soon as everything was settled in Northumbria.'

'There was no message.'

He frowned. 'I sent a man to Dinan. My father had written saying that Agenhart saved you and the child. He said that she deserved my thanks. I requested that the messenger continue here.'

'I see,' said Gunnhild, but she did not see. It rankled that Agenhart had received Alan's thanks and no doubt his gift. Yet, no word had come to Fréhel. In fact, the old count had never sent her any acknowledgement of his new grandchild either, nor had he sent a birth gift to Maud.

She shook her head sadly. 'You are here now so you had better meet your daughter.' There was nothing to be gained by quarrelling with Alan. She reached down into the crib, lifted the sleeping baby and placed her into his arms.

He seemed awkward as he held the child and looked down on the tiny sleeping face.

'Where is the wet nurse? Why were you suckling her, Gunnhild?' he asked.

'Because, Alan, I almost lost her and because I choose to,' she responded, relieved that Maud slept on despite the tension that was rising between them.

'It is not seemly. You are not a peasant.' He handed Maud back to Gunnhild saying in a more kindly tone, 'She looks cast in your own image, a Saxon princess of King Harold's blood. That will bode well in the marriage market.'

She mused that Baby Maud had the look of Elditha about her too, fair and green-eyed. She showed the promise that, like her mother and her grandmother, she would one day own a very elegant neck. For a moment she felt sad that it was unlikely that Elditha would ever know Maud, her granddaughter.

Aloud she said, 'Our daughter will not be bought and sold, Alan. I want no talk of that. She is still a baby. '

'Girls from noble families marry into other wealthy families and it will do us no harm to be on the lookout for a suitable match for her. So you called her Matilda?'

'I chose Maud because you requested the name.'

'The Queen will be pleased to hear that you have called her so.' He paused. 'And you are churched?'

She nodded. 'Hubert and Ann are her godparents.'

'That will be convenient enough. We can save the nobility for our son. Though I would have thought my sister Matilda a more suitable choice this time. '

'I do not know your sister.' She tucked the sleeping Matilda into her crib. Looking up she said, changing the subject, 'Brother Gregory is to return to his old monastery in September.'

'His was a temporary appointment. There is to be a permanent priest placed here from the Abbey of Landévennec, a studious and kindly man, which is good, because I am here to bring you back to England with me, and I intend leaving the new priest from Landévennec here. He will not allow the villagers to let their faith slip again.'

Gunnhild said neutrally, 'That is good.' She looked over at her basket of strawberries, then leaned down, lifted it, held it to her chest and studied him over the mound of fruit that hovered between them. She should be pleased to return to England but she was not. For months she had learned to live without him. She added, 'I shall be sorry to leave. This has become my home.'

'There will be another home, a safer home since it is a fortress. Sit down, Gunnhild. I have something to say.'

Gunnhild sank down onto the stone bench again, still holding the basket. He began to speak. 'I have been in Rouen for several weeks in conference with the King getting agreement concerning your mother's lands. I am to have her estates in Norfolk and Lincolnshire. They will be managed by my loyal stewards. I intend to take stock of them. Other lands your mother has title to are held by the King until such time as he decides to distribute them. Wilton Abbey apparently claims the Reredfelle villages and those lands she had in Essex. The King refuses and will have his stewards manage them for now. I shall claim them.' It seemed that her mother's lands had been whisked at the stroke of a pen from Elditha's name and, indeed, from her own. It was unfair.

This revelation explained why he was dressed so finely. He had been with the King. With realisation she knew that she was married to a more calculating man than the one she thought she had known when she had run away with him from Wilton.

'My brother, Niall, agrees to dwell with us. As I hoped, he will help me train the new knights that King William intends billeting on us. It will be a great expense.'

She returned his hard look with a questioning one of her own. 'Why, Alan, is King William billeting knights on us?'

'King William intends that there will be no more rebellions. He does not want to bear the cost of the mercenaries himself. He is placing soldiers in every great castle in the land.'

'I see. So, when do we depart?'

'As soon as we are ready. I have appointed a new man to look after Fréhel. Hubert will accompany us to Richmond. I have need of him there.'

'You have done all this without coming first to me and your daughter. Where have you been, Alan, as well as Rouen?'

'With my father in Dinan.'

She felt her stomach heave and somersault as if she was tossed around in a basket at sea. There was no need to ask. She knew in her heart that he had been with Agenhart and maybe intimate. 'There will be much to pack,' she said with brusqueness. 'I must go and tell Ann.'

She called for a maid who had occupied herself with sewing on a bench by a distant apple tree, far away enough to give Gunnhild privacy but near enough should her mistress have need of her. 'Take Maud to the bower,' she commanded. 'Then order hot water for my lord. He will want to bathe.' Gathering her cloak about her, clutching her basket, she excused herself and went to seek out Ann who was busy brewing that day.

On a fine day with a blue sky and fleeting wispy clouds, Gunnhild, Count Alan, Dorgen, Baby Maud, her nurse and Ann and Hubert gathered in the bailey. They, and a small group of retainers, made ready to mount their horses. Carts of clothing and provisions waited in an orderly line for their departure. Alan had prepared for the first part of their journey home to England, even down to the finest detail of how Fréhel would prosper during their absence.

He climbed onto his stallion, twisted back towards Gunnhild and said, 'Come on, get up on your mount. I want to see you seat the new sidesaddle. Give Maud to her nurse. They will travel in the wagon. You and my son will ride beside me so that all our villagers can see their lord and lady depart for England.'

Gunnhild gave Maud over to her new wet nurse, Dame Elizabeth. Although Gunnhild liked her and trusted her, she felt sad to lose Maud into her care.

'My dear wife,' Alan had said calmly and persuasively some

weeks previously, after he had sent to Rouen seeking a reliable wet nurse. 'It is the way our nobility behave, just as you must now learn to ride sidesaddle. Besides, we must set about providing Maud with a brother.'

She had looked askance at the cumbersome cushioned saddle with a seat which looked as if it would hinder rather than facilitate her freedom of movement, *just as a husband tries to limit a wife's freedom.* She was supposed to hook her right leg around the pommel. She practised but it was uncomfortable even though she had a platform at the side on which she could rest her left foot.

She said, 'My lord, I shall do my best with that saddle but if I find it delays my riding or holds us up, then I do not care what way the nobility of Normandy behave. I shall ride as I find comfortable.'

'You are competent. You must not hold us up,' was his firm response.

With the help of her groom, Gunnhild mounted Shadow, sat awkwardly in her new saddle. She let her knees grip the pommel, trotted a few clattering paces forward and took her place beside her husband. She knew that in this saddle every bone in her body would ache by nightfall. Dorgen already had his legs thrown over his prancing pony and he trotted to the other side of his father. Alan spoke warmly to Dorgen. 'Ready?'

On his return to Brittany he had told Dorgen that he was his father and Dorgen was even more in thrall to him. Was it that now Alan had some of her mother's lands she was of no more importance to him than a brood mare? He did not speak warmly to her as he did to his son. As she rode out through the gates of Castle Fréhel her heart felt heavy and she wondered when again she would see her gardens, the cove which she loved, the kitchen she had added, the solar with its painted walls and her airy bedchamber that looked over Fréhel's walls towards the sea.

* * *

A month passed during which they rode with pennants flying

and carts rattling up the great North Road. They made many stops on the way, to visit Alan's sister, Matilda, and to show her the daughter who took her name, to allow time to rest, and to break the journey in abbeys and great castles on the way to Yorkshire. Finally they rode through the gates of Richmond on a late August afternoon fat with the promise of a ripe and glowing early autumn. There was a dry breeze on the air and a sky above which crossed the Dales with puffy scudding clouds tinged with gold and pink. Gunnhild had finally mastered the sidesaddle on their long yet interesting journey. With her head held high she trotted through Richmond's great gates on the high-stepping Shadow, past waving servants and the people of the small town about the bailey gates. She caught a posy of Michaelmas daisies thrown by a child.

As they rode under the new portcullis, she looked up at the grandeur of Richmond's stone keep and surveyed the great paved courtyards below. When they reached the tower she thought to herself, I shall be mistress of one of the greatest castles in the land. *It is my right, my destiny as a Godwin princess to rule my kingdom here in the north with care.* She turned to Alan smiling. 'This is more than I expected. I can be happy here, my lord.' Alan reached out to her, and as he placed his gloved hand over her own he said, 'We must make many heirs to inherit my lands.'

She buried her head into her little posy of late daisies and for a moment smelled their dry elusive scent. 'And what if there is not another child?' It was her fear because the midwives had hinted that she might not conceive again.

His brow darkened. 'Then my brother has all, even though we had different mothers and after that Stephen who is still with Brian in the south.'

'Why?'

'It is the way our wills are made. All follows through the male line so long as my father recognises his sons, and he did. So, Gunnhild, provide me with a son.'

She gritted her teeth at that thinking to say, *my womb is unfit*. But she held her silence. He might think that it was God's punishment and send her to the convent.

She heard a shout and looked towards the great entrance to see Niall striding across the cobbles. He was so handsome, laughing and carefree, that she forgot her present anxiety and had to suppress an urge to stare at him.

'Welcome to Castle Richmond, welcome home, my lord brother,' he said as he bowed to Alan. He reached up to Gunnhild. 'My lady, my mistress of the castle, what a cumbersome saddle; may I help you down off your horse?

15

Castle Richmond, March 1079

Two years slipped by. Alan was always away fighting for King William in Normandy or patrolling the borders with Scotland or seeing to his many mercantile interests. He left his brother, Niall, to watch over the Honour of Richmond, reminding her that if he had no son by her, his legitimate wife, Niall would inherit.

Niall dwelled in the gatehouse alone with a few servants to care for his small though towering abode. He was kind and he made Gunnhild laugh, so that she often thought if it was not for Niall and the company of the two children, life at Richmond could be bleak as life in an abbey. At times she found herself longing for his company, looking forward to his presence at her table, admiring his tall, agile figure as he leapt onto a horse or down in the bailey or was showing a youth new manoeuvres with his sword. His quick movements matched his quick wit. She was glad, too glad, she sometimes thought, of his care of Richmond during Alan's absences. She would catch herself sighing, thinking if before long he would decide to remarry. He never spoke of his dead wife and she never broached the subject. It would be bold to do so, though she wondered if he ever compared them. In truth, she wanted Niall to admire her for herself and not as a duty to a brother's wife.

She was alone again and had been so for many long months. If it had not been for Alan's younger brother she might have despaired. She sensed he warmed to her, even liked her more than a little. Sometimes, when she found herself in conversation with him, seated before the pale linen napery at dinner time, she would catch herself not listening to his words but watching his countenance. His eyes fascinated her. They were extraordinarily dark, a deep, deep brown that was almost but not quite black; they were magical eyes, a moor's eyes, rich and soft like that rare and valuable cloth they called velvet. She quickly looked away thinking, *but I am a married woman. I chose my destiny and this is wrong. I have no business admiring my husband's brother's eyes, nor anyone else's eyes. It is a sin, and indeed more than once a sin since I have admired them too often.* She prayed in the chapel for forgiveness and for weeks cast her own eyes to the earth whilst in his company and concentrated better on listening to his words, a resolution which was also difficult since the sound of his voice was lighter on the ear than Alan's harsher cadences.

In March a great gale blew in from the north, sweeping through the dales, rattling shutters and felling branches. Outside, anything not tightly pegged down banged around with a fearsome noise. On the third morning of the storm Gunnhild ordered fires to be made high in the two vast fire-places that were built deep into Richmond's walls.

Both children had taken chills a week earlier. Maud had made a full recovery. Not so Dorgen. He had picked up something new and Gunnhild had wondered if the cause had been his insistence on playing sword fighting with a family of mercenary boys who dwelled in the bailey. She would have forbidden it but during a brief afternoon of sunshine she had taken pity on his longing to be free of the keep and allowed him out. Dorgen had sickened on the following morning after Prime and had worsened by Compline. Her night-time vigil had brought no change in his condition. His fever had not abated, his eyes hurt, his small child's head was sore and by daybreak his chest, trunk, arms and legs were smothered with a rash.

After cock-crow she could bear it no longer. She sent Niall to the House of St Cuthbert on the road to York, with orders to bring back a leech-man. Given the storm's ferocity it was unlikely that he would return before dawn of the following day, and she fretted that Dorgen might not hold on that long. By now he had all the symptoms of the spotted fever.

Ann insisted that the measles had come into the castle with a new troop of soldiers from the continent. If it was not contained it would cause panic inside their fortress which since the previous autumn had been filled to overflowing with the King's mercenary soldiers, their wives and children.

When Dorgen sickened she sent two-year-old Maud into quarantine up in the solar with orders to the nursemaid Elizabeth that Maud was not to leave it, not for any reason. Her ladies, too, were banished into quarantine until the danger of infection had passed. Only she, Ann, who had had the disease as a child and had recovered, and Dorgen's nurse, Amelia, would tend the sick child.

Determined to stop the disease spreading she unlocked the storerooms. Stored there since last summer, were small sacks of strewing herbs with rue and camomile scattered amongst them. The servants must spread them amongst the floor rushes. These herbs would keep infection at bay.

Then fighting the wind and rain she struggled through the courtyard and into the brewery where she ordered small beer to be sent across to the hall. She fought the wind all the way round the yard to the dairy and demanded a pail with fresh milk for a posset for Dorgen. Returning to the hall, she shook off her sodden mantle, selected a small key from her great household ring, and climbed the steps to the dais where she unlocked a squat oak-wood chest.

She fumbled amongst neatly coded pots and jars of ointments until she found what she needed. Lifting a candle to see better she drew out a stone jar which had a purple thread around its wax stopper. It contained a salve of burdock that might sooth Dorgen's angry spots.

She called down to Ann who was preparing his posset by the fireplace, 'Bring this up to his chamber too. Can you take over from Amelia? She must go down and check on the bailey children.'

Ann hurried over to Gunnhild. Wearily she pushed a stray lock of hair under her wimple. 'The posset is ready, my lady. I am on my way. I shall fetch you if there is any change.' There were dark circles around her eyes. At first Gunnhild had tried to forbid her to nurse Dorgen, but Ann had insisted, 'I cannot catch it again. I may be pregnant but I am safe.' As she took the salve she grasped Gunnhild's arm. 'When the leech-man comes, he will know what to do. My lady, get rest while you can.'

Gunnhild feared that only a miracle could save Dorgen. I am tired, she thought as she dragged herself up to her chambers. I am exhausted by everything, this castle, a husband who is never by my side, soldiers tramping around the bailey, two long winters and these storms and now this terrible illness. If he dies … she shook her head. *I will never forgive myself.*

She glanced into the solar on her way up to her chamber. Her women, four ladies, sent to her from minor noble houses for their education, were hugging what paltry warmth they could get from the central brazier.

'My lady, what news?' Elaine, a young girl, rose to come to her.

'None yet. The leech doctor is on his way from the monastery.'

'St Cuthbert's?'

'The same. Stay back. I may carry infection,' she said as Beatrice came closer. 'And keep Maud away from the hall.'

'She is fast asleep, my lady, and well.' Elizabeth put down her sewing and called over. She pointed to a curtained alcove. 'She has her poupées for comfort.'

She longed to hold Maud close, to go to her pallet, gather her into her arms and smell her living, healthy smell but she dared not endanger her. 'That is good,' she said turning back to the stair that went up the castle's heart. She bent over, feeling old beyond her years with anxiety, and climbed the stairway up into her own chamber.

Stretching out on her coverlet she fell into an uneasy sleep. It felt as if only a few heartbeats had passed when she woke up in a panic from a dream in which Dorgen was swimming through a dark deep pool. Already the chapel bells were ringing for Vespers. The leech-man must not have come yet or they would have sent for her. Too early of course, she remembered, her mind dimmed by lack of proper sleep. She scrambled to her feet and hurried down to Dorgen's bedchamber behind the hall.

She pressed a compress against his forehead but he was tossing and turning, muttering words that made no sense.

Gently she examined his small body. He was covered from head to toe with the rash and he was hotter than ever. He burst into coughing but when she took him in her arms and tried to hold him up, he did not seem to know her.

Dorgen had loved her as if she were his true mother and since they had come to Castle Richmond she had returned his affection, treating him as if he were her own child, trying not to feel broken-hearted that she had not yet conceived again. From time to time she wrote to Dorgen's mother. Alan took her letters with him to Normandy but never brought replies. She began to wonder again about the true nature of his relations with Agenhart. Did they renew their old affection when Alan travelled to Dinan to see old Count Eudo?

Lightning flashed through the narrow window embrasure, so close it seemed to light up the small room. Dorgen twisted away from her again.

'Hush', she whispered. 'Sweeting, the doctor will come soon.'

Around midnight Dorgen's breathing became shallow. She reached down to press a compress on his forehead again and felt someone slip into the chamber beside her. Ann had returned. She looked at Ann with tears gathering in her eyes. She felt the child's forehead. 'He is burning up, Ann. It is as if the devil and all his demons are seizing him from us.'

Ann was breathless and her mantle was dripping rain. She must have run all the way up from the bailey. 'The doctor has arrived,' she said catching her breath and removing her sopping cloak. 'Just now, as the midnight bell rings. He will be on his way up in a moment.'

'I pray to holy St Cuthbert that there will be no one else with this contagion. Has Amelia returned from the bailey?'

'Not yet. Hush, don't fret, my lady.'

At that moment, the doctor, a leech-man known as Brother Matthew, pushed through the curtain into the chamber. He took one look at the boy, shook his head and lifted the leather satchel he had dropped by the foot of the narrow bed. Opening it he said, 'If I can bleed him, it brings down the fever.'

'What if it weakens him further?' A sense of despair washed over Gunnhild because she could not think of an alternative. She had tried everything to reduce the fever, even bathing him with cool water. The rosemary she had hung about his bed, the worm-wood tonic she had tried to get Dorgen to sip that afternoon, the milk, cowslip and honey possets; the meadow-wort she had strewn amongst the rushes and the amulet of betony that she had hung about his neck had not taken away the heat; nor had they dispersed the evil that hung about the boy. She shrugged and said, 'Do what is necessary. What can I do to help?'

'You can pray,' the leech doctor said, quiet-voiced, 'and hope that in bleeding him the devil spirits within his disease will leave him be.' He gazed into her face and she felt he was looking into her soul. 'And pray that the infection does not spread throughout your household. Have you sent for Lord Alan? The boy is his son, is he not?'

Gunnhild nodded. A grudging tone sneaked into her voice as she replied, 'He is Alan's son by a leman.' She paused. 'Alan loves the child well, as do I, but he is in Normandy with the King.'

Brother Matthew raised his head from the prostrate little body about which he was gently feeling for a place, the correct place, to make a cut. 'Count Alan is often away,' he remarked.

'They have been fighting King William's son Robert who has brought the King of France against his own father,' she added by way of explanation.

'Evil times, my lady, when sons turn against their fathers.' The leech-doctor crossed himself and laid out his knife and cup on a small oak table close by Dorgen's cot.

Gunnhild watched closely. 'Can you save him?' The doctor did not reply. Dorgen looked so damp and fragile, like a little bird caught in a snare, struggling for its life. She felt angry at a God who could allow this to happen, angry at herself that Dorgen was ill. She sank down by the side of his bed again and tried desperately to pray that he would recover.

'I shall hold his arm,' Ann said, always practical in a crisis.

Gunnhild stopped praying and watched. As blood dripped into a cup, Dorgen became utterly still, as pale as the linen curtain that hung about his bed so that the livid spots seemed even more vicious. She leaned over him, sure that he was not breathing. His little soul was quivering as if on a cobweb about to float away, but still it clung to life. 'Oh, Dorgen,' she whispered, her voice choking. 'If you die, know that I have loved you.'

Alan would blame her care of him. She shuddered as she recollected how angry he could become if he thought that he was crossed by her. Moreover, they had not managed another child and recently he said the fault was not with him since he had had a son with another woman. She complained that he was never at Richmond so how could she fall pregnant. If there was fault the fault was his neglect of his family. He had raised his arm to strike her but thought better of it and strode off down to the bailey yard and his soldiers. She never repeated the accusation.

It was Niall who managed things in the garrison when Alan was in Normandy and it was Niall who always spoke gently to her when Alan's anger flared up. It was Niall who took her and the children riding, and who brought them small but beautiful gifts made of woven wool when he led a garrison up north into Northumbria. She knew that it would be Niall who would comfort her now.

She looked around the chamber. Dorgen's russet riding cloak hung on his clothing pole along with his breeches and small tunics. Sadly, she studied the chest which contained his stocking and linens. She counted the child-size shoes and boots neatly lined up below it, their dyed leather chosen especially for him and made carefully to fit his growing feet by the shoemaker from the village. There were two pairs of each.

Brother Matthew wearily put away his instruments, lifted his cup and went out into the hall. Moments later he returned to say that he was needed in the bailey. Amelia had returned with the bad news. He had to see a family with the contagion. They were in a bailey cottage, a groom's children.

183

'Oh no, not them too,' Gunnhild whispered. 'They were all playing together.'

The leech-doctor shrugged. 'It is God's will, my lady. Try to get Dorgen to sup a little wine. I shall return soon.'

The candle clock slowly burned down through the marked hours. Ann sat beside her, praying over Dorgen as they waited for the doctor to return. They kept the child's lips moist but he would not swallow. He was fading.

Brother Matthew returned before Compline with Father Christopher, the castle priest. There was nothing more he could do for the family in the bailey cottage. They were all dead already.

'All of them?' she asked.

The priest nodded. 'All excepting the father. He never caught it.' Gunnhild looked down on Dorgen. Her lips moved in prayer. Her eyes filled with tears. The priest knelt by the child's bedside and prayed beside her.

The castle was still. The wind seemed to have dropped. Gunnhild could hear the distant dragging of benches over the hall's floor. Just after dawn Niall came to them and reported that many of the servants were in the chapel praying for Dorgen's recovery. The priest said in a soft voice, 'I fear it is too late for prayer. They must now pray for God's care of his soul. Our father in Heaven has claimed him.' Gunnhild's agonised wail echoed around the castle. Niall held her close and whispered, 'Gunnhild. It was God's will.' She wept great tears of anguish into his surcoat.

Gunnhild sickened the following day. She was too unwell to attend Dorgen's burial. Brother Matthew, the same leech-doctor, tended her with great diligence and kindness. She heard him say quietly, 'Shall I bleed her?'

Niall's stronger voice was saying, 'No, you must not. Let us wait and see.' She fell into a sleep and for several days was mostly insensible.

Ann nursed her because the doctor was needed in the bailey. After two nights her fever abated but she was still covered from

184

the crown of her head to her toe nails with an itchy, vivid rash. Ann bathed her skin with juice of blackthorn and persuaded her to sip drinks containing dill to ease her into sleep.

As the hour clock burned down and day after day was replaced with a new candle, Gunnhild slept as if trapped within an enchantment. The wider life of the castle continued. Five days later, she woke up feeling a sense of peace and she knew that since she was not in Heaven already or in Purgatory she would recover. Ann told her that there had been other deaths. 'But, my lady, thanks to your precautions all of your ladies have escaped. And Maud is safe.'

As April passed the castle recovered but a deep lethargy seized Gunnhild and she refused to move out of her bed. Ann tried potion after potion to build up her strength.

'I am at peace here. Leave me alone.' She turned her head away, finally turning back to Ann who possessed great patience with her. 'What is it this time? Must I drink it?' she muttered from her pillow.

'Cuckoo-sorrel amongst other things, my lady. In any case, you are well. Time to be up. This is foolish.'

Gunnhild turned away again. 'I cannot. I can't face anyone.'

'You did not fail Dorgen.' Ann stroked Gunnhild's forehead. 'God called him.'

'God spared me, and he was just a child.'

'You have another child. She has been asking for her mother for weeks.'

Gunnhild studied Ann's face for a brief moment and burst into tears.

Ann wiped them away with a piece of soft linen. 'My lady, you cannot change what has been. It is harsh and it is sad and we all miss Dorgen but it is God's will. Sit in the sun at the window. It will raise your spirits.'

Gunnhild shook her head and fell back into a deep dreamless sleep.

Ann brought her more possets with snippets of news concerning Maud. Occasionally she smiled. A week later, she decided to rise. Slowly easing her legs from out of the covers she sat on the edge of the bed. 'You are right, Ann. Maud needs me.' Shakily she stood up. Her legs were surprisingly more solid than she had realised. She looked up at Ann. 'Does his father know?'

'Lord Niall has sent to him and he told him of your illness. I think it is time you wrote to Count Alan yourself. He will want to know of your recovery.'

'Did he send a message back to Niall?'

Ann shook her head. 'Not yet, but it has been less than a month since the messengers rode out.'

'I see.' And Gunnhild did see. She saw that Alan must not care. If he had he would have written.

Her green silk gown caught her eye as it hung from her clothing pole. She had everything she had wished for, almost; she had all the gowns she desired, a castle, servants, a lovely child – though Dorgen would haunt her thoughts for many a year and she would never forget him – but she knew deep in her heart now that she lacked a husband's love, nor would Alan grant her forgiveness.

Dorgen's death would lie between them. She could never forgive herself that she had not taken better care of Alan's only son.

Part Two

Richmond 1082-1089

St. Cecilia

St Cecilia (picture from Wikipedia)

16

June 1082

Five-year-old Maud was watching her mother in the castle laundry.

'Are you ready, Maud?' Her little girl nodded and took her place at the long bench.

In the three years that had passed since Dorgen's death, Gunnhild had watched over Maud like a she-wolf guarding her brood except that there was only Maud. She never conceived again. Gunnhild lifted the glass smoother out of the steam. Handling it with a wrapping cloth, she watched Maud lift up her own smoother. This was a flat round glass stone that was a miniature of her mother's smoother but not heated. 'Maud, remember that you must never touch mine. It is too heavy and it is hot,' she said, pointing to her own.

'I know. It is hot. Mama, you say the same thing every time we come here.' She began thumping her tiny glass iron on her poupée's little cloak.

'And you are not to come here on your own, do you hear,' Gunnhild added as she pressed her gown, protecting it with a linen cloth. She moved the smoother carefully from bodice to sleeves, half listening to Maud with a smile on her lips. Maud was muttering to her doll in a language of her own.

Gunnhild pressed the glass iron down onto the stiff green silk, taking great pleasure in looking at Aunt Edith's beautiful overgown once again. The overgown had remained in her coffer for three years, wrapped in linen amongst bags filled with fennel seeds. With the death of that little boy she could not bring herself to wear it. Dorgen had loved the dress, but tonight, she decided, she must lay the past to rest. She would wear Aunt Edith's gown for St John's feast and let go her sorrow for the loss of Dorgen's short life.

The maids bustled about carrying baskets of trestle napery from laundry to keep. The hall had been thoroughly swept and fresh strewing rushes sprinkled with camomile laid down in complicated patterns on the floor. The cooks would be busy making pastry coffins all morning and already a hog was roasting on a spit and small birds plucked for at least one of the many dishes they would eat later.

She had almost finished pressing the dress when from outside, beyond the courtyard, came the sound of chains rattling and clanking as the castle portcullis was raised. Moments later a single set of hoofs clattered over the cobbles. With a thundering noise, more riders followed. Gunnhild laid down her smoother and raced to the entrance, Maud trailing behind her. If Alan's retinue was returning from the borders she must drop everything at once and see to his needs. That way her peace would not be disturbed, her sense of harmony unpolluted and her ability to co-exist with him would continue.

Alan had not blamed her for Dorgen's death but he had blamed her for not conceiving another child during the two years that had followed his return from Normandy. He rarely lay with her now and she suspected, yet again, that he had found comfort elsewhere. Any excuse and he was clattering with his men down the Great North Road to London, to inspect his estates in the south, or off to fight for Normandy with King William and into Brittany to see to his trading vessels. He was away so frequently she wondered that she ever saw him at all.

When Alan was home at Richmond, to her surprise, he had taken an interest in Maud, saying that she was growing into an intelligent and pretty girl. Maud, in turn, admired her warrior father, loving to sit before him on his stallion, reaching up for his pommel and riding with him through the town below the castle and into the hamlets that had grown up along the River Swale.

Gunnhild stopped to catch her breath. She need not have hurried because, this time, it was not Alan who was climbing down from a stallion. It was Niall. He, too, had been patrolling the borders between Northumbria and Scotland. Her heart flipped over. It was always a pleasure to be looking up into Niall's dark eyes and to see them smiling back at her. There seemed to be an understanding between them, though neither had yet spoken because, she realised, neither of them dared. They did not step across that invisible and forbidden line. Yet he had never remarried and more than once she wondered what prevented him from doing so.

'Where is Alan?' she asked, feeling herself smile as Niall walked his horse forward to greet her.

He bent down from the saddle, lifted her hand to his lips and whispered so low no one else could hear his words, 'Ah, if only it was me you come running to, to welcome home.' He shook his dark head. 'Gunnhild, you look as fair as the swans on the river, and, well, a never more welcome sight too after a hard campaign, have I ever met. You are truly the loveliest of countesses. I shall rename you, swan-daughter!'

'A swan-daughter?' she repeated, remarking the playful tone in his softly accented voice. 'Ah, you mean my mother and her long swan-neck. Did you ever see her on your travels?'

'Only from afar. Would you like to see her again?'

'Yes,' Gunnhild said without hesitation. 'But as you well know all members of my family are destined to be kept apart from each other, in case we foment rebellion.' She sighed. 'Perhaps one day I can visit Canterbury.'

'Forgive me, my lady, I should not have spoken of her.' He slid down off his horse with concern in his eyes. Her heart contracted at his care for her feelings. He touched her arm and said in a cheerful tone. 'Count Alan rode on to Edinburgh with Prince Robert to broker peace with the Scots. He sends his greetings.' Niall glanced up at the castle keep, then back at Gunnhild. 'And he says, "Niall, tell my lady Countess I am sorry that I cannot preside over my own board at St John's feast."' His black eyes were now dancing with mischief. ' "You must do so in my stead."'

He lied of course. Alan had said no such thing. He would never show concern that he could not attend a feast with her at Richmond. He owned many estates throughout England, other places he could visit, some of which had once belonged to her own family, rich lands and manors that were fast accumulating great wealth.

Niall cleared his throat and continued, 'He has asked me to act as his proxy and sit beside you in the great chair.' He waited, his dark eyes still dancing. Gunnhild felt colour rush into her cheeks.

She glanced about the yard and, noticing dairy maids and approaching grooms close by, she replied loudly for all in the courtyard to hear. 'If my lord asks you to preside over the feast in his stead then so be it.' Surveying the dismounting riders accompanying him, she added, 'Take your men into the small hall and I will have Ann send them dinner from the kitchens.' With a smile playing about her lips, she returned to Maud who stood by the laundry door listening with wide, watching eyes. What does she see, thought Gunnhild? There is nothing to see, nothing between me and him.

'Maud, I have tasks to finish,' she said gently to her watchful child. 'Go and play with Ann's little girls.'

Maud groaned, 'Ailsa is foolish and Maggie is a baby.'

'You were three years old once. Now run along and share your dolls with Ailsa.'

Maud studied the poupée cradled in her arm. 'Maybe the others, but not Catriona.'

'As you wish.' Gunnhild knew that the doll was special. It had been carved in Paris, a name-day gift from Alan, and no one was allowed to touch this poupée with its golden hair and its blue gown. She finished pressing the overgown and held it up, pleased to look on it again. This gown belonged to her. It was a part of her heritage, not bought for her as others had been. She would be glad to wear it once more.

Its pearls glowed in the dim light, and fingering them Gunnhild became possessed by thoughts of the feast ahead. It had to mean something. The dress was magical and if she wore it tonight she would feel its power again. She was to preside over the feast with Alan's brother, she reminded herself, and on this night for the first time in many years she would wear Aunt

Edith's dress and the Godwin embroidered slippers. Take care, Gunnhild, she whispered to herself. Do not give away your heart. Do not risk everything for velvet eyes and a gentle voice.

17

St John's Eve 1082

Already the spell has set its well-known stamp on my heart. O winged loves, how is it that you are able to fly to us, but have no strength to fly away?

> *The Greek Anthology*, Meleager, 6th century, edited by
> D.L. Page, 2008

The mid-summer's evening threw long shadows on the courtyard and over the garden below Gunnhild's bedchamber. She peered out of the window embrasure, pulled her head back, wrinkled her nose and sneezed loudly. Smoke was drifting into the bailey and towards the keep from the fields where villagers had already lit bonfires. The village children had collected bones and other rubbish to burn on an enormous fire in the fallow field to purify the air. It was a popular tradition and a yearly event at Castle Richmond, one Alan frowned upon but was powerless to forbid because, just as with Beltane night in Brittany, this tradition stretched far into the depths of past time. Here in the north of England, St John's Eve marked the summer solstice, the night that witches could meet and dragons would poison wells. Gunnhild felt its power. Anything could happen, anything on this night when some people thought the membrane between worlds was thinnest.

Smoke flew through the half-opened shutters as if the witches and dragons were racing into instead of away from the castle. Coughing, she shut them on the unpleasantness. A long spell of hot dry weather had annoyed her throat more this year than ever before. She hoped that the breeze would drop and the ashy drift from the fires would settle before they visited the fields after the feasting to join in with the dancing.

By early afternoon Maud was so excited she could hardly stand still. Gunnhild and her women clothed her in a dress similar to that worn by her poupée, Catriona. It was embroidered at the neck and edged along the flowing sleeves with green leaves and with white and purple daisies. Maud danced about the chamber in a little blue mantle.

'If only Papa could see me,' she said as she pirouetted, kicking out with her blue slippers. 'He should be here for me.'

And for me too, thought Gunnhild, but he never is. 'Uncle Niall is with us tonight and he will be very impressed. Come here.'

Maud danced back to her and she pinned Maud's cloak with a silver swan. 'You know your grandmother had a swan's neck. I believe you have one, too. She was so lovely that even your father, who was a very young man then, younger by far than your grandmother, admired her.'

Maud reached out and touched Gunnhild's stiff silk overgown. 'But, Mama, you look beautiful, too.'

'Thank you, sweeting, I hope so.' She laid her hand on the gown. 'This gown once belonged to your great-aunt Edith who was a famous queen. I married your Papa wearing it.'

'So you always say. I remember everything.' Her small voice held an impatient tone.

Gunnhild studied Maud's earnest face. 'I know, you clever girl, but stand still for a moment.' As a final touch she placed a small wreath of cornflowers on Maud's golden hair. Sometimes Maud dwelled in a faery world of her own making. Yet she could be astute, and very observant.

Gunnhild slipped on her silver bracelets and hung a string of tiny amber beads about her neck, the only jewellery she possessed, along with a poignantly remembered but never worn coral necklace, Gytha's chain and cross and a few brooch pins for her mantles. Alan still locked the Penthiévre jewels away in his coffers. He concealed the key to his treasure chest about his person. She really would not care, except that those jewels not only contained the Penthiévre ruby but also gifts that had come to her from Countess Gytha, her father King Harold's mother, who after the battle at Hastings had fled with Thea, Gunnhild's sister, to Exeter in the south-west. There, the countess had held out against William's forces back in 1068. She had died in exile in Flanders.

Many years later, a parcel of gifts to Gunnhild came with messengers from Flanders to Richmond. Alan had also removed a book on hawking once owned by her father, five gold arm bands and two strings of pearls, a torc with a large garnet set into it and a brooch that had special sentimental value. Her father had worn it on the Christmas old Uncle Edward had died. Into it was set a piece of amber as large as a goose egg.

How could Alan be so cruel? These were all the memories that were left to her of her mother, father and grandmother. She tapped her toe as if ready to dance and smoothed down her skirt. It was fortunate that he had not taken away the dress she was wearing tonight. And, had he remembered that it had once belonged to her Aunt Edith, a queen, he might have done so, lest she remove the pearls and sold them to buy inks and parchment.

'Come, my love,' she said reaching for Maud's hand. 'We are ready.' She turned back to her ladies. 'Make a line,' she commanded. 'And follow us down.'

The hall trestles were covered with flowers tied into posies, bound with red thread signifying love. A posy of five different hedgerow flowers lay on the white cloth in front of the great chair that Gunnhild was to share with Niall. She lifted it and, pressing her nose into the nosegay, inhaled its sweet scent. In that moment she had captured the essence of wild roses and peonies, cornflowers and daisies and foxgloves, fragrant summer flowers that she had often included in her manuscript work.

'I wonder whom my lady will grant her favour to this night.' Niall's voice hovered by her ear below the clash of cymbals and the ringing of bells. She kept the flowers by her nose and ignored his whisper for a moment. How she wished everything was different. She longed to respond to this black-haired brother of Alan's. It was wrong. She should not but tonight the devil was tempting her sorely. Still holding the posy, inhaling its seductive scent, peeping over the flowers, she tried to distract herself from her true feelings by watching a Danish skald gambol around the hall disguised as a fool as he led a band of youths in rolling a great wheel through the trestles.

After the skald had passed by the high table she set the nosegay back on the cloth, the red ribbons trailing between her and Niall as she locked eyes with him. 'Be careful what you say. People see things that are not there. They see what they want to see. There are those who could cause mischief for us both.'

It was true but perhaps if they were very careful ... no ... the Devil hung by her shoulder whispering into her ear. *Take him for your lover.* Did Leviticus not forbid communion with a husband's brother? *That was a long ago law.* The Devil murmured into her ear, '*Did not Deuteronomy say that a brother should take to wife his brother's widow?*' Neither applied here since Alan was alive and she would never ill-wish him. '*Yet,*' spoke the Devil, '*you are living in a widow-like state since Alan is so often absent.*'

Niall broke into her thoughts 'Not Ann and probably not the children. No one else is close enough to watch you.' She shook her head.

The Devil was gone and for a while her reason returned to her. 'Yes, Niall, yes the children. They notice things. Maud is very astute. And there are servants, a hall full of them, and then there are my ladies.'

'Who wishes you ill, not them surely?' he said, with amusement in his voice.

'The priest would for a start and those two monks,' she whispered, turning her glance to where the priest Father Christopher sat beside two monks who were visiting from St Cuthbert's Priory.

'But we have done nothing to bring about their suspicion,' he whispered. 'And more's the pity.'

She ignored the remark and turned to ask Ann to pass the bowl of strawberry sauce for her duckling wing.

From the corner of her eye she saw that all three of the monks had cleared the posies from their part of the trestle. They wore narrow, watching faces as if they felt that St John's Eve was already disintegrating into a charade of frivolity. Yet, Gunnhild noticed, they did not refuse the special midsummer ale prepared in her brewery, nor did they abstain from the slices of pork or the pies filled with thrushes, the chickens and duckling and the sweetmeats, fresh stuffed salmon from the river or the rich sauces prepared in her kitchens.

Gunnhild set her face into a fixed smile and pretended to watch the skald's antics as many courses of delicious dishes continued to circulate about the trestles. The skald approached the dais. When he asked her for a favour she plucked a rose from her nosegay and gave it to him. He bowed and promised her a poem in return for a kiss. Laughing, she stood up, leaned over the trestle and kissed his balding head. Cheers and whoops followed her action. The skald tucked the flower into his cloak pin and bowed to her. There was further applause as he danced up to Ann, reached over, snatched her hand and kissed it. The children laughed and cheered.

As the candle clock burned down, the children began to nod and when midnight approached their nurses swept them off to bed. The doors of the hall were flung open and the remains of the feast was carried away to the bailey and out of the gates, over the second drawbridge to the villagers who lived in wattle-and-daub dwellings strung along the river. Led by musicians many of the castle inhabitants followed the servers who were carrying the baskets of bread and cheese, left-over meats and pies and flagons of ale.

'Come on,' said Niall, taking Gunnhild's hands. 'Why don't we join them?'

'It would not be seemly.' She looked down. 'Besides I might ruin this gown. It belonged to my Aunt Edith … and …'

Her protest faded as he interjected, 'We can ride out to the edge of the woods by the field. Why not? Your people will be pleased to see you.'

Reason was prevailing though she was beginning to detest reason. 'They will see us both. I am not sure that is a good idea,' she replied sharply.

'Nonsense, there is no harm in it. Wait in the courtyard. I shall get our mounts.' He disappeared through the hall door before she could refuse. And he was right, what was the harm in it? The Devil was in it though, she thought, as she searched around for Ann and for her four ladies but they had already vanished with the dancing crowd. Only the men of the garrison and the servants who were moving trestles into the alcoves to provide sleeping areas remained inside. The Devil reached deep into her heart. *What is the harm in a ride out with him on a festive midsummer's eve?* If I did not feel as I did why there would be no harm, none at all, she reasoned.

Gathering up her dress she threw her legs over Shadow and rode astride out through the gate-house and over the drawbridge. Others raced past them, hardly noticing that their lady was out. Occasionally someone shouted a greeting her way. Once they were on the pathway behind the straggly village, Gunnhild saw couples entwined amongst the shadows under trees. 'Tomorrow is St John's Day,' she said, thinking of the sour-faced monks. 'The villagers are bold tonight.' She could not hold back her laughter. The wine had made her feel giddy, reckless even.

'The witches are out and the dragons, too,' Niall said softly.

'The villagers won't dare sport tomorrow.' She felt relieved, as she glanced back over her shoulder, that the pious monks were not in evidence. 'They had better make the best of tonight. Tomorrow they can pray for forgiveness.'

At the edge of the field they could see the huge crowd of castle servants and villagers, making merry as the music-makers played pipes and clashed cymbals. A loud cheer seemed to shake the air like thunder when a group of youths hoisted a makeshift dragon, painted green and red with a trailing ragged tail, on to the bonfire. It burst into flames that crackled and hissed as the dragon began to burn away. Its enormous papier-mâché painted eyes, bulging at first, seemed to look out through the licking flames with an expression of anger.

Niall lifted the reins of her horse and turned her towards the woodland pathway.

'Would you ride on, Gunnhild? I think we can have a while to ourselves and I have a hidden place to show you. It is somewhere you can always find solitude if you ever want to be alone.'

She raised an eyebrow, surveyed him, hesitated and pulled on her reins so that her horse drew closer to Niall. 'Is this wise?' she whispered.

'Yes,' he said. 'You will be delighted with it, I promise.'

Her heart beat with anticipation and the delicious sense that she was enjoying an adventure with someone she cared for and whom she suspected cared for her. No words of romance had been shared. There was no need. She forgot the Devil and his temptation and just felt the romance that was hovering about them, a fragile thread that linked them but could easily break. They were alone for the first time ever, and, truthfully, though she was always in the company of others in Castle Richmond, she felt the loneliness of one unloved.

When she had first ridden out from Richmond in the early months, much of the countryside around them had been laid waste. Close to the castle, swathes of woodland had been charred and in many places only isolated areas of ragged shrubbery and stumpy trees remained. On the hills and in the valleys abandoned huts were crumbling into the earth and empty fields appeared blackened where King William's troops had scorched the earth to starve the rebellious population into submission. Count Alan had put many of the old British and Norse thanes in charge of outlying estates and villages and slowly the woods, the fells and the dales were lush with growth again. People came north from his estates in the south and repopulated the empty land. Tonight these tenants, villagers and servants were out in the field celebrating, making love in the hedgerows, dancing about a dragon on a great bonfire, as if the terrible destruction of ten years earlier had never happened.

Tonight she felt the heart of Richmond had stopped beating. She was in a faerie place between heaven and earth where rules were undone. Caught up in a sense of her own momentary happiness, she forgot her safety. She forgot the Devil at her shoulder. Her pulse increased as they passed through the moonlit trees, through the rustlings of wild creatures and the scent of trampled heathers. The path forked and Niall led her to the edge of a dark glade. She looked up. Through the canopy she glimpsed the moon hanging fat in the starry sky. They paused. He pointed. The moon cast its light on two ancient oaks with canopies that had joined above their paired trunks. A crude lime-washed wattle-and-daub shelter was fashioned between them, a hut of sorts. It had a door with a handle carved into a bird of prey, an eagle with a broken wing. Close by the door Gunnhild saw a shuttered window, and above that an exit for smoke. Niall rode up to it. She followed. He pointed. To the side of this strange hut, the tree trunk sweated oak galls.

'So this is what you wanted me to see, oak galls for ink?' she exclaimed, feeling a slight sense of disappointment.

'Yes, but inside there is more to see. I think that before the great rebellion a maker of inks must have lived in this place. There are shelves in the cottage with evidence of his craft, pots, jars of dried out inks; and all are abandoned.'

'Let us look,' she said, excited now. She shook her right foot out of the stirrup, threw her left leg over her saddle and began to slide down onto the bracken. Her dress caught in the stirrup. She swore, reached up and pulled on it, causing the linen undergown to rip. 'I would have to be wearing Aunt Edith's gown.' She unhooked the undergown from its trap, lifted the silk overgown carefully away and twisted around to inspect the underdress.

He jumped off his horse, knelt down on the bracken and placing his hands on her own removed them from the gown. She stood still, hardly breathing. He gathered a handful of silk overgown into his own hands. As his fingers lightly touched her legs he remained kneeling, for a moment, holding up her dress.

'Only this,' he said, looking up. 'Just the one little rip that is the perfect size for my middle finger. I am afraid, though, it penetrates right through both layers.' Before she could protest he had put his finger through the rips and was gathering up a fistful of silk and linen, exploring, so within a moment he was touching her naked thigh just above the ties that held her stocking up. 'And you are wearing nothing under it,' he said, looking up at her with mischief in his black eyes.

She stood still, lost for words. She wanted him to continue. She felt dampness seep between her thighs, but as she swallowed her gasp of pleasure, he removed his hand. He allowed her clothing to drop and stood up, swept his hand gently along her overgown and said, 'There is nothing a good needlewoman cannot repair. Shall we take a look at what the maker of ink has discarded?'

For a moment Gunnhild felt bewildered and without saying a word she followed him, her boots crunching through the fall of last year's leaves. They approached the deserted hut. As she glanced back over her shoulder she noticed that their two horses stood together in the moonlight, by ancient tree roots, their necks reaching for the foliage. Apart from the sound of their horses grazing, the world of the forest was quiet.

Niall pushed the door open. He stooped down and entered. 'Careful, Gunnhild, it is dark. Wait there.' From the doorway, she heard him rubbing flints. A heartbeat later she saw the spark and the candle glow that filled the space inside. 'Now,' he said. 'Come, look.'

When she stepped over the threshold her eye was drawn to the high shelves set into the wall opposite. She counted six of these, one above the other, each filled with an assortment of pots and all except those on the lowest shelf draped with cobwebs and below them a sturdy wooden table with the remains of quills and dried-out ink pots. Near the table a plain wooden chest sat in the corner. She crossed the earth floor and pulled open the lid. It was empty except for a few pieces of vellum. She leaned in and lifted one out, Niall's presence momentarily forgotten with the thrill of discovery.

'There are no marks on the parchment, nothing,' she said turning round. She saw pots by the hearth. 'Whoever lived here took his writing with him and departed in a hurry because he has left all those pots of ink and look, Niall, he has left his copperas and bits of iron, too.' She indicated the scraps of metal lying in a pile by the empty hearth stones. There was a hint of sulphur in the air, a smell like soured eggs. She crossed to the hearth and lifted a clay pot. 'And there has been gum Arabic in this. He would grind it up.' She sniffed the empty vessel. Her eye caught a basket. She reached into it. Her fingers came out covered with dirt. Reaching in again, this time she felt around. 'It is filled with oak apples. He made gall ink, the very best.'

'I wonder where he is now.' Niall stepped over to her and lifting the candle so they could see better peered into the basket, his face close to her own. Her heart beat fast as they looked into it together. His closeness, their twinned concentration; it was perfect. If only he would kiss her. What would it be like, a deep kiss, a real kiss, not just a greeting kiss? He said, 'He made ink with colour. These pots are all dried out. The hut has been abandoned for some years.'

Gunnhild tore herself away to the shelf and lifted the small pots off, one by one. 'So he did,' she remarked. 'He has made red inks – yes sulphur and gum Arabic and egg whites,' she sniffed at each pot, 'and vinegar.' She lifted another and another, brushing dust away, pulling out their wax stoppers. She dipped her little finger inside one. 'Bring the candle here.'

Niall held the candle up by her shoulder. There it was again, that closeness, that longing for a kiss. 'Blue ink,' he said touching the dust on her finger with his own.

Again she felt his breath on her neck. She replaced the ink pot and slowly turned round. She must not desire him so. Instead, with difficulty, she mastered her self-control. She must first be sure he felt for her what she felt for him, *very sure*. 'How did you find this place?' she said aloud.

'I was hunting nearby last year. One of the hounds led me to it. I have come to this glade a few times since. It is as beautiful by day as it is by night.' He lowered his voice. 'A place to share.' His breath was on her cheek, his mouth near her own. She could smell his cold sweat.

She could not help herself. She lifted her face to his, her

fingers to his cheek. She touched his hair. It was longer than was usual for a knight in Duke William's cohorts, longer than Alan's hair. She traced his mouth with her finger, then let it drop and said, 'But, Niall, who else knows about it?'

'Oh, my love, none. No one has discovered it. Gunnhild, how I have longed for years ... I never dared to hope ...' He pulled her close and whispered into her hair, 'Just you, Gunnhild. Only you, I promise.'

'Then?' she said knowing full well that she could not help herself, understanding what they both desired. 'I cannot help what I feel either. I have tried so hard, prayed and prayed, cursed the Devil for it, but I cannot help myself. I cannot, Niall.'

'Nor I, Gunnhild. Come. Not here,' he said. 'It is better under the stars where the air is clean.' He took her hand and led her out of the cramped hut. 'This cannot be wrong. It is love,' he murmured. 'Love is not wrong. We are human. It is human to love no matter what the monks tell us ... or the nuns.' He scooped her into his arms, lifted her up and set her down on a bed of bracken and dried moss. She stood where he placed her.

'Let me,' he whispered into her hair. She could not resist him. He unloosened the lacings on the sides of her gown. Carefully, he drew it over her head and laid it aside. The first kiss they shared was soft and light. He found the hollow in her throat and kissed that. She clung to his arms. He drew off her linen undergown and laid that aside, too. She was in her short shift when he took her face in his hands and held it lovingly. This time his kiss was more penetrating and this time she slid down with him into the moss. Then she was fumbling with his clothing. He was kissing her breasts and stroking her quim. His penis was stiff in her hand.

Afterwards they lay in each other's arms. The moon had dipped in the sky.

'No one, no one must ever find us out,' she said. 'I shall be sent away.'

'If Alan finds us out,' he said, 'my life will be forfeit.'

'No confession,' she whispered. 'I cannot believe that God will punish us. I cannot believe in an angry God who would wish ill on us for this.'

'Just a furious husband who must never know what has passed between us. If he does you will lose everything, Gunnhild.' He kissed her hair and allowed it to trail through his fingers. 'I have long loved you. I have wanted you but never allowed myself to believe that you might feel the same for me or that if you did we could dare come together.'

'I do,' she whispered. 'I do love you.'

'Then, we must return before we are missed so let us see if we can get back into the castle. It will be a challenge.' He kissed her on her forehead, drew her close and said, 'When we reach the edges of the wood we separate, Gunnhild, sweetest of swans, I think we know that if there is to be love between us, it must remain secret for both our sakes.'

Gunnhild rode back to the castle alone. The enormity of what she had done terrified her but she felt loved and she knew that, in turn, she now truly loved for the first time in her twenty-five summers. She moved her lips in a brief prayer as she rode. 'St Brigit, intercede for me because what we have done tonight is love, mutual, and for ever, and I cannot stop it.' The Devil had won the toss. Fortune had spun her wheel.

As she trotted along the lane she could hear the echoing of rambunctious merry-making in the field. Her mouth curved into a drowsy smile. Clearly her people intended to squeeze every pleasurable moment out of this night. She joined a group of her servants close to the gate house, entered the bailey amongst them and called for a boy to take Shadow to the stable. Ann came bustling towards her from the hall entrance. 'Where have you been, my lady? Messengers came looking for you. I sent them into the big field.'

'Where are they now?' Gunnhild asked, looking around. 'I was there. They cannot have looked hard enough.'

'In the barn, sleeping. They have news of Count Alan. They say he expects to be here tomorrow.' She walked inside with

Gunnhild, through the disarray in the hall to the staircase that led up to the chambers above. 'My lady, speak with them after Prime. You need your bed.'

Wearily Gunnhild climbed the staircase.

The following morning she slept through Prime, and only when it was almost noon did she venture into the hall. As she descended she observed that she was not alone in sleeping late. Scant effort had been made at clearing the mess from the night before. She looked about her at the wakening servants, all the time wondering where Niall was, if he had even returned to the castle keep.

She sighed. All this disorder must be put to rights before Alan returned. She approached Edward, the gangly slate-headed steward who was shouting at servants to clear away the debris of soiled cloths heaped in corners. As she crossed the hall to him she trod on filthy rushes and knocked into benches that lay askew. Hounds were racing in front of her, barking and brawling over left-over scraps. She was snappy with tiredness. She felt irritation as she side-stepped a band of castle cats that prowled about the overturned benches and slid into the way of kitchen boys. The boys were balancing swaying piles of dirty wooden cups that they had started to remove from the tables.

'I told you to clear it all last night.' She heard her steward complaining at the boys as he kicked away one of the dogs running ahead of her. 'But no, you leave the job half-finished and run off into the fields.'

It was always so after a feast. The only difference this time was that Count Alan would be furious if he arrived on a saint's day into a hall that held such chaos and to a delayed dinner.

'No one here breaks their fast until the mess is cleared and the hall put to rights,' shouted her steward. The rest of the servants adjusted clothing that was half off and half on and scuttled to their tasks. He spun around unaware of her advance and yelled after a group of maids, 'Clear this dirty hall straw and refresh it.' They ran to do his bidding.

Gunnhild stopped walking, thinking she should leave him to

207

it and return to the quiet of her chamber. She needed to be alone, to reflect on the previous night. She desperately wanted to return in her imagination to the woodland glade, rather than to wait in Richmond's great hall for Alan's return. Nor did she wish to dutifully attend endless chapel services by Alan's side later that day when all she really desired was to be with his brother.

The steward spun around and finally noticed her standing lost in her thoughts. He broke into them with a firm tone, 'My lady, Count Alan will expect order here.' He pointed his long rod at two men crouched over a hunk of left-over bread and cheese. 'Those messengers say he will be here by Vespers.'

'Then, Edwin,' Gunnhild said with a conviction she certainly did not feel, 'we shall all be prepared for him.' She crossed herself and said calmly, 'For now, I intend to break my fast and I shall then oversee the setting of the table for an evening repast of herb pottage, fish and barley cakes. After I have greeted those men, I shall insist that the cooks are ready again.'

Pushing the memory of last night into the recesses of her mind she hardened her resolve not to let her guard down. If she was to see Niall again as her lover she must dissemble. She turned away from Edwin and hurried towards the bench where the men were sitting watching her approach. She took a deep breath, steeled herself to face them, prepared to show them courtesy.

Alan rode into Richmond after sunset. She need not have concerned herself because by the time he thundered up the stairs to seek her out, everything was returned to order and she was seated at her needlework. In and out of the linen cloth, her fingers flew making neat stitches on the shirt she was embroidering for him, in and out as if those same fingers wished to flee from everything he was. He was Alan who locked away her jewels, who blamed her for childlessness, who had a mistress in Dinan and who had wanted her for her mother's estates.

18

'Rest assured that I will be your knight for the remainder of my life.'

'Tristram and Isolde', *The Death of King Arthur* by
Peter Ackroyd, 2011

Alan did not remain long in Richmond that summer. Within two weeks he had ridden south to be with the King and to advise him on military tactics in France. Odo of Bayeux was arrested under secular law as the Earl of Kent, a traitor because he had overreached his ambition. He supported the King's son against his father. It was even whispered that he aimed at the very top, to be the Pope himself. The King's son, Robert, had rebelled against his father again and so Alan was again with the King in Normandy.

Gunnhild and Niall snatched whatever brief moments they could in the forest. During these short expeditions Gunnhild felt elusive happiness again as she glowed within the forbidden, secret circle of Niall's love. In the Hall they were distant and polite to each other, recognising that their romance was as fragile as the spider webs that hung thickly on the hedgerows that autumn. Christmastide passed. Another summer flew by and still their love remained secret.

The year turned through its seasons. Early in November of 1083 Queen Matilda died of a mysterious illness that had gripped her during the summer. When Alan returned that autumn, Gunnhild wondered if her romance was a dream, invisible to all. She and Niall had been lovers for over a year and if there was talk it never reached her ears.

Late in November Niall sat with Alan in the private room behind the great hall, poring over a document concerning a new land entitlement, a place they called Middleton, close to the other lands Alan was accumulating around his Honour of

Richmond.

Gunnhild looked down at her outline of St Cecilia, her mother's name-day saint, who had dedicated her life to music. She had made the saint resemble her mother as she had last seen her, hair that was golden gathered into a knot behind her long neck. She tried to lose herself in the beauty of the small figure. This page would be bordered with golden harps and white swans.

Alan was speaking again. Her fingers were icy and she shivered in her mantle even though it was thickly lined with rabbit fur. It was so cold that the fire only warmed a semi-circle directly before it. She found herself listening to Alan and Niall's discussion.

Alan started up from the document he was studying. 'Richmond is in capable hands. Good steward, competent reeve and yourself, Niall, when you and Hubert are not taking troops north. I may be gone all of the winter.' He added that he would set out for Normandy the following day so he could reach Caen in time for Queen Matilda's funeral.

Gunnhild started. Of course Alan must be part of the funeral cortege, but she, though she was all but estranged from him, was his wife. She said with her voice cutting through the crisp air, 'Ought I not to return to Normandy to honour the Queen?' She set the drawing on a small table, folded her hands into her lap and waited patiently for his reply.

She had but a heartbeat to wait for it. He turned to her and said acidly, 'You, Gunnhild, why would I want you there? You lost me a son. Your place is here with our daughter.' He was saying what he had long thought and had not voiced until he had given up hope that she would bear him another child.

'Why, because I am the daughter of a king and as you well know Dorgen's death was none of my fault. I cared for him, too,' she retorted bitterly.

'Then it is more the pity that you cannot provide me with another to take his place.' He turned his back to her and busied himself with the scroll, closely scrutinising its contents. She was of less importance than a land agreement.

Niall glanced at her sympathetically but dared not intrude between them. 'I will take good care of Gunnhild and Maud in your absence, Brother. I love them both dearly.'

Alan looked up, stroked his beard thoughtfully and said one terse word, 'Good.'

She watched him from behind her drawing board, feeling anger bubble up inside her as Alan stabbed a finger at the vellum weighted by stones on the table. 'You must see that this pays, Niall. There can be six plough lands here.' He peered more closely. 'Ah, I see it belonged to Kari.'

'Kari?' Niall said, his black head close to Alan's red head.

'Kari was an outlaw, Brother, long dead, during the great rebellion. His son is an overseer in charge of one of the five villagers there. Watch him. He is named Uhtred. Remember that name. He may have been a child then but he is a man now, and lucky for him that the King's men spared him.'

'Not many left in that village to work the fields.'

'Make them work all the harder. Set Alfled to drive them.'

Gunnhild grimaced. Alan had hardened towards his tenants. This was not the way he had been when they had first come to Richmond. Then, he had felt that the King and Bishop Odo had alienated the peasants. Though tough in many ways, he had done much to help their villages' recovery. She puzzled at the harsh line he was now taking. Alfled, the reeve, was a hard man. He would show no mercy.

'So I am to remain here this winter, not to go up to Scotland, Alan?' Niall said.

'This estate and its manors cannot be left to the care of women and mercenaries.'

'When can we expect you again?'

'I shall visit our father this Christmastide.' Alan shrugged. 'He is old, ill. God could snatch him from us sooner than the winter snows melt. You must go to him when I return here. Spring, by Eastertide.'

The log in the fire hissed and burst into a flame. Gunnhild turned to it and stretched out her cold hands. She could not care any more about Alan's concerns. 'So be it then,' she heard Niall say with an edge to his voice. 'We all carry out your wishes here. I shall visit our father in the spring.'

If Alan recognised Niall's sarcasm he chose to ignore it. He rolled up the parchment, tied it with a thin red cord, placed it in an oak chest, locked the barrel lock securely and put the key back on the ring that hung from his belt. He strode to the door and shouted into the hall for lady's fingers and hippocras. Both arrived moments later. He came over to her, looked down at her without any emotion, no word of missing her or needing her help, just, 'This winter I shall be away for months. You must see that all the church services are observed here and in the villages. I do not want to return to laxity. No matter how cold it gets, remember we are a Christian people.' He looked closely at her old cloak. 'You need a new mantle this winter. It will be bitter. The cloak must be of triple-lined wool.' That at least was considerate so she forced a smile.

'Thank you, my lord.' She calmly put away her charcoal and parchment into a small chest by the window and returned to her chair. As she bit into her lady's finger she thought of the dark cloud that had descended over their marriage, even darker now because of her relationship with Niall.

19

Winter 1086

Niall was hanging around the doorway into the barn, his eyes casting quick sidelong glances across the freezing yard. She saw him duck back as she hurried over snow, its softness absorbing the sound of her boots. The darkness had hidden her as she had climbed from her bed, pulled her overgown over her night shift and then her hose and thick boots and thrice-woollen mantle. Hurrying down the stairways, avoiding the solar where her ladies slept soundly and the sleeping hall, she left by the back door and took a track down the hill into the bailey. Had the weather not been so bitter she would have been discovered. No patrols ventured anywhere; it was not necessary to make rounds on such a cold night. She slipped through the door which he had pushed half closed when he knew that she was approaching.

Moments later she was in his arms. It had been weeks. For two years they had met when they could, secretly and with a stealth she did not know was possible. For two years they had seen Alan rarely. Count Eudo had died during Niall's visit the previous spring. This winter past had been particularly difficult with two long months of confinement inside the castle keep. Wolves howled outside at night and the Richmond garrison went hungry. They brought desperate families from outlying places on the fells into the castle. It was not wise to leave Richmond's strong walls and venture out into the frozen dales. Dangerous times had returned again and, with the weather so cold, the hungry to feed, she had not had a moment to herself.

'My love,' he said softly. He pulled back her hood and was whispering into her hair. 'I sit by you at table. I watch you lift a morsel to your lips and wish that I was that piece of bread. I look but I dare not touch.'

'Niall, everyone is hungry. Do not speak this way. I am hungry. Maud is suffering. All the children are hungry. There is famine everywhere.'

He opened his palm and she saw that in it he held a fat dried fig.

'By Christus, where did that come from? I have not seen such a fruit for months.'

'I have more from a merchant who crossed the snow with them yesterday. I shall bring a small barrel of them up to the keep tomorrow and you shall have them stewed in honey for your supper.' He popped the dry purple fruit back into a pouch and laid it down on the straw. He offered her his flask.

'What if someone was to come?' she said as she sipped from it. Warmth coursed through her blood. She wiped her mouth with the back of her hand.

'Tonight! No one but us here, and the wolves beyond the walls.'

He fetched a lighted lantern from the depths of the empty barn and set it close. He threw a skin on the ground and they sat on it as if they were peasants. He took a loaf of dry bread from a satchel and broke it. She took half of it and ate greedily. He held her close and stroked her hair. 'If only it could be different. My brother does not deserve you. Yet, there is nothing we can do but snatch moments like this. And pray that no one sees us.'

'But tonight no one is out,' she sighed, almost content.

'We are safe.' He slid his hands beneath her mantle, drew her to him and kissed her, a long lingering kiss. It would be all she could keep of him for now, but she had desperately wanted it. She wanted the memory of it to linger with her through the deep cold of winter; for who knew when it would be possible for her to escape from the keep again.

As they kissed they did not see the shadow that crossed in front of the barn, the thief who had like them realised that a guard on the castle would be lax and who had found a secret way into the bailey across the frozen moat; a thief who stole cheese from the dairy when they thought the barrel lock was secure; a sneak in the night who disappeared back through a hole in the castle wall concealed by a scraggy bush, one that was only big enough for a small man. This was a creature of the night who came from Uhtred's village desperate for food and wood and who was able to slip in and out of small places taking away only a little at a time of the scant stores needed to feed Richmond's hungry garrison. If they were hungry, he was hungrier.

The thief peered through a crack in the barn door. He had noticed the lamplight seeping out over the snow. Through the slit he saw Lady Gunnhild, her bright hair curling loose about her mantle. The man she was kissing was not her husband and though her lover was in shadow the little man was sure it was Count Alan's brother.

He departed as silently as he had arrived, dragging his sledge behind him keeping close to the buildings until he reached the hole in the wall. This information he would ferret away. One day it might be useful.

20

Summer 1086

'Yet as the old books tell us, Tristram and Isolde were steadfast in their love.'

'Tristram and Isolde', *The Death of King Arthur* by
Peter Ackroyd, 2011

Gunnhild glanced up from the book she was sharing with Maud. These moments alone with her daughter were special. Spring had come late again, cold and wet but there was new growth on the trees at last. The hedgerows were fat with hawthorn and the verges smothered with wildflowers. May arrived with the song of the cuckoo and the sparrows that rutted below in the herb garden. That morning, sun had shone through the castle's arched windows so she had risen early and ordered that all the shutters be thrown open to let in its light.

She studied the page of her book, bound between deerskin-covered boards. The title, St Margaret of Antioch, was burned into the leather and painted in gold lettering that curled and waved as if it had its own rhythm. St Margaret smiled serenely from the opened page. The angel that Gunnhild had so delicately painted years earlier hovered above the saint's head. Miniature shells decorated the margins interspersed with sea grasses. She loved this tiny illustration. She considered it her best work, perfection itself. She traced the figure with her finger. How this saint had suffered, endured imprisonment, tortures and death by the sword for her devotion to God. Gunnhild knew she could never live such a life; she had sinned. There was no help for her aching, desperate love for Niall, a love that ate into her soul and damned it.

Nine-year-old Maud stopped reading. She spoke Gunnhild's own thought aloud as if she knew her mother's mind. 'How can we read about the purity of saints when you are not a good

217

person, Mama …' She trailed off, biting her lip.

Gunnhild reached out to Maud but the child pulled back her hand. This accusation hurt. It bore deep into her conscience. The chamber felt chill. Maud was about to say more, explain her rudeness perhaps, but she held back her words. Instead she stared at the wicker-worked cage hung by the shutters in which a small nightingale lived. The creature warbled, squawked and rattled the cage bars as if it felt Maud's anger. It ruffled its orange feathers. It seemed to sigh at last and the air stilled. There was silence except for the everyday sounds beyond the chamber – those of chambermaids shouting, coffer lids shutting, a gardener banging the gate as he entered the herb beds below the window.

Gunnhild studied Maud closely. She could not know. They had been discreet, rarely visiting their oak tree refuge during the last summer before the worst winter in memory gripped, one even colder than the famine winter of two years previously. She tried to think back. It had been difficult to meet Niall in secret as she usually had to bring Ann with her. She left Ann in the village tending the sick, delivering gifts of cheese from their dairy, or to talk with villagers, whilst she rode on with Niall to collect oak galls for her inks, the excuse being that Niall would protect her from danger. Ann never questioned or criticised her mistress, nor as far as Gunnhild was aware did she say anything to Hubert. There had been only two assignations in the deserted bailey barn during the past dark winter. Fortuna had smiled on them as her wheel turned. Until now they had escaped discovery.

She bit her lip and said quietly, swallowing her concern, 'Maud, what is wrong?'

'Everything. My uncle sits closer to you at table than does my father and when I see my uncle's hands around your waist after you climb off your mare's back I do not like it. It is not seemly.'

It was true. Niall had become bold but Gunnhild smiled because the truth was simpler than she had at first realised. Maud was jealous. Gunnhild put the beautiful book aside. 'I am sorry that you feel like that but, Maud, it is perfectly seemly that Niall helps me down from my horse and sits with me at table. Your father is always away protecting us from enemies, and your uncle helps us organise our estates here, so that one day when you marry you will bring a great dowry to your husband.'

'I shall not marry,' Maud said angrily.

'Marry you must, Maud, because Uncle Niall will inherit Castle Richmond should your father die.'

'He will take our lands! That is why he is always here.'

'Maud, that is the way wills are made. It is not his fault and it is certainly nothing to merit such an unkind comment'.

'If I am to have a husband, my spouse could live here.'

'You will live with your husband in another castle. He will be wealthy and maybe handsome, too. Now, Maud, I will hear no more unkind thoughts about your uncle. Your father is too often away. Your uncle is good to us both.' She closed the book. 'Enough of this talk for today. Go now, my sweet, and find Ailsa in the garden. Ann has marigolds to plant. Just think, by the time your papa returns from Normandy you will have things for him to eat from your own garden.' Maud ventured a weak smile. Growing food was important to her. They had known hunger pangs that winter, though Gunnhild mused at how easily the memory of them slipped away when now there was plenty to eat from their garden and fresh game and mutton from the woods and hills. 'We can read a little more tomorrow,' she added.

Suddenly Maud's green eyes brimmed with tears. 'It is just that I have not seen my father since my name day. He has not even watched me ride Merleswein.'

'I think we shall see your father very soon, before midsummer in fact and when he returns you can ride into the woods with him for a picnic. We all can.'

After Maud tripped off, Gunnhild bit her lip and tears leaked from her eyes. There must be no more caresses, no more stolen kisses, knowing glances and no touching of hands below the folds of the linen trestle cloth at meal times.

A sob caught at her throat. They would burn for eternity because of their sin. Her own would be worse than his because, after all, Eve had tempted Adam and so she, too, had inherited the sinfulness of woman. What sort of nature did she possess that she had for years stolen away with her husband's brother, flouting the laws of the Church, and behaving like a common leman? Looking sadly at the nightingale dozing on its perch, its small head buried in russet feathers, she said, 'Little bird, our song is ended.'

Stirring herself, she crossed to the doorway and pulled her mantle from its peg. A moment later she was hurrying down the stairways and outside into the family chapel. Father Christopher was in the village outside the castle walls saying mass for a villein who was dying of a fever. She would be alone. Entering the still chapel she knew she must prostrate herself before God's altar and this time pray for forgiveness.

It was her barrenness that had angered Alan more than anything else. She hurried by the font that had never once been used to baptise one of her own. A painting of heaven above, filled with singing angels, and hell below, decorated the chapel wall. She shuddered, and glancing up, realised that those ladders with tumbling devils ready with their spears and spitting fire could be her fate. Sobbing, she dropped on to her knees in front of the altar and prayed to St Brigit to intercede with God for his forgiveness. She muttered pater-nosters over and over. Whispering the Latin words, she realised that she could not remember when she had last poured her heart out to the saint with such humbleness.

That evening at supper she slipped quietly into her place beside Niall. When he leaned over to pass salt for her fish she whispered to him, 'I must speak with you alone, Niall.' His black eyes brightened but she could not meet his look and contemplated the lonely slice of salmon that sat on her plate marooned in a pale-coloured sauce. She poked at the limpid fish. 'How was York?' she asked loudly so others could hear.

A couple of yapping dogs chased about the hall. She watched them momentarily as they kicked up dust from the straw. It needed changing. They had been lax of late. Niall carefully laid his eating knife on the board, lifted a hunk of bread, chewed it for a bit, swallowed, took his cup, drank deeply, set it down on the table and, furrowing his dark brows, said in a voice much lower than her own had been, as if he wanted none to hear his news, 'When Lord Alan returns, he will bring with him tax men, monks and scribes and goodness knows who else, mercenaries no doubt. The King intends to record all that my brother has in his possession.' Niall drank deeply from his cup, before continuing, 'And my own brother has helped the King organise a land survey of everything in the whole of England. They will hate this.' Seeing her startled look he leaned closer and said in so low a voice that now she could hardly catch his words, 'Yes, even you, my sweet, and me, too. We are all the King's possessions.'

The servers passed by them with dishes, a salad of greens and another with purple carrots dressed with vinegar. They served pigs trotters and hunks of pork. Good times had returned. Her empty pantries were thankfully filling up with food. Another servant hovered behind her with a flagon of watered beer. She thought as she waited for him to move on. *This is not good news. It could bring about a new rebellion.* 'My lady?' the servant said. 'Will you drink?' Absently she held out her cup to be filled. Ann called over from her place beside Maud, 'Lady Gunnhild, are you ill? Your face is ashen.'

There was the thump of plates and rattle of eating knives. 'I am well, never better,' she replied evenly. She turned back to Niall. 'When are they coming?'

'Soon,' he said. 'The worst of it is that once the word goes around the countryside this castle will need to be fortified again, and if there is an attack on us, Alan must return with an army.'

'How am I to feed all these people when there is just enough for us, the guard we already maintain, and the servants?'

'Simply you must find a way. Send the fishermen out. We can hunt deer in the woods.'

'It will never be enough. We won't have bread. The mills at Bedale and Brampton can hardly feed us all here.'

She had heard Alan speak before of how the King was planning a survey. Alan had said at Easter that just as he was getting rich the King wanted to know how much tax he could raise from the lands cared for by all his tenants-in-chief. He intended a survey of every corner of England. The King had decided on it during his Christmas court which he had held in Gloucester and which Alan had attended, yet again spending the season in a royal household without her. King William was organised in a way that her father, King Harold, would have disliked. There was tax in the old days but more men were free then, and women, too. Many heiresses ran their own estates in those days. Now there was always an appointed guardian watching over them. 'Is it to be thorough?' she said aloud.

'Yes. The villagers will resent the counting of sheep, the measuring of their lands, the questions and the numbering of everything they own, the marching over their fields full of newly growing wheat and barley, the labelling of their scant possessions, all of this, but it will be exact. I fear for everybody. This accounting of everything will bring new misery here just as the villagers and cotters and sokesmen are recovering from the famines of past winters.'

'How many visitors must I expect after Saturday?'

'A goodly number I believe; scribes and judges and the chief investigator and their retainers.'

'I see. There is much to prepare.' She studied the translucent fish in its congealing sauce for a moment. Then she looked into his worried eyes. 'What can we do?'

He gave her a weak smile. 'Nothing, there is nothing we can do. Just pray that the taxes are not overly vicious. The clerks won't be here before Saturday.' His eyes grew warmer. 'We could ride into the woods tomorrow to find you oak galls for your inks. It will be good to be out in the air.'

She drew in a breath. The necessity of parting with him was tearing at her fragile heart. She said carefully, 'Niall, there is no need any more. Bishop Robert from St Cuthbert has sent me a gift of inks.' Laying down her eating knife, she picked up her napkin and dabbed at her mouth. Her eyes were swimming with tears. 'If you will excuse me, Niall, I must go. I need to see to one of the servant girls who burned her hand this morning.'

She detected surprise in his voice when he said, 'Surely the wise woman can see to this?'

'No,' she said softly, '*I* shall.' Her voice was breaking like her heart.

Although it was very difficult she bowed her head to him, took her leave, and walked to the staircase, never glancing back, feeling his eyes following her. She made her way to the private door she had used that morning. A path wound around the side of the castle past the chapel to the courtyard. She hurried towards the infirmary. The medicine chest she had once kept on the dais had been replaced by a low building, a small hospital for wounded soldiers and in here there were shelves of salves and the makings of healing possets.

Just as she rounded the corner the first horsemen were galloping through the gatehouse. She stopped short. Stable boys appeared from the barn, racing across the paving stones to help with mounts and to catch and steady the rumbling carts that rattled in after the riders. The strangers were dismounting. She had no choice but to step forward to greet them.

A narrow-faced, silver-haired man in a black cloak and a tunic and hose the colour of damsons bustled forward to meet her. 'I see the Lady Gunnhild has had warning of our coming. We are here on the King's business.'

She stared at him before saying, 'You know who I am, but who are you who is here on King William's business, and what precisely is his business?' Gunnhild drew herself tall, trying to appear every bit her father's daughter, by rights a princess. She looked beyond him to the group of dark-clad men who were descending from the carts. Severity washed off them in waves and with it a cold authority that was meant to be felt by all who encountered them.

'These are my clerks,' the man said testily as she studied them one by one. 'I am Edward d'Arcy. I am here to make accounts for the King's new geld-tax.' His eyes narrowed, becoming slits in his lined face. His lofty disposition was not to

223

be trifled with.

'There is table and board for you and your clerks inside the hall,' she said chillily and gestured towards the great oak door that led in from the yard. 'Go in and join the table. I will see to you later.' She was about to show them her back. She did not give a fat fig for what he thought of her, and began to turn towards the infirmary building when behind her she heard the great hall door dragged open. She spun around. Niall exited followed by Edwin their steward, a band of servants and several men at arms.

On seeing that Edward d'Arcy was with the visitors, Niall ordered the servants back inside to make ready beds in empty chambers high up in the keep. He went back in briefly himself and she could hear him calling to the others to refresh the table.

Moments later he returned. Sir Edward was waiting patiently. Gunnhild stood beside him, this time not sure whether to rudely move away, or remain as lady of the castle.

'Welcome, Sir Edward,' Niall said evenly. 'We did not expect you before Saturday. Come, eat and after you are rested we can discuss your business here.' Niall's brow creased as he ushered the knight and his stern clerks before him into the hall. He looked back at her and dropped his voice. 'Send Ann to that girl. Tonight you must act the lady of this castle, even if it is distasteful to you. Please be helpful, Gunnhild. We must not antagonise them.'

Gunnhild bristled but followed the last clerk into the hall and told them to sit wherever they could find a space on benches which already were emptying. Word had spread about the survey faster than an adder could pounce. Her people wanted none of these strangers. She sent maids for bowls of water so the visitors could wash their faces and hands and Ann to the infirmary in her stead. For a moment all felt chaotic, a great fuss. She indicated Ann's empty chair to Sir Edward. Finger bowls, bread trenchers, fresh food and drink appeared and silently the clerks began to eat, munching with eyes darting around suspiciously, no doubt thinking that one of her sullen servants would stick a knife in as fast as filleting a fish.

She made a brave pretence of eating the food that had further congealed on her plate but quickly laid down her eating knife. Nothing was palatable now, nothing. She made strained conversation with Sir Edward, asking him about his journey, and where he had been before Richmond. Niall smiled generously at her and as the meal concluded she won her paltry reward. He suggested that their guests visit the chapel before retiring for the night. Summoning Father Christopher he said to Sir Edward, 'My lady must see to her household. She will speak with you in the morning after Lauds.'

She had done her duty well.

Before they departed for the chapel she inquired how long the survey would take. Sir Edward frowned. 'That depends, my lady. We may be here some time.'

'I see, Sir Edward. In that event, I hope you will be comfortable. We have suffered famine here and my people are only now beginning to recover. They cannot afford King William's new geld-tax.'

'They must. The whole kingdom will accept it and that is the long and short of it.' Sir Edward sniffed. 'No doubt these Saxons *can* survive. They are a hardy race.'

Gunnhild bit back a bitter retort. *How dare this interfering clerk insult them?* 'Are there soldiers following in your train?'

'King William's soldiers will ride in tomorrow. His men are hardened mercenaries who will deal ruthlessly with any hint of rebellion from your villeins. They will be assessed and they will pay their dues to the King. And you should be grateful for a new garrison, my lady. Rest assured that should there be a rebellion, this castle will be safe.'

With those words he swept away with his four dark-garbed clerks. Niall touched her arm, and bent to her ear. 'It is best to say as little as possible. I shall send warnings out to the larger manors. They must give the impression of co-operation even if they intend evasion. I shall summon our reeves and request representatives from the freed men to the hall within days.'

* * *

A crack of thunder awakened Gunnhild from a deep sleep. She

threw back her covers and jumped out of bed just as a flash of lightning crossed the room. Running to the window she flung her hand out and struggled to draw closed the opened shutters. Another blast of thunder was followed by a high whistling wind that drove the rain through the square embrasure drenching her. She dragged the shutters over and began to fasten them. Peering through the wooden slats she saw that two pails left behind earlier were crashing and tumbling against each other, bumping along the pathway as if Satan drove them forward. A wicker fence was bending with the gale and it was clear that it might not hold. She forced a bolt to keep the shutters firmly closed and ran back to the safety of her bed covers. She pulled her bed curtains close trying to lessen the noise that had begun to swirl around the castle. There could be no land survey. The route-ways would soon be flooded and the castle yards a quagmire. No one could ride across the estates and through their fields and villages whilst the sleeting, drenching rain lasted, but then she worried as she huddled under her covers, if such weather continued through the summer as it had done in previous years, famine would return to Yorkshire by winter.

High up in the great square keep, the sound of the storm must be even harsher. It would be miserable and damp in those dank chambers. She smiled to herself as she thought of the leaks and the chill draughts that the clerks were to suffer that night. Well, they were monastery men, pious-looking creatures, and ought to be used to lack of comfort.

Niall was as good as his word and sent messengers to all the outlying halls and estates that owed fealty to Count Alan. During a brief conversation with Gunnhild, Sir Edward confronted her objections and insisted that the survey was a military necessity. Otherwise how would the King maintain his army and protect his realm? He needed a new geld tax and for that he needed to know what he owned.

'The King owns everything,' he said.

She was tired of hearing this. Not me, she thought to herself. If I can avoid it, I shall not be recorded in his ledgers by these scribblers.

Sir Edward and his clerks took up residence in the antechamber behind the hall. When they asked for details of the estate, Gunnhild indicated the locked oak chest that stood in the corner. 'There are contracts there,' she said. 'My lord has the key. He is in Brittany.'

'Ah yes, he will be returning soon.'

Gunnhild's eyes widened. No message from Alan, no warning. He would bring the mercenaries of course, she realised.

'So how can we feed them, the men that come with my husband? Can the King tell me that?'

'My lady, you had better send out to your villages for salmon and pike, and whatever grain, peas and beans they have concealed.' His thin-lipped smile was an irritant. She disliked him even more. 'Now, if you will send us candles and sconces, we can prepare questions for your reeves and chief tenants.'

The clerks opened their travelling boxes and withdrew portable desks that they hung about their necks. They covered her oak table with their inks, parchment and pens. She stared down. Her eyes widened. They used fine goose quills. She would have taken one or even two when they were at prayer, but for the fact that her servants might be accused of theft.

Outside the rain was still blasting down, descending around the castle in torrents. It hammered at the shutters and lashed down the outer walls. The messengers Niall had sent out the night before were unlikely to ride back through it. Their jurors, for that was what they would become, those chief men and clergy and the free sokesmen of the hundreds, could not be recruited in a day, nor could they set out in such weather.

'I'll send for candles and sconces. It will be days before you can progress,' she said to the clerks with a tight-lipped smile.

Sir Edward grunted but never replied. She wondered if she had made an enemy.

'I'll send in a boy with logs for the hearth,' she offered later in the morning. Still no word of thanks from Sir Edward, just a grunt and a nod. His clerks' eyes followed her with suspicion as she turned and swept through the tall arched door, glad to be away from their taciturn faces. She was, after all, King Harold's daughter.

'I hope Count Alan can make it through to us in this weather with a fresh garrison. We may need it once we do begin the survey.' She heard Sir Edward call to her retreating back.

21

He [King William] ruled over England, and by his astuteness it was so surveyed that there was not one hide of land in England that he did not know who had it or what it was worth, and afterwards set it down in record.

1086/1087, The Anglo-Saxon Chronicles, trans. and ed. by Michael Swanton, 2000

'I cannot understand why Niall did not give up his gatehouse to these men. Why I am giving Sir Edward my own lodging,' Alan grumbled as he prowled around Gunnhild's bedchamber some days later. He touched this and that, her linen chests, her clothing pole, the cushioned winged chair and the stool by the blonde wood table on which lay her two completed books St Margaret and St Cecilia. 'Very nice, Gunnhild,' he said picking them up and glancing at the carefully stitched-together pages one after another. 'You could still make a good nun.'

'Not my calling, my lord.' A shudder ran through her. She wondered what he suspected.

He snorted and laid the book for St Cecilia back on her table. 'I recollect that St Cecilia is your mother's name-day saint. She is a nun. After I am gone you might take your vows, too. After all, my wealth goes to Niall and then to my younger brother, Stephen. I hope Niall considers marriage soon. I cannot understand why he does not. His outright evasion of my words to him "get ye wed" becomes tiresome.' He sighed, 'As for Stephen, we hear little of *him*. He remains in Brittany where he has married Hawise de Dol. Stephen has had nothing to do with Richmond, Gunnhild, nothing, yet he and his brats could get everything I have striven for here.' He gave her a hard look. *Was he giving her a warning?*

Alan pinched the heavy fabric of her new bed curtains between his finger and thumb. It was as if he was measuring its value as Sir Edward measured the value of their lands. 'What need have you of new bed curtains? The old ones have a half

229

century left in them, more than all our life times and our daughter's, too, and maybe her sons.'

'I gave the old curtains to Ann for the bailey hall, for their chamber there.'

Alan sat heavily on the bed. They had been married for over ten years and, well into his fourth decade he was still lean and muscular, strong and agile. Yet the years had taken their toll on his countenance. His hair was greying and his face weathered and lined. He beckoned her to him. Hesitating a moment, she left the bench by the window and approached him. The nightingale set up a squawk. 'Send that bird to the solar. If I hear it sing tonight I shall wring its neck.'

'Yes, my lord.' She stood before him, her head held high, steady-eyed, determined not to allow him to intimidate her.

He studied her for a moment. His voice became gentler. 'How do you think we will get on tonight, Gunnhild?'

'Comfortable enough,' she said, carefully looking at the width of her bed.

'Well then help me off with these.' He pointed down to his boots.

Slowly she knelt and began tugging on his right boot. To her discomfort he reached out and began unpinning her veil. He loosened the pins that bound her plait.

'You had best unpin it yourself.' He pulled her onto her feet. 'I shall get my own boots off. You are too slow.' He bent down, pulled off one boot, then the other and kicked them aside. 'Go on, you finish this,' he said. 'First the hair, then the gown. I want to see Eve as God made her.'

She inhaled a deep breath and obediently removed the final pins and shook her hair loose. Could he possibly know that she had sinned with his brother? Could he see her as Eve banished? She felt her knees weakening as she removed her gown. However, when she stood before him naked he simply gasped and said, 'By the Virgin, what a beauty. Gunnhild you have not aged since I first took you on the crossing to Normandy, in a storm.' He laughed. 'You have ripened like a peach in summer.' He looked around the chamber. 'Bring me the pot. I would take a piss before I take you.'

She hesitated and said, 'My lord, please do not offend me. It is there.' She gestured to a wicker screen in the corner.

He slowly stood up, loosening the ties on his hose. 'As you wish.'

When she heard him make water she leapt into bed and pulled the coverlet over her nakedness.

She leaned back against her pillows. She did not want his caresses. Nor did she want to respond to him. She lay as if she were a carving on a tomb. Her desire had gone, but then *a women's desire was wrong, so said the Church*. Afterwards, she lay wide awake, feeling sad it had become so, listening to rain beat on the outside stone. Tonight she was more of a leman than she had ever been with Niall. She was Agenhart's replacement, their roles once again exchanged.

Sir Edward and Count Alan spent two days delivering questions to the agents selected from the villages and halls on the Richmond demesne. Throughout a week of drenching rain a gaggle of representatives from the villages trailed into the castle hall to be interviewed by Count Alan and Sir Edward. The clerks looked like toads, wearing their portable writing desks strung from their necks by leather straps. They watched on and scribbled, recording the information. The ten men sullenly returned to their homes with a store of further verbal questions for their neighbours and underlings.

During these interviews, Gunnhild sat quietly on a bench with two of her ladies, her head lowered over a piece of embroidery, a napkin for the table. She peeped out from her wimple at the proceedings. She noted the questions that sadly reminded her of a world of English names that she had known as a child before that world became a lost world. Now it would recede further into the past. She had a feeling that with the great survey there would be new changes and she felt for those who had lost their land twenty years past in a time of greater freedom and individuality. Who owned the land when King Harold lost the great battle, who owned it now? What had the geld tax been then? How many in each household? What were their names? What did they possess in the way of sheep and cattle, geese and hens? How many ploughs and who were the ploughmen?

She heard Uhtred mutter, 'We'll not take this easy.' She noticed the sly looks between Uhtred and Gospatrick of Ellerton on the Swale, but kept silent thinking that if anything was amiss Alan would see it, too. But Alan did not because he was conscientiously questioning his other chief tenants, Robert of Montiers and Bernwood of Well. Both were nearer his social class. They were knights and loyal to him. These men could give Sir Edward intelligent answers and create a better impression than the assortment of English freedmen and clergy who dwelled on The Honour of Richmond. The tenth juror was Enisant Musard of Brough Hall. He was an old friend to Count Alan, a Flanders man who had carved out an existence in Yorkshire for himself after the troubles of 1070. Yet now, too, he found it impossible to pay the tax levied three years past, never mind what was to come after the survey.

During the days of soaking rain, Sir Edward and his clerks were shut away in the chamber behind the hall like moles buried in a peaty-smelling, earthy gloom, punctuated with the acrid scent of ink, where they absorbed Alan's total attention. Sir Edward was as keen as a fox with its snout into the wind, determined to get as much gain as he could squeeze out of their lands for the King.

Some days later the rain became a slant and then a drizzle. At last it stopped and Alan announced, 'Tomorrow we ride out to the villages. Gunnhild will ride with us. As King Harold's daughter she has respect amongst the villagers.'

Yes, you recognise that, she thought to herself, but it will not save us if the villagers turn against us all.

On the following morning, Maud slipped through the curtain that separated her bedchamber from her mother's, smiling to see her father seated on the coverlet pulling on his riding boots. She curtseyed to them both and pertly said, 'Merleswein needs exercise. My father has not seen me ride him.' She took a step forward. 'If it has stopped raining I need to be out on my pony. I want to come, too.'

'Maud, now your father is back you do not enter this chamber until sent for. Stand still and be quiet for a moment.' She glanced at Alan, seeking agreement from him.

'Your mother is right, my girl. You do not enter her bedchamber without permission. What would Walter d'Aincourt's family make of you?'

Gunnhild turned from Maud and stared at him open-mouthed. 'Whose family?'

Ignoring her, Alan hoisted a thick greying eyebrow at his daughter. 'Yes, my girl. You are to be betrothed to a knight and as part of your dowry I shall be giving him a portion of your grandmother's lands in Cambridgeshire and a few hides of land here in Yorkshire. As for you, you will be bedecked with jewels on your wedding day.' He raised his eyes to the beams above them. 'Pray God it is soon.'

Gunnhild felt profound irritation. It was not that she resented anything granted to Maud but she suspected where those jewels would come from. She gave him a look brimful of anger. 'Not Gytha's jewels.'

He reached over and patted her arm. 'I have not decided yet.' He looked back at Maud. 'I think it right that Maud rides out with us. We have a guard. All will be well.' Maud's rosebud mouth broke into a smile. 'I shall get Elizabeth to bring me my boots and mantle,' she said in a very grown-up manner, before spinning round daintily to push back through the heavy gold-and-green embroidered curtain. She was clearly pleased with this outcome. She stopped, turned and said with a mixture of delight and wonder in her voice.'

'Truly, I am to be betrothed soon, and to a knight?'

'I believe so,' Alan said.

'I shall want us to live here, Papa.'

'You shall be mistress of your own estates. Now hurry! Go and find your mantle and boots, my sweeting.'

* * *

Gunnhild rounded on him the moment Maud was gone. 'What

233

sort of man is this Walter d'Aincourt? Why did you not tell me of this scheme? I raised Maud when you were off fighting and ...' She could not bring herself to mention Agenhart, not when she wore the stain of Eve's guilt herself. '... and now you return and reorganise all our lives.'

Alan pulled his heavy woollen mantle from a peg and fastened it across his shoulder. 'I will do as I feel right,' he said as he headed for the doorway, 'for the child. It is me who has provided her dowry and do not forget it.'

'You? My mother's lands. You are giving away my mother's lands!' She called after him, unable to contain her fury. 'My lands!'

He turned back and for a moment she thought he might strike her. 'Do not raise your tongue to me like some worn out *whore* who is past her reason. I need to speak with you about your mother, but not now. Not today. Today, Madam, I shall see you below. Wrap up well. There is a chill in the air. I want to be on the road by daybreak. You will have an opportunity to show great care for our daughter today.'

She was dazed, hurt by his choice of words, wondering what he wanted to say about her mother. Changing her red slippers for riding boots, she struggled down the curving stairway into the great hall below. The hall was busy but she sensed sullenness from the servants as she broke her fast. If only these clerks would ride away and leave them alone.

After Prime she hurried out into the courtyard, a chattering Maud beside her. As Alan gathered together a band of the new mercenaries the bailey bustled with the clanging of swords and the snorting of horse. Their breath ghosted through the misty air. Ann hurried about wrapped in a heavy cloak. She had seen the men fed, and promised that she would oversee the dinner preparations that day in Gunnhild's absence. As Gunnhild looked about the heaving bailey with its restless horses and barking dogs she could not see Niall anywhere. Since Alan had taken up residence in her chamber, Niall had avoided her and though she was determined to bring their relationship to an end, she found that already she missed him. As if he read her mind Alan announced that today Niall was to stay behind with the castle guard. At least Alan had not made any further attempt at intimacy but rose early and was at prayer in the chapel before daylight. How different he was to his brother, who was passionate and kind, whereas Alan had grown cold and dismissive.

They mounted their horses, Gunnhild on her mare, Blackbird, since Shadow had died two years past, and Maud sitting erect and proud on Merleswein. Alan and Sir Edward took up their positions at the head of the column. The clerks followed. Surrounded by a sinister army of ghostly seeming shades, namely their new guard, they headed out through the clinging mist, over the drawbridge, past the row of lime-washed cottages that straggled through the town beyond the castle wall, and then deep into the dales. As wooded lanes narrowed the soldiers fell back, taking up the rear, ready to surge forward if there was trouble. A scout who knew the route to the large village of Well rode ahead, occasionally doubling back.

At a trot, they moved through the thinning mist, past arable land and pasture. Every now and then Alan stopped the column and waved his gloved hand towards the great fields, showing Sir Edward how green shoots were rising from the muddy furrows. She could see he was assessing for himself just how hard his peasants were working along the mucky mire of the troughs. Sunlight broke through the morning mist and was glinting off helmets, their soldiers a warning to anyone who hindered their passage. Occasionally stands of beech trees rose up on the edges of the great wood, where somewhere deep inside stood a double oak tree that had sheltered Niall and herself during long, easy, summer afternoons. This same wood, once friendly, seemed to her now as if it could be a secret place for enemies to plot resistance. As they rode through it, conversation ceased between Gunnhild and Maud, drowned out by the raucous clamour of rooks in the trees above their heads, as if the creatures seemed about to swoop down on the moving column and as if the birds were intent on warning the village of

Well of their approach.

They rode along a lane into Well just as the church bell rang out the midday hour. As they approached the hall she heard Alan call to Sir Edward that this was one of the most profitable villages, with ten or more households, fourteen plough lands and seventeen plough teams. He dismounted and led his stallion through the village, scattering clucking hens and squawking geese, all the time watched by women who followed him and his soldiers with suspicion in their eyes. When they saw Gunnhild and Maud they sank on their knees to them. They had remembered how she had sent them food and visited their sick during the winter famines.

'I see they give my wife the deference they owe their lord,' Alan remarked as he slowed his pace to walk his stallion beside Blackbird, as if Gunnhild, a dispossessed princess, provided them with legitimacy. He never looked at the peasants who had ignored him.

They rode into the yard and stopped in front of a long wooden hall with a thatched roof. Sir Edward dismounted. As of one accord his clerks came off their scruffy nags and began to unfasten saddlebags that bulged with ledgers. The village headman, Alfred, met them at his doorway and ushered them into the building, a simple hall but clean. Inside, Alfred's wife, Ingar, had a long trestle near the round raised hearth laid with cheeses, meats, bread, watered beer and an enormous jug of buttermilk. Shabby servants scurried around. Dogs yapped over a bone and a family of new-born kittens mewed from a corner. They sat down to eat. Maud clung close to her mother. 'You know these children,' Gunnhild said. 'You must talk to them.' Maud refused to speak. She looked away from Ingar's brood and busied herself breaking her bread into a myriad of crumbs.

It was early afternoon by the time they were finishing the plain fare proffered by Ingar. She was a comely woman, tall, handsome and proud. She came from old Norse stock. Alan liked her and patted the bench between Sir Edward and himself saying she should rest a moment and eat with them. The servants could serve. The woman shook her head. 'Thank you, my lord, but I have fruit tartlets just ready. Best when they are hot.'

After she finished her rhubarb pasty, Gunnhild laid her napkin aside and suggested that she and Maud would visit a weaving shed whilst the survey continued. Alan nodded but warned her to keep an eye on Maud and not to let her wander loose around the village with the children.

'Come, Maud, we shall see if there is any cloth we like here.' She studied Maud's green mantle. 'There might be some russet woollen stuff for a new riding cloak.'

Maud glanced around the pleasant hall and said in a precocious manner, 'This would make a fine place for a new hall, Papa. I think my knight and I should very much like it as a wedding gift. I do not want to move far away when I am married.'

'It is not your father's to give away, Maud,' Gunnhild said crossly and tugged her daughter's hand, anxious to get her out before she further insulted Ingar and Alfred.

'Oh yes it is,' Maud said quickly. 'It absolutely is. My father owns everything here. Sir Edward says so.'

'I think Ingar and Alfred here have rights, too, according to the King's law,' Sir Edward said. 'You would agree Count Alan?'

'Yes, indeed and now we will see what he does to earn those or Maud will have them off him.' He slapped Alfred's shoulder. 'Come, Alfred, while the lady Gunnhild is inspecting your weaving shed we can finish here and ride on to Middleton before the night closes us in.' He pulled his long legs from under the bench and pushed past Gunnhild, tweaking Maud's chin as he went. He shouted over his shoulder 'The privy calls my member first. Then we are ready, Alfred. Get your pen shovellers together, Sir Edward.'

Alfred grunted. His wife bustled about for a bit and called her brood to the table to finish up what remained of the meal. She looked askance at Maud and Gunnhild. Maud whispered to Gunnhild 'Was it what I said?'

'No, it is what your father said. Alfred is very proud. He was lord here when your grandfather was the king. Your father should not throw his weight about, nor must you. They don't like this survey. It will mean a bigger tax for them. Come on. Let us get into the air before your father returns and changes his mind.' She politely thanked Ingar who was smiling at something her smallest son was saying. The woman's temper was slowly recovering.

'Watch where you step, watch your boots! Mind the dung there,' Gunnhild scolded Maud as they followed a pathway behind the hall to Alfred's weaving sheds. Through gaps in the hawthorn hedge she could see the dozen or so soldiers they had brought to Well. The sun was glinting through the branches and was reflecting off their breast plates. They had removed these and were settling down with the remains of the repast, slouching against the rough stone wall that marked the boundary of Ingar's vegetable plot.

Glancing the other way through shrubbery she could see the mill which stood across a rushing stream. Alfred and Alan were approaching it followed by Sir Edward and his clerks, but since their voices competed with the mill wheel's crashing through the river she could not make out their words. She clutched Maud's hand tightly. Something was not right. The mill owner, a lanky man with yellow hair tied into a pigtail, had rushed onto the pathway and was shouting at Alfred and the gaggle of clerks. He pointed over the gurgling stream towards the weaving shed in front of her. Then he was flapping his arms and yelling.

Gunnhild stopped and pulled Maud to her and considered turning back but at that instance a familiar voice called to her from just inside the door of the long weaving shed. It belonged to Uhtred, the lord of Middleton, whose village they had hoped to visit later that afternoon. She took even tighter hold of Maud's hand. Maud squeaked, 'Let go, Mama, you are hurting me.' She loosened her grip intending to ask Uhtred what was happening.

'My lady,' he called to her. He beckoned her into the dim

light of the shed. It was an old hall building with a back entrance.

'I am coming.' As she hurried inside she realised that the atmosphere within was very still. Five silent men stood around inside watching her. With a glance she saw that she knew them. That winter she had thrown caution away and had ridden with Niall into this village leading mules with saddlebags of provisions, salves and tonics, all to be distributed from here to cotters in the fells. She had ridden to Middleton, despite the danger all around them, with Father Christopher in tow to help bury their dead during the two winters of famine.

She realised too late now that this time these men were not welcoming. They held clubs instead of weaving tools. Gripping Maud's hand, she turned to escape but found her way barred. One of the men stepped forward. It was Clac, their foreman. Before she could protest, he spat his words, a gob of spittle flying towards her, 'We have naught against you or Lady Maud, my lady. She is the granddaughter of a king, and she is your daughter no matter who is the sire, but we intend to keep your daughter with us for a while. I swear to you she will come to no harm. Lord Uhtred will see to that.

Before Gunnhild could prevent it, Clac tore Maud away from her, swept the shocked child off her feet, and carried her struggling and protesting through the opened back door. The other weavers, still clutching blackthorn clubs, hurried after them. Uhtred lingered just a moment to say, 'No harm will come to Maud. She returns when we are assured that the geld will remain unchanged. Keep Count Alan and his hounds away from us or his lands will not produce another ear of corn, his mills will stop grinding and the weaving sheds will close. Your daughter will return unharmed if he helps us. '

'You demand help!' she cried. 'He will string you up, send your innards to the four corners of the shire. He will burn your villages. Have sense, take heed. He is not to be thwarted.' She opened her palms in supplication. 'Take me instead or let me come, too,' she begged.

'No, my lady. You will see that he complies.'

He turned on the heel of his boot and hurried after the others, only pausing briefly at the doorway to throw back at her. 'And we won't betray your secret meeting in Castle Richmond's bailey barn some winters past, not if you help us.' Gunnhild froze and bit her lower lip from fear. *How did he know? He had this information either himself or from a spy. She clapped her hand to her mouth, remembering how once she had heard rustling outside the barn. It was not this past winter but the one before. Yes, it must have been two winters past. They had waited for the best chance to use such information against her. Uhtred would have known the survey was soon to reach their lands. He had planned all this.*

She heard horses canter out of the village by the back way where deep beech woods ran through the valley. On hearing a row behind her she stumbled to the entrance. Alan and the miller, Alfred and Ingar and her gaggle of shocked children, Sir Edward, his pasty-faced clerks and a half-dozen mercenaries had arrived on the pathway. The soldiers' swords were drawn, and all of them were running towards her. She gathered her wits, shouted and pointed at the back entrance. 'They took Maud. It is Uhtred of Middleton!'

'You fool,' Alan hissed at Gunnhild. 'By the Devil's spawn, you useless Eve; you stupid, idiot pretence of a woman, get out of my sight.' He turned back to the soldiers, 'Ambush the bastards.' To Alfred he growled, 'If a hair on my daughter's head is harmed not one of you here will live to tell the tale to your grandchildren or their children. You will be burned to ash and your dust cast onto the fields.' He seized Alfred's youngest child, the tow-headed boy Gunnhild had seen Ingar laughing with not a quarter hour before. 'He comes with me.' Reaching out he roughly grabbed the boy's tunic. He turned again to Gunnhild who was still shaking with shock and shouted an order into her face. 'You, my lady wife, get on your nag and get back to Richmond.' He pointed at Alfred. 'You too, and your brat.' He glared at the guards. 'You, you, you and you will ride with them.' He counted out six of them and turned to the gaping pen men. He addressed Sir Edward, 'And you too, Sir Edward, and your scribblers. Be gone, the lot of you. Your work here is done.'

Alan pushed his way through the crowd that had gathered and was blocking the path towards his horses. He whipped his sword from its scabbard and raised it at the cowering villagers. 'Get back to your huts and pray for deliverance.' Following his example, his soldiers raised their weapons. The peasants, mostly women and children and a few old men ran, falling over each other, scurrying into hiding as if wolves of the forest were in pursuit. It was clear that Count Alan's soldiers would spare none who hindered their passage.

'Come, Lady Gunnhild,' Sir Edward said quietly, 'You have had a great fright here.' He took her arm in a gentle way. 'Let us do as he says and be gone from this terrible settlement. It is only fit for wild beasts. Count Alan will get her back, and I pour scorn on those here when he does. Their fate will hang in the balance. I shall see you safely home to your bower.' It was the kindest word he had ever spoken to her and she was glad too of what he said next. 'God smite me dead if I ever speak to my lady in such a manner.' He lifted his arm about her shoulder and guided her back to where their horses were grazing along the shrubbery within Alfred's hall compound. Alfred and his family followed, herded like animals over the pathway by an angry, stony-faced guard.

She glanced back as they rode away from Well. Alan was at the head of his galloping swordsmen, knees gripping his mount, forging through the hamlet, set on plunging his pursuit deep into the forest. Ingar stood sobbing on the pathway, her other children clinging to her. Not one soul remained about the cottages. Even the hens and geese had flapped into hidden roosts and bushes, terrified of the tempest that had engulfed the village.

22

The land of Count Alan: In Middleton Tyas, Ulf had a manor, with sake and soke, of 6 carucates to the geld, and there could be as many ploughs. Uhtred has it now of Count Alan. In demesne is 1 plough and 5 vellans with 4 ploughs. Tre worth 40s now 20s. The whole manor is 2 leagues long and 4 furlongs broad.

> *Domesday Book, A complete translation,* edited by
> Dr A. Williams and Professor G. H. Martin, 2003

'You must keep up your strength, my lady,' Ann said as she tried to comfort her mistress when she rode sorrowfully into Richmond's bailey that evening. 'Her father will get her back.'

Gunnhild shook her head. 'It is my fault. We should never have taken her to that village.'

'You can't change what has been, my lady.'

'No, but we can try to change what will be,' Gunnhild said.

Three long nights passed, and during that time she neither slept nor ate. She felt as if she was a collection of fragile bones rattling about the castle keep. By the fourth afternoon, when Niall came to her chamber, she was seated by the window with a book of prayers open on her lap. She hardly glanced at it. God had abandoned her. All day she had watched intermittent showers of rain slant down on the herb garden below and felt overcome by sadness as grey as the weather.

Niall knelt by her bench and took her hands in his own hands. 'Gunnhild, my love, they promised no harm would come to Maud. If Lord Uhtred promised this, he will make good that promise. We have sent another troop out to the hall at Akebe to help Alan.'

'What good can another troop do? There are so many hidden places out there in the woods. Anything can happen to her.' She waved towards the window embrasure and cried out, 'There have never been such downpours in May! Where has Uhtred taken her?' She drew her mantle closer, feeling cold, as if icy fingers were reaching into her heart and were tugging it from her husk of a body. 'Two days and no word, no message and no return.' She choked on her welling tears. She turned to him, 'You know what he said. He said he knew about us.'

'Uhtred said this? What, how?'

'He said he would not tell about the barn if we sent the King's clerks away. Well, if Alan did.'

'This is nonsense. He thinks he knows but what he thinks and what he really knows may well be different. He is blackmailing and it won't hold weight.' He thought for a moment. 'Unless he has a spy and has been storing this knowledge up but even so, he could be accused of mischief-making.' He held out the cup of hippocras to Gunnhild that Ann had left earlier. 'Take it. Drink. I doubt Uhtred knows anything real. I do not think he will say anything even if he does for the simple reason that he likes my rule here. There is no love between Alan and him. Try not to worry. He will not harm Maud.'

She drank the sweet, honeyed wine. For a moment it warmed her, and she wiped her tears away with her fist. 'Tears will not bring her back. If Alan does not return, I must go out and look for her myself.' Looking up at him she said, 'And those scribes are still scribbling, counting everything, as if nothing matters but their survey, that endless counting of stuff. If it wasn't for Maud, I would approve of Uhtred's rebellion.'

He nodded. 'Yes, though stealing a child will not get rid of the King's men.'

'If they took themselves away from our lands he would give Maud back to us. The fault is theirs.'

'Sir Edward has to finish his job.'

'Has he ridden out again?'

'Yes, he rode out with the extra troops that came in from York two days ago. The villages are on our side now. They call Uhtred an outlaw, a nithing and they say they will co-operate.'

'Even though they know it will increase their geld?'

'They are angry with him for what he has done to you.'

'And when do you suppose the King's men will leave us in

peace?'

'They may not even wait for Alan to return.' He paused then said, 'Will you not come down into the hall, Gunnhild, and speak for yourself?'

She shook her head, 'No. Sir Edward has unsettled us. I cannot.' She was thoughtful for a moment, 'Alfred and the boy?'

Niall crouched over and clasped his hands on his knee. After a moment he spoke quietly, 'Listen, my love, Alfred and his son are safe in my quarters. He has an idea. It is dangerous but I think we can discover where they have taken her.'

'What do you mean, "we can discover"? You mean without Alan?'

'Yes, Alan would frighten them off, well, in this case. That is if Alfred is right.'

She leaned closer and grabbed his hand. 'Explain.'

'It is only a guess, of course, but Alfred thinks that Maud has been taken to Hallikeld. Not there at the great hall, but to a nuns' house nearby. The Bishop of Durham owns the estate but he is never there. The nun's house is hidden in the woods and the nuns themselves are long forgotten by the world. They are like hermits, secret and quiet.'

'But the bishop is Norman. Why would they take her there?'

'Well yes, but Uhtred is a friend to Bishop Robert and the nuns are English. One of the nuns at this house is Uhtred's sister. Alan will never think of that forgotten nunnery. There are only four nuns living there now and they devote themselves to prayer. They are good women, Gunnhild.' He hesitated. 'But if she is there, and she could be, would they keep her hidden to protect their own?'

'Maud is an English king's granddaughter.'

'And that is why no harm will come to her. That is why it is better that Alan does not barge into their nunnery with troops.'

She gave him a stern glance. 'If you are going to look for her I want to come, too. They might listen to me.' She looked at him with hope on her face for the first time in days.

He considered. 'Yes, but it has to be done with stealth,

during the night. I intend taking Alfred and Hubert but no others. Alan must not know so if by chance he rides back today, it is off.' He rested his chin on his fingertips. 'Alfred's boy must stay safe with Ann in case Alan returns and finds Alfred, Hubert and myself gone.'

'When do we leave?'

He took her face in his hands. 'In truth, I expect Alan will not return before morning, if even then. You may come with us but only if you do exactly as I tell you. You are to stay out of sight when we reach the nunnery; at least until I know it is safe for you to approach. After that we can see.' He stopped. She nodded. 'Then, it depends on this. We have to return by daybreak whether we have Maud or not. Do you understand? Alan always has to be in control. I risk my brother's anger for this and even more for taking you with me when he has ordered you to remain here at Richmond though if we do have Maud back with us perhaps he will be forgiving.'

'Can I get out by the gatehouse and over the drawbridge without being seen? I am in confinement here. Alan is furious with me.'

Niall thought for a moment. 'I have a plan. During Vespers Ann will send your maids away. She will bring you one of Hubert's mantles. In this weather you won't be recognisable.'

He was on his feet. 'And you must eat first. I shall send Ann with sustenance and do not refuse it.' He gave her a warning look. 'This will not be easy.'

She nodded. 'I shall do anything if it helps to get my daughter back.' She managed a weak smile. 'Even eat.'

As the chapel bell was ringing out for Vespers, Ann entered her chamber with a tray of food and a sack of clothing. 'Hubert's mantle and we have a tunic, belt and hose too, my lady. It was left behind by Hubert's young nephew at Eastertide. Wear your riding boots.' She drew the bed curtains closed and, turning round, saw that Gunnhild was picking at a slice of mutton pie. 'By the Holy Virgin, wolf it down or else you are staying behind with me.'

246

Gunnhild ate quickly. She lifted the clothing and ran her hand over the warm woollen tunic and mantle. They would be comfortable. When she pulled them on she found that they were a good fit, too. She drew the belt about her waist and fastened the wooden buckle. Lifting her silver looking glass, she loosened her plait to allow it to fall down her back, and twisting it tightly she looped it up with a length of cord that she generally used to keep her pens neat.

'Good,' Ann said, standing back to survey the result. 'My lady, it will work. You look like a squire now but there is little time before the maids return from Vespers.'

Without further hesitation, they hurried down the stairway past the bower into the hall and out of the back entrance. It only took moments to follow the muddy pathway around the chapel, from which they could hear Brother Christopher intoning the plainsong. Stumbling with as much speed as they could, down the private path that side-tracked the garden fence to the bailey hall, they found Niall waiting at the bottom with a roan for Gunnhild.

'Your own horse, Blackbird, would be recognised. This is Argos.' She patted the roan's nose and stroked him allowing him to get her scent so he was used to her. A glint of humour flashed through Niall's eyes. He touched her arm and gently pinched the thick wool of the tunic. 'I doubt that you will be recognised in that gear.' He grinned and helped her mount the brown roan. After he gave a low whistle, Hubert and Alfred emerged out of the drizzling rain leading the other three horses.

'My lady.' Alfred came close to Argos and whispered, 'My lady, I had no knowledge of it before Sandi the miller warned us. He had his suspicions of those weavers. They were confirmed when he saw them talking with Uhtred of Middleton behind the mill that day.'

'Pity we had not known sooner. What happened has happened. It is not your fault.' She reached out and touched his mantle. 'Do you really think she may be in the nuns' house at Hallikeld?'

'That Count Alan has not returned with her already makes

me think that she is not in any of the Richmond villages. Count Alan has set himself up at the old hall in Achebe so he can cast his net wide through the meadow lands and woods. The villagers and the priest, Alfric, at Achebe are helping him.'

'He could have sent word,' she muttered below her breath.

'Does Alan ever stop to send word?' Niall said. The others mounted and she tugged on the reins and turned her roan towards the gates.

Niall called out as they reached the gate-house. The soldiers on guard recognised the darkly-clad lead figures trotting through the bailey to be Lord Niall and Hubert. They shouted for the drawbridge to be dropped down, not daring to question Niall's business outside the castle. It was none of their business, but just in case, Gunnhild and Alfred tugged their hoods over their heads and tried to look like servants falling in behind their masters.

Once they were beyond the town they wove along the edge of the woodland, riding south towards Well. Hallikeld lay further to the south east. The rain ceased as they rode further from Richmond. Evening became night and a pale moon broke through the clouds lighting up tracks that were empty of humankind. Now and then overhanging branches caused Gunnhild's roan to start as he sidestepped them. She mastered him easily and reined him in. A long-eared hare stood up in a field sniffing the wet night air, ears pricked in points as it watched them pass. Moments later a pair of stoats scampered across their path. An owl's sudden hoot made Argos nervous again. He leapt up but Gunnhild found now that she could calm him with a word. She never once allowed herself to fall behind Alfred who was leading them. As they neared Well, they turned into meadowlands. The mill and the village church were just about visible as they splashed through the stream that turned the mill. She had no desire to encounter Alan and anxiously prayed to St Brigit that they would miss any of his patrols.

'We must avoid my estate,' Alfred said reading her thought, and dug his knees into his horse's flanks pushing him into a canter. 'Come on, my lady, let us get up a gallop here and see if we can make speed across country. It is all fields now in this dale, river and meadowland as far as the eye can see. The nuns' house is hidden inside the Hallikeld woods. It will only take us an hour or more if we keep up a good pace.'

They took his lead, dug their boot heels into their horses' flanks and spurred them on. Gunnhild overtook them and easily galloped past Alfred, Alan and Hubert. Her seat bones would suffer in time but she didn't care. She rode fast, easily managing her roan through the gorsy meadows and over the tracks that edged the fields. The rain kept off and the moon appeared to grow fatter as clouds dispersed. Great beams of moonlight now slid over the fields lighting their way forward and sheening the wet grass with a wet glow. God's will was with her again. The faster Argos flew over the landscape the more she allowed hope into her heart. She would recover Maud.

After a gallop through fields and over the stone walls that separated them, they began to find trees growing in dense stands. Gradually a wood closed in on them. They trotted in single file into a sunken lane where beach leaves reached over and sheltered them, a mixed blessing because this new growth also hid the moonlight. They hunched their shoulders and crouched low over their mounts, splashing through elongated puddles, riding carefully to avoid the water-filled tree roots that stretched across their path, attempting with difficulty to overstep them where possible. Raindrops wet her face as the foliage brushed past her. Gunnhild could hardly see Alfred in front because the darkness here had so completely closed out the moon's glimmer but soon, thankfully, the lane finally levelled out and it became easier to ride towards where a track opened up to the left. Alfred halted at the divide. He pointed to the left. They grouped behind him. Riding very slowly now in single file, he led them into a glade filled with patchy wet grasses, nettles and bluebells.

'This is where we tether the horses out of sight,' he said, as he threw his leg back over his mount and slid onto the earth. 'We keep our horses back and our voices low. Uhtred and his men could be close by.'

'With luck, he is in the hall at Hallikeld tucked under a sheepskin, a skinful in his belly, a servant girl in his bed,' Hubert grunted. 'He will not be holed up in these damp woods tonight, you can be sure.'

Niall said softly as he came off his mount, 'Hubert, you will stay with Lady Gunnhild and settle the beasts. You know this wood. Whistle twice, long and low if you hear anything that is not winged or small.' He pointed to his right where the ground sloped up. 'If you go up to the top of that bank over there by the oak trees you will keep dry.' He sniffed the air. 'There could be another downpour before dawn. We must hurry. Alfred and I will go ahead on foot.'

Alfred beckoned Niall to a gap in the trees. 'Look there, Lord Niall. The nun's house is in the hollow down there beyond these trees. I can just about see it.' He gestured back to Gunnhild who had come off her roan and was unceremoniously rubbing her backside. 'Come over here and look, my lady.'

She hurried to his side. She could make out the shadowy outline of a grassy roof rising above the treeline in the valley below. 'It looks such a secret place, so well concealed in that wooded dip, it is as if no one could ever discover its existence,' she said, putting a hand on Niall's arm.

'We shall be as stealthy as foxes on the prowl.' Niall softly touched her back. 'And return before their Matins bell sounds.' He glanced up through the canopy. 'There is enough of a moon again to see by, and enough to remain invisible, too.'

Hubert tethered the horses to the heavy branches and efficiently hobbled them. 'Come, my lady, there are none of Uhtred's people out here tonight. There is nothing human besides ourselves but we had best climb up the mound and get under the trees like Lord Niall says. The horses are well hidden and up there we can discover if anyone *has* set up a camp nearby.'

They climbed the bank and made themselves as comfortable as they could on damp grass. Despite her heavy mantle she shivered as they waited. Somewhere far out in the woods a wolf was yipping. The sound came closer, an eerie elongated howl, and then retreated. Moments later she started. Something shadowy was moving towards the horses tethered below them. At first she thought that Niall and Alfred were pushing through the brush again. But it was the wolf. He was moving silently, belly low, clearly intent on reaching the hobbled animals. She froze, but Hubert was quicker than the wolf. He lifted his hunting knife and slipped back down the bank, weaving in a silent zigzag so he did not slide. She saw the outline of the wolf turning and Hubert leaping forward. Without a moment lost Hubert had his knife in the wolf's throat, before the creature could sink its fangs into him. There was a short struggle. The horses were snorting and pawing the earth. Hubert called up, 'I got the bastard. Another moment and he would have got the horses there and maybe us, too.'

Her heart raced and she wondered for a moment if it was madness to be out here in a strange wood, but as doubt crept in she felt as if the forest were speaking to her. She knew with certainty that Maud was close. She sensed it. Resolutely she stood up and leaned back against the tree trunk. The bitter tang of blood hung in the damp air. Hubert finished off the wolf and seemed to be murmuring into their horses' ears. She leaned into the tree bark, trying to become invisible Wolves ran in packs. The dead wolf's brothers could be close. And what if Uhtred of Middleton was somewhere in these woods, too?

A new sound rustled from the undergrowth. This time it was Niall pushing through the foliage with Alfred at his heels. When he saw the wolf lying in a pool of blood he stopped. Hubert spun round.

'By Christ's holy bones did you do this work, Hubert!' It was a statement not a question but Hubert just said, 'Do we take the skin?'

Gunnhild half slid and half tumbled down the slope landing uncomfortably close to the dying beast. She was never to be so glad to see another human again as she was to see Alfred and Niall return.

'Pity not to,' Niall replied to Hubert. 'But, we had better

make haste now in case there are more about,' Niall was saying as he pulled out his sword and thrust it deep into the wolf's heart. 'They usually travel in packs. If we're lucky this may be a lone one.' He thumped Hubert's back and said, 'Good work. Are you willing to wait here with Alfred while I take Lady Gunnhild to her daughter?'

'We'll whistle if there is anyone about though I doubt you would hear it,' Hubert said.

'I've roused the nuns.' Niall turned to her. 'They have Maud safe and will give her up when I show you to them. So, as well you came.'

'Uhtred, is he anywhere?'

'We searched. He is not here. Come, I'll help you into the lane.'

They pushed through heavy foliage down the lane to the hollow below and squeezed through a small broken gate into a compound consisting of what seemed to be a tiny stone chapel and a tiled-roofed, two-storied timber building. As they approached the nun's house the Matins bell rang. Four nuns stood waiting between the church and the hall. A thin boy scuttled from the church wearing a loose gown emulating a monk's habit tied by cord around the middle, hood flapping behind him. He stopped beside the nuns, completing an odd convening, and stood beside them. Gunnhild crossed the yard in a bound and was about to demand her child but the four nuns of one accord pressed their fingers to their lips. One stepped forward, clearly the senior nun. She wore a threadbare but neat habit and wimple. Her bearing was proud. 'So you are King Harold's daughter,' she said to Gunnhild. Indicating the scrawny waiting creature by her side, she added, 'The boy will bring her. After he fetches her you must take the child and go.' She gave Gunnhild a weak, thin-lipped smile. 'And God go with you.' She turned to the boy monk and said something in the Norse tongue. He immediately raced to the low building and disappeared through the doorway.

A second nun stared at her. Turning to the prioress she lifted a hand in a halting gesture and said, 'Not so quick, my lady prioress.' She addressed Gunnhild. 'You are Gunnhild of the English?' she said carefully. 'Have you proof of it?'

'Would you rather I sent for Alan and his army?' Niall said in a firm voice.

'Be silent, knight. Let the princess speak.'

Proof she was a daughter of King Harold. Silence stretched between them all like an invisible thread. She had no seal ring, no jewellery, nothing left to her now of her old life except long ago memories of her father. But, of course, there was her mother, and this gave her an idea. Gunnhild spoke quickly in the English tongue in case the nun changed her mind and called the boy back. 'When my father was slain at Senlac, it was my mother who knew him. She went to the grey apple tree on the ridge and saw that field of slaughter for herself. She recognised my father's broken corpse by marks only known to her. I know them, too.'

'And?' a second nun finally spoke. 'They were?'

Without hesitation Gunnhild leaned over and whispered into the nun's ear. The little nun stretched up her plump goose-like neck, listened, smiled and nodded. 'My father was there that day. Though they took him for dead, he saw what Edith Swan-Neck saw and he lived long enough to tell us children.' Her pale eyes became sorrowful. 'I believe that you are the youngest Godwin princess.' She added, choosing her words carefully, 'It was a great wrong that my brother did to you when he stole your child away.' She reached out and touched Gunnhild's hand. 'Forgive us, Lady Gunnhild, for we have no way of leaving this place as Uhtred well knows. We could not have brought the child to you had we wished to do so.' She waved her hand towards the church. 'We are solitary. People bring us food here and we have our church and our garden. We have prayer. Despite the great wrong my brother has done you, God worked a miracle tonight for he has brought the child's mother to us. And,' she added with emphasis, 'rest assured that we have cared for her well this past week ...' She looked around. 'But here she is. I can hear her footsteps.'

Gunnhild peered into the space beyond the group of nuns.

Maud was stumbling out of the hall's gloom into the moonlight, her hand in the child monk's hand, looking confused and very sleepy. She was wearing the same mantle as several days before, now mud-splattered and dirty, though her face was clean. Maud cried out one word, 'Mama' and ran the last few yards to her mother. Gunnhild knelt down and gathered her into her arms. Maud clung to her. For a moment, Gunnhild's eyes swam with tears of relief and looking up through a mist, she whispered to the nuns, 'Thank you.'

'We did our best to soothe her; we gave her a posset of camomile and honey to calm her, but I fear she is as frightened as a little doe,' the prioress said, her voice sad. She looked away towards the chapel. 'And now that you are reunited, my lady, we must go to our prayers.'

'Not so fast.' Niall's hand caught the nun's arm. 'Where can we discover Lord Uhtred and the weavers he took from Alfred's estate?'

She shrugged. 'Unless you have a guard with you, armed and fast, avoid him. He is at Hallikeld Hall. His men are out in the woods yonder. Now be on your way, Lord Niall, since you have what you came for. When my brother rides in here I shall say Lord Alan and his men came for the girl. Ride back to Richmond with as much speed as you can make. Get away from these woods, and God go with you.' She shook him off and with agility beyond her years she whisked around and walked towards the chapel. The boy-monk and the three other sisters followed her through the arched low door. It was over.

Niall walked quickly away from the hall with Gunnhild and Alfred following behind, Gunnhild clutching Maud's hand, chivvying her forward. When they reached the broken gate Niall said firmly, 'Maud, I am going to carry you. You are too heavy for your mother to lift.' Maud clung to her mother's mantle until Niall gently unpeeled her. He lifted Maud into his arms and carried her through the shrubbery and along a sodden track back to their waiting horses. Gunnhild hurried beside him. Niall said to Maud, 'And everything will be fine now. You are safe. But we have to make speed. You will be back at Castle

Richmond in time for breakfast.'

Gunnhild rode with Maud before her on the saddle so that Niall, Alfred and Hubert were free to defend them should they encounter an ambush. Just as they came onto heathland edging the Bishop's estate, they saw shapes etched on a hillside. As if they were moving as one great dark shadow, riders were coming down the slope towards them.

'That,' Niall hissed through his teeth, 'is not a sight we need to see. We must outride the bastards.'

'I'll take the rear,' Hubert said. 'You, Alfred, keep Lady Gunnhild between Lord Niall and my horse.'

They dug heels into horses' flanks and galloped, keeping a steady distance between them and the pursuit. Gunnhild's arms ached with the effort of riding and making sure that Maud did not slip from her arms. 'Hold tight to Argos's mane, sweeting. It won't be long. I am going to get us home.' Fear overcame her gathering fatigue. She rode as if the Furies were in pursuit.

They slowed down momentarily as they came to a rushing wide stream. 'It will hinder them, too,' Niall called back.

'Let me take Maud for a bit,' Alfred said, steering his horse alongside her. Gunnhild allowed him to loosen the child's hands from Argos's mane and lift her onto his own saddle. They pushed on through the trees until they were into water meadows.

Surely they will fall back here, Gunnhild thought. She glanced round. There was no sign of the riders. They had turned away as they had left the borders of the Hallikeld estates and had neared Alan's patrols. 'They will expect Alan's men here,' Niall said. 'It is a wonder we have not encountered them either this night.'

As a watery dawn broke, they were plunging into the wide fields close to the village of Well. Niall signalled to them to pause into a steady walk once they had reached the narrow track that skirted the great field beside the village. He stared up at the brightening sky. 'Somewhere else got that downpour.' He pointed to the encroaching horizon. 'Beyond that is Richmond.'

Well was very close. Again Gunnhild feared passing it. She gritted her teeth as she rode. Once past the edge of that dark wood into which Maud had been spirited less than a week before, Niall reined in his horse and signalled to them to stop, turned in his saddle and called back, 'Hubert should ride over to Achebe and tell Alan we have Maud safe, and that Lord Uhtred and his ragtag army are holding up at Hallikeld.'

'Lord Niall,' said Alfred. 'They are not likely to return to Hallikeld. They will look for shelter elsewhere. They will be expecting Lord Alan soon after this.'

'Go and tell him he has to hunt the bastards down because if he does not, as soon as my lady and her daughter are safely inside Richmond's walls, I shall.'

'I'll ride over to Achebe. They made their biggest mistake by following us because now they will have to retrace their ride. With luck, their mounts may tire.'

Moments later Hubert had turned his horse around towards Achebe and was gone with a backward wave, riding off down the lane. They glimpsed him moving through a barley field, on the periphery of the tree line and after that he was swallowed up by the Achebe woods.

Count Alan returned to Richmond late that afternoon. He had sent a troop after the rebels but he himself had ridden straight to the castle to see Maud, doubting that his wife and brother could really have so easily found her and carried her safely home. He praised Gunnhild's part in the rescue, grunted at Niall, and hurried off from the hall again, because a rider had come with news that they had taken up the four weavers.

The following day, Gunnhild was idly batting rose petals about the tub Maud had used before her. She felt warm and happy except for the ever-present worry that Niall could be wrong about Uhtred and they were close to discovery. Yet, Maud was back in her bed asleep just beyond the heavy tapestry, close and safe and for now that was all that mattered.

'My lady,' Ann was calling to her softly. 'My lady, do not fall asleep in the tub. Lord Alan needs you in the hall. You have little time to get ready.'

'He wants me,' she repeated, guilty anxiety creeping into her voice. 'What about Maud?'

'Sleep heals. Let her sleep it all off. I shall send the nurse to watch over her. Hurry, my lady. Count Alan has a look of Thor about him.' Ann sped around her bedchamber gathering up the garments that Gunnhild had discarded on her return, as well as the old gown she had hastily pulled on when Alan had ridden in. Gunnhild splashed flower petals onto the floor tiles as she pulled herself out of the tub. Ann handed over linen cloths with which to dry herself, insisting all the time, 'Get dressed, my lady, and I'll call for the maids to clear this all away.' She took the cloths from Gunnhild and helped her, rubbing fiercely at the hair that Gunnhild had loosened and allowed to fall into the bathwater. 'That will do. We can plait it round your head and pin the veil on it.' She rummaged amongst the garments on Gunnhild's clothing pole.

'Anything will do,' Gunnhild called from the bench where she was rubbing a salve on her naked feet and between her legs that were chaffed and sore from her wild ride. If Alan had discovered her infidelity then what she wore did not matter. He would lock her in a nunnery and throw away the key.

'Anything will not do. They are holding a court in the hall. Sir Edward and his men have agreed to be judge and jury. Alfred has been dragged into it because Maud was taken on his land.'

She stopped rubbing the salve into her legs and relaxed her guard. 'They have brought Lord Uhtred in already?' she said as she began to furiously brush her hair.

'Lord Uhtred got away. He has powerful friends who will protect him.'

'The Bishop of Durham?'

'Amongst others, according to Hubert. Here, my lady, this overgown will be better.'

Gunnhild pulled on the garments and Ann laced them and smoothed down her mistress's overdress. Ann called for maids to take away the water and clear the spilt petals from the floor tiles. She began to plait Gunnhild's damp hair.

'You know, my lady, you said that there was a boy at the nun's house when you took Maud from it?'

'What of it?'

Ann lowered her voice. 'He is the child of Grettir, the nun, Lord Uhtred's sister. That boy monk is Bishop Robert's and Grettir's love-child. Uhtred of Middleton has friends in high places.'

Gunnhild twisted round to look straight at Ann. 'So who exactly *has* Alan got down below?'

'My lady, be still. They found the weavers in a woodland camp south of Well. Lord Uhtred and his armed band rode away at the very sight of Count Alan's outriders. He abandoned the weavers. So Count Alan took them but Lord Uhtred vanished. The dogs could not even track him over the rivers or in through the great south woods. He may be near Durham itself by now. Alfred, Alan and Sir Edward's clerks will all condemn those men today.'

'But it is Uhtred who should be punished. He led, they followed.'

'Yes, my lady, they followed and they should not have followed him.'

Gunnhild came slowly down the stairway, her head high, knowing that she commanded respect. She had ridden out in the night with only three others and she had accomplished what Count Alan had failed to do. As she took her place on her chair in the centre of the dais between Alan and Niall, she heard a murmuring throughout the hall. Sir Edward sat on a bench at the head of his scribblers, seriously clerk-like with their portable desks strapped from their necks. One of them had been charged with the task of recording the trial and that clerk was seated by a trestle that had been moved into place in front of Alan as if it was a safe barrier between him and the anxious-looking crowd gathered below it. Alfred leaned back against the wall. His face was drawn and he was still wearing the mud-splattered garments he had worn yesterday morning. Clearly, she thought, he had endured enough already and needed his family and a day of sleep. Now he had to listen to judgement on his weavers, men who would be difficult to replace. But they took my child, she reminded herself. *And what if they, too, know about Niall and me? What if Uhtred has told them the words which he has threatened to speak to Alan?*

The hall was crowded with soldiers, servants, priests and a group of villagers. She was sure that they had walked all the way to Richmond with Count Alan's soldiers. These were the wives and children of Well's weavers. Gunnhild glanced to her right. There was an empty space inside a roped-off section of the hall just by the dais. It was not empty for long because once she had uncomfortably settled into her place Alan shouted, 'Bring in the scum who stole my daughter.'

A ripple of voices flowed through the crowd below the dais, as a way parted, and four bloody men were dragged through the hall door into the body of the hall where they were manhandled into the heavily guarded empty place near the dais. Alan called to them that they would face judgment. He boomed out, 'The devils of hell will thrust flames into your rotting flesh.'

The outcome had already been decided.

Sir Edward read out the charges, those of obstructing the King's survey and kidnapping Lady Maud, daughter of the King's tenant in chief, Count Alan of Richmond. Gunnhild did not wait a moment longer. She could not. She stood and addressed both Alan and Sir Edward. Leaning forward, turning from one to the other, she exclaimed, 'My lords, I ask you to spare these men. It is Uhtred of Middleton who influenced them. And the geld tax is heavy. It is an unfair tax.' She looked straight into Sir Edward's cold eyes. 'They did it because of the King's survey. Have mercy, Sir Edward. Reduce the tax on our villages. My child has not come to harm. She has been returned to us. I ask this one favour of your court. I beg you to forgive the weavers but to seek your revenge on Uhtred of Middleton. It is he who instigated this crime.'

'Sit down, Gunnhild and be silent,' Alan said through his teeth.

Gunnhild sank down again. There was a heavy silence. She glanced at the pathetic group of men. Their eyes were desperate. They knew there was to be no mercy.

Sir Edward looked over at her and said clearly for all below them to hear, 'A fine speech, my lady, but you see the King must have order in his kingdom. These men's fate will be an example to anyone else who dares flout the King of England's authority.'

He leaned over and spoke with his clerks. Alan glared at Gunnhild. Niall seated to her right looked surprised, as if he did not know how to respond. He shook his head.

The verdict was quickly reached. Sir Edward rose and addressed Count Alan. 'These men shall hang by the neck and before they die their innards will be cut out. They will watch as their hearts are torn from their bodies. Their rotting corpses will hang in the village of Well for all there to see that the King's justice has been done.'

Alfred hung his head. He did not say a word. Gunnhild felt his anguish and his shame. She stood up again and shouted, 'No! If they must die, Sir Edward, they die a clean death and they are to be taken down and buried. I will not impose this on our villagers no matter what these men did. They will have mercy.'

Alan's face turned thunderous. He pulled Gunnhild back down and said, 'Silence, you are not judge and jury here, woman.'

He was about to say more but Sir Edward cut across him. 'So be it. The King is merciful. They will have a clean death, no mutilation. They must hang for two nights and a day and then their families may bury the corpses.' He turned to the scribe. 'Write it down that this is the decision of the King's court at Richmond on this first day of June of the year of our lord 1086.' He summoned the priest. 'Father Christopher, go with them, hear their confessions. They will die before noon on the morrow.'

The weavers were dragged away weeping because they were not brave men. Gunnhild glared at Alan, 'I have seen enough.

Mark well, I do not intend to ride to the village of Well, so do not expect this of me.' With those words she rose and, with her head held high, she swept from the dais. Ann dutifully followed in attendance.

After Compline, Alan swept into their bedchamber. He loomed over her as she sat alone with sewing in her lap, so distressed she could not bear to be in the company of her ladies. He glowered at her. 'You must attend, Gunnhild, and you will attend. Sir Edward has made this easier for you. You do not have to ride again to the villages. They will die without quartering in the bailey yard. Their bodies will then be carried to the village of Well and strung up in the market place as a warning to all who question the King's survey. After two days their families will be granted permission to cut them down. They may bury them as they will.'

Gunnhild rose and, dropping the crumpled veil she was sewing, she spun around to face him. 'Very well, Alan. I shall attend this killing in the bailey yard, though I have no heart for it.'

'Thank you. See that Elizabeth keeps Maud away from the scene. As dawn opens the sky tomorrow, these men meet death.' He came closer to her, so close she could feel his breath on her neck. 'I know it is difficult, but remember, Gunnhild, you are my representative here when I am away. You must be seen to be firm and loyal to the King. No more disloyal outbursts.'

She never spoke. She fingered her grandmother's cross and made a silent prayer that these men's ordeals would be short. He stood close to her, waiting for a response. When none came, he turned to go. Finally, she called to his departing back, 'So that is decided. What is not clear is when Sir Edward is departing.'

He turned at the door. 'He will be gone to York by the week's end and will return in August to double check his accounting. Interestingly, he has the Bishop of Durham's Yorkshire estates to account, too. Perhaps he can find Uhtred there and bring him to justice.'

'Kettle, was he involved?'

'No, he was not. He does not seem to have had anything to do with their plot.'

'That is something. So some of the Norsemen remain loyal to us?'

'Most of them are. I have always been fair. If they remain true, that is. But justice must be seen to be done.' Alan studied her for a moment. He took a step back inside the chamber, crossed over to the sideboard, gestured towards a flask of red wine and lifted two palm cups. Turning to her, holding two empty cups, one in each hand, he said, 'Share a cup with me, wife. I want things to improve between us. What you did was courageous. You succeeded where I failed. I shall ask for a reduction in the geld tax because of what they have suffered up here in Yorkshire.'

She reached out for the proffered cup. He poured wine for them both. That night they lay as man and wife, though the experience was one that smacked of duty.

Part Three

St Brigit

(Picture from Wikipedia)

23

'I cannot agree to this marriage,' she said quietly.

Alan paced the antechamber, his expression tight-mouthed. He circled the brazier with its glowing coals and the great oak table where he stopped momentarily to pour a cup of wine and drank it down in one swallow. He crossed to the window embrasure, glanced out at the afternoon downpour and turned back to Gunnhild, who was seated on the bench with the veil she was embroidering in opus anglicanum, delicate raised stitches particular to English embroidery, lying abandoned across her knee.

'You, my lady, must comply. Maud will live in Lincoln after her betrothal to Walter d'Aincourt. Their marriage ceremony is to be held in the new cathedral at Lincoln and within the month. His family will raise her to be a suitable wife to a Norman knight in his father's household until she is old enough for it to be consummated. That is an end to it. She is unsafe here as events in May proved.' He lifted the d'Aincourt letter from the table, waved it at her and put it down again. 'It is arranged. Maud must be able to ride out freely without fear. And she needs to learn wifely duty.'

'She can learn that from her mother. God knows I know more than enough about my wifely duty. She is still frightened of her own shadow. She needs her own mother.' She picked up her exquisite sewing. 'What age would she be when it is consummated?' she added, recognising that she would not win this battle, but perhaps she could set parameters.

'She is ten years on her next name day. If she has her courses by her twelfth I shall make them promise no earlier than thirteen or fourteen. Otherwise not before she has bled for a half year at least.'

Gunnhild stopped sewing and considered. That was something. Ever since the incident at Well, Maud was closely guarded if they ever rode out of Richmond. Lincoln was a thriving town. Maud would mix with new people, young people of her own status, and she might even be presented to the King when he stopped there on his way to York. She wondered what sort of family Walter D'Aincourt had behind him. Walter's aunt was Matilda, Alan's older sister through her marriage to Walter's uncle. She was a kind woman. And, Gunnhild mused, Alan did love Maud. He indulged his daughter, bringing her gifts from York, baubles for her jewel casket, silk for gowns and a set of ivory combs for her hair. Although he was often still cold, he had also brought Gunnhild lengths of linen, silk and wool and latterly new brushes and fresh inks. She sighed. After Sir Edward had departed, a tentative truce lay between them. If Alan had suspected that she had been intimate with his brother he never said it. He stayed at Richmond throughout the summer, seeing to trade and to his great estates in Yorkshire and he was kind to them all, until now that was. Yet surely Alan would not send his cherished daughter to an unkind family no matter what this alliance gave him?

Alan rapped his fingers on a tall side-table, leaning against the wall plaster. 'Our daughter needs to learn her duty as a woman, and not from a mother who contradicts her husband at every opportunity.' He paused, allowing the cruel words to fly through the damp air. She opened her mouth to protest but he continued, 'After the wedding you will travel with her as far as Lincoln, then on to Canterbury. We must be clear about my estates, including Reredfelle. Wilton Abbey has dared to claim them. Reredfelle, for instance, is temporarily in Bishop Odo's name but he is still in Rouen. He supports the King's son, Robert Curthose.' He laughed as he said *Robert Curthose*. 'If it is not the bastard bishop, then it is the Abbess of Wilton who is after what is mine by right of our marriage.'

'How do you know?'

'Sir Edward told me.' He studied Gunnhild with a dark look and swept a hand through his thinning cropped hair. 'I shall have a grant written out making Reredfelle and other properties made over to you. You will take it to Canterbury for Lady

Elditha to sign. It must go straight to King William, himself, before the survey puts them all down as Abbey lands. I expect you to be persuasive.' He gathered his mantle from the bench threw it over his shoulders and made for the door.

'Before you go there is more to say, Alan,' she called after him. 'When did you say I travel to Canterbury?'

He turned around. 'After the wedding.'

'And who escorts me? You?'

'Your mother will certainly not wish to see me again. I shall organise an escort. After the marriage ceremony I shall return to Brittany.'

She drew in a breath. Her lands indeed. By the old English laws a woman could dispose of her own property as she wished. Not so now the Normans said that a woman's property belonged to her husband. Dear God, let Walter d'Aincourt be generous to her daughter. She hoped that Elditha would refuse. Alan had land enough and had already acquired much of what had belonged to her mother.

Alan had tried to marry her mother after the Normans came to England, built castles and quashed any rebellion afoot, sending her grandmother, Countess Gytha into exile in Flanders, killing one of her rebellious older brothers, keeping her youngest and dearest brother Ulf a hostage in Normandy.

And, of course, no one had heard of Ulf for years. He had simply disappeared. Ulf was a difficult topic and one they never discussed. All Alan would ever say was that Ulf was part of Robert Curthose's household. He was probably, by now, more Norman than English. What age would Ulf be? She counted. Maybe, he was already twenty-four years old since she was twenty-eight.

'I see,' she said aloud, now finally setting her embroidery aside and folding her hands. To see her mother again after so many years had passed was a joyful thought, but parting with Maud would be accompanied by deep sorrow. 'And when are we to expect d'Aincourt?' she asked.

'By mid-month and it will be a quiet event. I leave it to you to arrange chambers for our guests.'

'And the betrothal feast?'

'That must be as fine a feast as is fit for the female kin of King William, including my sister and her husband Hugh. They will stand as witnesses. You may order what is necessary from York.' He swept out through the doorway and returned to the hall.

She picked up her embroidery and made a few neat stitches on the hem, but her mind was not on acanthus leaves and miniature flowers. Her thoughts worked fast. Ann would help her to prepare Maud for her betrothal. There would be the castle to make ready for guests, food to order and new gowns for Maud. The loss of her daughter would be tempered by the anticipation of a visit to see her mother. Elditha had been informed of her marriage to Count Alan years before but after that there had been no communication. This visit was to be welcomed. It had never been permitted before but now that it was a question of land suddenly it was permissible.

A few days later, Alan and Gunnhild sat with Maud on a bench in the garden. A yellow sun shone down hotly and the roses suffused them with a soft perfume. The rain had stopped. Summer had arrived at last. Together they gently broke the news to Maud of her imminent betrothal. Alan told Maud that life on a great manor and in a noble townhouse in Lincoln would be much more exciting than life at Richmond. 'We shall visit you often, my sweet,' Alan said. 'Although you will be married, Alice d'Aincourt and her ladies will see that you continue your education. They will introduce you to their bower and teach you how to organise the dairy and stillroom. You will be happy there and get to know your bridegroom. He is a kind and handsome young man. His father, Sir William, is my trusted friend. I knew him at King William's court when our King was just the Duke of Normandy. You will grow up amongst good people and I would not have it otherwise.'

Gunnhild was grudgingly impressed with Alan's approach to the changes in their daughter's life. She took Maud's hand in her own. 'We shall both travel with you to Lincoln and settle you in with your new family.'

'But I shall miss you, Mama and Papa.' Maud looked from one to the other.

'There will be new things to see and learn. We shall miss you, sweetheart, but I think your father tells the truth. You are going to be pleasantly surprised.'

'And can I bring my Merleswein and Pippet?'

'Yes,' Alan said quickly. 'Your pony and your dog will be part of your retinue. And Elizabeth will stay with you so you will always have her company.'

'I would prefer Mama's.'

Gunnhild blinked back the tears that swam too easily into her eyes. 'I must stay here at Castle Richmond, but if you ever need me, send for me and I shall come to you.' As she said these words she prayed to St Brigit that Alan would permit her to fulfil her promise.

From the bailey yard to the keep's turrets, Richmond prepared for the d'Aincourt arrival. The hall was swept out and the timber boards scrubbed; tiles in the bedchambers were freshly washed with vinegar, lemon and water. Dust was swept away and garlands and banners were hung in the solar and the hall. Guest chambers were prepared on the upper two storeys and in its four turrets. Soft feather mattresses were delivered and fresh linen was trundled upstairs in huge baskets to make these chambers comfortable in a way the neglected upper rooms had never been before. Walls were freshly limed and hung with tapestries which Alan had kept hidden away for years in huge coffers. Braziers were placed in every room so that if the weather was cold and rainy the d'Aincourt party would have every possible comfort. Frankincense was burned in all the braziers throughout the castle to freshen it. Finally, camomile and lavender were scattered amongst the floor reeds.

Supplies came on sumpters from York and from the countryside. There were exotic spices, sacks filled with flour, honey, wine, raisins, dried fruits, venison and birds that would be spiced with cinnamon and encased in pastry coffins for the betrothal feast. New cooks rode in on a wagon dragged by a team of four horses, lent to Count Alan for the duration by the custodian of York Castle. A team of five seamstresses arrived from York with bolts of material and within two weeks Gunnhild had a new overgown of blue silk with trailing sleeves, trimmed with raised roses and embroidered with gold thread.

Maud exclaimed over the sumptuous overdress and mantle that she would wear for her betrothal ceremony. Her betrothal dress was made of pale gold damask with a matching mantle, yet she favoured her wedding dress of scarlet silk, hemmed with hundreds of pearls and the delicate veil with a gold circlet that she would wear for the wedding ceremony in Lincoln.

Thankfully, September was dry. Gunnhild looked at the sky hourly, hoping that fine weather would continue for the visit. At last, on a day of perfect skies with only the odd scudding wisp of a cloud, the d'Aincourt party rode into the castle bailey with clattering hooves and rattling litters. Matilda d'Aincourt and her husband Hugh, who had ridden in from York some days earlier, now hurried to Alan and Gunnhild's side to make the introductions. They were a kindly couple and Gunnhild had been grateful for the older woman's help, though Matilda warned her that they would depart after the betrothal ceremony. They, too, were to face the survey clerks. They would ride south to London taking a route through the midlands where Sir Hugh had estates that were part of the King's great survey.

Gunnhild and Alan, with a very excited Maud standing between them, came into the courtyard to meet Sir William and Lady Alice. Their four young d'Aincourt daughters tumbled out of a long litter that clattered over the paving stones, stopping before the castle's entrance.

The girls seemed to range in age between four and ten. An older girl of around twelve years rode on a little brown mare beside her brother, Walter. He climbed from his white roan, helped his sister to dismount and led her forward to join his parents. He knelt in front of Maud and took her tiny hand in his long elegant fingers and kissed it. His manners were impeccable. Gunnhild smiled at him. He was a beautiful young man of around eighteen years of age with even facial features, nut-brown hair that curled onto his shoulders and a figure that was well formed. His height when he stood again was middling for a man, around five feet and eight, though Gunnhild guessed that he would stand an inch or so less without his riding boots. When he lifted his head he smiled back at her with eyes that were blue and clear and which caused his whole countenance to light up. Gunnhild could see from Maud's smiles that her daughter was well pleased with her bridegroom. She prayed that happiness would follow. In four or five years' time this marriage would be consummated and the pair would move to their own household. As nine-year-old Maud solemnly curtsied, Gunnhild considered that the groom and bride had both made a good beginning.

On the following morning, Gunnhild and Alan watched proudly as their daughter was betrothed to Walter d'Aincourt. The young man looked even more handsome today in a green tunic trimmed with gold bands and matching hose. His linen mantle was secured across his shoulder with a large golden pin fashioned like a goshawk. Momentarily, as she gazed at it, Gunnhild wistfully remembered the hunting bird she had once owned in Brittany. When they hunted close to the Castle Richmond it was deer that Alan enjoyed chasing or, if not deer, she often suspected it could be women.

The d'Aincourts crowded the chapel with their bevy of exquisitely gowned, excited daughters, their servants, maids and nurses and their personal guard who stood watchfully at the back. Bishop Thomas had arrived from York to officiate. Brother Christopher swung an incense censor, scattering a light but pungent scent over everyone present. Gunnhild turned away. She had never liked this smell. It reminded her of death, of her aunt's funeral at Westminster more than ten years before, of Christina and of the miserable years she had endured under Christina's rule at Wilton.

Today, she could not help but reflect on the losses life dealt. There was her father, her brother, her grandmother and her aunt, lives all destroyed by the conquerors with whom she had now united, and with one of whom she had created the beautiful child who stood before the altar alongside a son of the enemy.

Although the betrothal ceremony was held inside the church, the marriage ceremony, later that month, was to be sanctified in Lincoln Cathedral porch, where afterwards there would be a lengthy mass in the nave to celebrate the union. Today the betrothed would make vows and Bishop Thomas of York would bless them. There would be a pater-noster and a small sermon from the bishop and after this the ladies and children would return to the bower hall briefly before the feast later that afternoon.

Gunnhild had been diligent in preparing the castle's great hall. To ensure the occasion was light-hearted she had summoned musicians from York. Later there would be dancing. She knew Maud was looking forward to this because over the past month she had been practising every dance step she had ever learned so that she could impress her bridegroom, Walter, with her little steps, weaves and turns.

Ann and Gunnhild had trained Maud well for her part in the betrothal ceremony and now she stood, with her small frame straight. She seemed self-possessed, a princess who would have made her grandfather, King Harold, and her grandmother, Elditha, very proud. The chapel was beautiful, scented with candles and filled with slanting rays of light. The day was perfect. Beams of sunlight scattered through the decorated glass set in long narrow windows, creating patterns of coloured light over the tiled floor. Bunches of purple Michaelmas daises were placed in three of the window embrasures around the small church lending it a festive atmosphere. As Maud knelt at the altar with her bridegroom the pearls on her silver head band caught the light and gleamed, and under it her hair, freshly washed with soft rose-scented soap and camomile, shone like spun gold. It rippled in waves onto the flowery, straw cushion below her knees.

Gunnhild blinked back her tears as she watched her daughter's betrothal blessed by the elderly bishop. Lady Alice,

272

too, dabbed at her eyes. She seemed to Gunnhild a lady of sound sense, an elegant woman with a longish face and dark laughing eyes. Sir William, her husband, studied everyone and everything through gentle, studious eyes that were kindly and thoughtful. Gunnhild felt great relief. He would be as serious and considerate surrogate father to Maud as Alice would be mother.

'I like Sir William,' Maud had said that morning as Gunnhild straightened her daughter's pearl-studded cap and twirled her around to check that it was pinned securely on her head. The gold dress fanned out. Maud's new shoes, calf skin dyed a pale yellow and studded with tiny pearls peeped below her gown. As she spun she declared, 'And I like my new family.'

Gunnhild had said, 'You look perfect and you will have sisters at last. Katherine, the eldest, clearly wants to be your friend. Study her and learn.' Katherine was sweet and delicate but Gunnhild knew that they would soon marry her off. Maud must befriend the others, too. As she watched Maud turn and leave the nave alongside her betrothed, she considered that her child was fortunate. She hoped, too, that Lady Fortune would continue to smile on Maud and allow her a happier marriage than her own had been.

During the feast that followed the betrothal ceremony, Lady Alice turned to Gunnhild, 'What an excellent table you have provided today.' She looked down on the snowy cloth, picked up her napkin and daintily dabbed her mouth. 'I know what it is to part with a daughter. My eldest, Adelaide, was married last year and now she is in Normandy.' So Katherine was the second eldest. There was a tear in her eye when Lady Alice added, 'I shall miss the birth of our first grandchild.'

'Are you from Normandy, Lady Alice?' Gunnhild asked quietly. She was puzzled because Alice's English accent was light in tone, like that of a small songbird, not heavy and guttural in the usual way of the Norman French.

'No, I am French from Montmartre, but I am here now, and

here we shall stay. Walter has been accumulating lands in England, though we have an inherited estate near Bayeux and I brought our French lands to the marriage. Walter will visit them with Maud, when she is old enough, but that is still some years off.' She leaned towards Gunnhild. 'Gunnhild, rest assured, I love your daughter already. She is self-possessed and full of energy and enthusiasm for life. She is a credit to you.'

'My lady.' Niall had appeared from his place on the high table and was bowing to Lady Alice. 'Would you partner me?' The musicians struck up a traditional round and the space in the middle of the hall filled up with dancers. Alice hesitated a moment and turned to Gunnhild, 'Our conversation must wait, it seems.'

'Go,' Gunnhild encouraged. Lady Alice tripped off into the widening circle with Niall, who looked back and smiled at Gunnhild and, in that moment, her heart leapt at the warmth in it. She felt guilty watching his slim form and his easy movements as he led Alice into the dance. She still desired him but, biting her lip, she turned her gaze elsewhere. She must not betray her feeling for him, not here, not ever, and especially not with Alan deep in conversation with William and Walter. Alan put down a half-eaten morsel of marzipan and called her over, 'Gunnhild, this young man has a promise for us.' He looked sternly at young Walter d'Aincourt. 'Go on, say it to my lady.'

Walter jumped to his feet in a coltish manner and bowed to her. 'Madam, I promise to cherish your daughter. She will be my greatest treasure and I shall value her above my own life.'

'I will hold you to it,' Alan said frowning. 'Maud is an heiress and granddaughter to the great Earl Harold of Wessex. Remember it, lad, and remember it well.'

'My lord, always.' The boy seemed awed by his future father-in-law. For a moment Gunnhild saw Alan as he may have been at this youth's age, filled with notions of knighthood and honour. Life had hardened him and the Conquest had made him the tough middle-aged man he was now, a cold, religious man who was once fair to his tenants but lately appeared determined to extract impossibly hard work despite the famine winters and worse, since he was determined to extract the King's new tax from them.

At that moment Maud broke away from the dance, her sisterly retainers tripping after her. They dutifully smoothed her gown and generally fussed about her, four pairs of eyes filled with admiration. Katherine said to her brother, 'You must lead your lady out.'

'Well, my lady,' Walter rose, bowed and holding out his hand, addressed Maud, 'Shall we?'

Gunnhild watched her daughter leap in the dance, to be caught by Walter, her skirts swirling and her hair loosened from the jewelled cap so it was flying about her in a cloud of gold. She was only nine years old and already her dancing was perfect.

Alan's sister, Matilda, leaned over and said, 'Maud reminds me of your mother whom I once saw at King Edward's court. She was very beautiful, too.' She laid her hand over Gunnhild's and lowered her voice. 'I wish you were happier with Alan, my dear. I fear you are not. He cannot be easy to live with. He is a soldier and a merchant. He does not understand women.'

Some women, Gunnhild thought, as she twisted her napkin. Yet, she would not be disloyal. 'We manage well,' she replied.

Matilda, to her horror, glanced at Niall who was leading one of Gunnhild's ladies into the dance. 'Now our younger brother is more carefree than your husband. It is a wonder he never remarried. Hugh has suggested many matches for him, heiresses, ladies of high birth, but he will have none of them. His heart was broken when Constance, his wife, died, and their child gone to heaven with her. God rest their souls.'

'Indeed I have wondered it, myself, Matilda,' Gunnhild said with neutrality in her voice, though her heart was breaking for love of him as he danced with Hilde, a sweet girl, newly come to her from York and already her favourite lady. She felt a tinge of envy that it was Hilde who swirled and tripped over the rushes alongside Niall. If only it could be her.

On a late September evening, a week after the d'Aincourt

family trundled away on the route to the Great North Road, and back towards Lincoln, Alan summoned Gunnhild to the antechamber. After he asked her to sit in the armed chair, he poured her a cup of hippocras and brought her a plate of almond cakes that the cook had freshly baked that morning. He spoke cheerfully of how in a two-week space they would all be setting off for Lincoln and asked her how their preparations were going, how many wagons they would take, how many coffers Maud would need for her new gowns and her possessions.

She said that she had been organising and overseeing their packing for two weeks. He stretched out his feet to the hearth, contemplated the flames for a moment, before turning towards her. He stroked his greying beard. She knew he was about to tell her something significant because he cleared his throat and coughed.

She was not prepared for their wounds to be opened. They had just spent a pleasant week in moderate harmony, but he said with halting speech, 'I have selected the jewels that Maud will bring to her marriage. Come and see for yourself. I want you to agree.'

He stood up and she rose and followed him to the oak table. The jewel box sat on the linen cloth. He pulled a key from his belt purse and carefully unlocked it. Her jewels gleamed up at her.

'I should not have to watch you unlock my property,' she said, remembering how even for the betrothal she had worn lesser pearls and sapphires rather than bring herself to ask him for permission to wear these exquisite settings.

'They are not your property, Gunnhild. What is yours is mine. Most of what is here I gave you in the first couple of years of our marriage. They are the Penthiévre jewels. Others belonged to your grandmother. You do not resent your daughter having these?'

She reached into the box, took out a ring with a cluster of garnets set in gold and slipped it on her finger. She lifted a necklace of pearls and another of silver beautifully engraved with tendrils and roses and put it up to her neck. She fingered a sapphire pendent and touched her silver bracelets. They had gorgeous engravings. Some were studded with amber. She touched the ruby that had caused the rift between them so many years before. As she removed the garnet ring from her finger, she measured her words. 'I am happy for these to go to Maud, but why not give her the ruby now and leave the rest here? She will inherit them all one day. It is not right that a daughter takes all of her mother's jewels into marriage during her mother's lifetime.'

'Very well. You are right on this occasion. She shall have the Penthiévre ruby and I am sure she will take good care of it. The rest will remain here.' He banged the jewel chest shut and put the key back into the purse on his belt chain. 'Such a pity, wife, you are not able to give me a son, unfortunate that the one I had died young.' He did not add the words 'in your care' but she suspected that he still thought them. He added, 'While you seek our lands from your mother I intend to return to Brittany. Agenhart is with child.'

She felt colour drain from her face. 'And the child is yours?' she said, gripping the edge of the table. Her legs were about to give way with the shock of this revelation.

'Yes,' he said.

'I see.' Gunnhild whispered with sinking heart.

She determined to rise above this crushing statement. Never again would she be lulled into a false sense of security with Alan. Her nagging guilt dissipated as she remembered how Niall had moved amongst the dancers at the betrothal feast. She remembered how he had looked at her with longing as she had passed him in the dance and how she, determined to keep true to her decision, had prayed that no one noticed. Now she was tempted to make a counter revelation. Yet, it would be unwise. Alan was her husband. His adultery would be of no consequence, hers would. That was the unfair truth of it.

Alan broke the silence that had descended over the jewel box. 'You have taken this well, Gunnhild, as a wife should.' She did not reply. 'Niall and a guard will escort you and one of the wagons south. They know where you must rest for the night, which abbeys and castles. And hopefully the weather will hold.'

'Niall ...' she began, wondering if it was wise. She thought the better of it and said, 'As you wish, Alan.' She turned away from him and swept out of the chamber without saying goodnight, but she hoped that he stayed in Brittany with his mistress for a very long time.

24

October 1086

Isolde had managed to escape from her confinement at the court of her husband, King Mark, and by secret means had travelled across the borders of Cornwall, out of the reach of her husband.
'The Reunion of Tristram and Isolde', from *The Death of King Arthur* by Peter Ackroyd, 2011

Gunnhild gathered what was necessary on a journey such as this into her saddlebags, ointments for bites, powders for weakness of the stomach, cleansing treatments in tiny jars, a change of linen for herself and Maud and a spare gown each. These she would keep with her on Blackbird. Packs for the sumpters were piled up in the courtyard in the bailey. The pack animals themselves were drawn up and waiting. Youths came forward and carefully loaded them as Alan watched, making sure he knew what held what. He had sacks filled with new wool that he intended taking on to Brittany and now he oversaw them loaded safely onto sumpters. He supervised the men, too, as they loaded carts with Maud's possessions. Within the hour their cavalcade would set off from Richmond to York and then turn south-east towards Lincoln. If the weather remained fair the journey would take four days. Gunnhild knew that to travel from Lincoln to Canterbury could take a week but she looked forward to it. It allowed her a sense of freedom, but most of all, she looked forward to seeing her mother at the end of it. Many years had slipped by. So much had happened during that passage of time. 'My mother,' she whispered into her pillow on the night before they were to set out, 'I hope you remember me.'

Maud descended into the bailey courtyard with Pippet snapping at her heels and her nurse, Elizabeth, watching over her protectively. Her father helped her up onto Merleswein's broad rump. She sat pertly on her velvet-cushioned saddle with her reins set firm in her hands, impatient to be on the way. A bemused smile played about Gunnhild's mouth. What a precocious girl her daughter had become. Pippet was relegated to the wagon where he was held secured on a leather lead by Elizabeth. Gunnhild's two personal ladies, Emma and Hilde, climbed in after the nurse. Ann and Hubert and their three small daughters waved them goodbye.

After the emotional leave-taking of Ann, Hubert and their daughters, the long cavalcade processed through the bailey gate and over the drawbridge. Gunnhild turned back to wave one last time. Ann raised her hand and waved back. Gunnhild leaned from her sidesaddle and spoke to Maud. The child bride turned back and gave Ann a final wave. Gunnhild wondered how many moons would set before Ann and her daughters saw Maud again.

With a jingling of bridle bells and a clattering of hoof, they were trotting through the village, their horses' hooves thumping the dry earth road. Count Alan's azure-and-gold chequered pennant fluttered in a breeze, held high in their advance by a young squire. It was a wonderful sight. Gunnhild remained smiling, pleased that their villagers had come out to throw pink roses and golden broom in their path, and to cheer for Maud.

What Gunnhild did not count on was that she and Alan were to share a bedchamber when, five days later, they arrived at the d'Aincourt manor house on the edge of Lincoln. They stood on either side of the comfortable bed in their night mantles preparing to share a feather mattress for the second time in a summer. Determined not to spoil the joyful atmosphere with which they had been received, Gunnhild climbed the wooden step up into the high bed and made a cheerful comment on how enthusiastically they had been welcomed.

'Our daughter brings a great dowry with her,' Alan grunted as he rose from his lengthy prayers, 'as well as the Penthiévre ruby. They ought to show gratitude. Tomorrow will be a long day.' With those words Alan climbed into the bed, pinched the candle, turned over on his side and almost immediately began to snore.

Gunnhild lay in the darkness longing for sleep but her mind was too alert. From outside in the garden she heard an owl hoot. She sat up wide awake and through the window opposite she saw a harvest moon that was framed by it. It was a great white ball hanging in a sky of stars. Slipping from the bed, she found her deerskin slippers and her mantle. Clutching her mantle close, she slid from the bedside, lifted the latch, and pushed the chamber door open and tip-toed down the staircase into the hall.

She stole past bodies that were wrapped in sheets on pallets in curtained alcoves and hurried out through the back porch, gently opening and closing the heavy oak door behind her. Outside, a shingle path to the side of the swathe led towards the manor's gardens. She followed it into the walled garden that Lady Alice had proudly shown her that afternoon. There was a garden seat somewhere close. She discovered it halfway along the inside pathway. Sinking on to the stone seat she inhaled cool night air scented with the perfume of late roses.

She glanced up at the fat mellow harvest moon which cast shadow and light over the peaceful garden, over neat rows of berry bushes, herb beds, marigold patches and semi-circular-shaped espaliered apple trees. The owl hooted again. She peered past the sundial that stood in the garden's centre. One of the garden's shadows seemed to move through the trees, advancing towards her, growing larger as it drew closer. Her pulse beat faster and she sat very still. She thought she recognised its owner and shuffled to the end of the bench into the shelter of an arch of trailing white roses. Momentarily she blinked. The shadow had vanished. From behind her a voice whispered softly, 'Gunnhild. It is me.' She stood up and looked around the arch. Niall moved forward to stand beside her arbour.

'I suspected as much,' she murmured.

'I could not sleep,' he said.

'Nor me.'

She gathered her mantle around her like a carapace between them. He sat on the bench beside her and lifted her hand. 'We have not shared a moment together for many months.' Despite herself, she held his hand back.

'So much has happened …' she began.

'Since that business with Lord Uhtred,' he finished her sentence and looked up. Opened window shutters loomed above them. He laid a finger on his lips. 'I doubt anyone is watching but we should move into the trees.' Stepping forward, he slipped into chestnut trees that grew around the garden's boundary. She waited for a moment then followed.

'It is a full moon,' she said quietly. 'A good omen.'

'For Maud or for the harvest this year?'

'Both,' she said.

'And for us, Gunnhild? Is it a good omen for us?'

'I don't know.' She felt a blush rise and looked uncomfortably down at her slippers. 'Agenhart is with child.'

'Alan is the father?' Niall took a long breath and let it out slowly.

'Yes, he is the father,' Gunnhild replied. 'It was a shock when he told me.'

'That was cruel, Gunnhild.'

'It is the way it is. Alan says a wife must bear such with patience and understanding. I possess neither.'

'I am sorry that you must suffer this.' He lowered his voice further. 'Do we still matter, Gunnhild? I must know.'

'If Alan suspects me he will not hesitate to set me aside, put me in a nunnery.' She gave him an anxious half smile. 'The rules for a wife are different.'

'We are to be together on a journey that may take some weeks to complete. Am I to suffer because I shall be with you and without you?' He leaned over her and his lips touched hers. In that moment she felt the melting she always felt when Niall kissed her. She pulled away but he was quicker and caught her. He drew her towards him, his hand entangled in her loosened hair, his mouth again claiming hers. She gently pushed him away again.

'It cannot continue, not now, Niall.'

'Then when?'

'I know not. It is for the best. I must go back to bed.' She turned away from him and hurried from the garden, away from Niall, confused. Life was very, very short and there might never be an opportunity again for them, but would God forgive her, her broken vows?

Three days later under a blazing autumn sun, Gunnhild's retinue set off for Canterbury. Her small train, consisting of Niall, Hilde, Emma and a maid, was escorted by a half-dozen guards. She rode Blackbird behind Niall and two outriders, no sidesaddle on this long ride; instead her dress was comfortably fanning out on either side of her legs.

As they trotted out of Lincoln and rode over the old Roman roads south, Niall remained courteous but quiet. He was focused on the road ahead, often sending one or other of their outriders on before them. Since he was so lacking in conversation, Gunnhild and Hilde rode either side of the slower wagon which held Emma and their maid, Greta.

Happy to be free of Richmond, she listened to her ladies' chatter. They discussed the wedding which her ladies thought had been very beautiful; Maud's fabulous gown sewn with pearls, her hair of gold, her little cap and her delicate veil and that ruby. It must have been beyond price. She overheard the maid, Greta, remark on how magnificent Count Alan had looked in a scarlet mantle and how Lady Gunnhild had been more elegant than royalty itself in her gown of stiff silk.

'And that wedding feast! I never tasted larks tongues before,' Greta exclaimed.

'Nor rabbit either. It tasted like chicken,' Emma added.

Gunnhild smiled to herself. Nor had she.

Sir Walter had introduced rabbit warrens from Normandy and he had brought over cooks to prepare the wedding feast which was splendid: doves, larks, blackbirds, pigeon, rabbits, chicken pies, almonds and other sundry nuts introduced into sauces as were mushrooms, boar and deer dressed with rich wine sauces, honey cakes, spice cakes, lady's fingers and a subtlety that was a miniature castle decorated with sugared flowers, roses and honeysuckle, shaped perfectly and nestling amongst sugared tendrils of deep green acanthus leaves. It even possessed a moat with tiny dragon ships, and d'Aincourt and Richmond pennants entwined that flew from the castle's miniature towers.

Their conversation comforted Gunnhild, who was loath to allow her precious memories of Maud to easily slip from her. Hilde joined in adding her own reflections, swearing that of all the ladies present Gunnhild was the most magnificently dressed. Hilde was young, sent to Richmond by her English father, a merchant of York, so that she could learn the ways of the nobility. Gunnhild smiled to herself. She would make an excellent court lady one day if she married well. It was Hilde who had dressed Gunnhild for the wedding in the blue silk gown with trailing sleeves and it was she who had plaited her hair into a knot at the nape of her neck and placed her opus anglicanum embroidered veil over it. With her pearls released from captivity, Gunnhild knew that she had looked her best.

She reached over and squeezed Hilde's hand. 'One day soon you will be a beautiful bride, and you will have a handsome and very wealthy bridegroom.'

Hilde seemed delighted at the thought, smiling like a cat offered a rich lick of cream even though she said, 'My lady, not for some time. I would not leave your side too soon.'

As the first stage of riding stretched though the warm September morning, Gunnhild began to smile, too. Hilde was easy company, compensating a little for Niall's aloofness.

At night they stopped at monasteries, pushing on at daybreak, unfurling a linen cloth under trees at midday and picnicking on pies and pastries, bread and cheese washed down with watered ale. Trees shivered dryly and leaves rattled if the slightest breeze caught them. The south possessed a warmer climate, one she remembered fondly from her childhood. Ducks on ponds quacked, tame geese honked, marsh birds, corncrakes and wild geese common to these flatlands of Norfolk flew above them criss-crossing the flawless sky above. They met pilgrims who travelled in bands, moving over trackways towards shrines, generously scattered like manna, along the way. They rode with merchants who possessed huge sacks on their wagons and who were followed by their own small private armies. They passed villeins heading out to the great fields with sickles and knives preparing to bring in the last of the grain harvest and stow it away safely in tall barns. There were encounters with travelling monks and, as they entered Cambridge, a choir of canons came towards them chanting plainsong and then veered through a gate that led into the precinct of yet another new monastery church. As they rode through Essex they could smell salt pans bringing the fresh smell of the sea on a breeze inland. She slept well at night sharing her bed with Hilde, her mood lightening joyfully the further away from Richmond they travelled.

Gradually Niall thawed. Nearing London, they rode close together again as they had done many times over the years in the north, but on this occasion they avoided conversation about themselves. They discussed Lincoln, the wedding and the d'Aincourts, the towns they had passed through, the clement weather and even the stars shining down from clear night skies.

Slowly she found herself renewing the feeling of closeness they had felt before Alan had returned from Brittany that year. Simply, Niall made her heart lift and her body longed for his. It was an illicit love and deeply sinful. She could never deny her love for him, though sadly she wondered if she must endeavour harder to control her desire, as must he.

It took them a further day of travel to reach the north route into London. As they rode from the Essex villages down gentle slopes towards the city's walls, Gunnhild exclaimed, 'It is a city of bells. Even in my childhood London's bells always peeled. for every hour.' Again they rang, this time for Vespers, following each other, pursuing and competing, as if announcing that travellers were entering a city of monasteries, abbeys and nunneries.

Niall said back, 'You will find it changed, Gunnhild. London is a city reborn, busy with commerce. Wait until you catch a glimpse of the wharfs and the new streets strung out along the river.'

She twisted from side to side looking with excitement at the many two-storied houses and gardens that stretched towards the old city walls. Then they were through Cripplegate.

'One night here and then on to Canterbury,' Niall said as they dismounted in the courtyard of Bermondsey Minster and Abbey. Their guard took possession of their mounts, intending to get stable boys to rub them down whilst Niall went to inspect the place where they were to lay their heads that night.

On his return, Niall swept them up as if he was the monastery's custodian. 'Come, my ladies. The abbot is waiting to greet you. He is a friend to Richmond and a distant relative to my own mother.' Gunnhild had never asked him about his mother. He never mentioned her, but it was reassuring to her that Niall was not a full brother to Alan. Surely that made their sin a lesser offence in God's strange reckoning?

Early the next morning they met in the pilgrims' refectory to break their fast on bread rolls and buttermilk. The abbot, an aged man whose face was creased like crumpled cloth, joined them. 'So, my lady is to Canterbury? Did you know that the great Abbot Anselm of Bec has been in residence at the Bishop's Palace in Canterbury since the calends of August? You will meet that noble and fine human, though he is made of such goodness he is more like an angel.' He lowered his voice. His long face sank towards his dark chest. 'He will be Archbishop after Lanfranc ...' He paused as if he was over-reaching himself. Then he threw caution away. 'Lanfranc is well past seventy years. Anselm will be a breath of fresh air.' He patted her arm in a fatherly manner. 'And your mother, Lady Gunnhild, I met her a year since. She is a most gracious lady.' He looked from Gunnhild to Niall. 'Ah, how times have changed. I pray every day that this land will settle into a more comfortable age as King William himself ages. Ah, indeed, indeed, like myself, too.' He let go a sigh.

Niall lifted his cup, drained it of buttermilk, and said, 'Abbot, we pray for peaceful and plentiful times too.' He stood and pushed his chair back. 'But we must be on our way if we are to be in Canterbury by St Calixus.'

The old abbot studied Niall, his small inquisitive eyes steady below the ridge of his dark brow. He looked at Gunnhild again, then back at Niall. 'Your brother is this lady's husband is he not? Where is he? What nature of man is he who leaves a beautiful wife in another's care?'

'Alan has business in Normandy trading wool and then he intends visiting his estates in Brittany. There is a family land dispute we must discuss with Lady Elditha in Canterbury.'

'I see. Ah, the great survey. The clerks have been to me as well. We have been counted, our goods and chattels outside the city, too. We have lost some lands and gained some lands.' He sighed again. 'It is God's will. Fortune's wheel is turning, I fear.' Then he patted Gunnhild's arm with his bony hand. 'But may it turn in your favour, my lady.'

They knelt for the abbot's blessing, the others following their mistress's direction, and the aged abbot made the sign of the cross over each of their heads. 'May God and His holy angels be with you.' When they rose, he once again looked from Niall to Gunnhild with a flicker of concern in his grey eyes. She silently whispered her own prayer to St Brigit, 'Protect us all.'

Hilde rode in the wagon with Emma and their maid. Her mare was in need of a new shoe and Niall said that once they were on the Canterbury road they would stop at a blacksmith's forge that he knew from other journeys south. He tethered the mare behind the wagon and told the guard to watch it carefully. Gunnhild smiled to see Hilde peering out through the curtains as it rattled over the stony streets past churches and shops with opened shutters selling everything one could desire, saddle decorations, bridle ornaments, materials, leather goods, ribbons, silks, bobbles for the ladies. The girl exclaimed at the crowds of people, the knights with bright armour that gleamed rosy in the rising sun's glow, the morning street traders with trays of bread and pies, the barking of dogs, shrieking of cats as they were kicked to one side, the chirruping of caged birds, the rat

287

catchers, their poles strung out with their prey, and general toing and froing.

Gunnhild stayed close to Niall as they rode on through London's narrow streets until they were approaching the bridge that crossed the wide river. It was even busier here. Niall shouted back to his soldiers, 'If we are separated regroup at the sign of The Hawk. It is the last inn out of Southwark. Do not take any side lanes, forge on straight.' He reminded their guard, 'Men, you must stay by the wagon. I shall stay with Lady Gunnhild.' He took Gunnhild's reins and drew Blackbird closer to his own horse, 'Hold onto the pommel. I want your horse neck and neck with mine in case we lose you to the crowd.' He touched his sword hilt as if to emphasise potential danger.

Gunnhild bent over and grasped her saddle pommel. As if he spoke just in time, a procession of carts crossing the bridge stopped the wagon's forward movement. Glancing back, Gunnhild saw their guard protectively gather around the wagon. Niall called to her, 'They shall be safe. Wulfric will make sure the men stay with your ladies.'

They clattered on over the bridge. About midway across a band of lepers surged forward from the shelter of buildings that ranged along each side, ringing bells and with streams of incoherent words pouring out of their ruined mouths. She loosened her grip on the pommel and dug into the purse she kept safely concealed below her mantle, but there was only a silver penny. 'Niall help them, please. They are God's chosen.' Niall reached into his own purse and withdrew a handful of coins. He tossed them into the crowd of outreached fingers, crippled limbs and ghostly faces that had gathered around them. 'Now go, and with God's peace,' he called down in a gentle voice. 'Let my lady through.' He caught her bridle, tugged on her reins, clicked his tongue at their horses and forced them both through the crowd. The lepers scattered, clutching the alms.

Once they had come off the bridge she caught glimpses of the gleaming white tower rising on the other side of the wide river. It was the greatest symbol of the Conqueror's power. It made her feel sad for a moment for all her people had lost. At last, they left it behind and were riding along the road that ran through Southwark's huts, halls, orchards and copses, but every time they looked over their shoulders they still could not catch sight of their wagon or their guard. They were lost amongst the crowds that were still swarming in both directions. She felt Niall's breath on her cheek as he bent down and released her reins. In that moment she glanced up at him and their eyes met. He took her reins back, drew her mare close again, bent his head to hers and kissed her on the lips, unconcerned that there were still carts and pedestrians passing them. She lifted her head to receive his kiss and then she returned his with one of her own that was equally as deep.

'Look out!'

At the shout, Gunnhild started and pulled away, though Niall, oblivious to the cry in front of their horses, held onto her reins with her hands folded into his own. She jerked her head up. There was something familiar about the sharp voice she had heard shouting at them. A monk was seated on the platform of a long wagon that was stopped ahead. Now that he had caught her attention he called up to her, 'If you sin, you will reap God's wrath.'

His wagon was waiting by the left verge. Four dark monks in long habits were lounging by its side. One spat a huge green gobbet at Blackbird's hoofs. 'Shameless!' the monk shouted up to her. 'God will punish you both.'

'What is going on?' a harsh voice called from the apple orchard to the side of the track. Gunnhild and Niall together looked in the direction of the apple trees to where a group of nuns had gathered around a travelling screen. A trickle of yellow urine flowed from it, out and along a gully in the road. The owner of the harsh voice emerged from behind it, hurrying as if rushing from a storm, straightening her black habit. She paused, looked up at Niall and then at Gunnhild, her eyes widening with recognition. She studied them for a moment, her small beaded eyes still recognisable in her yellowing complexion. Just as Gunnhild recognised Christina of Wilton,

Christina had clearly remembered her.

'Lady Christina, my greetings,' Gunnhild said clearly. 'Are you well?'

'As well as the good Lord permits. What brings you to London, King Harold's daughter? I thought you to be in Richmond with that thief.' She straightened her dark cloak and adjusted her wimple. 'And who is this? Unless Alan of Richmond has grown younger and changed his appearance, he is not the one who holds your hands now.'

'Whore,' grumbled the monk.

'Be silent, Brother Francis, do you not recognise her? No, you would not. She is grown up since your time in her mother's household.'

Gunnhild glanced from Christina to the aged monk. 'Brother Francis!' she whispered, her words hardly audible. The last time she had seen this monk was at Wilton years before Aunt Edith had died. She was sure he had accompanied Alan when he had passed through the abbey on his way to Exeter in 1068. Since then she had changed from a ten-year-old girl into a woman approaching her thirtieth year but he was still the same, just older, but still thin and mean-looking.

'You are clearly full of whore's tricks. You deserve to be whipped naked about the churchyard,' the monk croaked.

Christina interjected, 'Harsh words, Brother Francis, though certainly penance is in order.' She turned her attention to Gunnhild. 'You belong in Wilton,' Christina said. 'You are our property, do you hear me, you and your lands. You never belonged elsewhere and certainly not with that man who seized our rightful inheritance when he took you to be his concubine.'

'We were married in God's house, as you well know,' Gunnhild said with courage, inwardly shuddering as passers-by were pausing to watch. Unless their guard caught up, the gathering crowd was capable of dragging her off her horse and marching her into the nearest churchyard for her penance.

Christina ignored them. She shouted at Gunnhild. 'God will be your judge. A flighty girl you were then and clearly you are a flighty woman. You still need the discipline of the convent and God's forgiveness if you are not to burn in the fires.' Christina gathered her cloak closer as if to shut out evil. 'We must press on to Wilton to do God's business. We have loftier things on our minds this day than a woman who has sinned and is still sinning.' She could not resist the boast. 'We have preparations to make for a visit from the eminent Abbot of Bec.'

'Abbot Anselm?'

'The same. I expect you are on your way to Canterbury. You will have no joy there if you are after estates in Kent and halls in Canterbury. They all belong to Wilton now.' Christina curled her upper lip, stared for a moment from Niall to Gunnhild and added. 'I shall pray for your redemption.' Christina, still agile, climbed into the curtained wagon followed by her darkly clad nuns, all with a swish of dusty skirts and the wearing of sour faces, all except for one who paused and looked lovingly back at Gunnhild. She smiled and with that smile her face came alive. Gunnhild started. She could never mistake that wide-eyed look or the smile that lit up that gentle face. It was Eleanor. Memories flooded back. She opened her mouth and closed it as Eleanor mouthed, 'God speed, Gunnhild.'

The crowd began to disperse as Brother Francis climbed on to the driving board, took the reins of the cob, and flicked a hazel switch at its rump. At that the horse slowly moved forward. 'Wait, brother!' one of the armed monks shouted. The wagon halted further along the road. Two monks ran to the verge, folded the portable screen, hurried after the litter and loaded it into the back of the wagon. Without another word the group moved off. Eleanor glanced back at Gunnhild and lifted her hand in a small wave. They were gone, rattling along the road, mingling into traffic, vanishing into another crowd. Gunnhild lifted her hand and waved to the disappearing wagon. Eleanor's life belonged in a place behind latticed screens, a life of prayer in candlelit chapels and contemplation in quiet cloisters.

'What an unpleasant woman,' Niall said to Gunnhild, giving her the reins again. 'We should wait here and allow some distance between us and that parcel of bitterness. Thank the Virgin that they are not on the road to Canterbury.'

'But they will have conversation with Abbot Anselm.'

'There is little to tell.'

'A kiss,' Gunnhild said softly as Blackbird stepped through the drying yellow stream that Christina had left behind her. 'A dangerous kiss. That crowd looked like they wanted fun at my expense. The priest had only to say the word and they would have had me out of my saddle.'

'They would not dare. One precious kiss. Pray, my lady, it is not the last.' He reined around. 'Our guard is coming.' She turned her head back towards the bridge.

'Yes, they are,' she said. 'And lucky they missed the Wilton nun.'

'Lucky for us, perhaps, that we did not need them.'

On seeing them waiting, Emma shouted out hardly able to contain her excitement. 'My lady, did you see the jongleurs on the bridge?'

'They were dancing and throwing yellow balls into the sky. They were catching them even through the press of people and wagons,' Hilde added, reminding Gunnhild that until meeting Christina the journey to Canterbury had been light-hearted, filled with new experiences for her maids. She determined not to darken their mood because of one unpleasant encounter on the road.

'Indeed, and did you see an angel and the devil on a cart?' she laughingly said back.

'We did, we did and they said they were off to St Paul's to cast judgement over the sinners. The devil chuckled and pointed his sceptre at us and we nearly tumbled from the cart in fright.' Emma gave a little pretend shudder. 'Then the angel leaned over, kissed my head and blessed me.'

'So we are on the road to Canterbury,' Hilde said, peering around at the orchards that opened up on each side of the road. She looked up at Niall. 'My horse needs his shoe. Then I can be back riding alongside my Lady Gunnhild.'

Niall waved them forward. 'The blacksmith's dwelling is

292

less than a furlong away.' He lightly tugged his horse's reins and set him off at a walk with Blackbird following.

25

In the city of Canterbury King Edward had 51 burgesses paying rent and 212 others over whom he had sake and soke, and 3 mills rendering 40s. Now there are 9 burgesses paying rent. Of the houses 11 are waste in the city ditch, and the archbishop has 7 of them, and the Abbot of St Augustine's 14 others in exchange for the site of the castle ... Ralph de Courbepine has 4 messages in the city which a certain concubine of Harold held, the sake and soke of which are the king's; but hitherto he has not had it.

The Domesday Book, a Complete Translation, ed. by
Dr Ann Williams and Professor G. H. Martin, 2003

When the ancient city walls of Canterbury reached up before Gunnhild, she turned to Niall and said, feeling uncomfortable and anxious, 'My mother owned houses and weaving sheds here. Now she is a nun. How everything changes.'

'If she is content, that matters,' he replied, putting her at her ease.

They rode through a high archway and found themselves on a long cobbled street. The town had grown over the eighteen years since Gunnhild had last seen it as a child and had become a spider's web of lanes and streets. Even so, it was not difficult to find their accommodation since it was one of the most elegant buildings in the town, set in its own courtyards, surrounded by pollarded trees. The bishop's palace stood close to the new castle that overlooked the town.

As they rode into the palace lane and crossed a rushing stream, a gatekeeper popped up behind the thick wooden bars of a gateway and asked their business. When Niall said that Lady Gunnhild, wife of Alan of Richmond, daughter of Harold of Wessex, was expected, he bowed low and had his boys rush to open the entrance gate. 'God bless the lady,' he said, bowing again as they rode in, followed by the wagon with Gunnhild's ladies and the inquisitive wide-eyed maid who stared all around as their driver guided the cart towards the palace buildings.

They were welcomed by Bishop Odo's steward, a tonsured, plump, smiling man, who, when he realised that the visitors from Count Alan's Honour of Richmond had arrived, welcomed them with warmth and told them that their chambers were prepared. He showed the women their sleeping chamber and immediately disappeared with Niall back down the wide stone stairway. Clearly Niall was to sleep in a distant part of the palace.

Gunnhild directed their maid to unpack her travelling coffer in the large room where the ladies had beds with feather mattresses. She remarked to Hilde, 'We should be grateful. In comparison to the beds we have been sleeping in, this is luxury.'

'It is heaven.' Hilde bounced on one of the two beds and fingered the rich curtain.

Gunnhild supervised Grete's unpacking of her travelling chest. Her clothing included her aunt's green silk dress. She would take pleasure in wearing it when she visited her mother. Retrieving it from the deep leather coffer, she held it up, asked Hilde to brush it and hang it on the clothing pole by the window. Hilde dutifully set to work, hanging it where light shone on it. The gown looked beautiful, still not a moth hole in the silk. The flowered hem with its pale jewels glowed in the beams of patterned light. Gunnhild sank onto a cushioned bench by the large bed and stared at it and then at the undergown hanging beside it. The longer she looked, the more convinced she was that the small darn which, though it had been carefully mended with the tiniest of stitches, remained visible, a reminder of a long-ago midsummer's eve.

That evening she walked in the cloisters with Niall. Hilde walked behind at a distance, looking down at a small book which she held opened as she followed them. Anyone watching would suppose that they were all slipping quietly to prayer.

Niall spoke in a low voice. 'Your accommodation, Gunnhild, is it better than the flea-ridden hole we slept in last night?'

'It is a great chamber, and its windows are set with coloured glass.'

'Good. Now, tomorrow, when you visit St Augustine's, do you want me to accompany you? The land problem could be difficult to explain.'

'No, I must do this alone. I shall take Hilde. She will enjoy meeting Abbess Elizabeth.'

'Of course.' He glanced over his shoulder. Hilde had paused at a statue of the Virgin. Her head was bowed and her lips moved as if in prayer. Niall clasped Gunnhild's hand into his own. 'Tell me, truly, was your mother as beautiful as they say?'

'Who says? Alan?'

'Her beauty was renowned. I caught a glimpse her myself as a young soldier when they brought her to the camp at Hastings. Her skin was white and once I saw her hair I think I was half in love with her. It was thick and the colour of corn.' He reached up and touched Gunnhild's hair where it escaped from the veil that covered it. 'Golden like your own.' He looked at her with longing. 'How I would love to unpin your hair now and watch it fall.' He playfully tugged her veil. She moved away from him.

'I think it not the right time, Niall.' She glanced about her. The cloisters were deep with shadows. A sundial stood in a square of moonlight. An archway opposite stood empty. Yet she sensed movement, as if someone was watching from it. She blinked and caught Niall's sleeve. What she had thought to be a cloak had moved into the archway's hollow. 'Just look over there,' she whispered. 'I am sure somebody is waiting in the shadows.'

Niall followed her glance, looked hard for a moment, turned back to her and said, 'If there was, he has gone. And, there was nothing for him to see; just two fellow-travellers on their way to prayer with their maid close behind them.' He took her hand and squeezed it. 'Never fear, sweeting, nobody knows.'

She let go of his hand-clasp. *Except God, and perhaps Christina who thinks she knows and would put such knowledge to use if she thought she might gain from it.*

The following day she rode out to St Augustine's priory, recently rebuilt after a fire had destroyed its buildings. The new priory gleamed white amongst placid meadows. The two women handed their horses' reins to a stable lad and crossed a green swathe to the receiving hall. There they were greeted by Prioress Elizabeth who gave Hilde over to two nuns who would show her over the buildings whilst Gunnhild spoke with her mother. Gunnhild followed the quiet Prioress through the cloisters and left her by the door into the apartment where Elditha was dwelling in considerable comfort. With trepidation bubbling Gunnhild knocked. A voice called out, 'Enter'. Prioress Elizabeth touched her arm and said softly, 'I shall return later, my child.' She could hear the nun's departing tread as she hurried back through the cloister.

She stood in the doorway unable to speak. Her heart foundered until her mother turned from a desk by a long window and stepped forward to greet her. She was as tall as Gunnhild had remembered, her hair concealed by a wimple and her face serene. She reached out her hands to Gunnhild and said, 'I have been anticipating this for days, ever since the messenger came to say you were on your way south to visit me. And yesterday when the Bishop's messenger came to say you had arrived, well, I need not tell you, sleep eluded me last night.'

She came closer, her hands outstretched, all the time gazing at Gunnhild's face. 'Welcome, daughter.' Elditha reached out and clasped Gunnhild to her breast. She held her back and studied her. For a moment they stared at each other without words. Although so many years had passed, Gunnhild was surprised at how familiar her mother seemed. Her eyes were the same green with flecks of hazel and though she wore a close-fitting wimple of starched linen, a little of her grey hair escaped onto her cheek. Elditha's dress was a nun's plain overgown of wool with loosely hanging sleeves. Pleats of snowy linen peeped below them at the wrist. A silver belt cinched her small waist and from it hung scissors, a thimble and a bunch of keys.

They let go another long embrace and for a moment Gunnhild looked away. Her mother's chamber was light and smelled of late autumn roses. There was a wide bed with green linen curtains, decorated with a border of gold. A harp lay on a side table in a corner. *She must still play it.* Gunnhild looked at her mother again, a tall, serene lady who, now past fifty, was still handsome.

'Let us walk to my bee hives,' Elditha said. 'You are grown up, Gunnhild, and I hardly know what to say to you. And that gown, do I recognise it perhaps?' She tapped her chin with a finger. 'Ah, I believe it belonged to your Aunt Edith? Come, if we walk in the sunshine we can relax with each other's company and you can tell me about life in the north. '

'This gown did belong to Queen Edith, Mother. I inherited it and now I wear it for special occasions such as today.' She absently touched the small leather satchel by her hip. It contained the land document and a gift for Elditha. But these could wait.

'You are a beauty, Gunnhild.' Elditha touched her daughter's face and as she did a frown crossed her brow. She turned away from her daughter and lifted the latch of a door that opened into another cloister. Gunnhild followed her out into a garden.

'Well, tell me, how has this marriage treated you, Gunnhild?' Elditha said as she opened a low gate to a herb garden.

So that explained her mother's unease. It must be the marriage to Count Alan.

Gunnhild breathed in the scents of thyme and lavender. Dare she tell the truth to the woman who had rejected Count Alan many years before? She breathed the scent of lavender again and then found words. Now that she was with her mother she could not hold back. Once she began, her story began to pour out as they walked, her satchel swinging softly by her hips. She hardly noticed that they had already passed through the garden and had reached a pleasant apple orchard. Gunnhild stopped speaking. She had only spoken of her leave-taking of Wilton.

299

There was so much more to explain.

Elditha indicated a bench by a pile of woven skeps and Gunnhild spread the skirt of her gown and sank onto it. 'We have privacy here,' Elditha remarked. 'There are many wagging tongues in this place. Tell me the rest ...'

Gunnhild told her about the happiness of her early days, Brittany and their return to Richmond with a small daughter, how after that terrible labour all those years ago she had never conceived again. She told her about the winter of measles and the deaths, of the winters of famine and the visit of Sir Edward earlier that summer. She then recounted how they had rescued Maud and how she had been betrothed, married at nine years old and sent to her husband's family in Lincoln. Yes, thankfully, Maud was going to be happy there. She finally said that Count Alan was rarely with her but that his brother helped her with her care of Castle Richmond. When she saw that Elditha was frowning at this part of her story she could not resist saying, 'I heard that Count Alan wanted to marry you, my lady mother.'

Elditha's frown turned into a smile. 'That is an old story. He was hardly older than your brothers. And, of course, he was responsible for the destruction of Reredfelle.'

'I thought King William was responsible.'

'They were both responsible and I cannot forgive them.' Elditha folded her hands and said, 'Now, daughter, have you come with a request?' Gunnhild inhaled a long breath. The question hung in the air.

She clasped her hands together and said, 'Mother, Alan asked me to show you a land document that he has had drawn up.' She opened her satchel and drew out a tight scroll from which a seal dangled. When she handed it over, Elditha broke the seal, opened it, laid it on her knee and began to read it slowly.

She glanced up. 'Gunnhild, this refers to my Kent properties. It includes Reredfelle. Many of these estates will go to Wilton Abbey. Some belong to the crown, others to this convent and the monks' church of St Augustine.' She smiled. 'They could never be your lands anyway because by Norman law all that goes to you becomes your husband's possessions.' She reached over and placed a hand on Gunnhild's hand. 'They are disputed estates, but some of them must go to Wilton because one day, my daughter, you may seek sanctuary there.'

'I could never return to Wilton, my lady mother.'

'I hope then that that day does not come, but it is wise to be pragmatic. I have your interests at heart, and your father's family have always had their daughters educated in Wilton. We have long given Wilton our support. I cannot and will not allow Count Alan to purloin the Wessex properties. So, my dearest daughter, this must be an end to a gathering of Wessex lands.' She handed Gunnhild back the scroll. 'Take it to him and tell him I say no. In any case, a petition from me will make no difference to the outcome. Alan may be a cousin to the King but I believe that the matter has been decided by Archbishop Lanfranc.'

Gunnhild nodded. 'It will not please him. I have done my duty by him and clarified the matter with you. I have no desire to take land from Wilton or from St Augustine. In fact, it pleases me to think he will not get his way on the matter.' She smiled and tucked the charter into her satchel.

Elditha rose. 'Now let us take a look at my bees. After that we can return to my chamber to eat honey cakes and take a cup of wine together.' Gathering her dark skirts she rose from the bench, slipped her arm through Gunnhild's and walked her around the bee hives. For a moment, as Gunnhild peered into a skep seeking the queen amongst the bevy of singing bees, she understood why her mother was enchanted by this peaceful orchard, by the minutiae of nature. She keenly felt the presence of the mother for whom she suddenly felt an overpowering love. Yet, it was mingled with the sadness of loss. As she discovered the queen bee at rest amongst the labouring bees, she wondered if she would ever meet her mother again this side of heaven.

* * *

When they returned to the abbey building and were sitting

companionably with cups of honeyed wine and small sweet cakes, Elditha spoke about Gunnhild's brothers and sisters. 'I wish it had all been different. I am old now and I accept everything has changed out in the world, except one thing. I cannot believe your brother Ulf is a squire at Robert Curthose's court and still a prisoner. I suppose I must be grateful that this Robert who wars with his own father has befriended our Ulf.'

'My sister?' Gunnhild asked. 'She is well?'

'She is wed to the Prince of Kiev. If I were not approaching my dotage I would travel across Europe to see her. She has children of her own. She called her first son Harold for her father.' With these words Elditha's eyes appeared to cloud over. Gunnhild reached out to her, 'Mother, perhaps you still can visit your grandchildren.'

'I think it unlikely.' Elditha wiped away her tears with her hand. 'It seems I have all but lost my children, all of you, whom I love so much, and though I may not see you, you all dwell within my heart. Remember this, Gunnhild, in case we never meet again. You are part of me. You will always be so. I have prayed for you daily since you were nine years old and will continue to do so every day that remains to me.' There was a gentle rapping on the door. 'Come in,' Elditha called. The Abbess Elizabeth pushed it open and stepped inside. 'My lady, Anselm of Bec has come to see you.' She glanced at Gunnhild. 'But should I send him away?'

Elditha said, 'Send him in, Prioress. He must meet my daughter.'

Gunnhild, knowing her allotted time was drawing to a close, laid her cup down and lifted her satchel from the floor. She withdrew a book from it. 'It is for you, Mother, a book of St Cecilia.'

Elditha took it to the table and opened it. She gasped as she saw the perfect calligraphy and exquisite drawings – St Cecilia with her harp, and the creatures peeping out from roses, cornflowers and daisies that danced along the margins. She carefully turned over a page. There was her saint again, this time kneeling in prayer with a golden halo placed above her head. With a delicate touch, Elditha traced the gold leaf on the miniature hovering circle.

Abbess Elizabeth came to the table where the book lay opened. A tall elderly man in a simple monk's robe slipped in behind her and stood silently at Elditha's elbow. The man looked down on the beautiful drawings and illuminations, and delicately drew back the tiny scraps of linen that protected many of them. 'This is a work of great beauty,' he sighed as he turned the pages carefully again and lifted another fragile curtain to see the illustrations. 'Where did you come by such a precious thing?' He addressed her and as he did, seemed to look into her soul. In his countenance she saw wisdom so profound and intelligence so sharp she immediately felt at ease.

'I made it, Abbot Anselm,' she said simply. 'I was allowed to work in the scriptorium when I lived at Wilton Abbey. I drew and I wrote. I preferred the drawing of letters to embroidery. I work on vellum when I can. Mostly I use parchment.'

'You have a great talent. It is Wilton's loss that you saw a different calling, daughter.'

Elditha sighed. 'She brings this precious gift for me, Anselm.' She touched Gunnhild's arm. 'It is too valuable, Gunnhild.'

'It took me many years, but, yes, my mother, it is for you, my gift to my mother who has suffered so much.'

'And who has found peace.' Elditha closed the curtain covering the last page and then the book. Looking up she said, 'It will give me such pleasure to look on this when you are gone.' She clasped Gunnhild close to her and whispered, 'My sweet child, now I must speak with my old friend, Abbot Anselm, today, before he journeys on to Wilton.'

Knowing their meeting had come to its end, Gunnhild lifted her satchel and followed Abbess Elizabeth to the door. For a few hours it had been as if time had paused, as if she was a small girl once again, pouring out her heart to her mother as she had done in her childhood. She glanced back and saw her mother watching after her. 'Come again, daughter,' Elditha called softly.

303

'Before we depart Canterbury, I shall come to say goodbye.' She took one final look at her mother's pretty chamber, her small altar, a painted Madonna hanging above it, the carved table, shuttered windows and her bed covered with green linen curtains embroidered with gold.

Gunnhild collected Hilde from the refectory where she was chattering with a group of novices over a cup of elderberry cordial. She patted her satchel as, accompanied by the jingling of their bridle bells, she rode out of the courtyard reflecting that she did not care a fig for Count Alan's disappointment when he discovered her latest failure.

Alan had not returned from Brittany when they rode into Richmond after a slow, uneventful journey up the Great North Road. Gunnhild spent October at Richmond preserving fruit in jars, which she sealed with wax stoppers, pickling onions in vinegar, clearing her herb garden and gathering apples in the orchard which she carefully laid by in straw to see them through the winter. She missed Maud but kept busy, passing her evenings writing her new book dedicated to St Brigit, her own name-day saint.

As the month passed and Alan sent no word of his return, Niall slipped through the castle after the midnight bell rang and discreetly shared Gunnhild's bed. He disappeared back to his gatehouse before dawn. If Ann and Hilde or any others close to Gunnhild harboured the suspicion that Niall visited her chamber under cover of darkness none spoke of it.

Count Alan clattered over the bridge and through the gatehouse entrance on a November morning of clinging spider webs and swirling mists. He discovered Gunnhild in the still room supervising the making of beer, an apron wrapped about her gown and her hair escaping her close linen work wimple.

He never embraced her, nor did he greet her with any semblance of affection. He had not ridden straight to Richmond from York but had stopped to spend the night in Alfred's Hall at Well. 'Wife, I must speak with you in private,' he said to her, his brow darkening. There was anger in his face.

She sent her maids away and told them to return to finish the brewing after they had changed the linen on his bed, dusted and prepared a bath tub for him. Turning back to Alan, she said, 'We are private here.' She poured him a cup of beer. 'Drink. Then say what you have to say.' She pushed the cup over the table to him, refilled a jug and sat it beside his cup.

He gulped down the beer and wiped the froth from his mouth remarking, 'It is good beer.' He paused. 'Uhtred of Middleton has been allowed to return to his estates. He remains as under-tenant on my estates. The King has pardoned him for his attempted abduction of Maud when the bastard should have been punished. Robert of Durham had a hand in that decision.' Alan set his cup down on the table and pointed a gauntleted hand at her. 'And you, Gunnhild, you have not helped matters. You were sent to Canterbury and your mother refuses her help. The King has granted her Wessex lands to Wilton, to St Augustine in Canterbury and to that greedy bishop, his half-brother Odo, who has begged the king's forgiveness. He is another bastard who has managed to get your mother's lands, our lands.'

Gunnhild wiped her hands on her apron. 'They are not my mother's lands to grant away. The King owns everything. They were never "our lands", Alan.'

'Mind this,' he said. 'The King gives lands and castles into the care of his barons. I am one of his most important tenants in chief in England. With the numbers of soldiers William is billeting on my castles in the north and on my houses elsewhere I need rent from all the land I can get to feed them.' He glared. 'I should never have trusted you or your mother, Gunnhild. You did not represent our case.'

She raised her left eyebrow. '*Our case*, my lord? Surely you mean *your case*. In this world I am nothing, at least not in your world. Must I remind you I am a woman with little power? Now, if you are finished I think you should go and cool your temper in the bath tub. I have work here.'

He did not move but instead poured himself another cup. In a more reasoned voice he said, 'You do have your own property, Gunnhild. You have a dower castle in Brittany. And I can vouch for it being a very comfortable castle too.'

Gunnhild sank onto the bench opposite him. 'You have been there?'

Alan grunted, 'I did not stay in Dinan.'

'And Agenhart?'

'A girl. She gave birth to a girl. I took Agenhart to Castle Fréhel to recover from a difficult birth.'

Gunnhild bit her lip and swallowed her furious retort. Agenhart had stayed in her castle, had used her bedchamber, eaten in her hall. She did not ask how they had named the child. She could not bring herself to complain and for good reason, except to say with bitterness for all that was lost between them, 'Are they still living in Fréhel Castle, Alan? If so I do not want her there.'

'No, they are back in Dinan. Agenhart has her own property in the town. She has maids and cooks and skilled silk workers.' He looked up from his beer cup. 'She has her own cloth business in Dinan, you know. She brings silk cocoons in from Spain. My merchants sell her fabrics for her.'

For a moment, Gunnhild felt envious of Agenhart, a woman with her own business, and her own independence. Alan was staring at her as if he had noticed her for the first time since he had stormed into her still room. 'You look in good health, glowing. Clearly travelling to Canterbury has done well by you.'

She ignored his compliment. 'How long are you with us, this time, Alan?' She busied herself with jars, moving them around a shelf.

'I shall stay in Richmond until after the Christmas feast, then I shall return to Normandy. There is a suspicion that in the spring Robert Curthose will march against his father again. This time Niall will accompany me. We need all the commanders we can muster.'

She closed her eyes. Both of them would march to war and both could be cut down. Alan was experienced, but it had been years since Niall had been in the field. As the enormity of this sank in, she began to hurry about the still room repositioning small barrels. 'How long do you think this war will take?' she asked, turning to face him again.

'We should be done by summer. Curthose will be firmly brought to heel this time.'

'What about the estates here? Niall always acts as tenant in chief during your absences.'

'Hubert will train the troops here and in my castles elsewhere in Yorkshire. If there is trouble he will see that Gregory and the other reeves do their jobs properly.' He jabbed a finger at Gunnhild. 'And you will preside over the manorial courts with Enisant Musard. This time you must do the task I give you properly. All disputes should be settled firmly and fairly. If there is to be a hanging you see to it that the twelve just men act as judge and jury. Enisant Musard of Brough Hall will act as seneschal of Richmond and Uhtred of Middleton will not be one of the twelve judges in the manorial courts.'

'As if that man will ever sit in my hall,' Gunnhild remarked with ice in her voice. She remembered how Lord Uhtred had hinted that he had knowledge of her liaison with Niall. Fearful of what he might know, she bit her lip. He must not accuse her. Thinking quickly, she said, 'I want to visit the abbey of Mary Magdalene in Lincoln this spring, and also, Alan, I can visit our daughter at the same time.'

Alan shrugged. 'I have no objection. A month or two in an abbey will serve you well, wife. It will soften your sharp edges.' He rose to leave. 'I shall tell Enisant Musard that you will not sit in the shire courts with him during the spring sessions. He can have Father Christopher by his side instead. I trust the priest.' He did not add that he never trusted her.

In late January, a few days before Alan and Niall were due to set out for Normandy, they rode with Enisant Musard around the Richmond estates. To Gunnhild's distress, they encountered Uhtred of Middleton, with a tattered-looking servant man, at the fork in the road over the dales, a parting where one track led towards Middleton, the other to outlying villages on the Honour of Richmond.

'Good morning,' Uhtred grunted, reining in his fine piebald stallion.

Alan stared at him, his face darkening. Niall moved his gelding closer to his brother's stallion. Niall spoke first saying, 'You are no friend to us, Uhtred. Be on your way.'

Uhtred looked from Gunnhild to Niall, then to Lord Alan and back to Gunnhild, more than simply a look; it was a penetrative stare by the time he had returned his attention to her. She wondered what he would say and prepared herself for the worst possible scenario. Her legs tensed around Blackbird's girth as fear washed through her. She held his look, however, and did not turn her head away from it. He opened his mouth and closed it again. The soldiers with Count Alan paced forward and drew their swords.

Alan lifted his hand to stop their progress. His words to Uhtred were clear and not intended to invite any communication beyond the necessary. 'Whatever you were going to say, do not say it. Get back to your lands at Middleton and keep to them. And let me remind you that Enisant here will expect the full geld portion, paid on time, on rent day in April.' He turned to Gunnhild. 'Ride on, my lady; we do not waste our time with child abductors.' With these words, Alan reached forward and took hold of the sagging reins which she, in the effort of gathering her self-control, had allowed to drop, and guided her mount onto the path leading away from Middleton and towards his other lands. 'Good riddance,' he muttered to Gunnhild as his guards sheathed their weapons. If Alan suspected her, he was clearly not going to punish her. Her grip around the horse loosened.

On the last day of January Gunnhild watched from the battlements as a troop of their best horsemen rode through a scattering of snow with the azure-and-gold chequered Richmond pennant flying before them, drooping limply as the snow-fall gradually increased. As she watched the column vanish into the snow she sank to the ground clutching the stone wall. Ignoring the chill on her knees she held up her sapphire cross and began to pray. 'Dear God in Heaven, bring them both home safely. Forgive me Lord for my great sin. I care for my lord Alan because he is my lord and we are bound together in your sight and for Niall because despite my greatest will, I cannot stop loving him.'

'My lady.' The call came from the stairway. She rose to her feet. Ann was waiting with a woollen shawl. 'My lady, come in from the battlements. You will catch a chill here.' Gunnhild took the shawl gratefully and allowed Ann to help her descend the steep stone steps. She was at that moment very sad, for Niall, for Alan, and for what should have been between them as husband and wife. Yet she was happy that she had loved, too. When she contemplated the years she considered how life owned great complexities. She wondered if there was any possibility that this love and its accompanying guilt was what God had intended her to experience.

26

Spring 1087-1089

He [King William] who was earlier a powerful king, and lord of many a land, he had nothing of any kind but a seven-foot measure; and he who was at times clothed with gold and with jewels, he lay then covered over with earth.

The Anglo-Saxon Chronicles, trans. and ed. by Michael Swanton, 1996, 2000

The brothers returned safely despite Gunnhild's concerns. King William had died in Normandy on the 10th day of September 1087. Bells pealed for a new king. Now, Alan and Niall found themselves fighting to protect their lands in Normandy from Robert Curthose who had not inherited England, even though he was William's eldest son. The King had divided his kingdom. Curthose inherited Normandy. The dead King's younger son, William, inherited England, which had brought about further strife. 'I shall give William our loyalty,' Alan insisted as he read yet another letter from Westminster, turned it over, laid it aside and continued his game of chess with Niall. He moved his bishop close to his king. Looking up he said, 'He is a young cub, too.' His voice turned bear-like, growling, 'But Curthose is not acceptable to us. We have spent too many years fighting him.'

Gunnhild glanced up from her sewing. 'I am sure that is the best decision.' Niall flipped over the queen he was playing, replaced her, slid her into checkmate and said, 'Game over, new king, new ways.' He lifted a pawn. 'And here *we* are.'

Some of the younger Norman barons supported Robert Curthose's right to inherit it all, England and Normandy, and for years there would be skirmishes in the south. When a summons came to Richmond, Alan would say, 'We go to our young King's aid, Niall. To arms and to London.'

Gunnhild kept a sad silence. Although she had become

resigned to their many departures, she could not become resigned to Alan taking Niall away with him when they were summoned south by the new King, this time to fight rebel barons, supporters of Duke Robert, in the southern counties.

During these years of rebellion, Gunnhild and Niall had no opportunity to meet in the barns or in the woods and certainly never in her chamber. By keeping Niall close it was as if Alan was deliberately blocking their liaison. She was always busy. When they were gone south and, later, after the baron's rebellion was quelled, across the sea to Normandy, she helped the seneschal, Enisant Musard, in whatever way she could.

She presided with him in the hall court on rent days, sitting on the dais with one of her ladies beside her in discreet attendance. At the monthly judgement sessions she helped him and their clerks settle disputes. Together they worked in partnership and gradually she looked forward to Enisant's visits. He was a red-faced man, now past his prime, a grandfather, squat, with a great beard and bushy greying hair. The tenants liked him and she recognised why Alan trusted him. For all his jovial behaviour his mind was sharp as a scimitar, and she recognised another reason for their friendship. Like Alan and Niall, he had fought at Hastings.

'You killed my father,' Gunnhild whispered in a serious tone before they began the first session in the hall. 'Are you about to kill his people?'

'No, lady, and I have wounds to show what a fierce fight your father's army gave us.'

It was true. Enisant could never go to war again. He had taken sword strikes to his legs that caused him to limp. As a consequence, he walked with a stick. His sword arm was weak. She observed grooms helping Enisant on to his horse by the mounting block, and, during the long, frost-rimmed, snow-filled winters he complained to her that his bones ached. 'You are stiff again today, I see, my lord,' Gunnhild said one February day. 'Ann has a remedy, a new cure for your rheumatism. I shall ask her to give you the salve and a prayer.'

'The salve might help but the prayer, perhaps not.' He

312

shifted his weight uneasily on his chair. 'I have prayed enough for relief from the Devil's stiffness. It has not eased in all these years.' He twisted ungracefully into a more comfortable position. 'It is worse.'

'Then the salve without the chant.'

'Maybe.' He shuffled vellum scrolls around. 'So, who do we have today, Gunnhild? Well, my, my, looks like Lord Uhtred wants to cheat us of two chickens, four turkeys, five sacks of wheat and by the Virgin's veil, he has the audacity to withhold a pig.'

'Alan insisted on firmness before they went to fight the new king's enemies.' Gunnhild said as she looked at the document. 'Let us make Lord Uhtred pay.' She glanced up and set her lips into a determined purse. 'I know, let us tell him he owes us six hives' worth of honeybees as well.'

Enisant laughed. 'Done, my lady. Six bee hives. I hope you intend to settle them in your orchard.'

'I do, I do,' Gunnhild replied. She looked to her other side where Hilde was stitching a hem on a napkin. 'I think Hilde might enjoy learning a new skill.'

'What me, my lady?' Hilde glanced up from her lowly stool on hearing her name.

'You will be mistress of my bees. How like you that, Hilde?'

'Very much, my lady, if I am to be excused my lady's chamber pot.'

'Agreed,' Gunnhild whispered.

'Hush, ladies,' Enisant Musard said. He banged his fist on the papers before him, making the ink pots jiggle in a dance as he called down the hall, 'Lord Uhtred of Middleton, step up.'

It was Uhtred's reeve who stepped forward. 'Uhtred,' Gunnhild observed wryly to Enisant, 'clearly has no desire to show his face.'

'We are blessed.'

They passed judgement and Gunnhild was half-a-dozen bee hives richer. She had once heard Hilde boast how she had a way with bees and so Hilde was made mistress of six hives of hibernating bees. When the other ladies asked her about the task she would undertake once the bees awakened, she insisted that she knew all about bee-keeping from her life at her father's home in York where she had often helped their beekeeper when she was a young girl. She looked mischievously at Gunnhild and said she was very happy to be excused toilet duty in my lady's chamber. 'Clouts as well,' she reminded her mistress.

'Yes.' Gunnhild glanced up from her inks and turned round to face the chattering maids. 'Those, too.' She waved a hand in their direction. 'I shall choose one of you for that.' Ignoring the mutters of complaint she returned to her manuscript.

Each spring she set out for Lincoln and stayed in the quiet nun's abbey, but often she would take a cubicle in the monk's scriptorium sometimes helping with the abbey's work of illumination and at others her own new work. She felt the seasons so keenly that she had introduced a calendar into her Book of St Brigit, carefully painting pictures to represent the seasonal tasks on their own lands – winter wood gathering, crafts such as weaving baskets from reeds that grew along the River Ure's edge, the Christmastide feast, the snows and the frozen landscape. She outlined her ladies as they were bent over their spindles. For spring she drew her villeins sowing grain and planting cabbages. She depicted sheep on miniature hillsides, monastery fish ponds and fishermen netting salmon in the rivers. She carefully included the thatcher's repairing of cottages and her ladies in the church procession at Eastertide.

For summer she settled on her own garden fat with produce – salad, onions, beets, carrots and cabbages. Now her ladies were gathering herbs and flowers and in a later illustration seated on a bench under the plum tree stitching embroidery. There were tiny vignettes of haymaking and groups of cows and pigs in the field.

Autumn was golden with beech and oak leaves, tiny grain carts, the mill at Richmond, the church and the priest, red berries, trees full of apples and miniature spiders making miniature webs on tiny neat hedgerows. She included her ladies in this scene dancing a roundel at the harvest feast.

In each seasonal picture Maud, too, had her place with the ladies. Smaller than the others, she wore a blue mantle like the Virgin's cloak, her hair cascading in gold-touched curls down her back. The creamy pages of soft rich vellum grew over the two springs she passed in Lincoln – April in the abbey and throughout the month of May at the manor house in the country where she enjoyed Maud's company.

Maud was growing up. She had reached her eleventh year. The tumbling, loving family of daughters with whom she lived in the great manor house outside Lincoln became her sisters and from them she learned skills such as stitching fine needlework, opus anglicanum, churning butter and how to make new herbal remedies. By the time Gunnhild came for her third annual visit Maud was grown up. She had experienced her first menses, her flowers, and could now be considered a woman.

Walter, her young husband, was learning the skills of war as he joined Niall and Alan to fight the young Norman barons who supported Curthose.

'What household task do you enjoy best?' Gunnhild asked one soft May afternoon as they were cutting out a tiny dress for the latest little sister to wear during the d'Aincourt midsummer revels. The child, Lady Alice's last baby, toddled about the solar getting in their way, demanding her mother's attention.

'Go and play with your kitten.' Alice shooed the toddler off, giving her a bobble on a string with which to tease the creature. 'Well, Maud, what do you enjoy most of all?' she asked, echoing Gunnhild's question. Gunnhild smiled because Lady Alice was not just a good mother. She had become a trustworthy friend.

Maud wrinkled her brow as she considered. 'I enjoy making simples. I like to help sick people get well.'

'In that, sweeting, you follow in your grandmother's footsteps,' Gunnhild said. 'She had cures for everything. She still has.' Elditha had written many times to Gunnhild since her visit to Canterbury, and sometimes sent her a recipe she had discovered to ease the discomfort of winter colds. Her newfound communication with Elditha compensated for the long years of silence. 'Everything changed for my mother when King William died. She can write to me now,' she voiced her thought.

'Of course, everything must change, Mother,' Maud said, glancing up from her stitching. 'There is a new king.'

'Well not just that, but there is something I must tell you, and Lady Alice, too.'

'Oh?' Lady Alice said glancing at her with an eyebrow raised. She bit off a blue thread.

Gunnhild thoughtfully chewed her lip. This would be both difficult and joyful. She had received a letter from Alan when she was staying at the abbey. She began to explain. 'My brother Ulf, your uncle, Maud, was King William's prisoner and now he is set free. Alan has written to say that my brother is to be a knight.' She looked at Maud and Lady Alice and continued, choking back her emotion. 'Alan said that this is Robert Curthose's doing.' Maud's face was wide-eyed, and the other women sat still, their scissors and needles at rest in their hands. Gunnhild swallowed as Alice leapt to her feet. 'But Gunnhild, this is happy news. You will see him again.' She placed an arm about Gunnhild's shoulder. 'When you least expect it he will ride into Castle Richmond with a sword in his belt and a squire by his side.' She put her other arm about Maud's shoulders. 'And he will come to see you in Lincoln, Maud. Won't that be a happy occasion, to see an uncle who has been lost to you?'

'I shall pray for my Uncle Ulf. I hope he comes to see us,' Maud said. It was obvious from her blithe tone that she could only feel for her uncle in a distant way. Gunnhild frowned. Maud was a new generation, half Breton and half English, and even though she was the granddaughter of a king, her daughter could never really understand how deeply her grandparents had suffered when the Normans came and conquered.

Gunnhild said sadly, 'Yes, but only after England and Normandy make peace and Curthose permits him to come here.'

That night Gunnhild cried herself to sleep, for all that was lost, for her father, her brothers, her sister, her mother, for Niall

316

and for Alan who had shown her kindness when he had returned to Richmond last Christmastide. He had, too late, presented her with her jewels on New Year's Day. 'My dear, forgive me. I should never have kept these from you. I am sorry I have not been a kinder husband to you.' This was a strange change of heart. For a moment she scrutinised Alan's face but she saw nothing untoward except that he had grown older and lined. It had all happened so slowly that she had scarcely noticed, but he seemed to be mellowing as age claimed him. She had set the box aside. She had no interest in the jewels now.

Long after he had gone she opened the casket. Inside there was not only her jewels but a new emerald disc brooch for her mantle. She lifted it and turned it round and round and she had a feeling that she had seen Lady Emma wear it at Dol years before. Alan had said, 'Enisant tells me, you have been diligent in your duty here. He says you are Richmond's custodian, not he.' She scrutinized Alan's countenance with concern when he had said this. He had looked haggard and tired; his hair was streaked with more grey than ever and his red beard was turning to white. She wondered if he was ailing but soon after this the brothers burst into renewed action. Obeying a fresh summons, in February they rode out again.

Alan had stood by his great brown stallion, Achilles, as she had held up a cup of warm wine first to him and then to Niall. She gave them both her blessing. Niall's longing for her was achingly obvious on that frozen February morning. After the Richmond pennants batted through an icy wind, she hurried into the cold chapel, knelt before a statue in a wall niche and prayed to St Brigit that both of them would return safely.

From Suffolk to the easterly counties and as far as the northern valleys of Yorkshire, Alan was, she knew, respected as a fair overlord, yet he could be harsh if crossed. He was trusted in a way that Saxon under-lords and Bretons settled on his lands never had faith in King William. That February, Alan and Niall had sailed for Normandy and Brittany where Robert Curthose threatened their lands across the Narrow Sea.

That evening when she retired for the night in the manor

house outside Lincoln, Gunnhild tossed, turned over in her bed, and buried her head in her pillow. She worried about her long-lost brother dwelling at Duke Robert's court and she then began to worry about Niall and Alan. She felt uneasy. Something felt wrong. Towards morning she fell into a restless doze with the sense that Alan and Niall both faced great danger in Normandy.

The following day was so bright and clear that Lady Alice suggested they all passed it outdoors enjoying a break from their usual tasks of sewing, gardening and brewing ale. Maud laughed and said, not her, not today. She wanted to gather herbs in the garden because she was making simples in the still room. She would see them at supper time.

The sun beat down on the women as they sat in the orchard, crumbs from a picnic of soft buttered bread rolls and sweet cakes scattered around them. They plaited daisies into crowns and with sharp-eyed glances from time to time, they watched the younger children climb the apple trees.

It was around mid-afternoon that a sudden wind swelled up causing blackbirds roosting in the hedges to chatter loudly and flap their wings. Gunnhild shivered. A shadow blew through the trees. On the periphery of her vision she noticed a skinny, aged monk appear through the gap in the hedge accompanied by a youthful messenger. Wondering who could be seeking them out, she stared as they came closer. The young man carried a scroll with a familiar seal. 'Brother Francis!' she exclaimed, recognising the monk, her small string of daises crumpling into a pile in her lap. She scrambled to her feet, the daisy chain dropping onto the grass. She trampled them as she moved forward. 'What brings *you* here?' she said, her voice sharp, cutting across his pasty, expressionless face.

Brother Francis folded his hands into his habit sleeves. With a sideways twitch of his head he indicated the messenger who held the letter with the Richmond seal and its dark blue tags. 'This,' he said. 'Your husband has gone to the angelic host which is more than awaits you, Lady Gunnhild, when Death rattles your latch.'

She gasped, caught her breath at his bluntness. 'Explain yourself, monk. What exactly is your meaning?'

'Once, long ago I was a monk in Count Alan's service, one of his priests after the Great Battle. The Count deserved better than an ungrateful member of your family to wife. He deserved better than a woman who shows favour to his brother.'

The youth looked shocked at the priest's rudeness. He knelt and thrust forward the letter he held. With shaking hands Gunnhild took it from him. It was as if an ill-wishing wind was blowing and an icy spell was settling over a happy summer day. After the monk's cruel words, its chill enchantment possessed her from the silken slippers encasing her feet to her lips which had frozen, refusing to open into further speech. Rising, the boy cried out in distress, breaking the terrible spell, 'My lady, I came from Brittany as fast as was possible. First, I rode to the King in London ...' He indicated the monk who had not moved since his outburst. 'Brother Francis was with my lord Anselm of Bec and the King. He said that he would take me to you here ... that you were not at Richmond ... but that you would be with your daughter in Lincoln ... Oh, my lady.' He glanced at Brother Francis. 'My lord Niall sent me, my lady. I am truly sorry. Count Alan is dead.'

She stared down at the seal, afraid to break it. Brother Francis offered in an almost, though not quite, remorseful tone, 'I was on my way to St Mary's in Lincoln this week. I knew you where you were. The nuns told me you came every spring.'

She stared at the missal, still unable to move her fingers to break the seal and open it. Lady Alice stepped forward and, ignoring the monk, addressed the messenger, 'Go and find food and drink in the kitchen. I shall let you know if there is a reply.' She turned to Brother Francis, 'Thank you, Brother Francis for bringing us the messenger. I hope you have a place to rest. You are not welcome here. Your disrespect for Lady Gunnhild, who was Count Alan's very good wife, precludes any possibility of a bed here for you. Be on your way.'

Brother Francis shrugged. 'No matter. I must continue to St

Mary's. You can find me there if you need me.' He turned tail and began to stride back through the orchard.

Gunnhild felt her legs weaken. Alice caught her as she began to collapse. 'What do you know of my lord?' Gunnhild called out to the monk's retreating back. 'What else do you know?'

Alice took her arms, shook her gently and stopped her from following him. 'Gunnhild, the monk knows little. Let him go. Come back to the solar. Read this in private, and with something to revive you,' she said in her quiet manner and called down the orchard to Hilde, who was gathering cornflowers for vases in the hall and had been oblivious to the short encounter. 'Hilde run to the bower and set out a jug of hippocras.' Hilde took one look at her mistress's face, which was pale as parchment, and ran.

Clutching the letter with its seals still unbroken, Gunnhild stumbled back to the bower. Glancing out of the window into the courtyard, she saw Brother Francis clamber onto a palfrey, kick its flanks and tear off through the gate towards the road into Lincoln. St Mary's was Alan's priory, which meant that Brother Francis must know Prioress Ann from the nun's house. He surely would not be so evil as to bend her ears with his slanderous hints. Cautiously she lifted the silver letter knife from a small sideboard, sank into a chair by the window, cut the seals and began to read its contents.

My dear lady,

Greetings from Niall, lord of Richmond, wishing you perpetual health in Christ.

This missive must be brief, but rest assured, my thoughts and concern will be with you and my niece, Matilda, at this terrible time. My brother and your husband's life expired yesterday in the castle at Avranches. He had been hawking in woods close to the castle, was ambushed and took an arrow wound to his stomach which caused him to drop from his stallion. As a consequence he hit his head on a rock. We had not expected any ambush and Alan was without helmet and other armour. His end was swift and that is a blessing. Alan is now with Christ, since a good man cannot linger long in Purgatory. As he often requested when we were on campaign, his burial will be at Bury St Edmunds, three weeks hence on the feast day of St Thomas, the third day of July. I set out for Bury St Edmund with his embalmed body forthwith. Messengers have already gone out to everywhere my gracious brother and lord was known in this world. May you order masses for his soul and may you find strength in Christ at this difficult time. Lord Niall of Richmond.

Gunnhild clutched her stomach, hardly aware of Alice holding her upright and forcing a sip of the honeyed wine into her mouth. 'This will help with the shock, my dove. Ease back in the chair and then breathe. He is gone. There is nothing you can do to change what is. We must be practical and strong, order masses in Lincoln, though no doubt that sorry priest has already precipitated the singing of masses for a man he never knew.'

'Evidently, he once knew Count Alan very well,' Gunnhild said. 'There was a time when Brother Francis was a part of my husband's retinue. That monk has the uncanny ability to appear when he is least expected.' She laid the letter on the table. 'I must tell Maud right now. She is in the still room. And we both must ride south to the Bishop of Bury in the morning. I expect he is already arranging Alan's funeral.'

She touched the letter feeling deeply saddened for Maud and for the loss of a husband she had tried to love but could not. Never would she have wanted him gone. She closed her eyes and in squeezing them tightly shut she could almost imagine once again the day when she had first seen him at Queen Edith's funeral in Westminster. She thought of him standing beside her as the Breton priest joined them in hasty matrimony and she remembered their midnight ride to the coast, the storm at sea, their journey to Castle Fréhel. There was Agenhart, Dorgen and Alan's determination to accumulate a great fortune. She had been part of that plan. Shaking her head she opened her eyes. But, mostly, he had been a fair lord to his tenants and there were many who would remember him fondly. His life was not black as the darkest night, nor was it as light as a day. Sadly she thought that Alan's life, like all our lives, was for the most part composed of the in-between.

'What will you do?' Lady Alice asked Gunnhild when later that evening they returned from the church in Lincoln. 'Maud is broken-hearted. She loved him so.'

'I know it and I hope that in time her heart will mend.'

'We can care for Maud's heart. But what will you do, Gunnhild? What do you wish for your future?'

'I do not know. It is too soon to decide a future. Niall will be Count of Richmond. I think I should travel to Brittany for a while. Fréhel is my dower castle and now I must claim it. Alan wished it to be so. I shall take whichever of my household wish to accompany me. I shall be welcome here, too, I hope?'

'Of course, of course you will, always.'

Hilde raised an eyebrow. 'My lady, I think Lord Niall will be unhappy with your decision.'

'That may be truth indeed, Hilde, but it is the best decision I can make.'

'Are you sure, Gunnhild? Do you really wish to leave your home?' Alice asked.

'I cannot explain but I shall not return to Richmond.'

Hilde spoke up again. 'I shall come to Brittany, if you will have me.'

'O Hilde, I would be glad of your company but what would your father think? He will expect you to marry soon.'

'I shall tell him that there are great lords in Brittany and I shall have my pick of them,' Hilde replied.

Gunnhild sent to Richmond for her possessions. They arrived in three long wagons and they included her bedding, her books, her inks, baskets and chests with clothing and linen. Ann knew what she required. Hubert and Ann accompanied the guard travelling south and brought with them the ladies and maids whom Gunnhild had requested.

On seeing Ann in the courtyard of Alan's manor in Bury, Gunnhild fell into her arms. A moment later, wiping away tears with her hand, she drew back and said, 'Go to Maud, Ann. She is in the solar and will be pleased to see you. When you have greeted her we shall walk in the garden. I have something to tell you.'

As they walked in the garden, Gunnhild told Ann that she intended to make a visit to Castle Fréhel as she intended to establish her rights over her dower castle.

'Brittany indeed. We shall miss you, my lady. But, then again, we can only hope that you will see your place is with us and return to us,' Ann said. 'Return soon, Lady Gunnhild. Do not remain long at Fréhel. Your place is here.'

'You must know I cannot stay. Indeed, however, in time I shall return to Lincoln to be with Maud. Perhaps a part of my widow's third can be this manor house at Bury.'

'I think Lord Niall would want you to stay in England.'

'That I must not do, so make an end to such thought. This is what a dower castle is for and I shall be glad to see mine again.' Gunnhild replied. They had returned to the house and were climbing the outside staircase to the solar without even noticing.

Count Alan's funeral was attended by every loyal magnate from Kent to Northumberland. The magnates rode to Alan's manor of Bury where Gunnhild was waiting to receive them but when Niall rode into the courtyard a few days after their arrival, Gunnhild was shocked to see how tightly drawn his countenance looked, how stooped with grief his manner.

He said at supper, 'The lords of the north object to Bury. They say Alan's remains should be interred in York. But, Gunnhild, Alan expressed a wish to rest in Bury and for the choir there to sing his funeral masses. He said there was no sweeter choir in the whole land.' She saw Niall's eyes well up with tears as he spoke.

'So be it. You are tired, Niall. Rest and we can talk later.'

Maud jumped up from the hall bench where she was seated with Alice's daughters and burst into a fit of weeping. She would not be consoled despite the comforting arms that reached out to her. 'I want to see my father before everyone comes.'

Gunnhild wrapped her in a long, long embrace. 'Sweetheart, he will rest by the altar in Bury for two more days. We can ride over to the church tomorrow,' Gunnhild murmured to her in soothing voice. 'And we shall observe a midnight vigil for his soul, all of us who are his family.'

That evening Niall and Gunnhild sat in the manor garden. It was edged with a wild rose hedge, and they chose a bench under an arch of honeysuckle. Gunnhild breathed in its sweet scent. 'So much life in the midst of death,' she said. 'Even the flowers have their season.' She turned to look into his eyes. 'Tell me now Niall, how Alan died.'

'He died well and in peace,' Niall replied. 'He seemed to recover, but he was not in good health. Remember how after Christ's Mass he took to his bed with a heavy chill? The chill weakened him but he ignored his weakness and when we set out last February he fought harder than ever to protect his castles in Maine and Normandy.'

'And his attackers? Were they captured?'

Niall nodded. 'All of them. They are no more.' Niall took Gunnhild's hands in his own. 'Gunnhild, you must not blame yourself for any of this. He would listen to none of us. Count Alan lived the life he chose. Many admired him. He was a warrior first, a landowner second, and in the end there was not much left in his heart to give to you. There was a time when you did not exist for him. You are free now to make choices. But his last words to me were, and I swear to this, "Care for Gunnhild, Niall, for I know the love you bear her. Tell her I forgive you both." So those were his final words.'

Her tears welled up. He *had* known, but he had ignored that knowledge and forgiven her. Yet, her heart had shattered for what might have been and for what could not be. 'I need to rest,' she said rising from the bench. She stared up at the white crescent moon, a small bowed sliver in a black starlit night. 'Tomorrow will be a very long day.'

He caught her hand. 'What of us Gunnhild?'

'It is not our time, Niall. You are my husband's half-brother

324

and marriage is impossible between us.' She smiled through her damp eyes. 'I cannot stay and I am sorry that I must not. I shall go to Fréhel. It is for the best. You are Count of Richmond. Look after it well. Find another to love and be by your side. May God protect you and watch over you.'

Before he could reply, she leaned over and laid a kiss on his forehead and was gone back into the hall, her tears overflowing.

Nobles, priests and retainers gathered in Alan's hall at Bury. Hounds and children ran through their legs as servants brought out watered wine and great platters of meats, breads and cakes to feed the company. At midmorning, the procession filed out through the manor gates. Gunnhild sat on Blackbird at its head with Niall on one side and Maud on her other. Maud's young husband and his family followed, and after them rode the thanes and barons of the north and eastern counties. The burghers of Bury St Edmunds thronged the streets and bowed their heads as the funeral procession passed. They hung dark cloth from their windows and stood praying by their doorways. They prayed that Count Alan's soul had a swift exit from Purgatory through St Peter's gates and into the gilded world of angels and His presence.

Gunnhild sat up erect on a sidesaddle, her horse covered with black cloth. She wore dark midnight blue for mourning and a starched wimple of fine linen which covered her hair. The colours of Richmond, borne by Niall's pages hung before them. Following the family were all the monks and barons and wives who had gathered in Alan's hall that morning.

Pages and boys raced across the pavement in front of the church, helped Gunnhild and Maud dismount and took charge of their horses. Gunnhild entered the long nave where she slowly walked towards the altar through banners and amongst sombre colours. A quire of monks had gathered around Alan's coffin. Tapers illuminated the simple carvings of leaves that circled the lid and sunlight glinted through the decorated window glass, casting lozenges of colour onto the tiled floor. Moved by the solemn dignified beauty before her, she sank onto her knees, and then prostrated herself before the tableaux, her lips moving in prayer, both forgiving and in search of forgiveness.

As she rose again she glanced around. The church was crammed full and many more mourners stood outside beyond the great arched doorway. She lifted her head to see that Anselm of Bec was officiating and that one of his servers was none other than the skinny monk of Reredfelle, Brother Francis. She drew breath. The Bishop of Bury had the responsibility for her husband's funeral. She had not realised the Prior of Bec would lead the funeral mass instead of the aging Lanfranc, who had obviously sent Prior Anselm north-east in his stead. Nor had she expected to see Brother Francis either. He clearly had inveigled himself into Anselm's train of monks.

The press of bodies, the stale odour of the unwashed, the heat from hundreds of candles and the intense smell of incense made for an atmosphere tense with urgency, as if God were calling on the mourners to be whisked away into the after-world with Alan. Disappointed that Prior Anselm had brought Brother Francis to Bury, she prepared to endure what would be a long mass before Count Alan was lowered into the ground.

Towards the end of the mass, Gunnhild's eye strayed around the nave. She saw then that a group of nuns stood close. Yes, the nuns from St Mary Magdalene at Lincoln. She smiled, thinking how good it was of them to come south in such uncomfortably hot weather, but her smile turned into a frown when she observed one studying her with speculation on her face – Christina of Wilton, another unwelcome mourner. In that moment she knew that her departure for Brittany was imminent. Never would she return to Wilton, never.

Several hours later they filed from the church into bright sunlight. She stopped at the west door to speak with Anselm of Bec, to offer him alms to be distributed to the poor of Bury that day, and for prayers to be said for a whole year at Bury every day following her husband's funeral, prayers that would help ease Alan's journey to paradise.

'It will be done, my lady.' Anselm lowered his voice. 'I know the loyalty you and Count Alan bore each other, but now,

326

perhaps, it would be wise to consider your future.' He had selected his words with care. How could he understand the torn and damaged love hers for Alan had truly been?

'Prior Anselm, it is too soon to make such a decision,' Gunnhild said.

Christina sidled up and stood straight-backed in front of her. 'You will be welcome at Wilton, my lady. We await your return to the abbey where you belong.'

Gunnhild bowed her head graciously, 'I think not, My Lady Christina. I have business elsewhere.'

'Richmond?' Christina raised a quizzical eyebrow. 'You husband's brother is lord there. He will soon find himself a wife.' Her words stung like an unexpected insect bite.

'Elsewhere,' Gunnhild said. 'Now, if you will excuse me, I have other guests to speak with.' She looked for her lady. 'Come, Hilde, we have much to do. I must bid farewell to the tenant lords of Yorkshire, and, after that, we can return to the manor and the funeral feast for my husband.' She bowed to Prior Anselm. 'My lord prior, the cloister is not my vocation.'

Anselm looked at her with kindly eyes. 'I hope you change your mind. You have a great talent that can be used in God's service.'

'No, my lord prior, I have completed my testament to St Brigit. I intend secular writings from now on, poetry, romance, perhaps a story of a great love,' she said and turned on her heel, not looking back once.

During the calends of August, Gunnhild said goodbye to Niall with heavy heart. He did not try to persuade her otherwise, knowing that she was resolute, but he took her hands in his own and said sadly, 'Come back soon.'

'It would not be the same,' she said, 'though it breaks my heart to leave.' She kissed him, a very public kiss and therefore chaste. She slipped a token into his hand, a curl of her hair, still golden and tied with a scrap of scarlet silk. He tucked it away into the tunic underneath his breast plate and whispered, 'Close to my heart.' Moments later he took up his position at the front of the retinue that had travelled south from Richmond. Seated high on Aragon, his piebald stallion, his train moved off following the unfurled Richmond banner carried by his squire. Gunnhild, her two ladies, Hilde and Emma, and Grete and the other maids who were to accompany her to Brittany, climbed to the upper chamber of the two-storey manor house at Bury. They watched the colourful cavalcade vanish into the late August sunshine, over the flatlands to eventually become swallowed up by a corridor of beech trees still heavy with summer leaf. As the long train disappeared into the woods she wondered sadly if she would ever see Niall, Ann, Hubert and Father Christopher again.

Her leave-taking of Maud a fortnight later was not so sorrowful. She knew that they would meet when Maud and Walter travelled over the Narrow Sea. Alice promised that she would visit her in Brittany. 'And, my dear friend, my home is your home, is it not, my husband?' She turned to Sir William.

Sir William reached out to Gunnhild. 'You were Alan's wife, not an easy marriage, I suspect.' He looked penetratingly at Gunnhild. 'But I like you very well, Gunnhild. And not just as my old friend's wife but for yourself, so return to us soon.'

Gunnhild bowed her head. She had not really known what Sir William thought of her. She seized his calloused soldier's hand and kissed it. 'Thank you, Sir William. I am fortunate that you have care of Alan's and my child.'

On a blue sky day with just one little cloud tinged with gold floating through it, Gunnhild and her carefully guarded group of women, ladies and maids, along with a band of young faithful knights, set sail from Norfolk for Normandy. They had enough sealed boxes, chests and baskets to overflow the hold of the ship; these were along with their palfreys, a covered cart and two lean hunting hounds with jangling bells on their collars. The sea was still as a polished mirror. It swished and gently rolled while they dined on small cheese pasties, fish and oatcakes cooked on a brazier on the deck. As night fell the women gathered their mantles and sat under an awning where they told each other old stories. Above them there was a wash of stars some men called the Milky Way. Gunnhild pointed up. Tears gathered into her eyes as she said, 'If I could wish on one of those stars, I would wish that my lord Alan were there above them with a host of angels, for I believe that in the end he meant well by us all.'

Hilde squeezed her hand. 'My lady, I am sure that he is at peace.'

'When we reach Brittany I have a mind to visit my brother Ulf in Rouen, if Duke Robert will permit the wife of an old enemy safe passage into his city. My brother was King William's prisoner for many years and now he has his freedom. He was only five years old when I saw him last. I shall never see my sister again, I know, but at least I have seen my mother. I never really knew my older brothers. Now I would like to see Ulf. He was my childhood companion.'

'My lady, if that would be possible, I think it would bring you great happiness.' Hilde said and her other ladies crowded round agreeing. She felt at peace. A new life was opening.

27

Brittany, 1089

My only crime was to love Isolde.
'Tristram and Isolde' in *The Death of King Arthur* by
Peter Ackroyd, 2011

Late in September a messenger from Lincoln crossed the sea to
Fréhel carrying two letters, one from Alice and a second from
Maud. There was nothing from Richmond. Nor did she hear
anything concerning the new Count of Richmond from pilgrims
who sailed over the Narrow Sea, stopping at her castle on their
long journeys south. She prayed daily for Alan's soul in the
little bailey chapel at Fréhel and although she meant her prayers
with all her heart, it was Niall whom she missed. Frequently her
hand flew to a silver and emerald brooch pin that Niall had
given her a year before as a Christmas gift. Sometimes she felt
such longing for his touch her whole body would ache from the
lips he had kissed to the fingers he had so often held.

Another kind of melancholy had set in during September,
making her even more uneasy and restless as she began to
search for her brother. Just as Niall was King William Rufus's
man, Ulf was Duke Robert's man and as such he could not
return to England unless there was peace between the two royal
brothers. She sent a messenger to Duke Robert at Falaise asking
for news of Ulf. The agony of waiting began. She waited
patiently during a long golden October and then through the
chill mists of November, but no news returned to her.

As December opened and her messenger returned without
news of her lost brother, another route of enquiry occurred to
her. It simply was brilliant. Her new idea, something she had
remembered from fifteen years before, dropped into her thought
as she planned Christmas provisions to be purchased in Rouen.
She wrote to William, Rouen's archbishop. This archbishop,
once a young bishop, had been a friend to her aunt. She would

send him a Christmas gift of a precious psalter that contained depictions of the many strange beasts that were saved from the great flood. After she wrote to the archbishop she sprinkled sand over the wet ink and sealed the parchment with her personal seal, a garland of heart's ease, alongside Alan's family motto 'Live in Harmony'. Surely this would elicit his response. Fulk, her steward, could deliver her letter when he journeyed with the cook to Rouen to oversee their purchases.

As she approached the kitchen intending to seek the steward out, she overheard him involved in a conversation of a personal nature. 'Lady Gunnhild is nobody's fool,' Fulk was saying. 'Good it is to see a woman with wits about her and a sense of economy.' She stopped short and cautiously peered through the half-opened door. Her steward was talking to the cook.

The cook replied, 'Even the kitchen servants speak well of her. They are dressed in new garments which she has provided. None will go cold this winter.'

'Or hungry, and glad they are to serve her,' Fulk replied. He added, 'Now, Cook, do you have that list of goods my lady has given you?'

The steward, a busy little man with gesticulating hands, stopped talking, coloured and opened them wide as Gunnhild pushed open the door with a flourish and entered the kitchen. 'Fulk, I wonder could you come to the antechamber for a moment since I have a letter for Archbishop William? You can deliver it when you travel into the Norman city tomorrow.'

Moving his hands constantly and nodding, he followed her from the kitchen and listened to her request in the antechamber. He bowed and took the letter and held the psalter delicately, as if it were made of thin glass.

God willing, there would be a reply from Rouen.

Two days before the Nativity Eve, Gunnhild woke up with her mind fogged, as if she had just shed a nest of uncomfortable dreams. She dragged herself out of bed and, not waiting for Hilde to come to her, lifted a faded gown from her clothing pole. Careless of her appearance she pulled it on. Hilde sleepily appeared from the small chamber next door. Gunnhild sent her down into the hall to ask for soft rolls, butter and honey and followed slowly, thinking sadly that had she still been at Castle Richmond, Niall would be in and out of the hall bubbling with excitement, anticipating celebratory happy evenings of music, dance and feasting.

In Fréhel's hall the yule log glowed comfortably in the hearth. Resolutely she drained a cup of buttermilk and ate the rolls. Maybe, she told herself, hoping for cheering news, her wagons would return today and she would have a reply to her letter.

The morning became busy. Her servants showed enthusiasm for the festival by rushing about, placing holly in great jars and winding mistletoe around the tall candle sconces. She supervised the spreading of new green reeds and camomile over the hall floor. She found herself glancing towards the door, wistfully looking for Niall, even though she knew that she would never see him tramping through the hall towards the antechamber.

In the late morning she climbed upstairs into the solar where her ladies had comfortably established themselves by the fire and were embroidering belts and purses for New Year's Eve gifts. Momentarily, she watched their needles whisper in and out of fine cloth. She could not help wondering what gifts Niall would have that year.

Just as she was about to unpin her mantle and join her women, a shout barrelled up from the courtyard. Curious, she crossed to the window and peered out. A lone outrider had ridden in and was calling out that the wagons were returning from Rouen. She ran from the solar and raced up all five staircases to the battlements, fighting a gusting wind all the way to the edge of the tower, where she leaned over the wall and watched the road. Her goods wagons were slowly approaching the castle, but there was no pennant with the archbishop's colours flying in the wind, no sign of a messenger.

A gust caught her veil. She took a step back. Her cloak was threatening to pull loose from its silver pin. By the time she had refastened her mantle the provision wagons were crossing the drawbridge into the lower bailey. Behind them rode a lone figure dressed in multi-coloured garments, scarlet, green and blue. She felt a sense of hope that this was a messenger but he looked more like a glee-man, an entertainer. Struggling with the wind, she returned to the narrow door that led on to the staircase, pushed it opened and slowly walked down the steep stairways back to the solar.

She peered out through the solar window again. The carts were awkwardly moving forward towards her keep from the lower bailey, swaying a little under their heavy weight, slow and unsteady as they climbed up the hill.

'There is a gleeman following our wagons,' she called back to her ladies, who were still sewing and chattering as if nothing unusual was happening. But when they heard the word 'gleeman' they looked up, dropped their fabrics, leapt to their feet and crowded round her by the window embrasure.

Anna-Maria said from behind her, 'No, no, my lady, that is never a gleeman. He is a new kind of singer, a troubadour.' Before Gunnhild could respond, Hilde called out, 'Oh no, they will take a tumble now.' Gunnhild leaned out over the ledge, anxiously drew in her breath and exhaled with relief as the wagon righted itself. The four carts were now struggling through the upper gateway.

'A troubadour,' she said, turning to see which maid had said this new word. 'Have you seen one before, Anna-Maria?'

'Yes, my lady, it is the new sort of entertainer. Some years past one came from Spain to my uncle's castle in Occitan. He sang songs of love. He sang to the ladies.' She giggled.

'Oh!' Gunnhild said, and leaned out again to see the brightly clad troubadour leap off his sorrel palfrey.

The ladies clucked amongst themselves as he began remonstrating with servants in the courtyard. 'He is arrogant,' Hilde remarked. The servants pointed up to the solar window. Gunnhild stepped back. From the corner of her eye she saw the young man sweep his cloak behind and run up the steps into the keep after Weylin, the cook.

'Return to your stitching,' she ordered. Obediently they scurried back to their places by the hearth. She closed over the shutters. The air outside was icy, the sky heavy with fat white clouds. There could be snow before Christmas was over. Just as she had begun to remove her mantle, her ladies glanced up at a knock at the door. She gestured to them to stay seated and opened the door herself. The maid, Grete, curtsied. Looking up, the girl said, 'My lady, a man has come from Rouen to pass the Christmastide feast with us. His name is Ranulf and he says that he wishes to speak with you in private.'

'Where is Fulk?' Really, her steward should deal with the gleeman, not her.

'He is busy … in the kitchen, my lady. The gleeman begged me to ask you to grant him an audience.'

She glanced back over her shoulder. All her ladies had dropped the purses and belts back into their laps. They looked up with hungry looks in their eyes, eyebrows arched. There was a chorus of, 'My lady, do you wish us to accompany you?'

Gunnhild said in her sternest voice. 'I shall see what this young man can provide.'

'Ask him if he knows the old stories, my lady,' Anna-Marie said.

'Ask for Tristan and Iseult,' Gretchen peeped up. 'After all the troubadours sing love poems.'

She smiled back at them. 'I shall,' she promised. Her ladies liked to entertain themselves with stories as they spun thread, mended hose and tunics and embroidered altar-coverings for the chapels in small towns like Dinan. The tale of Tristan and Iseult was popular with them and often as they embroidered they would piece the romance together. Gunnhild could hear the anticipation in their voices as she swept from the room, smiling to herself, secretly delighted that such a storyteller had found his way to her castle, hoping too that Fulk would have news of her brother. She stopped at a turn in the lower stairway and said to the servant who followed her, 'Give the troubadour drink and meat. After he has eaten send him into my antechamber.'

Fulk's hands fluttered wide open as he came rushing across

the hall to greet her. 'Madame, can you come to the kitchen this instant and check over your goods, before we store them all away. We need your help. I am trying to keep up with all of our accounting.'

Gunnhild hurried after him. 'Has the archbishop sent any word with you?' she asked, the moment she caught up with Fulk near the kitchen archway.

'Alas, no, my lady, but perhaps the man he has sent to sing for you might know something. The archbishop has sent him to you.' He pointed to the hearth. 'Over there!' He gestured towards the colourful young man who sat on a bench strumming at a stringed instrument. Grete was approaching him carrying a platter and a cup. As the maid spoke to him, the troubadour removed his hat. Gunnhild observed that his hair was as fair and fine as her own, and that he wore it in the new fashion for young noblemen, longer than the Normans had worn their hair in old King William's time. It was curled under at the bottom of his neck. She noticed, too, that he was gathering interest from servants who were still busy placing greenery in enormous pots about the hall. When he stood up to follow Grete towards the antechamber, their eyes followed him as he vanished through the doorway behind the hall.

'He spoke with Weylin on our return journey. He might have gleaned something from him,' Fulk said. Then the steward flicked his hand towards the kitchen. 'My lady, it will only take a moment to come. Before you speak to the glee-man, speak to Weylin and come and see, too, what we have purchased for you.'

The cook was supervising the last bags of goods coming through the outer door from the yard. He shouted at the boys who were carrying sacks on their shoulders to have care. Pointing to various corners, he showed the kitchen servants where to stack them. As Gunnhild entered he came over shaking his head. He said, 'My lady, the archbishop has not sent you a message, but he has done well by you. He has sent you a troubadour to play for you this Chistmastide. The singer says that you will be pleased to see him.'

336

'Perhaps he is a messenger.'

'I do not know, my lady,' Weylin said, shaking his head again. 'We did ask, of course, but he says he is just a troubadour sent in return for your beautiful gift.'

'Ah.' She tried to conceal her disappointment by poking her head into a sack where she smelled currants. She moved on and examined fine white flour, allowing it to sift through her fingers, praising its quality and then she bent over a small white bag with sticks of cinnamon and inhaled a pungent heady smell. 'Good quality, too, Weylin. You have done well.'

Trying to keep disappointment from her voice, she told Fulk to make a new tally of everything. She turned to the cook again. 'So his name is Ranulf. It is odd that Archbishop William sends us such a person.'

Weylin shook his head. 'The archbishop's man delivered him to the very house, Count Alan's big place ...' He stopped short. 'Sorry, my lady, I meant Count Niall.'

'You can speak of Count Alan. It is an understandable mistake. Go on.'

'He arrived the day after we delivered your gift and letter, my lady, saying that Archbishop William was sending him to Fréhel with us to see Lady Gunnhild. He is pleasant enough company, always playing a flute or that odd stringed instrument he carries. Though, I would rather he made us laugh as the old gleemen did.'

'What does he sing, Weylin?'

Weylin scratched his thinning hair. 'Truthfully, it all is gibberish to my ears, though tuneful enough. He sings his songs in a language of the south. Why, we asked him, do you sing songs in a foreign tongue, and he said he learned them from a man of Aquitaine called Guilhem de Peitieus. We told him to sing in Norman-French and he did, pure sounding as a nightingale, too.' Weylin scratched his balding head. 'My lady, where is Aquitaine?'

'South and west of Brittany. What songs did he sing?' she repeated.

Weylin looked abashed, colour spreading from the neck of

his brown tunic up into his face.

'Weylin, answer me please. Of what did he sing?'

'Love.' Weylin spat out the word with great difficulty and looked at his flour-splattered boots. He peeped up through his strands of hair. His face was crimson. She could not hide her smile.

'He sings songs no archbishop would wish to hear!' Weylin added.

Gunnhild began to laugh. 'So ...' She wiped her hands on her apron, a length of linen cloth tied at the waist to protect her gown, and turned again to Weylin. 'You finish this. I must go and meet our troubadour. I am puzzled as to why an archbishop, who sees women and carnal ways as both sinful and foolish, would send us one who sings of love.' She repressed a snort of laughter. 'Especially at Christmastide.' She tossed her apron into a basket. 'We shall have an interesting feast.' She set off across the hall for the antechamber.

The young man scrambled to his feet as she entered, knocking over a cup from the side table with his elbow, causing it to splash wine red as blood too close to a new Eastern carpet. Gunnhild called back through the opened doorway for a maid to clear the mess.

'A clumsy gleeman, I see,' she said. 'That carpet cost me much silver coin.' She narrowed her eyes, opened them wide again and stared at him. 'Have I met you before, gleeman?' There was something in the young man's mischievous face, something uncannily familiar that she could not place. She raised her voice a decibel, 'Speak, I said, do I know you?' The maid came and began to collect broken shards of pottery and mop up the mess. The troubadour moved neatly out of the servant's way and with his dainty side-step, Gunnhild recognised that he was delicate in his movements. The servant slid back through the curtain into the hall.

The young man apologised and with great grace bowed low. 'My name is Ranulf. Archbishop William sends thanks for your gifts and greetings. He has sent me as a Christmastide gift for your castle, good lady.'

Gunnhild waved for the young man to sit again. 'So I am told.'

The troubadour sat on the edge of the stool studying her.

'Do you have a message for me?' Her voice was sharp.

The troubadour shook his head. 'I carry no message, just my harp and my pipe.'

She took the great chair. 'Then, perhaps you can explain why they send you here,' she said.

'I come because my lord has no need of me this Christmas. He says the Lady Gunnhild has grieved enough, that she will desire songs of good cheer and should be heartened by simple entertainment after the loss of her husband.'

'Is that so? Well, I hardly ever saw my husband at Christmastide; he was so often with the King. I am used to entertaining in my castles without him.' She leaned closer to him, scrutinising him. The young man's cloth smelled of jasmine warmed by the fire into a pleasant odour. 'So, then, Ranulf, how can you entertain us at our Christmas feast?' By St Bride, the young man was bold. This was no ordinary messenger. He was too finely dressed and overly familiar, a nobleman perhaps by his bearing. He was fair. His eyes were as green as hers. At this thought a smile twitched at the corners of her mouth. Could her suspicion be correct? She would make him wait. After all, she could be mistaken. She must be sure. 'In any case, you had better earn your keep here' she said, 'I shall arrange a sleeping space for you. You will have your food for Christmastide if you can prove your voice ...'

He interrupted, 'My lady, I promise you I shall more than earn my keep here.'

'Who are you? You are not a poor man.'

'But I am a poor knight, also one who sings of knightly feats. I know many stories and songs of Armorica. You will not regret my presence here.'

She heard the swish of the curtain as the maid entered with a fresh jug of wine and cups. She decided that for now this interview was over, stood up and said to the maid, 'Grete, take his wine to the cupboard chamber by the kitchen.' Turning back

to the troubadour she said, 'We shall try you out, troubadour.'
She liked how this new-fangled word tripped off her lips. 'And
be prepared to sing for us tonight. I hope that since you know of
Armorica you can sing to us of Tristan and Iseult? My ladies
have a liking for that story.'

'My lady, tonight then. I know the story.' He scrambled to
his feet, bowed, picked up his satchel and made ready to follow
the maid.

'And, I too, so tell it well,'she called after him.

That evening the candles seemed to burn more brightly than
was usual. Gunnhild saw to it that the trestles were laden to
overflowing – the cooks had been busy all afternoon creating
wonders with their fresh ingredients. Those servants who could
be spared from serving, clearing, cooking and housekeeping,
knights and noblewomen, feasted together on desserts of
pastries stuffed with preserved fruits, dishes of wafers, honey
cakes and suet puddings. At last the troubadour stepped forward
from his lowly bench into the centre of the hall. He bowed,
raised his flute to his mouth and played his first tune so
perfectly that a hushed atmosphere began to circulate around his
audience. His haunting melody seemed to touch the hearts of
all. They fell silent.

Ranulf began his story. He told of how the Breton knight,
Tristan, had killed a terrible beast of a dragon and as a
consequence won a bride from Ireland for his uncle King Mark
of Cornwall. This noble lady was known as the fair Iseult. On
their journey from Ireland to Cornwall the ship was becalmed.
The poet told how Tristan and Iseult were playing chess to pass
time, when Tristan called for a drink. By mistake, Iseult's maid
brought them a flask of wine intended for her bridal night.
Tristan drank and passed it to Iseult. Neither knew that it held
for them a lifetime of suffering and hardship. 'After some
hesitation Tristan and Iseult confessed their love, and it was
soon consummated.' He said the words quietly, so quietly it
seemed to Gunnhild that even the candle flames bent in to
listen.

Thinking of her love for Niall, Gunnhild allowed a sigh to flit from her lips. When Tristan fell in love with Iseult it was because they had mistakenly drunk a love potion prepared by a dwarf for her wedding night with King Mark, and then the pair were so deeply enamoured with each other they could not bear to be separated. She had not even the excuse of a love potion, but she loved Niall just as passionately.

'Woeful it was,' Ranulf was saying. 'When they reached the shores of Cornwall, King Mark claimed his bride.' A soft groan ran around the hall. Then there was a chuckle when he said, 'But Tristan and Iseult met in secret. They managed to avoid the King's wrath through deception.' For a moment Ranulf played a little lilting tune, then paused and said. 'A few years passed as Tristan and Iseult continued to deceive King Mark, loving each other so deeply that they could not help their love. Meanwhile, the bad dwarf was determined to trap them. When Tristan climbed in through her window he saw the little meddling dwarf scattering the flour and slip out through the door, and when he realised that their footsteps would be revealed, Tristan put his feet together and jumped the distance to the King's bed. But he had taken a hunting wound that day and now it bled. "You are guilty," the King said to Tristan when on the following morning he discovered Tristan's blood on his wife's chamber floor. "You may be sure that you will be put to death tomorrow."'

'"Do what you will with me but, sire, for God's sake, have pity on the queen."' The troubadour bowed his head as he said the words spoken by Tristan.

He looked up again. 'But there was no mercy. The King's barons bound the queen. Tristan escaped into the woods whilst Iseult was sentenced to burn as her punishment.' Ranulf revealed how Tristan had escaped through the window of a chapel on to the cliffs below, a feat no one else would dare for fear of breaking their bones. But Tristan had nothing to lose. He leapt and God's angels protected him. He hid in the forest and rescued the princess by snatching her from her guards as they led her to her trial. 'He led her into the forest where for a time they hid, safe from harm.' As the troubadour said these words he looked straight at Gunnhild.

She looked down at her clutched hands and could not meet his gaze. Her earlier suspicions were correct. She knew him. 'Enough for tonight and it is a good place to stop,' she called out. 'My ladies will dance for us.' How could he take on such a guise? Why would he?

The troubadour laid aside his flute, bowed to great applause and took his place at the very farthest end of the servant's long trestle.

Gunnhild stood, and rising to her full height commanded in a clear loud voice, 'Sir Ranulf, I would speak with you a moment. You sing well. Come and sit with me whilst my ladies are dancing.' Musicians struck up a tune at her invitation. Cymbals clashed, flutes were raised, strings plucked. Led by Hilde, Gunnhild's ladies took up positions beyond the high table. They began to weave in and out, making an interlaced chain around two long tables, daintily stepping the length of the hall, moving at first with great grace, then faster, disturbing the neatly laid patterns of floor reeds as they twisted and turned. As they had become absorbed in the dance others from her household joined them. When Gunnhild knew that no one was watching her she turned to the waiting young man now seated by her side. 'I have observed you closely tonight, Sir Ranulf. By the Lady Mary's grace, I am convinced more than ever that you are not who you say you are. Tell me who are you, in truth.'

The troubadour sighed. To her surprise his eyes welled with tears. For a moment she remembered her mother – those eyes, that hair so flaxen and thick.

He spoke softly, so quietly she had to lean closer to hear. 'My lady, do you recall the skates of bone, the winter at Reredfelle and your brother from whom you were separated so that you could have an education at Wilton Abbey?' He grasped her hands. 'Do you recall our grandfather's great window of green glass and our mother who read riddles to us, and the day the priest found us dressed in chasubles and chastised us because we asked him to wed us?'

'Ulf, Ulf, Ulf.' She whispered the name over and over. 'You are my brother, Ulf, but why this curious concealment?'

'I am indeed Ulf, sister. Let us step into the alcove behind and I can explain.'

They slipped away from the emptied trestles and behind a thick pillar. He took her hands again and held them tight. 'One reason was that I needed to savour your presence and see the person you are now. I have been a captive almost all my life. There is much in my heart that is missing, a father, a mother, a sister and my grandmother, whom I never really knew. Grandmother Gytha is just a glimmer of a memory, a blurred shadow on the very edges of my vision. It hurts to think of the childhood I lost. The second reason for my deception is that Duke Robert thinks I am with the archbishop's cousin in Rouen. My freedom is hard-earned. I am the Duke's man and he will fear that if I associate with you I shall give my allegiance to his brother, William of England. I beg you, Gunnhild, to permit me to continue my deception here as Ranulf the troubadour.'

She drew him further into the depth of the alcove, threw her arms about him and hugged him. He clasped her close. 'Oh, Gunnhild, I never thought to see you again.'

'Yes, Ulf Godwin,' she whispered. 'I know you well and I shall keep your secret. There is much to say in private.' She felt overcome with emotion. 'Our mother has long desired to find you again. She is old now.' She untangled herself from his embrace and peered into the hall. It was as if they were children again creating mischief, secretly watching the world of adults as they had once done on feast days. The music had slowed. Her ladies gathered in knots, mopping their brows with discarded veils, chattering to young knights who had come up from the castle's lower bailey for the feast. She returned to him and lifted his hand to her lips. 'Oh, my dearest brother, clearly I cannot see you alone now. That is if you wish us to keep your secret, but perhaps I can allow my trusted ladies with it. Come to our solar in the hour before Vespers as we embroider and we can withdraw to a private corner and talk. You can tell me what you have heard of us all these long lost years at the Norman court.

343

And, I, well we can talk of the others, our sister, brothers and of our mother.' She smiled through tears. 'I shall show you my books. Now, dearest brother, go back to the servant's table and tonight, sleep well, knowing you have made your sister happy.'

She slipped back into her carved chair and Ulf discreetly returned to his place. Calling for Hilde to come with her she left the merry-making. As they walked to the stairway she told Hilde she had to speak to her.

'What have I done, my lady?'

'Nothing wrong, Hilde. I have something to tell you. It is a secret that concerns my brother. Come with me up to my chamber now. None of what I say must be repeated'

'My lady?'

'Oh, cover your hair, at once. The priest is already horrified by my ladies tonight. He will condemn our troubadour and accuse him of bad influence.'

'Yes, my lady,' Hilde said with contrition in her voice as she fumbled with her veil and her silver fillet.

Gunnhild glanced back from the turn in the stairway and saw that her ladies had descended on Ulf and were, she realised, begging him to sing them one last song. He looked up, caught her eye and winked at her.

Each afternoon as Gunnhild and Ulf talked of their lives, her ladies protected him and no one was any the wiser about his true identity. They sank into recollection, often weeping, clasping hands, sometimes laughing and at other times asking questions of each other. Their lost years fell away like leaves from an autumn tree and grew afresh once again, as spring yields new flowers.

On the twelfth day of Christmas, Ulf examined her manuscripts concerning St Brigit. 'It is a work of art, Gunnhild. But when it is finished you must write down the story of Tristan and Iseult. That tale has words that twist and change like a dance, a story embroidered in poetry.' He lifted her hand to his lips. 'But, tonight after I tell the final episode I must return to my lord duke.'

She clasped him to her. 'I wish you could stay.' She swallowed. There was one more secret to tell him. She lifted a pen, laid it down again and looked into Ulf's eyes. 'I have something I must confess.' Through that long wintery afternoon she recounted the story of her own love. When she was finished she said, 'Love between a widow and her husband's brother is forbidden by the Church. Yet, I cannot help my love for my lord Alan's brother. You are a story teller. Can you understand what it is to really live such a story as they sing, to have lived with such deception in your heart?'

He enclosed her in his arms and held her close. 'God will forgive you. Love is complex. I do not judge you, my sister.'

'Thank you.' She gave him a half smile that reflected her sorrow but also it held for her the relief of unburdening. 'Ulf there is something else.'

'Yes.'

'You must go to our mother, even if you must do it secretly. It broke her heart to lose us all, but especially you. She is in a nunnery attached to St Augustine in Canterbury.'

'I have never forgotten her. My sister, I shall cross the Narrow Sea this summer and we shall be reunited. This I promise you.' Ulf knelt and lifting Gunnhild's hand kissed it. Looking up at her, he repeated, 'I swear it.'

Ulf rode away on a day sprinkled with a first snowfall. Gunnhild sat by her table, with her inks and brushes in front of her and thought of Tristan and Iseult. Night after night, during the darkness of deep winter, she drifted into sleep dreaming that one day Niall would become her Tristan, and that he must come for her, to ask her to return to Castle Richmond.

Epilogue

'Every good story has its ending,' I say. 'This tale has a happy one.' The hall, already hushed, becomes so quiet that even a candle's slightest splutter can be heard. I have touched their hearts with my tale.

'It was a summer's day, early in the morning of the feast of St John, and Gunnhild was decorating the chapel at Fréhel with flowers and shells for the midsummer mass. She needed a great conch shell for a window embrasure, so leaving the chapel she hurried down into the cove below the castle. After a careful search amongst the great rocky outcrop she found the perfect shell. Cradling it in her hands she took pause, stood on the highest rock and looked out across the sea. The waters were still as if a spell was cast, though in the distance a sailing ship marked the horizon like a thin miniature, a line drawing, not yet filled in. She studied it, thinking to commit the watery grey image to memory. It grew larger and closer, and as it moved into the bay, it seemed to her that a craft was being lowered over the ship's side. She fled, gathering up her skirts, climbing fleet of foot up the steps, back up into the safety of the castle bailey. Hurrying back into the small chapel carrying her shell, she pondered who was about to land on her shore. Brittany was at peace. The ship could not bring an enemy, not on the Mass of St John, but perhaps a merchant ship had lost its way. She must tell her steward, though Fulk was visiting the village and would not be returned yet. Her guard was alert to any intruders. They would take care of the ship's crew.

For an hour the sun rose higher and higher and as the noon mass time approached Gunnhild arranged flowers and shells around the narrow nave. She became absorbed in her task, but started at a sound. She heard the clink of armour and the neighing of a horse out in the bailey. It came closer. It grew greater, louder, filling the chapel with echoing sound. She spun around to see a grey-and-white stallion pawing the stone by the opened chapel door. Her eyes strained to see who it was. The sun was full and at first she could not make out the figure on the horse. Rays of sunlight caught at the jewels on the rider's mantle. She withdrew to the altar, fearful now and about to shout out for help. The rider dismounted, leaving his horse by the door and approached her. Before she had time to speak or run behind the altar, he reached her and swept her up into his arms, lifting her so high she lost her breath. She looked down at her captor's face, his dark eyes filled with laughter, his hair, which had been black, now sprinkled with streaks of grey, brushed against her face as he kissed her and released her again.

His voice so familiar said the words she had clung to in her dreams. 'I have come for you, Gunnhild, if you will have me, for I cannot live out the rest of my days without you.'

'And I thee,' she whispered into his cloak. 'So you have come to me at last.' She held on to his hands for a moment, tears of joy streaming down her cheeks. Together, hand in hand, they walked through the chapel's nave and out of the arched door into sunlight.

'Is all well, my lady?' Just returned from the village, Fulk had come rushing into the bailey and was anxiously standing by the chapel doorway. Hilde stood behind Fulk, open-mouthed on seeing the familiar piebald stallion. Soldiers were moving through the yard ready to protect her.

'All is well, Fulk, very well. Send the soldiers away. Tell the priest to ring the bells for St John's Mass. Today we shall have a very happy feast to follow.' She looked at Niall smiling widely. 'This guest is most welcome.' She sent the castle soldiers away, and seated high on Aragon she and Count Niall rode up the hill to the castle keep.

The candles flicker. The yule log hisses softly. The people of the hall let their breath out in a collective sigh. It has been a long story of love and lovers and they always enjoy such stories of romance. After my tale is ended I lift my flute to my lips and play an older tune, one that holds long-ago memories, a soft lilting melody that belongs to the world of the English, before my father, King Harold, had lost his throne. Outside, snow bright as the white mink's fur softly covers the land.

Author's Note

There is little precise historical information about Gunnhild Godwinsdatter. What exists is intriguing. Most women from this early historical period are lost in the footnotes of history, even noblewomen. They are as shadows in a corner.

Gunnhild was the youngest daughter of Harold II, who was defeated at the Battle of Hastings by Duke William of Normandy, and his handfasted wife Edgyth (Elditha). Just before the Battle of Hastings, Gunnhild was sent to Wilton Abbey for her education, as had been her aunt, Queen Edith, years earlier. I imagined that Edith the Queen was close to her niece as Edith also was Wilton Abbey's patron. Dowager Queen Edith spent much of her life there after 1066. At Wilton a noblewoman's education would have included reading, writing and the knowledge of languages.

Norse languages as they were spoken in the eleventh century were very akin to Old English. People throughout the Northern world must have understood each other's tongues. Gunnhild would have had a rudimentary instruction in French, Latin and Greek and would have practised embroidery, music and possibly calligraphy. Carola Hicks, one of the Bayeux Tapestry's historians, believed that at least some of the Bayeux Tapestry panels were embroidered at Wilton as well as in Canterbury and that Queen Edith, a renowned embroideress herself, was involved in the Bayeux Tapestry embroidery. Generally, historians of the Bayeux Tapestry believe the fox and the crow image, which is repeated in the borders of the tapestry, to be deliberately ambiguous. I imagined in *The Swan-Daughter* that calligraphy and drawing, not embroidery, were Gunnhild's favoured occupations. While we know that her aunt was a skilled needlewoman, we know nothing about Gunnhild's talents.

After the Battle of Hastings women who were widows and daughters of slain noblemen often disappeared into convents for their protection. The alternative could be marriage with the enemy. King William always considered himself the legitimate heir of Edward the Confessor. He favoured integration with the remnants of the English nobility. Even so, they were subservient to the conquerors. King William employed many English middling sorts of men as clerks. His regime included a system of English common law that came down from the tenth century with very few changes. In addition an emergent feudal system was already in place in England before the Norman Conquest and was systematically developed after it. The King 'owned' everything and everyone in the land, from barons to lowly serfs.

Many noblewomen who fled to convents after 1066 never took vows. This became an issue in the 1070s as England settled into the new Norman-led regime. In 1073 Archbishop Lanfranc ruled that Anglo-Saxon women, who had at the time of the Conquest protected their chastity by retreating to convents, should make a choice to become professed nuns or leave the convent. Gunnhild would have been about fifteen years old when this was mooted. Her Aunt Edith, widow of Edward the Confessor and patron of Wilton Abbey, died in 1075. Therefore, I began the story of Gunnhild's elopement in early 1076, when she was around eighteen years old and possibly about to profess.

It is fact that Count Alan acquired many of Edith Swanneck's lands. This can be traced through Domesday accounts for East Anglia. Those who owned a particular place in 1066 were recorded, as well as those who owned the same properties in 1086. This was a thorough investigation aimed at reassessing tax and I have no doubt that it was unpopular, thus the name Domesday. Can you imagine how this must have impacted on the population at the time? As a writer of fiction I wanted to explore the emotions and possible responses to the Domesday investigation on Count Alan's lands. It is recorded that he was a fair tenant in chief and from Domesday evidence it is apparent that there were many men of Norse origin who were retained in important positions on his estates as well as

Breton incomers. Thus, I invented the kidnap story to create drama but also to reflect the survey's unpopularity with a population that had suffered horrific winters with famine.

It is historical fact that King William dispersed armies of mercenaries around the country, billeting them in his barons' castles – costly for his tenants in chief. Although the north was threatened by rebellions and by Scotland during the 1070s, one wonders how welcome all these mercenaries were.

It is also fact that Gunnhild eloped from Wilton Abbey with Count Alan. There are two differing accounts of her elopement or, perhaps more accurately, two interpretations. These are as follows.

First, it is recorded in Oderic Vitalis's accounts, written within fifty years of the Norman Conquest, that Gunnhild eloped from Wilton Abbey circa 1089-1090. He refers to Archbishop Anselm's letters to Gunnhild of 1092/93. I shall return to these, as it is a question of interpretation. In Oderic Vitalis's account, Count Alan, veteran of Hastings and a second cousin of William of Normandy, who would have been at least fifty by this date, came to Wilton hoping to court and wed Matilda of Scotland. Matilda was the sister of Edgar Aetheling, daughter of Queen Margaret of Scotland, and also Christina's niece. This princess, like Gunnhild, was educated in the abbey, except that Eadmer's Chronicle suggests that Matilda was at Romsey, not Wilton. Eadmer was an eyewitness to the events concerning Matilda. Oderic Vitalis's story suggests that failing in his venture to marry Matilda of Scotland, Count Alan eloped with and married Gunnhild. She would have been in her thirties by this date. Two dates are given for Alan's death, 1089 and 1092. After his death Gunnhild lived with his brother Alan Niger whom I name Niall here to avoid confusion, and who inherited his brother's estates circa 1089. In 1092 Anselm, Archbishop of Canterbury, intervened and told Gunnhild to return to Wilton. Anselm's letters to Gunnhild apparently were resourced separately from all of his other correspondence and, although they are considered authentic, the non-inclusion of this communication with his letters to others could suggest the sensitive nature of the correspondence or his own lack of accuracy. Gunnhild had never professed, but in his two letters to Gunnhild, Anselm treated her as a lapsed nun and uses this as his reason for the choice of Wilton as her destination following Count Alan's demise.

The second interpretation may be attributed to the scholar Richard Sharpe who writes convincingly in *Haskins Journal* explaining, with sensible reasoning and evidence based on scholarly papers, how Gunnhild eloped with Alan of Richmond during the 1070s. One important piece of evidence cited is that in 1675 a head tablet was discovered near the west door of Lincoln Cathedral. It recorded the burial of a son of Walter d'Aincourt, a lord of Brittany and of Branston in Lincolnshire. The child who was named William was born of royal stock and died young while in the fosterage of King William Rufus. William's mother is named as Matilda (Maud). Matilda bequeathed gifts of land to the cathedral. Sharpe tracks the relevant land history and is able to show how these lands are recorded in the Domesday Book as attributed to Count Alan of Richmond, but were previously those attributed to Edith the Fair, suggesting that Matilda was, in fact, Count Alan's daughter by Gunnhild. Sharpe argues that the correspondence between Anselm and Gunnhild refers in the main part to her union with Alan's brother rather than the previous union with Count Alan. Remember, the lands in question originally belonged to Edith Swanneck, Gunnhild's mother. Was King Harold's great-grandson the child buried by the west door of Lincoln Cathedral? Interestingly, Alan Niger's death is recorded as 1098. There is no evidence that Gunnhild ever returned to Wilton Abbey. Her death is unrecorded.

Eadmer of Canterbury's *Chronicle* is contemporary with the events of *The Swan-Daughter*. He does not mention Gunnhild's elopement with Count Alan, yet he goes into detail about the betrothal of Matilda of Scotland to Henry I in 1100. Henry I was the youngest son of William the Conqueror and succeeded the childless William Rufus to the throne of England. Gunnhild and Matilda are unconnected in Eadmer's writings. Eadmer was an eyewitness, based at the heart of events, in St Augustine's Abbey in Canterbury, so I suggest that Richard Sharpe is correct and that Gunnhild's elopement from Wilton Abbey occurred during the 1070s.

Sharpe's interpretation of the elopement is the basis for the time span of *The Swan-Daughter*'s narrative. It is an interpretation liked by many scholars interested in this period. I used secondary research into the eleventh century to develop a sense of what married life might have been like for Gunnhild. The big intrigue for me was why she married his brother, which would have been frowned upon by the Church, therefore explaining Anselm's letters to Gunnhild. I invented a love triangle. Both marriages may have been in truth handfasted marriages but there is no evidence for this either. In *The Swan-Daughter*, I emphasise Gunnhild's claim to lands, under Anglo-Saxon law, that had once been her mother's lands and estates and I integrate into the fiction what Domesday meant for ordinary people living and surviving in 1086.

Count Alan was a soldier. He was utterly loyal to King William, taking sides with him against his rebellious older son, Robert, against Bishop Odo and supporting William Rufus when many barons rebelled after Rufus became king. He did not support the earls' rebellion of 1075 after which Earl Waltheof was executed. The Breton earls who instigated the rebellion were imprisoned or fled England. Alan's elder brother, Brian, was not involved either, but he left England during this period and returned to his estates in Brittany.

The early part of *The Swan-Daughter*, set in Brittany, for the most part, follows historical fact, though I invented the castle of Fréhel. Count Alan died in Normandy around 1089. During his life he became one of the wealthiest noblemen in England with lands in Brittany and Normandy. As his obituary indicates he was widely respected at the time. In the context of this novel, which I emphasise is a work of historical fiction, I portray a man who was a soldier, a religious man but unfortunately one who was not compatible with Gunnhild and who in the end recognised this. He is depicted as not all bad, nor is he all good, yet he is human. I aimed to show the disintegration of a medieval marital relationship trying to keep this true to the period, with emotions that may, in truth, have often been repressed. Men had affairs without consequence and often they took long-term mistresses. Women, if they did likewise, had to be very secretive or the consequences would have been disastrous. This was a society that cannot be judged by today's standards, no matter the universal emotions involved.

I deliberately created a 'romance' (romanz) out of Gunnhild's historical story. Was it really a love triangle or was it simply survival? I am interested in the literature of the period, both chronicles, hagiography and prose poetry that is inspired by the poetic imagination and is linked to emergent concepts of chivalry. The earliest evidence of the troubadours' secular treatment of romance appears in France with trouvères in Northern France and in England with a new Anglo-Norman literature which emerges in written form during the early twelfth century. Troubadour literature appears circa 1090 in Aquitaine when Eleanor of Aquitaine's grandfather, Duke William IX, scribed stories of love and chivalry using the pseudo name of Guillèm de Peitus. The Occitan troubadour tradition was preceded by oral tradition and so I took the very old story of Tristan and Iseult as a parallel for the love-triangle, that of Gunnhild, Count Alan, and Alan Niger his brother, thus creating another layer in my telling of Gunnhild's story. *The Swan-Daughter* is a work of fiction rather than historical biography.

Ulf was imprisoned as a child hostage after the Battle of Hastings. According to John of Worcester, Ulf Godwinson was included in Robert of Normandy's court. He was released after King William's death and subsequently knighted by Duke Robert. He may have accompanied Duke Robert on the first crusade. I made him a troubadour in this work of fiction, although there is no factual evidence for it.

Christina can be traced at Wilton Abbey and Romsey Abbey during this period. Christina's personality is based on information concerning her in Eadmer's *Chronicle*, in particular, where her harshness towards the young Matilda of Scotland is apparent. Many of the other characters in *The Swan-Daughter* are, of course, figments of my imagination. I do hope this Author's Note clarifies not only how I discovered the narrative elements of this story and its personalities, but also how I used authorial license to elaborate on these elements and translate them into a work of historical fiction, albeit with a factual basis.

For any reader who is interested in a further glimpse of this early medieval time, I was helped by Richard Sharpe's article in *Haskins Journal*, by Henrietta Leyser's *Medieval Women, The Anglo-Saxon Chronicles* translated by Michael Swanton, *The Trotula* edited and translated by Monica H. Green and *Domesday Book, a Complete Translation*, edited by Dr Ann Williams and Professor G. H. Martin, but there were many other books concerning the period as well as the chronicles of the period which I consulted in the Bodleian Library, Oxford. I have occasionally used *The Death of King Arthur* by Peter Ackroyd in chapter headings because I like the clarity of his unfussy prose translation of his chapter concerning 'Tristram and Iseult'. In the final chapter of The Swan-Daughter I adapted Ulf's oral version of Tristan and Iseult (old spelling) from the early version of the story *The Romance of Tristan*, a translation of Beroul's original poem (Roman de Tristan par Beroul) first set down in the twelfth century. It is, if you are interested, *The Romance of Tristan: The Tale of Tristan's Madness* (Penguin Classics) by Berol.

The Betrothed Sister

First Chapter

1

A pale moon was reflected in the still water that lay along the island's shoreline.

Thea took a step closer to the water's edge and for a moment glanced up at the night sky. Then she stared down at the reflection of the moon that lay on the surface of the sea. For a moment all was silent. It was as if the world had paused to take a breath.

Edmund touched her hand. 'Hurry,' he said. 'Grandmother is waiting in the boat for us.'

Accepting her brother's help, his hand guiding her elbow, Thea ventured into the shallows. She lifted her skirts high in the hope that water would not drench her gown, and allowed Edmund to lift her into the skiff. Taking a place in the stern beside her grandmother, Countess Gytha, she leaned back against the last chest of Godwin treasure. A sense of relief swept through her. They were finally setting out.

Thea's grandmother sat stiff-backed and silent waiting for the boat to cast off, her stony gaze casting forwards towards the two dragon-shaped vessels that had remained out in the bay all day as the women made ready to leave the island. All that day Countess Gytha had not spoken, not since her grandsons had sailed to them in the shadowy morning light, and had told her about their defeat in Somerset and of her youngest grandson Magnus's death in his first battle.

Godwine and Edmund had told her they must leave immediately. Stoical but broken-hearted, Gytha had watched the sea from the monastery cliff-side, leaning on her eagle-headed stick as the boys and their Danish oarsmen collected the women's valuables from where they were stowed safely in caves. Thea's brothers and their oarsmen had worked hard all day long, sweat running in ribbons down their bared backs, shifting chest after chest out to the anchored ships. They must catch the evening tide and sail away into exile in Flanders before the Normans changed their minds about allowing them safe passage out and, instead, attacked their ships and seized their treasure. Now, as well as the one sturdy oak chest on their skiff, other coffers containing valuable items were already safely stowed aboard the *Wave-Prancer*, the second of two great ships that would carry the band of noble women and their children and maids to Flanders.

As for Countess Gytha, once the task had been completed, she had left off her watching from the monastery's north window, attempted to eat a good dinner and at last she, too, had made ready for her departure. Embracing the abbot who had cared for them since winter, the countess had smiled sadly as she presented him with a valuable relic, a fragile snip of the virgin's veil. This holy object was contained inside a small crystal and gold reliquary box which she had smuggled from Exeter after the siege, when she, her daughter Hilda, Thea and their women and children had been banished to Flatholm to await exile.

Thea knew that leaving England would bring Grandmother Gytha immense pain. Losing Magnus left a hollow in her own heart, already brimming with sadness for the death of her father at Senlac, the viciously thorough conquest of their land by the Normans, and her mother Elditha's decision to enter a monastery. Her thoughts raced as if they were shooting stars moving like quicksilver through the night sky above. My sister Gunnhild is trapped with Aunt Edith at Wilton Abbey. My little brother is a Norman hostage hidden away in one of their dark castles, she thought sadly to herself, and now that the Normans have killed Magnus, Godwine and Edmund are all the brothers I have left. So, with those thoughts, Thea looked away from the island of Flatholm glad to leave days there that had been endlessly marked by prayer and the work of a small monastery.

Though Flatholm had been their home for six months, since Exeter had fallen to the enemy, she had tried hard to make the best of it. She had gardened, applied herself to her embroidery and told stories to the small group of children belonging to the noblewomen accompanying them into exile. She had even discovered other tales, stories older than those she already knew, from a strange bearded monk who came to visit them from Denmark carrying word to the women of her brothers' summer campaign. He had brought them hope, if only for a short time.

Thea glanced up at the thin, fragile moon. Despite all that had happened since the Normans stole England, anticipation gripped her. By the time that moon grew fat again they would be settled in their new home. She moved her lips in prayer to her name day saint, St Theodosia. 'Gracious lady, grant us a warm hall, fine furniture and new clothing and take a care for my brother Magnus.' Surely her saint would answer her prayer.

Yet, Thea did not confess to St Theodosia her deepest and most secret wish. She wanted revenge on William the Bastard. She wanted revenge not only on him but on his whole House for his destruction of her father, the kidnap of her brother Ulf by King William, her mother's seclusion and the murder of her brother, Magnus. If St Theodosia knew what lay in her heart, she knew it already. Thea wanted vengeance and until she had it, her life would never be complete again. One day, the Bastard, William of Normandy, false king of England, would die an ignoble death, unloved by his children and preferably in great pain because she, Thea, daughter of the great King Harold, wanted him to suffer for what he had done to her family. And, she added this to her thought – one day she would marry a warrior prince who hated the Normans as much as she did and who would help her brothers recover their kingdom.

She started. Voices were falling towards them, dropping from the direction of the cliff below the monastery, coming closer. She twisted around to see the rest of their women following a monk who was swinging a lantern. Their ladies, who were wrapped in their warmest woollen mantles, came in a snaking line down the cliff path to the beach. All of them, even the five children, were carrying small bundles. When the group reached the shingle the women gathered up cloaks and skirts and, bunching the thick escaping material into their hands, they began wading out to climb into the fleet of skiffs. Edmund and Padar, their warrior poet, took an arm here, a hand there. They lifted the older women, swinging in turn each of a tiny band of confused children from one to the other over the lapping water. Finally, they deposited the women and their offspring into the assorted fishing craft that would ferry them to the big-sailed ships which were to carry them over the Narrow Sea.

The women's exile had been arranged months before by Aunt Edith, England's dowager queen, wife to Edward. Because of her influence, King William had promised them this safe passage. Of course, Thea mused, he would promise anything that would rid himself of the Godwin threat and hold onto Aunt Edith's good will. If he retained Edith's good will he might get England's sheriffs and officials on his side, those who had the running of the shires in the days of King Edward. Thea could not understand why her aunt was so devoted to Uncle Edward. She shuddered. Never could she wed with such a frost-bitten one, never, not even to please the family.

A final splash threw salty spray into her eyes. She blinked it away, looked around and saw that at last the skiffs were full. Padar climbed over two rowing benches and sat opposite them, squeezed in on the end of a third bench, wrapped in his old sealskin cloak. He grunted a greeting, and received a glimmer of a smile from Gytha. Edmund came down the rowing boat, placed an arm about Padar's shoulders. 'Look after them as we cast off, my friend.' Once, it seemed long ago but it was only a year since, Padar had protected her mother and now he promised that he would protect them.

Grandmother Gytha seized Thea's hand and spoke for the first time since Prime. 'Soon we shall be in Baldwin's court. Just think how he will welcome us with honour. His family was always friendly to us Godwins.'

'Will he be friendly, Countess?' Padar asked, taking his watchful eyes from the shoreline. Raising a bushy eyebrow and leaning forward, lowering his voice, he said, 'Will he really be a friend to you? I'd leave your coffers under guard when we reach St Omer. You'll not breathe a word about it, my lady Countess, either, if you are wise. Given half a chance, Baldwin will be like a crow ready to scourge the wheat field. He seeks the best opportunity. He straddles loyalties.'

Gytha narrowed her eyes, nodded and glanced at Edmund who had taken up oars. 'The boys will need it if they are to get back our kingdom.' She turned to Thea. 'You will need help, too, if you are to marry well. Sixteen, my girl, and high time we found you a match.'

Thea thought to herself that her brothers would use most of any coin and treasures they possessed to buy ships and weapons. But she would need a dowry if one day she were to marry well. She watched the waves roll about their craft as the oars beat on water and the dragon ships drew closer. How would Godwine get them off the rowing boats and up into those enormous ships? The ships' walls were as high as a giant's reach.

A loud greeting echoed over the sea. Glancing high above her perch Thea saw Godwine waiting at the nearer ship's side. He shouted down to them. 'Grandmother first. Edmund, keep the boat still as you can. I am coming down to you. I shall carry her up the ladder myself.' Before Gytha could protest, Godwine was on the rope ladder and climbing down to them. He jumped into the skiff, and lifted Gytha as if she were a bundle of fine light wool. 'Hold tight, Grandmother. That's it, arms around my neck,' he urged.

Gytha laughed as Godwine reached out and grasped the hanging thick knotted rope with one hand, his other arm hugging the Countess, and began shimmying up it with Gytha clinging to him, holding on as if her life depended on it. It did.

Thea glanced down at the dark waters below.

'You next, sister,' Edmund said. 'Can you climb unaided?'

She nodded. As she made ready to grasp the rope ladder, Gytha, apparently unaffected by her journey upwards into the dragon ship, stood safely with Godwine supporting her on a rowing bench inside and called down, 'Girl, bring my stick with you. I'll need it to steady myself and smash a few sea serpents.'

Padar reached up and handed Thea the eagle-headed stick. Her ascent would be even more dangerous now there was this in one of her hands. Thea climbed, holding on precariously with her left hand, her arm aching. She held the stick up to Godwine, who was leaning over the side waiting to help her over the top. He took it and turned to his grandmother with a 'Here it is. Grandmother, let Gunulf help you down on the bench before you fall and break something.'

Gytha grasped her stick and accepted the oarsman's help. Once down she waved the stick about her head so that all Thea could see of Grandmother Gytha was a carved eagle head poking above the side of the ship, and her grandmother's strong voice yelling, 'I hope the Bastard king sleeps uneasy in his bed tonight. I curse him, by the Nons' spells; I curse him by Thor's hammer and by Freya's bones I curse him. I pray that he suffers Hell's fires for his theft of our kingdom.' The eagle-headed stick was shaking up at the stars as if to emphasise her words.

Godwine's answering call echoed around the waters, 'He will pay for Magnus's death, for my uncles' deaths, for my father's death. We will harry England's shores until he wishes he had never heard of our kingdom.' He lowered his voice and called down to Thea, whose stiff fingers could hardly grasp the rope as she listened patiently to her grandmother's diatribe, wanting it over so that Godwine would get her over the side. At last he called down, 'Now, Thea, come further, hand over hand.'

Thea climbed the last of it steadily, crushing her terror of dropping back down, until, to her relief, Godwine grasped her and swung her over so that she fell past the rowing benches and on to the deck. One by one, the other boats drew up to the big ship. Led by Hilda, the ladies courageously climbed into the ships. Finally the children shimmied up and they were all on board. The *Sea-Dragon*'s sails were unfurled and the seamen seated in the ship's body began to row. The *Wave-Prancer* followed. This ship, Edmund explained, carried the rest of their surviving Danish warriors and housecoerls, all well-armed and alert. Thea glanced over admiringly at their coned helmets and at their great jewelled arm bracelets that glinted through the starlight.

She watched, thrilled, as Godwine raced across the great

benches that ran along the ship's length and shouted to the *Wave-Prancer*. There was an answering call as the warriors began to manoeuvre the ship into position beside the *Sea-Dragon*. When they drew closer Godwine climbed up onto the wall of the *Sea-Dragon*. With a yell he leapt over the narrow channel of sea on to the supply ship and was gone. He would command their protection from the second ship which carried the greater number of his men at arms and sailors who were also warriors.

The *Wave-Prancer* moved away again, oars moving in rhythm. It took up the lead position now. The *Sea-Dragon* followed and soon they were out from the headland and the island was left far behind.

Padar joined the women where they made themselves more comfortable by leaning against Gytha's coffer. Squatting down, he opened his satchel, drew out a large flask and pulled a wax stopper from the skin. He produced a silver cup and with his eyes twinkling he offered the first draft to Gytha. After the Countess drank, Thea, and finally the other women raised the flask to their mouths. It held a concoction of something that tasted of honey and bitter herbs, clashing flavours. Thea did not mind. The liquid coursed through her, for a heartbeat allowing her thoughts to drift away to far distant lands, kingdoms that marked the edge of the world.

'A distillation of barley and herbs,' Padar said as he took the flask back and knocked off the dregs, stoppered it and returned it to his satchel.

'Just what we need,' Gytha said as the ship ploughed its way out of the channel, southwards. 'Now, little man, lull us into sleep with the melodies of my homeland.' It was as if Gytha was remembering places far to the north that had long been hidden in her soul, the land of the Danes, the country of her youth.

As Padar pulled his harp from his big leather scrip, the children squeezed up against their mothers. They were all packed as closely as a line of drying cod, twenty of them in all, women and children, jammed into the stern of the *Sea-Dragon*.

Thea looked past them and behind for the necessary. She took note that it must be that covered pail that leaned against the ship's wall just at the furthest end of the ship where the stern curved upwards into a dragon's tail. They would need to be careful if they had to crawl around the chests and over to it. If the sea remained calm then no one would be sick. Aunt Hilda was famous for her weak stomach.

The Countess had huddled down amongst the fur covers. As Padar played his harp her eyelids closed. In sleep Gytha's aged face relaxed and the lines of long years of care settled. For a moment Thea glimpsed the fine-bred northern beauty her grandmother had once possessed. The water's lapping, the oars plash, the murmuring of the night breeze and the strains of Padar's music contrived to shift Thea's thoughts to dwarf kingdoms under the mountains. She imagined caves along which rivers twisted through pillars of ice. Gradually her own eyelids closed as she, too, was lulled into sleep by the skald's melodies and the gentle rhythm of the dragon ship as it ploughed through the waters. She pulled her sheepskin closer and drifted into the territory of uneasy dreams.

The Daughters of Hastings Trilogy
by
Carol McGrath

Carol McGrath

Carol's passion has always been reading and writing historical fiction. She lives in Oxfordshire with her husband and family. She taught History in an Oxfordshire comprehensive until she took an MA in Creative Writing at The Seamus Heaney Centre, Queens University Belfast. This was quickly followed by an MPhil in Creative Writing at Royal Holloway, University of London. Her debut novel, *The Handfasted Wife*, first in a trilogy about the royal women of 1066, was shortlisted for the RoNAS, 2014 in the historical category. *The Swan-Daughter* is the second in the trilogy. It is also a stand-alone novel. Carol can often be discovered in Oxford's famous Bodleian Library where she undertakes meticulous research for her novels.

Find Carol on her website: www.carolcmcgrath.co.uk.

For more information about **Carol McGrath**
and other
Accent Press titles
please visit

www.accentpress.co.uk

Find more from **Carol McGrath** at

http://scribbling-inthemargins.blogspot.co.uk/

www.carolcmcgrath.co.uk